My Counterfeit Self

JANE DAVIS

IN MEMORY OF

My golden cousin, Cathy

'It takes fifty years for a poet to influence the issue'.
Attributed to W. B. Yeats

PRAISE FOR THE AUTHOR

'Davis is a phenomenal writer, whose ability to create well rounded characters that are easy to relate to feels effortless'.

Compulsion Reads

'Jane Davis is an extraordinary writer, whose deft blend of polished prose and imaginative intelligence makes you feel in the safest of hands'.

J.J. Marsh, author and founder of Triskele Books

CHAPTER ONE

2014

"Christ!" Lucy's shoulders jumped in their sockets. How could Ralph have crossed the lawn without her noticing? But here he was, in his black suit, and holding out a stiff white envelope. "What are you doing, creeping up on people like that?" she snapped. There'd been too many shadows, too many ghosts, this past week.

Ralph shrugged the corners of his mouth. "It looks important. But I can take it back inside if you prefer."

"What kind of important?" Lucy narrowed her eyes and tucked the secateurs into her gardening belt.

"Well, for starters, it has an official seal." Her husband was right to think that black drew too much attention to his eyebrows, which had remained defiantly dark, long after the rest of his hair had turned white.

"Oh, give it here!" Lucy thrust out an ungracious hand and snatched the letter.

After a few steps, Ralph made a half-turn. "Don't forget. We need to leave for Doris' funeral at ten forty-five. That's *leave the house,* not time for you to start getting ready."

Lucy had done her best to ignore the time. The thought of the coffin's misshapen oblong shuddered through her.

1

"Miserable so-and-so. I always hated the bastard." The false-hood snagged in Lucy's throat. Inside she was wailing; cursing the God she didn't believe in. Angry at Dominic for leaving her. Guilty at the relief she felt now he was gone.

"I hope you don't say the same about me once I'm safely out of the way."

Huh! A harsh breath left her mouth. "You were never miserable."

"Well, you might find it in your heart to hate Dominic a little less –"

"What? Now he's no longer here to piss me off?" Her pooled eyes spilled over. Here she was, taking it out on the one person who didn't deserve the sharp end of her tongue. Ralph only said what he'd said because he understood the truth. For both of them, Dominic's absence was knife-like.

"Poor sod stuck around as long as he could." Ralph moved away carefully, as if he was thinking where to make each footprint.

By the time Lucy had recovered her poise, he was almost at the patio. Safe to clasp one cold hand over her mouth. To grasp at a memory so intent on freeing itself. A snapshot. Dominic's head thrown back; raucous laughter.

Not as he was when she'd last seen him, prostrate on a narrow cot, sucking something puréed through a plastic straw. No point in asking how he was feeling when the answer was etched on his face. Pretending she hadn't seen the unfinished letter he'd left on the wheeled table that slotted over his bed, she'd dumped her handbag on top of the words he'd written: *outlook bleak* – as if it was the weather he was forecasting. Her eyes came to rest on his watchstrap, metal links hanging loose, a precise measure of how much of him they'd already lost.

Unbearable. Dominic, who'd lived life more fully than anyone she'd ever met, who never just walked into a room but *arrived,* coattails flying. Reduced to eating baby food. As Lucy had told Ralph repeatedly over those last weeks, she was no good with hospitals, the corridors of magnolia, the flowered curtains, the chairs upholstered in wipe-clean PVC.

"It's just Dom. You don't need to put on a performance."

"It's alright for you," she said. "You're a man. You and Dominic can mull over the cricket for a good few hours." Besides, there was not and there never had been *just Dom.* Not for her and certainly not for Ralph.

Ralph, of course, had more experience of hospitals and hospices. He'd spent hours sitting by bedsides in the second half of the eighties and the early nineties, at the height of the epidemic. Sitting by a bedside, just holding a hand.

"How can you bear to do it?" she'd asked.

"It really doesn't seem like enough," he'd said. "Not when you see what they have to go through."

Lucy had tried to contain her fears when Ralph arrived home with words she'd never heard before. *Pneumocystis carinii* and *Candida, sarcoma lesions* and *cryptococcal meningitis.* First, there had been the fear of blackmail and exposure. Now this thing would cast another shadow over their lives. Ralph distanced himself with complicated terminology. To Lucy, the terrible disease would only ever be AIDS.

"You've been tested?"

"Yes, I've been tested."

She bit her lip. She was not his mother. She wouldn't continually ask if he was being careful.

Dominic's disease was cancer, not AIDS. But she knew how the well-thumbed liturgy of the bedside vigil brought it back for Ralph. All of those deaths. All of those dear loved ones.

On the final occasion Lucy visited Dominic – and by then he was in St Jude's hospice – Ralph wasn't there to act as a shield.

There had, though, been one small satisfaction. "You're wearing the pyjamas I bought you," she said, smoothing a ridiculously expensive silken sleeve. That had been her quiet rebellion, her refusal to buy cheap just because he wouldn't get much wear out of them.

Dominic didn't reply, at least not in any way she would have wanted. His eyes, huge in his skull, pleaded *I'm trapped.* An agonising moment. A voice, somewhere that might have been inside her whispered, *I'll do it. Whatever you want.* But before it could form itself into anything more concrete the moment was broken.

"Would you like me to pray with you?"

Lucy turned to see a woman standing in the doorway, dressed plainly, a silver crucifix hanging around her neck.

Dominic gathered every ounce of strength and barked, "Fuck off!" The woman shrank into herself, and, as she backed away, he actually hissed. The two of them had clutched their sides: Lucy, howling in joy and agony; Dominic shaking with the effort of trying to rein in his ferocious joy, lest he trigger another unstoppable spasm of coughing. It was the last joke they shared. The last words she heard him say.

Fuck off!

Though Lucy rarely prayed, the interruption had sparked something inside her. With her sides still aching, she pleaded silently: *Help him find it in himself to let go.* How could he carry on when there was so little of him left?

She excused herself, saying that she needed coffee when what she really needed was escape.

In the cramped ladies' toilets, Lucy splashed her face with cold water and blinked at her shocked reflection.

You can do this.

Because what choice was there? Five years ago, it had been a false alarm. Death had donned his black hooded cloak but Dominic had resisted. Not this time. By the time she arrived

4

back at his bedside, Dominic had slipped away. She noticed the silk scarf knotted around his neck, a cast-off of Ralph's. He would be pleased when she told him. She couldn't for the life of her remember if Dominic had been wearing it earlier. That detail would go on bothering her.

"You need to leave half an hour to get changed."

Lucy looked about her, bewildered to find herself standing in the middle of her rose garden, eyelids heavy. Ralph, she saw, had paused outside the French windows. "I'll go as I am. He won't be happy unless he has something to moan about. He never liked the way I dressed."

It's not that. It's just that I prefer you naked.

Ralph was leaning on the doorframe for support. "He can't answer you back any more."

"Oh, he'll find a way. Count on it." Lucy thought of Dominic's interruptions as his echo rather than his ghost. She'd heard them during his absences in his lifetime. Why should it be any different now?

"You might rack your brains for something... I don't know... *pleasant* to say about him. Just in case the press are out in force."

Lucy stifled bitter laughter. This was as close to sarcasm as Ralph ventured. A media tornado was about to descend. So much for being allowed to grieve in private.

Only half of her attention was on the envelope as she tucked a thumb under its flap and tore the seal, jagged centimetre by jagged centimetre. "They won't want something positive. They'll want something caustic to regurgitate as a headline."

"Then 'I always hated the bastard' it is."

Despite everything, despite the day and the fact that she'd been snapping at Ralph from the moment they'd woken, Lucy smiled. *I'm sorry,* her eyes said. Her husband was aware of the problem. For Lucy to haul herself out of an indigo funk, she needed to pick a fight. That was where Dominic had come in so useful over the fifty-odd years she'd known him. Never holding back on opinions of her – or anyone else for that matter – he'd been such an obvious target. Tooth and claw.

He'd always known how to goad her. *"Why must you constantly demand that I apologise? I can't help the fact that I wasn't born working class."* The permanent chip on Lucy's shoulder – that and her lack of formal education. And how, goddamn it, was Dominic so qualified to dissect whatever she produced? He'd known nothing about poetry when she'd met him. Not a jot.

"I'll leave you to your letter, but keep an eye on the time," Ralph said and entered the house through Lucy's office.

Unfolding the single sheet, she experienced a quiver of pleasure at the way both ends had been folded towards the centre, rather than the more usual *Z* shape. She admired the precision of it, reminded of the rituals of pre-email days: filling her fountain pen; blotting paper; blowing on blue ink until it dried. But her smile froze. *Dame Commander of the Order of the British Empire.* As her eyes zigzagged furiously downwards, it was as if she was being pulled underwater. The words massed and swam in shoals, becoming foreign to her. She, who dealt in the currency of language. Lucy pulled her glasses onto the bony ridge of her nose, but still her brow furrowed. The embossed seal felt official as she passed the pad of her thumb over it. If this was someone's idea of a practical joke, it was a very expensive one.

So this is how you thought you'd exact your revenge. Because it could only be the work of one person. And then she was cutting the paper. Cutting it with her stiff secateurs. Fierce little snips. Triangles and polygons. *Today of all days, you pull a stunt like this.* The shapes became the thing. A row of inward angled snips at one edge, then upwards, a deep cut linking them together. A confetti-fall of dissected words. A snowfall of envelope. The fragments clung to her clothes. They spangled and feathered the jewelled grass. The hand holding the secateurs took control. There was a level on which Lucy could see herself as an observer might. Quite detached, unaware of sending instructions from brain to hand, only that she mustn't stop until the job was finished. And there was another level on which she worked herself into a frenzy, an insult accompanying every snip. *Well, I shan't. You aren't the Pied Piper any more.* Once the secateurs had made short work of the invitation, they started on her rose bushes, conscientiously removing every head, so that rich velvet petals joined with the flurry of vellum. Great splashes of dew were released. The soft thud of heavy heads on mulched bark, one after another. To Lucy, the sound of each impact was amplified: great timpani struck with felt-tipped drumsticks, bouncing off the low ceiling of a basement jazz club. As she worked around and between the semicircular beds, tugging at the thorn-snared hem of her skirt, there was a mania to her movements. She gave herself up to the destruction of the thing she had created and loved completely. Dominic's voice was inside her head. *Swapped your wire cutters for secateurs?* The air filled with a heady blend of Turkish delight, violet, apple, clove, citrus, moss and honey – the *soul of the rose*. It buzzed thickly with insects. Track-marks appeared in Lucy's pale threadbare skin. She shook one knuckle-gnarled hand. Where her thumb had been punctured, a single bead of rich red blood stood proud. As she sucked at it, tasting iron, the hard topaz of her oversized ring was comfortingly cold against her cheek. She was ankle-deep in petals. Cleopatra had not done this much for Anthony.

"Lucy?"

As her familiar name sliced the potent air, Lucy saw that she'd been cutting deep into the sleeve of her boiled wool cardigan. Ralph was powering towards her, breathless. A dark tie hung loose around the raised collar of his shirt.

"Not bad news, I hope?" he asked, saying nothing of the surrounding chaos.

From the tightness of her eyes and the fogging of her glasses, Lucy realised she'd been weeping. Words erupted from deep within her. "I didn't do everything I've done to become a national fucking treasure!"

"No one could accuse you of trying to win a popularity contest, that's for sure."

"Then *why?*"

He looked at a loss. "Why what?"

"It's an invitation from the *Palace*. They've put me on the New Year's *Honours* list." Even saying the words, Lucy felt sullied.

"Ah," Ralph said, a slow, measured sound. "Now that, I wasn't expecting." His feet shuffled.

"No!" Her entire adult life, she'd spoken out against the government. From Suez to Iraq, she'd challenged their actions. What's more, she'd criticised those who compromised their work by accepting honours, justifying the decision by claiming they'd stuck around long enough to move from anti-establishment to establishment.

"Damned if you do…"

"Exactly." She was shaking.

"There *is* a third option…" Ralph's mouth curled upwards, into what Lucy understood was an awkward shrug, rather than the crooked smile others might have taken it for.

"What?" she scoffed. "Do a Westwood?" Lucy was friendly with Vivienne, but she'd said as much to her face: One does not simply *forget* to wear knickers, not to the Palace. It doesn't take the knowledge of a world-class dress designer to understand that circular skirts lift and hover when you twirl around. Every little girl knows that.

From the twitch of Ralph's shutter finger, Lucy could tell he was itching to ask. Her voice was a challenge: "Go on! Fetch your camera."

"The light's perfect," he said, as if there was nothing unusual about the scene. Just a stage-set plundered from his imagination.

The speed at which her energy drained ambushed Lucy. Sand slipping through an egg timer, an avalanche thinning to the finest trickle. Her empty hand reached for support where there was none to be found. She staggered slightly, righting a badly placed foot. What little enthusiasm she'd had was waning. She didn't think she could bear to hear the vicar say that Dominic had been 'called home' or that he was in 'a better place'. *This* was his home. His place was *here*, with *them*. Lucy had a clear idea of what hearing herself described as the 'friend of' or 'Dominic's poet friend' would unleash in her. And she wouldn't stand for any unthinking individual pinning the equivalent of these inadequate labels on Ralph. And yet Lucy couldn't be the one to abandon the idea. A lifetime of rebellion had left her sense of duty undiluted.

"What about the funeral?" she called after him.

Ralph turned. "Fuck the funeral. We both know what sort of thing it will be. All hymns and speeches. Dom wouldn't dream of going unless he had to. You're staying right there."

Relief flooded through her, countering the earlier sensation of drowning. Better to remain here, in the house Dominic had shared with them. She summoned her wits sufficiently to look at the devastation. *What have you done? You've disgraced yourself, you stupid old woman.* If only slightly, only privately. But time and time again Ralph had presented her with proof. Creation can come from destruction. This was what he did; what he'd always done. He would capture her in a way – perhaps an unexpected way. Something that would grace the covers of tomorrow's papers. A white-haired woman with trailing mascara, a shock of too-bright lipstick, standing in the ruin of her beloved rose garden. Even the tattered sleeve of her cardigan and the pulled threads of her ankle-length skirt would be saturated with meaning.

Her eyes like small slits, bleary, barely capable of remaining open; her leg muscles weak, she sank to the damp grass, crushing precious oil from scattered petals. A near-perfect triangle of vellum picked from her cardigan absorbed her completely. A moment passed in perfect misery, before Ralph's cold fingertips tilted her chin upwards. "Just a little. And a wee bit to the side. That's it."

He walked backwards over rose petals, flattening blades of grass, and took his place behind the tripod. If hers was a discipline, a religion, Ralph's art was instinctive. He gave no other direction. There was no need. She heard the rapid repeat of the shutter.

CHAPTER TWO

1948

Her father flung open the car door and, leaning in, scooped her up from its leather seat. Eyes wide, like a panicked colt's, she took in the close-quarter detail of his bow tie, the press-studs of his crisp white shirt. Without pausing to slam the door, he began to run. A ragdoll in her father's arms, bounced up and down, Lucy was helpless as she fought for breath. But the fact that Father was breaking one of his own rules made more of an impression on her than anything else.

"Slow down!" he was forever shouting. "You don't have a train to catch."

For the first time in her memory, Lucy knew beyond any shred of doubt *he hadn't the blindest idea what to do.* Him, the self-made man, with an answer for everything.

"We need some help over here. My daughter…" Feet came pounding from different directions. She was laid flat on a trolley. More running. A starched white apron. Corridors. Bright strip lighting.

"Can you feel this, Lucille?" a faraway voice asked. She had no idea what she was expected to comment on. "What about this? Anything?" The voice seemed to move further away. Wheezing filled her ears.

Adults loomed over her and exchanged serious glances. "We need to move her," a voice said. "Now!"

"Try and relax. Fighting it won't help." Feet first, Lucy was slid inside a seven foot long, eight hundred pound state-of-the-art coffin. Horribly expensive, she was told. "You're a very lucky girl, do you hear?" How quickly meanings changed. 'Lucky' now meant being imprisoned in a machine.

"See this big bag of air?"

The stiff foam collar clamped her neck in position, and Lucy's eyeballs would only move so far. All she could see was the rise of the machine's sickly-yellow casing and a short stretch of wall. There was no choice but to place her faith in the calm voice that seemed to be in control.

"It's going to breathe for you. One breath every five seconds." All around her, machinery rattled and sucked and squeezed like an ancient accordion. Breathe, bump, breathe, bump, breathe, bump. The thing was alive, Lucy was certain of it. Between each breath came a jerk. "You'll get used to the noise. You won't even notice the shaking after the first few days."

The first measure of time anyone had used. A few days wouldn't be so bad. Lucy had once been ill for a week.

Matron fixed an angled mirror above her head. "Like the rear-view mirror in a car," she explained. Lucy wouldn't be able to look at people directly but, "Look in the mirror, and you'll be able to see just enough."

What I need is a periscope, Lucy thought. From the soft scent of rose talcum powder, she knew that Mother already had her blind spots figured out.

Mother couldn't stand being around sick people. Lucy had grown up hearing her lament, "It's not that I don't *want* to do more for the war effort, it's just that I can't." She claimed to pass out at the slightest whiff of blood.

"Ridiculous thing for a grown woman to say." Cook sniffed

(despite running the house, Cook was always called 'Cook' – a hangover from the days when there were more staff, each with a different role). "With or without children."

Charity whist drives were Mother's limit. Organising. Hosting. Catering (by which she meant delivering a menu to Cook, who would raise her eyebrows, mumbling about rabbits and hats). A discreet collection box on the table in the hall. Embarrassed to ask, but if you could possibly see your way.

Mother insisted it wasn't easy for her to do the things others took for granted. She would catch whatever germs they had but, for her, it would be far worse. Last spring, when Freddie was struck down with a heavy cold, Mother visited his bedside pressing an alcohol-soaked flannel over her mouth. When she removed it there were red welts underneath.

"Just about serves her right," Lucy had heard Cook mutter as she thundered about, unaware that her opinion had leaked straight into the ears of a nine-year-old girl.

Lucy had an idea Mother had insisted she be put in a private room so she didn't have to breathe the same air as an entire ward of sick children.

Outside in the corridor, Father was making his presence known. "We're not short of money if that's the issue."

"Mr Forrester," came Matron's measured reply when he paused long enough for her to get a word in. "I'm well aware of who you are. I don't know how to put this any more simply, but I'm not waiting to be bribed before I spring into action." Father wouldn't like being talked back to. When he raised his voice, ordinary souls quaked. "The diagnosis has yet to be confirmed, but if it's what we suspect –"

"There must be something else you can do. What about penicillin?" Father was slipping back into his East End accent, as he did when angry.

"Shouting won't make the blindest difference. There *is* no medicine." Matron spoke slowly, separating each word. Lucy imagined that his elocution teacher must have sounded very much like Matron. "And penicillin might do more harm than good."

"So what do *you* suggest?"

"We do the only thing we can do."

"Which is?"

"Wait."

"*Wait?*" His tone suggested her proposal was preposterous.

"Yes, *wait,* Mr Forrester." She answered him as if he were a toddler having a tantrum.

"What? To see if she dies or if she's –"

Red alert: Lucy's brain started dispatching messages. To die just before she turned ten would be so unfair. After breaking into double figures, she thought she would finally be taken seriously.

Somewhere close by, Mother inhaled sharply. "I feel a draught, don't you?"

"No, I'm quite –" Having dodged Hitler's bombs, Lucy had assumed she was clear of danger until the next war, at least. She needed to know all there was to know. So this wasn't a chill she'd caught while playing aeroplanes in the rain. (She'd been studying Freddie's aircraft-recognition books.) Cook had bellowed from her post at the back door. Something about unladylike behaviour. Lucy, who fumed when a distinction was made between Freddie and her, had run two final laps – zooming past the tool shed, the rhubarb patch, the rows of peas and beans – Dog snapping at her heels before she hurtled into the scullery.

"Look at you, soaked to the skin. Off with those wet shoes and clothes, my girl. Oh, no you don't." Cook lunged for the leather collar around Dog's neck as he tried to follow behind. "And no running in the house."

"No running in the garden, no running in the house. Where am I supposed to run?" she'd sulked as she peeled off a sock.

"You're not, as you know very well, young lady."

No running, no kicking of balls and strictly no climbing trees.

Lucy remembered how, later that afternoon, she lost all feeling in one arm. At first, only advantages struck her: imagine it was the first day of the month with Freddie saying, "A pinch and a punch." January being the exception, it was never just one pinch and one punch. June was six of each; November was eleven, all delivered to the exact same spot so there was only ever one bruise. Rather than risk her brother calling her spineless, Lucy put up with it. Besides, Father had no patience with telltales.

Lucy experimented with a pinch. Nothing. She squeezed harder. Nothing. She wouldn't need to pretend it didn't hurt like the end of the world.

The next thing she knew, she'd fallen flat on her face – wham! There was no slow motion, no seeing it coming. Chin grazed, tongue bitten, the taste of blood. And when Lucy had opened her mouth to holler with the shock of it, no sound came. Her bottom lip trembled. This wasn't fun any more. Dog came whining and circling, before flopping down beside her. She was up on the fourth floor, the adults three storeys below. To keep panic at bay, she'd pretended to be playing hide-and-seek.

It had seemed like an eternity before Mother came to find her. "Lucille! What on earth are you doing lying on the floor?" she called from the top of the stairs. It was a relief to hear shouting. "You haven't been down to kiss us goodnight, and now you've made us late."

These days, when Father was at home, her parents often went out. 'Making up for lost time', Mother called it. 'Such a relief to finally be getting back to normal', not realising that, for Lucy, wartime *had* been normal.

"You *know* how important this evening is. It's about the future of this family."

There had been something about 'a deal' being sweetened with port and cigars. Mother's money bank-rolled Father's businesses. "We're a team." He would tap his head. "I supply the brains." Most of his ideas sounded boring; factories and munitions. But Lucy had sat up and paid attention to his latest prediction. "You wait. Once sugar rationing comes to an end, demand for ready-made cakes will rocket."

Mother had stood over her, hands on hips. "You know how your father hates to be late. Get up from there at once, do you hear?"

But Lucy couldn't do as she was told. She looked up at her mother, dressed in all her finery, and tried to make her eyes speak: *Help me.*

"Answer me when I ask you a question. Lucille?" Mother crouched and put one perfectly manicured hand on the floor. "Lucy?" Lucy's chest heaved but she couldn't suck in breath. *"Lionel. Lionel, come quickly!"*

Now, up to her neck in machinery and lying Sleeping Tigers still, it dawned on Lucy. Bit by bit, her body was shutting down. When the final part shut down, she would be dead.

"I think I'll close the door." Mother's heels clipped across the floor. Lucy wondered if she might carry on walking: out into the corridor, past Father (who was still shouting in the hope of changing Matron's mind) and down to the waiting car. Lucy's neck jarred as she went to twist it, but after the door clicked, her mother's heels clipped back. "There. Don't you think that's better?"

When the doctor at last came to give a name to the thing that was wrong with her, Lucy's world tilted. In her mind, her arms flailed as she fought to steady herself.

Polio.

It was as if she'd leapt onto what she'd thought was a solid stepping stone only to find it loose.

She was aware of a startled silence. The word had the same

effect on her parents as someone swearing at the dinner table. She might not have been able to see them, but Lucy *felt* herself being looked at.

Polio was the summer plague; it tainted the holidays, reducing healthy happy children to war veterans. Leaving her house to go to school, Lucy often saw one brave-faced girl hobbling about the square on crutches, legs trapped inside metal braces. Snatching Lucy's hand, her mother would say through her teeth, "It's rude to stare." But wasn't it ruder to ignore the girl's struggle? Ruder not to say hello when the poor girl seemed so desperate to catch Lucy's eye? Dozens of three-foot gravestones in the corner of the cemetery reserved for children suggested that the girl with the crutches was one of the lucky ones. Perhaps she'd taught herself to believe it.

"How?" Her father broke the silence. His one-word question would have fogged a mirror.

It was suggested that Lucy must have *done* something. Shaken the hand of someone who hadn't washed properly, eaten food from dirty china, or swum in contaminated water. All eyes might have been on Lucy, but Mother reacted as if *her* behaviour was being called into question.

"But we've kept her away from parks," she volunteered. "Swimming parties, the cinema, all the usual precautions." It had never occurred to Lucy that *precautions* were being taken.

While the adults racked their brains, Lucy hugged the truth close. She could hardly own up to kissing Cook's son. Her parents would assume it had been *Barney's* idea. Lucy hated all of the sitting and waiting that being ladylike involved. She'd wanted a taste of what she was waiting for.

"Ask someone else," Barney had said.

But she'd jumped onto his back, gripped his neck in the crook of her elbow and explained: "It has to be you, stupid." Kissing Freddie was out of the question and, anyway, he was away at boarding school. Underneath everything else, Lucy had a deep-seated fear that no one else *would* kiss her. Her eyes and her mouth were too large for her small face and her neck was far too long. Mother often joked that she looked like the painting of the orphan boy that hung in the morning room.

Finally, he caved. "Just get it over and done with." But Lucy insisted, *he* had to do the kissing. She wanted to know how it felt, and so she'd closed her eyes and made her lips go soft. By the time she opened them again, Barney had belted off at top speed, and she was left wondering what all the fuss was about.

Her father steered the conversation back out into the corridor. His words were chopped about in unexpected ways. "Two in every ten" reached Lucy.

So this was it. Lucy assumed that dying would be at least twice as painful as the time Father had trapped her little finger in his study door. He'd been furious, shouting that it was her fault for lurking somewhere she had no right to be lurking. Now that the machine was breathing for her, she felt brave enough to ask, "Am I going to die?"

"No!" came the reply from her blind spot, too fierce and fast to be true. "You're going to get better and you'll be coming home very soon. Do you hear me?"

She felt terribly guilty about making Mother lie, because lying was a sin. If she was going to die she should probably do something generous to redeem herself. "You and Father should go and have your dinner now," Lucy told her mother.

"Oh, never mind about that!"

"But the business. The restaurant will give your table away." She closed her eyes. "And I'm really quite tired."

Heels clipped towards the door and then back again. "Alright then, I'll fetch someone to sit with you. And I'll be back first thing in the morning so you're not alone when you wake up. How does that sound?"

Lucy did her best to smile.

"I'll say goodnight, then."

There was no kiss, Lucy reflected. And that was fine. She had lied, she knew that Mother had lied, and it seemed likely that Matron had lied about polio not being catching. She didn't think that Matron had lied when she said there was no medicine, because any sensible person would have done whatever was necessary to stop Father's shouting.

Had someone remembered to feed Dog? Funny it should be this thought that made the tears come. Dinner, she'd said to her mother, but there had been a finality about the 'Goodnight'. She'd been given up for dead.

There's no point being a cry-baby. How will you wipe your eyes and blow your nose? But pretending to be brave was difficult when there was no one to help carry the illusion. Just the living breathing gasping machine and the silent stiff-necked girl. If the machine could breathe for Lucy, perhaps it would also speak for her if someone came into the room and asked, 'Are you hungry?' That was daft. She was still the brain. The mouth, the eyes, the ears and nose. She was only machinery from the neck down.

To distract herself, Lucy dictated a letter to send to Freddie at his school. "Take this down," she told an imaginary secretary, who was sitting in her blind spot, a notepad resting on one knee. Lucy spoke in the tone she'd heard her father use with his London secretary. "Of course, Mother and Father are completely off their heads with worry, but I shall be fine. I have a machine with portholes, rather like a submarine." Freddie had spent hours over the Easter holidays, recreating on his recorder the precise eardrum-vibrating sound a submarine makes. A softness on the start of each four-second blast, a slight fade-out at the end. Lucy had cheered inside when Cook whisked the instrument away, declaring, "I'll have that now, young man."

"But I'm supposed to practise!"

"We shall all go insane if we have to listen to your practice a moment longer."

All Freddie could do was gawp as Cook stowed the instrument on top of her tallest cupboard. "There. Out of harm's way."

Of course, Freddie had taken it out on Lucy, lining up his toy soldiers and flicking them at her one by one. And she'd let him because the rules of their relationship demanded she submit if she wanted to be allowed to play.

It was no good. Freddie always had to outsmart her. If she wrote that the machine was a submarine, he would question her about its surface range and diving capacity. Lucy wished she'd paid more attention as he reeled off his boring statistics. "Scrap everything after 'brave face on it' and take this down: I shall hibernate like Tortoise until I recover." Every autumn, she and Freddie packed Tortoise away in a cardboard box under a crisp pile of brown leaves. Now that Lucy had the machine to breathe for her, she would put herself into a deep five-month sleep. Her heartbeat would slow, her body temperature would drop. She would even stop going to the lavatory.

Still no one came. Lucy imagined a row of adults crouching in the corridor, fingers to their lips, all waiting for her to die, her father repeatedly checking his watch. *She's taking her time about it.*

Fitful sleep summoned a nightmare. Lucy was singing an old nursery song, something she'd outgrown: 'Heads, Shoulders Knees and Toes'. First, she found she had nothing to point *with,* and then she found she had nothing to point *at.* The piano was very out of tune and the singing got faster and faster.

"Come on, Lucille!" Her voice shrill, Annette Mills was sitting at the keyboard playing out of tune. Strange, because she was normally on the television with Muffin the Mule and usually much better than this.

"Yes, come along, Lucille. You're not even trying."

Stuck inside the grand piano, with only her head sticking out, Lucy protested, "I am trying. I just can't." Every time Annette Mills used the pedals, a terrible jerk forced the breath out of her. All of the puppets were dancing on top of the piano. Those with strings had no trouble bending their knees and touching their toes, but Muffin was dancing in the clumsy way he always danced. Clack, clack, clack.

"I expected more of an effort from you, Lucille!"

Mr Peregrine Esquire was just opening and closing his beak and tipping forward slightly. "What about Mr Peregrine Esquire? You're not picking on him."

The piano playing stopped so abruptly someone might have said 'polio'.

Mr Peregrine walked over to Annette Mills, his beak clattering as he opened and closed it urgently. He was telling tales on her!

"No, you're absolutely right, Peregrine. What Lucille said was quite uncalled for."

Lucy's mouth opened. She twisted her head, intending to appeal to the audience, but the front row was made up of floating faces and they were all laughing at her. And then Mr Peregrine bent down and pecked her on the nose and Annette Mills was laughing too. Clack, clack, clack.

CHAPTER THREE

1973

"Your parents left you there to rot? Then they really were as bad as you've said."

"They weren't uncaring. Not deliberately, at least." Most days, Lucy didn't feel up to the truth: *she'd been given up for dead*. Today, she simply didn't want to return to that dark place. Not when she was lying naked and spent, crumpled warm sheets in a sunlit room. The broken sash window propped open, bustle from the King's Road drifted upwards and inwards, but life outside these four walls could carry on without Lucy as far as she was concerned. "They were just terribly busy." In her mind, she barrelled past her father, a severe-looking man in a severe-looking suit, who yelled, *Slow down! You don't have a train to catch*.

Dominic rolled onto his side, kissing her shoulder. "I don't like to think of you there all on your own. It would have been kinder to put you on the children's ward."

Quick to brush his tenderness aside, she said, "No, it wouldn't." This was what always happened. You gave as much as you were able to, then the questions began.

"But you'd have had company –"

"I'd have had a far better understanding of how slim my

chances were. Not just of getting over the thing. But of getting away with it." 'Getting away with it' was a phrase she hoped Dominic would understand. They often used it with each other. "Not becoming that *thing* my mother was so terrified of." In her mind, Lucy heard the clip-clip of her mother's heels as she strode towards the door.

Dominic propped himself up on one elbow "Disabled?"

"That's *so* twentieth century of you." She widened her eyes, hoping mock horror would lighten the mood.

"Crippled," Dominic countered. "Deformed."

Harsh words that struck the soft places between her ribs in unexpected ways. "Funny." Lucy winced. "Calling something by its name holds such shock-value these days." She gave a thought for the girl in the square; the girl with the leg braces and the crutches. She might so easily have been her, forced to adopt a brave and determined expression. "Instead, we look the other way."

"Perhaps it's a reaction to all those times our mothers told us not to stare."

Her breath caught. Offer Dominic a small glimpse and he turned mind-reader. *Rows of miniature gravestones. Primroses in the spring. Tinsel at Christmas.* Lucy needed to buy herself a few seconds. She plumped her pillows and rolled onto her back, half-sitting. "Do you actually believe that?"

"I have a certain sympathy, yes."

She reached for her cigarettes. As she nipped one between her lips and flicked her lighter, she could feel the intensity of his gaze.

"You shouldn't smoke, you know. Not with your lungs."

Lucy had tried giving up, but couldn't think nearly so clearly without nicotine. She'd had a machine to breathe for her and now she had a drug to think for her. "I shouldn't do lots of things." Aware that Dominic's gaze had drifted lower – as if acknowledging the difference between her left leg and her right – Lucy pulled her heels towards her body. "Stop it," she said, although it was far too late to start feeling self-conscious.

"Stop what?"

She gave him an insincere smile. "Drafting one of those observational pieces of yours."

"Ah well, if you *will* go to bed with your critic."

"Exactly." Always, that element of doubt. How far could she trust him? *Or* herself for that matter? Lucy feared the things she could tell him. *Imagine them rushing out in a great torrent.*

"Admit it." He walked his fingers up her arm. "You do your fair share of mental drafting."

"That's different." Her voice was coy but she drew deeply on her cigarette, distracted by the thought of something he'd written about her recently. *The consolation of art.* It had *sounded* like empathy, but implied that Lucy was in need of consolation because of her childlessness, which wasn't the case, as Dominic knew full well. Lucy had accused her parents of brushing anything unpleasant under the carpet, but their approach seemed to be something she had inherited. She had decided not to rise to it then, and was damned if she would spoil this moment by reacting to the memory now.

"How so?"

"I'm a poet. My subjects – *if* there are subjects – are anonymous." If Dominic recognised the sentiments he inspired, he never said so. She aimed a plume of smoke at the ceiling.

He was still observing her. "I'll tell you what I was thinking about, shall I?"

She gave a take-it-or-leave-it shrug. Dominic's kind of compliments were in many ways so much more than *I love you,* but were sometimes just that bit too clever. Too well-thought out.

"I was thinking that you –" He paused.

In Lucy's mind was the singular naked head-thrown-back her.

"You were victims of appalling timing. All that time, Salk was working on a vaccine."

Something inside her sank. Pretending to finish Dominic's sentence for him, Lucy said dryly, "Waiting until he had something suitable to test on humans."

At the time when the virus was reproducing in her mouth – the summer of 1948 – in her intestines, seeping into her bloodstream, invading her nervous system, Dr Salk was working to eliminate the possibility that there might be more than three strains of polio. Whatever his lab produced needed to target every possible variation. But elimination was slow work. Too slow for many children.

Her chest rose and fell. She would serve up a slice of truth and see how Dominic liked it. "There was a boy who'd been stuck on the children's ward for over a year. A year of lying on his back, most of it locked inside an iron lung. Five minutes at a time was all it was safe to let him out for, and then he was laid like a sack in a little cart that looked like a wheelbarrow." She took another long draw on her cigarette. "Anyway, he'd taught himself to play the glockenspiel. They propped it up in front of his face and he held the hammer between his teeth. Can you imagine anything so sad?" Her first choice of word had been 'pathetic' but that wasn't a compassionate word. Even censored, Lucy saw how uncomfortable her brittle tone was making Dominic. She decided not to spare him. "The boy asked the nurse to give his glockenspiel to me. He felt sorry for me because I was stuck on my own, while he had other children for company. That was my lowest day."

Beside her, Dominic lifted his hand to swipe at his mouth, making a noise that wasn't quite a cough.

"Don't you have anything to say to that? You usually have an opinion on everything."

"It was kind of him. Offering you the only thing that gave him any pleasure." Such an awkwardly worded reply. So un-Dominiclike.

"He was the *last* person I wanted pity from. And what was the gift he gave me? Something to turn me into a performing monkey." Her eyes focused on the ceiling, Lucy felt the two of her fingers that had been kept apart by her cigarette come together. Dominic had extracted it from its nook.

"We're all performing monkeys in one way or another," he said.

"Speak for yourself." She looked at him, curious, as he closed his eyes and inhaled. *Is everyone's life different from the way they make it seem? Do we all play a part?* "Anyway, I thought you didn't approve of my filthy habit." Dominic had become a card-carrying member of the anti-smoking campaign since he'd quit.

"It's your fault. You've depressed me."

"I've depressed y–?" Lucy's lips pursed, a small involuntary twitch. "Now, perhaps you'll understand why I don't like talking about myself."

"Have you ever thought of writing about it?"

She twisted round and looked him straight in the eye. "What the hell do you think I've been doing all this time?"

"Not poetry! Plain language."

"What? A memoir? *My mother was a self-absorbed cow and my brother was a bastard.*" Lucy felt no duty to reduce her poisoned childhood to plain English.

"And your father?"

It was as if she'd rounded a bend, found an armed road-block and was forced to brake sharply. "What *about* my father?" she said flatly.

"I don't know. You hardly ever mention him, that's all. In fact, I'm not sure I can remember you *ever* mentioning him."

"I really didn't know him. What with having his hands in everything from munitions to motor cars, he wasn't around very often." In past interviews, attempting honesty, Lucy had said, "I have no love for him. I have no hate for him. My father

26

was a fact." Her brow furrowed and she glanced away. She put her two conflicting selves down to having such contrasting parents, a mother with an ancient family name and money, her father 'a young upstart', but with looks that turned heads – or so her mother said. (By then the words hinted at regret.) Lucy's mother had been confident that she could do no wrong in her parents' eyes, and so her three-year exile had come as a shock. Mother was never allowed to forget she'd overstepped the mark. But for the arrival of a coveted male grandchild, her parents reminded repeatedly (often within Lucy's hearing), they might never have *spoken* to their daughter again, let alone allowed her to inherit. Freddie was also her parents' social salvation. Everyone had been waiting for the nod before opening their doors to the unfortunate 'love-birds'. Was it any wonder her brother had been cherished and she hadn't?

"Then let someone else write your biography."

She laughed at the idea, before Dominic's meaning dawned on her. "No. Absolutely not."

"You know I'd make a good job of it."

She could see his thinking. He'd earned his reputation as a literary critic by writing about her and he would earn his reputation as a biographer following the same tried-and-tested formula. "How could you possibly be objective? You're part of the story."

"Exactly. An eyewitness account." He handed back the cigarette.

"I'm sorry, but it's not going to happen. Pick on someone else for a change." She drew greedily on her Embassy. "Actually, no. You can write about me when I'm dead."

It was his turn to laugh. "Assuming you go first."

"This body's had a grudge against me since I was nine years old. Anyway," she changed the subject, knowing that Dominic would take note as he took note of everything. "Back in the hospital. I *did* have company. A bloody marvellous nurse by the name of Vivien. She changed the spelling so that it was the same as Vivien Leigh's."

"Virtual royalty." His voice was brooding. "Except you could get away with being rude about the royals."

"Don't sulk. We should drink a toast to Vivien, wherever she is." Lucy gave her left leg a helping hand off the bed. "How do you feel about whisky?"

"At this time in the afternoon? Against my religion."

"Ice in that?" she asked.

CHAPTER FOUR

1948

The hospital room was plunged into darkness.

"Hello," Lucy called out. Other than the ghostly caterwauling that drifted up and down the corridor, this was the closest she'd come to human contact for several hours. There was no reply. Nothing. Lucy couldn't afford to let whoever had flicked the light switch disappear. "Hello," she shouted a second time.

"Oh, I'm sorry. I didn't know anyone was in here." A woman's voice. Younger than Mother, Lucy guessed.

The light restored, Lucy squinted and tried to shield her eyes by turning her head a little to the right.

"Are you all on your own? No visitors?"

When Lucy woke, it had been pleasant to imagine her mother sitting in the chair, perhaps embroidering or reading. But of course, she hadn't come. There would be an excuse. A hand-written note beginning, *My darling, you can't imagine how terrible I feel...* It seemed shameful to be so insignificant; so low down your parents' list of priorities.

In the rear-view mirror, Lucy watched the approach of a white cotton midriff.

"What's your name?"

"Lucy," she managed.

The nurse came close, making sure she could be seen. "And how old are you, Lucy?"

"Nine."

"Well, my name's Vivien." Vivien draped herself around the machine, in a way that made Lucy imagine she was being hugged. "And I've just come from the training school for magicians' assistants."

"I beg your pardon?"

"We have them lined up in rows, all waiting to be sawn in half. I have to say, you have an excellent box." No longer a submarine, Lucy's machine was transformed into a magician's prop.

Father had once taken the family to the Finsbury Park Empire to see the Great Torrini. She had watched with a mix of fascination and horror as the magician worked his saw back and forth. *He couldn't... Not with everyone watching.*

The Great Torrini paused midway and removed his red silk handkerchief from a waistcoat pocket to wipe his brow. Lucy joined in with the trickle of nervous laughter, pretending to be in on the joke. Sawing through a woman – even a slim one – seemed to be awfully hard work. Freddie whispered: he had it on good authority that it took a good half hour for a surgeon to saw through a leg bone.

"That can't be true."

He'd shrugged. "Apparently, it gets quite boring."

When the tip of the saw dropped, Lucy moved to the edge of her seat to see if its teeth were stained with blood, comforted that the sawdust that littered the stage was pine-coloured. Torrini then strode over to his table of props and came back holding something that glinted like metal.

"Is that a *guillotine?*" Lucy consulted her brother the expert, as the magician raised one eyebrow, daring the pale-faced front row to object.

"Don't you know anything, you nincompoop?" Freddie hissed as the metal plate was slotted into the gap the saw had left. "It's to stop the blood leaking out."

"It isn't!"

But as Torrini slotted a second metal panel into place, Lucy felt a fresh creep of doubt. Then, flashing the red lining of his black cape, the magician swept the two halves apart – the box really *was* in two pieces.

Vivien was smiling down at her. The nurse would be the only one who didn't insist she was too busy to stop and chat. "Have you been asked to audition yet?"

"No!" Lucy said, not sure that she wanted to be.

After the theatre trip, Freddie had bullied her into being his assistant, but Lucy hadn't liked the look of his rusty saw, not to mention the sound of the surgeon's half hour. She drew the line at hiding in Nanny's wardrobe while her brother experimented with a variety of magic words to make her disappear. They put on a passable performance for Cook and, when her brother announced, "Mademoiselle Lucille Fifi," she stepped out, dressed in her white cotton underwear, one of her mother's stoles and some elbow-length gloves.

"Good Lord, child." Cook had herded her back to her own room. "Put some clothes on before you catch your death."

With one arm around the machine, Vivien added, "I'll let you know how the others get on, shall I? Then you can decide if you want to audition. What shall we do for now? I could read to you if you'd like."

Lucy couldn't remember the last time anyone had read to her. It seemed like the most wonderful offer. "Could you?"

"I have a copy of *Peter Pan and Wendy*. Shall I fetch it?"

As Vivien turned to leave, Lucy was gripped by panic. "Don't go!" she erupted, blinking back tears.

The nurse's face came back into view in Lucy's mirror. It was deadly serious. "Here's what we're going to do. You start counting, and by the time you get to ninety, I'll be back, I promise. Can you do that?"

Lucy's collar didn't allow her to nod. Her eyes itched and her mouth felt misshapen as she willed the words into being. "One, two –"

"Keep going," Vivien said, her shoes squeaking as she made for the door.

CHAPTER FIVE

1948

Nine years old, extremely ill and unimaginably lonely, Lucy made friends of words. Sounds planted themselves. Repeated over and over again (because time was one thing Lucy wasn't short of), they sent out shoots, voicing hidden feelings. Words were insulation and oxygen. Like the iron lung, they formed part of Lucy's new armoury. If she had a name for chains of them, it wouldn't have been poetry. Poetry was *The Lady of Shalott*, *The Highwayman* and *Stopping by Woods on a Snowy Evening*.

To Lucy, the chains seemed familiar, as if they'd always been inside her, waiting to be discovered. Sometimes she imagined that the submarine-magician's-prop delivered more than breaths at five-second intervals. As it jerked and spluttered, it communicated with her. *I am machine. You are machine.* No longer afraid that she was going to die, Lucy struck a bargain. We are machine. Geppetto had taken a block of wood and carved a puppet which sprang to life. Her story would be the exact opposite of Pinocchio's. A boy had sucked the breath from the bottom of her lungs and now an iron lung was giving her the kiss of life. Surviving meant that she would be changed.

1979: "Don't turn that off!"

"It's dinner time. I've made your favourite."

"Remind me what my favourite is." Lucy leaned to one side so that she could continue to watch the machine her father had christened the Idiot Box.

"Cheese soufflé. It'll spoil."

"Two minutes."

"What's so important? *Top of the Pops?*" Ralph's face was impatient as he turned.

A bleached-blond boy wearing black eyeliner. His eyes fixed on left of stage, alien and odd; stiff-necked as he manhandled the microphone. Some might have called his strangulated voice tuneless, almost as if he were talking. It was a voice Lucy had imagined often over the years. *We are machine.*

A musical break divided each line of lyrics. Lucy counted five seconds as a keyboard see-sawed and the boy curled his lip at the camera. Not like Elvis's sneer. This wasn't sex. It was a challenge. Mesmerised, Lucy found that she was holding her breath, as if she expected him to breathe for her. Of course, Dominic would have hated the song. A 'serious' music-lover, he was horrified by the *idea* of synthesisers. "This boy," was all she managed to say to Ralph. There was an-impossible-to-break-away-from intensity about him. Something in his words enthralled her.

He opened his mouth and let a sigh escape. "I'll bring your plate in on a tray."

"There's no need. Dish up and I'll be there in a minute."

Hearing the synthesiser swell, Lucy remembered saying goodbye to the machine. Such an intensely personal thing to do, something that proved difficult with her father tap-tapping his impatient rabbit-felt fedora against his leg. Vivien had crouched to Lucy's sitting-down height. They hugged, Lucy clinging to the nurse for as long as she dared without inviting comment from her father. But the machine, the cylindrical machine…

"You'll be glad to see the back of that thing," he said.

This view of this thing that had kept her alive had been hidden. Four rectangular observation windows on top, three portholes, the pillow where her head had lain, her rear-view mirror, and the whole thing on castors. Lucy spun the wheels of her new chair and rolled forward, until she could lay her hands on its cold metal curve.

"Excited about going home?" From the way his voice shook, she could tell that her father's hat was still tap-tapping. The rabbit, thumping its back leg.

"Yes," Lucy said, her back to him. *We are machine,* she communicated silently. But unhooked, it was no longer breathing. Lucy had a sense that she was leaving it to die.

"Well," her father held out one arm towards her, shepherding her. "Chop-chop."

Years would pass before she felt an affinity with another machine, this time a portable Olympia typewriter.

This boy on the television interested Lucy. She decided to write to him. Address the letter to his record label.

CHAPTER SIX

15 February 1995

Dear Freddie,

I am truly grateful for your reminder that this is my last chance to decide whether to cancel the reading tour that has taken six months to arrange so that I can attend Mother's eightieth birthday party.

On one level, it may well be as simple as you imply.

I could return the money to the investors and issue refunds to ticket-holders.

I could cancel my flights and hotel reservations.

There is the small matter that I might be sued for breach of contract, but you needn't concern yourself with that.

HOWEVER, don't you dare lecture me on duty.

If I have a duty, it is to Perivale Poets who took a chance on me when I was an unknown.

There are so many occasions I can recall when Mother decided that her needs took priority over mine.

Every time I needed her, I was made to feel as if I was an inconvenience and I'd fallen ill on purpose.

I was terrified. Do you understand? Terrified.

I don't care if you think I'm being melodramatic, and I

don't care if you think I should have 'got over myself by now', as you put it.

There was no room for anger at the time.

I was stuck in the belief that the blame was mine and, besides, I needed every ounce of energy just to breathe.

I coped by convincing myself that they'd forgotten they hadn't packed me off to boarding school along with you.

You have no *idea* what it was like.

There was I, putting on this brave face to protect everyone else from the truth that I might not be alright.

It always was a big house with too many empty rooms.

Populated rooms were the places I wasn't wanted.

Occasionally I might be allowed five minutes before I heard the words, 'Run along and play'.

As the girl of the family, I was expected to be well-behaved ('ladylike'), good in a way that never applied to you.

An assumption that I would be sweet-natured and accepting.

I spent my time in hallways, peering over banisters, perched on the stairs, haunting the passage outside the scullery.

Any place where I stood a greater chance of bumping into another human soul.

It wasn't your fault that you had to leave, I accept that, but my first experience of heartbreak was when you went to school.

Then, you arrived home for the holidays full of stories, expecting to pick up exactly where we had left off.

As if the loneliness of the in-between weeks could be erased.

And I went along with it because I didn't have the words.

The best I could hope for was that, by getting in the adults' way, I would prove so much of an inconvenience that I would be sent away as well.

So I began a campaign of silently standing in the doorway

of Father's study until he looked up from his papers and acknowledged me.

Of improving my grades.

Of insisting that I be allowed to perform the piano pieces I had practised, otherwise, what was the point in all those lessons?

But it was all for nothing, because I fell ill.

As an adult, I can't forgive you for not visiting or writing – not even once – while I was in hospital, or making it your business to come home more often while I was convalescing.

I couldn't allow myself to feel the misery of it at the time.

I had no concept of how long I would be bedridden, or if I would *ever* get better.

The best part of a year I was trapped in that one room.

I'm surprised you find the need to ask why I'm so protective of my writing. It's because it started during that gouged-out time, those deep-cut wounds.

If I hadn't made friends of the thoughts inside my head, I honestly believe that loneliness would have killed me.

So that we understand one another, let me spell out why your bully tactics won't wash: I will no more accept a lecture on familial duty from you than I will from Mother.

And there is no point telling me that she is old and might not see many more birthdays, because I was young and frightened and had very little chance of seeing my tenth birthday.

And, yes, I may have told her at the time that I didn't mind, but that was because she made it plain that she couldn't bear to be in the same room as me.

Of course, I minded.

If there was one small blessing, it was that I'd already had good training for being lonely.

Don't expect any thanks for the part you played in that – and don't give me your lecture about 'reconciliation'.

Let me put this as plainly as I can: even if I didn't have the tour booked, I would not come.

There is no point pressing me on the matter.
As a family, we are no good for one another.
I know that you understand this because you once looked me in the eye and asked, 'What else is there to say?'
Your sister,

Lucille

CHAPTER SEVEN

1948

"Ah," her father said, awkward to find himself face to face with a woman he was clearly unfamiliar with, in a bedroom of all places. "You must be Miss Finney."

Held in her father's arms, the way a much younger child might be carried upstairs to bed, Lucy looked begrudgingly at the young woman. To hazard a guess, she would say the new arrival was the same age as Cousin Bea.

"You've settled in, I hope. I trust everything is…" He seemed to struggle for an appropriate word. "…Adequate."

There was no explanation, no introduction. The door to the adjoining room was ajar. This was where the children's succession of looker-afterers had always slept. Miss Finney was staff.

"Perfectly adequate, thank you."

Once he had settled Lucy in the wheelchair, Father steered the new looker-afterer out onto the landing.

Not too much expected from Lucille. Nothing to wear her out. A little reading. A little drawing. Perhaps some spoken French. *So, Miss Finney was her governess.* Each item on the list punctuated by a pause. Not dead, then, but written off.

Lucy took in her new sitting-down view of her world. Had none of the adults asked themselves whether a fourth-floor room was the best place for an invalid child? But the attic rooms were where the children had always slept. Tradition couldn't be swept away because of an inconvenience (because that's what she was). Besides, she would take lessons and meals in her room. What need would she have to venture downstairs? There was nothing for her any more in the drawing room with its plush armchairs and framed photographs. Or the dining room, a place children were invited into on special occasions once they'd demonstrated that they could be trusted not to slurp their soup. Her father's wood-panelled study, a wonderful secretive place with its mahogany desk and bookcases, its studded leather chairs, cigar boxes and decanters. Before this moment, Lucy had never thought of having the run of the house as freedom. She turned the wheel of her chair, staring up at the room's unreachable window. She wouldn't even have a view of the square. She would be denied those ice-glassed mornings when she pressed her nose to the pane until the skin burned bright red. Closing her eyes, Lucy pictured the backdrop of rooftops, chimneys, and sycamore trees, and, below, the cracked cobbles, the railings, wrought iron beneath layers of glossy black, the spirit-level hedge, the hidden squirrelled, pigeoned garden within.

As she sniffed, she inhaled a sharp smell. A hospital smell. Something was amiss. Nothing she could put a finger on, but wait… She'd been so caught up in the strangeness of her homecoming that she hadn't thought. The fourth floor might as well have been Everest as far as she was concerned. Deposited on the bottom step of the staircase, she'd slumped while Father took her chair upstairs. After the repeated thuds of his solid, steady descent, he hadn't said 'Fireman's lift' as he would in playful moments when his paperwork was finished and there was no meeting to rush off to. He didn't even say

'Chin up'. She should have questioned then why Dog wasn't bounding ahead, checking to see why they were lagging behind. Instead she'd been trapped inside a memory of racing upstairs with Freddie in pursuit. The Stetson-wearing cowboy to her feathered squaw, while she whooped her war-cry.

"Where's Dog?" Lucy called out to her father.

The murmuring ceased and his head appeared around the door. "He's gone to stay elsewhere for a while. Your mother – that is *we* – had an idea that perhaps he was carrying the germs that made you ill."

The germs hadn't come from Dog, but how could Lucy say so without earning herself the most terrible dressing down? Her bottom lip quivered.

Father's heavy tread crossed the floorboards, his brogues a brown blur. "You do see?" he said, his voice above her. "It's impossible to control where a dog sticks his nose. And you would let him lick your face."

Lucy did see. Her parents had sent away her only friend – *if* she could trust that sending him away was all they'd done.

Rabbits had been kept in a hutch in the back garden during the war.

"No names," they'd been told. "They're not pets."

"He means they're for the pot," Freddie had said. She'd refused to believe it – right up to her first serving of rabbit casserole.

"You're not to worry," Father was saying. "He's being well looked after."

Lucy could tell he was lying from the way his feet moved. She wanted him gone so she could let out her hot angry tears.

"Lots of walks and fresh air." Father was waiting for her to say that she understood. Lucy understood alright. But that didn't mean she wouldn't hate him for what he'd done.

Wait until his steps are muffled by stair carpet. Not even bothering to cover her eyes, Lucy let out an almighty wail. In the midst of her misery, it dawned on Lucy that Miss Finney was sitting in the armchair. From now on every one of her tears would be public. Too late to worry about trying to fit the description of the cheerful child Mother would have painted. Lucy imagined Miss Finney's interview taking place in the morning room, decorated in shades of pale yellow, which glowed in the sunlight. *The best china please, Cook. Would you prefer milk or a slice of lemon, Miss Finney?* Or perhaps there was no lemon, in which case Mother would have said how mortified she was, not having the basics to offer visitors.

Lucy's nose was running, but there was no offer of a handkerchief, not a word of comfort. Still getting used to breathing for herself, sobbing caused Lucy considerable pain. All she wanted to do was lie down. As her disobedient wheelchair rammed itself into skirting board and furniture, she fumed.

Where *was* Mother, anyway? Perhaps she couldn't face seeing her so soon after Father had told her about Dog. "She's a little jittery. Give her time to calm down," he would be recommending, and she would happily agree, "You know best, Lionel."

She dropped the arm of the devil of a chair, but every time she tried to shuffle sideways onto the bed, it rolled forward. "Can't you see I'm struggling?" Lucy yelled in frustration.

Miss Finney set her book, pages down, in her lap and observed. "When you're lined up, put the brake on," she suggested, her voice vexingly calm.

Lucy's blood pulsed in fury. How had she known exactly what needed doing? She slid sideways onto the bed, then lassoed the foot that belonged to her weak leg with the leather strap.

"Once we've fitted you with braces," the doctor had said, "you won't need to bother with all this fuss."

Over my dead body is anyone going to fit me with instruments of torture.

"Will you please take my shoes off for me?" she asked. Her words were polite. Her tone wasn't.

Kneeling, Miss Finney attended to the buckles. Then the new governess came out and said it: "When we're alone, you can call me Pamela."

Stunned, Lucy was reminded of something she hadn't planned to remember. How she used to call her first looker-afterer *Momo* because she couldn't say *Maud* – though she couldn't think why. Perhaps she'd thought the name ugly. Thinking that Lucy was calling for her mother, the nursery nurse encouraged her, *"Mother. Moth-er"* and, tapping her own collarbone, *"Maud,"* then pinching Lucy's nose: *"Lucille."* But it was Maud's digestive biscuit smell that Lucy grew used to. Maud's lap she liked to snuggle in. She knew the precise give of Maud's arms when grabbed. The feel of one of her own small hands in Maud's.

To begin with, *"Momo"* produced the desired effect. The nurse scooped her up from her crib. But then Maud disappeared. Apparently she'd given notice because she believed that Lucy had mistaken her for her mother. Cook told her Maud had said, "She's getting too attached. It's not right."

Lucy knew the natural order of things, even if Miss Finney didn't. A governess was always a Miss. Still, Call-me-Pamela was no Vivien. The way she crossed her arms didn't suggest that fun would feature high on her agenda. Lucy thought of the pleasures of quiet rebellion. Notes written in invisible ink. A stolen kiss. A name that shouldn't be yours to say. *If this is all that's on offer, jump at it.*

Cook came heavy breathing, with an enormous tea-tray and eleven weeks' worth of bottled gripes. Pamela stepped into the adjoining room, clicking the door shut behind her. With Cook in full flow, Lucy wasn't expected to do anything more than nod. She found herself caught in a limbo, halfway between her hospital room and old memories. Sitting on *Momo's* soft-cushioned lap. (Later she would tell herself that Maud's nursery rhymes must have been her first experience of poetry, certainly of rhyme.) Vivien looking her directly in the eye, laughing as she read *Peter Pan and Wendy.* Wondering at everything that was different and everything that was the same.

"Knock, knock," came a cheerful greeting. Mother put on her surprised act at finding Cook seated in the bedside chair; Lucy propped up on plump pillows, tucking into a buttered scone. "No, no, Cook, don't get up. I came to make sure Lucy has everything she needs, but I can come back later." A flutter of slender fingers and she was gone.

"Timed to perfection," Cook scoffed, reaching for another scone. "Couldn't even look you in the eye." Lucy was still getting over the shock of being taken into an adult's confidence when Cook added, "Oh, before I forget, Barney sends his best. He's been proper worried about you, no mistake."

She almost choked. "And he's – He hasn't been ill, has he?"

"No, touch wood. Up to his usual scrapes though." She rolled her eyes. "I'd send him up to see you if I thought –" She stretched her mouth into an awkward smile as Pamela emerged from the adjoining room, not interrupting but indicating towards the landing. "But what with you in your nightdress, you can hardly have visitors."

Pamela paused in the doorway. "I'm sure Lucy would welcome a visitor or two."

They both reddened.

"It's – it's my son we're talking about, Miss Pamela," Cook stammered.

"You needn't worry. I'll make sure Lucy doesn't bully him."

It was extraordinary that Pamela didn't see the danger. Not to mention the fact that Cook's son had no business being in the house. But Barney was familiar and, what's more, he might have an idea where they'd taken Dog – *if* he's been taken anywhere, Lucy reminded herself.

"You don't mind if I make myself some tea while Lucy has you for company, do you, Cook?" Pamela asked. "I'll only be gone a quarter of an hour."

"Take all the time you need." Cook waited until the bedroom door closed, then turned to Lucy. "Well, young lady. I think we can safely say we've found a new ally."

CHAPTER EIGHT

1948

With hindsight, Lucy was amazed how quickly the governess sized up the cardboard stage-set behind the grand façade. A father who was absent three or four nights a week. A mother – the public face of the Forresters – whose pressing appointments left little time for her invalid daughter.

Barney's first visit was enough to make them both squirm with embarrassment. He shoved a bunch of snapdragons at her. "She made me."

They were quite obviously picked from the garden. Lucy gathered he hadn't told Cook about the kiss.

"How lovely." Pamela stepped in and, after putting the flowers in water, went back to pretending to be absorbed in the pages of *Animal Farm*.

They muddled through ten or so excruciating minutes' talk but their tongues loosened as they argued over how to make sure yours was the winning conker (Barney had cooked his, but Lucy thought he should have soaked it in vinegar). They were approaching something like normal conversation as Barney told how the frogspawn in the garden pond looked just like his mother's tapioca pudding.

She sighed. "I'll miss this year's tadpoles."

"You don't have to."

"How am I going to get downstairs? I suppose you're going to carry me, are you?"

"No chance. I'll bring some up in a jam jar."

Surprised there was to be a next time, she looked to Pamela, who said, "What a good idea."

Between the three co-conspirators, while Lucy couldn't go out into the world, they smuggled the world up three flights of stairs. Cook came with a mixing bowl hidden in a laundry basket and produced a spatula from a sleeve. "Cake mixture. So you won't miss out on scraping the bowl. But don't go getting it on the sheets. How's our Jeremy Fisher doing?" She picked up the jam jar and held it at eye level. "Oh look, he's got legs!"

Barney supplied perfectly-formed pine cones, a lucky penny, part of a blue patterned tile, even a bone the gardener had dug up from a flower bed.

"That's a femur," said Pamela, and to blank expressions she explained, "It's a thigh bone. Perhaps it belonged to a family pet?"

Lucy swallowed her fears. The moment she voiced them, they would become true. She waited until the governess was distracted then leaned towards Barney, meaning to whisper.

He jerked away from her. "Oh, no you don't. I'm not falling for that again!"

She widened her eyes and hissed, "I have a question, twerp. Could you find out where they've taken Dog?"

"Where they've taken Dog," Barney repeated, glancing at Miss Finney's back, and carrying on the conversation at a normal level.

"I think it must be the countryside, somewhere."

Then, one day, Pamela did something extraordinary, even by her standards. She produced a stack of newspapers, pristine and unopened. "Your father suggested a little reading. It's time we made a start."

Drop-jawed, Lucy looked from the pile to her governess and back again. "Where did you get them?" she asked, though it was perfectly obvious. Father had *The Guardian* delivered on weekdays and *The Observer* on Sundays.

"I rescued them. Cook throws your father's newspapers away when he's not at home."

Lucy thrilled at the idea of being the first to unfold the pages (the millions of other subscribers meant nothing to her) but Pamela flattened one hand on top of a headline.

"First, I need you to understand something. What you read is only one person's opinion. And clever people can make their opinions sound like facts. That's why we must question everything."

Chomping at the bit, Lucy nodded.

"What could we do if we wanted to separate the fact from the opinion?"

Lucy shrugged. "If it's a report about something that's already happened, we could check in a book."

"What makes you think that anything you'll find in a book isn't someone else's opinion?"

"I meant a history book, not a storybook." Lucy's cheeks flushed.

"I'm not trying to embarrass you. History's written by people who won the wars. What if there were facts they wanted to hide?"

Lucy thought of Freddie. "You mean they might have cheated?"

It was the governess's turn to shrug. "It's possible."

But quoting dates and facts parrot fashion was how you passed tests. "Then what *can* I trust?"

"Yourself. You must train your instincts until you can rely on them. Keep asking questions."

This was the exact opposite of everything she'd ever been told. "Cook says I already ask too many."

"People of Cook's generation tend to be non-askers of questions, but we won't solve the world's problems by repeating what's gone before."

That learning mattered beyond the classroom came as a shock. Lucy wasn't expected to cram for a test. She was expected to solve something.

"Now, where are my scissors?" Pamela looked about her.

"Scissors?"

"You didn't think I was going to give you a whole newspaper, did you?"

That was *exactly* what Lucy had thought. Cut-out columns were considerably less satisfying. Still, the child who couldn't run and play outside became better informed on world affairs than her mother, who preferred *The Tatler* to newspapers. Lucy read about the National Health Service – 'The taxpayers' burden'. Pamela cast Nye Bevan as a hero, while Dr Coates (son of the old Dr Coates, and a regular visitor to the fourth floor) was convinced of Bevan's treachery.

"So which is he? Hero or villain?" Lucy asked.

"You'll have to make up your own mind," Pamela told Lucy.

She read how the first photo-finish camera made its debut at the London Olympics in front of a packed stadium. Ewell, who'd been the clear winner of several track events, raised his hands in victory as he crossed the finish line of the 100-metre sprint. He danced sideways, grabbing the hands of fellow competitors to receive their congratulations. But the photographic image, developed in eight minutes flat, confirmed that his American teammate's chest had touched the tape first. Dillard took gold.

Lucy asked a question. "So, in the past, the gold medal could have gone to the wrong person?"

"I imagine quite a few mistakes have been made."

You expected mistakes at Freddie's sports day. You didn't expect them at the Olympics.

Sometimes when articles didn't need much censoring, Lucy received what still looked like a newspaper but with cut-out windows.

The *Windrush* docked at Tilbury with an exotic cargo of labourers, come to help rebuild Britain.

Cook sighed as she drew the curtain. "Who'd have thought *we'd* need help from the Islands?"

"Just see how welcome we've made them feel," said a cynical Pamela. "Putting them up in five-star accommodation." This was a decade when lodging houses displayed notices saying 'No blacks, no Irish, no dogs'. A deep air raid shelter in Clapham South had become home to many 'Sons of Empire'.

Over meals, girl and governess discussed topics that would have been considered unsuitable for the dining room. Lucy wondered what would come out of her mouth if Mother ever joined them. She wouldn't be able to pretend to un-know the things she'd learned. Safe subjects, then. The birth of the Next King of England. But in Lucy's remembered version of those eleven months, Mrs Forrester's appearances were rare. This may not have been the reality (her mother would almost certainly have disputed it), but that sense of being hidden from view was Lucy's truth. As she strapped the foot of her weak leg, sidled into the chair and wheeled herself to her desk, she couldn't forget that she'd been given up for dead.

Pages rattled and Lucy dreamt up more questions. Why pin medals on men who were responsible for hundreds of deaths but hang those responsible for just one? When Barney – two years her senior – repeated what he'd been taught, she challenged him. Pamela nodded approval, not because Lucy always arrived at the right conclusion, but because she no longer accepted what she was told as fact. There was no pretence that they were anything other than a governess and her charge, but piece by piece, brick by brick, the wall between the two came down.

In the outside world, beyond the house on the square, boundaries of all sorts were shifting.

Less than seven months after Gandhi's assassination, India gained independence. *Today the new Dominions of India and Pakistan are in being.* Historic words.

In Paris, the United Nations General Assembly adopted the 'Universal Declaration of Human Rights'.

The British Nationality Act granted British citizen status to all Commonwealth citizens.

"Are there any other countries which have six counties cut off by sea?" Lucy asked, after reading that the Republic of Ireland had come into being.

"Geography!" Pamela sprang from the armchair and Lucy rolled her wheelchair backwards so that the governess could get to the map of the world that was pinned above her desk. Taking a black marker, Pamela divided Northern Ireland from the south with a thick line. Lucy imagined it as a wall.

"Will we still be called the United Kingdom?"

"Not all countries are islands, but these are good questions." Unlike Lucy's father, Pamela was never embarrassed to admit she didn't know the answer.

Shortly afterwards, the proclamation of the Federal Republic of Germany split the East from the West. It was just approaching lunchtime and, after a difficult morning, Lucy was sitting up in bed, something Pamela normally discouraged.

"Lucy," said Pamela, handing her the black marker. "If you could please draw a line around the British and American Zones."

Propped up on pillows, Lucy watched in disbelief as the governess towed her wheelchair away from the side of the bed.

"And, while you're at it, circle the city of Bonn." She applied the brake.

Earlier, Dr Coates had said it was time he measured Lucy for a leg brace. Angry tears had sprung to her eyes. She'd clenched her mouth, refusing point blank. Rather than argue, the doctor turned to Pamela. Now Lucy was being tested. Either she took the ten steps across the room, propped herself against the desk and drew a line on the map, or Pamela would side with Dr Coates. Meanwhile Pamela had turned, her hands clasped behind her back. Instead of studying the map, she looked down from the window to the square below. "B-O-N-N. You'll find it in the Rhineland."

Lucy didn't have to rack her brains to guess who her governess was watching. *Don't stare, Lucille.* Crutches tight in her armpits. Shoes attached to leather knee pads by metal rods. Straps and buckles cutting off her circulation. Gritting her teeth, Lucy lassoed her uncooperative foot and helped it off the bed. *I will* not *be that girl.*

CHAPTER NINE

1949

Cook's eyes widened at the headline: *Scandal at Wimbledon Tennis.* "Good Lord!" With a thunderous rattle, she gathered up the paper – the most complete to date – from the desk. "That woman's underwear is on display."

Lucy's mouth fell open. She had only just glimpsed the ruffled lace trim.

Pamela calmly met Cook's gaze. "You had no objections about the photographs of the women's swimming team last summer."

Not to be intimidated by someone less than half her age, Cook folded the newspaper very deliberately, tucked it under her arm and picked up Lucy's lunch tray.

Pamela gently retrieved the paper and flattened it against her chest. "If it's inches of bare flesh that concerns you, they'd have won hands down."

Despite the moment's delicious unpredictability, the ten-year-old had no idea what she would do if asked to choose between two of the few people who were on her side.

"But that was swimming."

"So it's *tennis* you object to?"

The small sound Cook emitted made it clear that she wasn't going to waste another breath.

But Pamela hadn't finished. "Is it so wrong for a young girl to see what training can do for a body? Don't you think Lucy's capable of deciding whether or not she's offended?"

Cook shook her head and shuffled towards the door. "The world's changing and no mistake."

"We've already had two world wars," Pamela called after her. "We can only hope it changes fast enough to prevent a third."

Cook turned. Her eyes flared. "Stop that scaremongering! What I'm talking about is common decency. Perhaps you won't be so quick to point the finger when you've been around as long as I have." And because leaving the room was the only way that Cook could claim the last word, she made a hasty exit.

Pamela smiled to herself, as if she thought that Cook's reaction wasn't only predictable but was correct in the order of things. "I'm afraid the world Cook put her faith in is crumbling."

"Do you really think there'll be another war?" Lucy asked.

Pamela paused before answering. "Many people argue that Hitler should have been stopped much earlier than he was. Next time, politicians might not be so willing to sit down and talk. So, yes. I'm afraid I do."

A fierce explosion lit the back of Lucy's mind, a column of dense black smoke topped by a mushroom-shaped cloud. The little she knew about the bombs that were used at the end of the last war had given her nightmares.

"Now, here we are." Pamela laid the newspaper on the desk in front of Lucy, open to the centre spread. "Gertrude Moran." Photographers had jostled for positions where the shots they took of the tennis player made her already-short skirt look shorter still. In the Parliamentary debate that followed, Cook would side with those who accused the player of bringing 'vulgarity and sin into tennis'. Pamela thought it ridiculous that the matter was debated at all. But looking at the pictures, Lucy had no interest in the way the American's skirt billowed to reveal a ruffle of lace. Her attention drawn by the young woman's muscular thighs, Lucy's hand strayed to the top of her own left leg. It seemed no wider than the bone.

Seeing this, Pamela said, "You're so much stronger than you were."

"Do you think I'll ever play a sport?"

"Perhaps – if you continue working at the exercises Dr Coates has given you." Pamela cocked her head as if considering an alternative. "Can you swim?"

An ice-cold memory shuddered through Lucy. She'd been sitting by the side of the lido, dangling her legs, when someone running past had knocked her in. She plunged into deep water, sinking below the legs of others, bubbles streaming from her mouth. Moments passed before she remembered to kick. Since her illness, Lucy had lost all confidence that her limbs would do as she asked. "Yes," she gasped.

"It would be a good way to build up the muscle in your left leg."

These days choices weren't real choices. There was only ever the lesser of two evils. She tried to sound more positive than she felt. "Will you ask Mother?"

"You can ask me." Mr Forrester's deep tenor made them both turn sharply. The bedroom door already swinging on its hinges, Lucy barely had time to close the newspaper. She appreciated the reassuring squeeze of Pamela's hand on her shoulder as Father pushed his way into the room, followed closely by Dr Coates. A heady smell of cigar smoke suggested they'd been locked away in Father's study.

"Sir." Pamela stepped to one side of Lucy's desk.

"Miss Finney," Mr Forrester acknowledged the governess, then Lucy found herself caught rabbit-like in the spotlight. "Lucille, Dr Coates has just informed me that you refused to be measured for a leg brace." She felt betrayed, yet it should have been obvious that Dr Coates would have had to report back after this morning's disagreement. "Is that correct?"

Lucy wanted so much to resist the urge to cower, but her shoulders shrank inwards. If she'd had more sense, she would have planned what to say.

"If I may?" Pamela cut in, drawing the men's attention. "I can sympathise with Lucille. She's seen an older girl struggle about the square on crutches and wearing braces." There was no tremor; her voice was steady and true. "When she's shown no sign of improvement, is it any wonder that Lucille lacks confidence that braces are the answer?"

While Pamela had the men's attention, Lucy glanced at the desktop. The newspaper had gone. In her own way, the governess was proving to be a magician.

"One of the problems is that leg braces restrict movement," she was continuing. "Lucy can already walk short distances on her own." The girl worked hard to keep the surprise from her face. She had progressed from the ten steps between her bed and the desk, but had yet to make it as far as the square. Three flights of stairs stood in the way. "What she needs is strength-building exercise."

Father made no attempt to conceal his displeasure. "I rather think that Dr Coates is best placed to advise on Lucille's medical needs."

"Then perhaps I can ask *you*, Doctor?" Pamela had a miraculous way of twisting everything the men said, so that it seemed to be exactly what she'd wanted to hear. "Lucille's worked hard at the exercises you've given her, but we were just discussing the possibility of adding swimming to her regime."

A gruff sound stuck in the back of the doctor's throat. "My recommendation would be both a leg brace *and* a course of swimming."

"But you didn't recommend both."

Lucy's breath caught. Was her governess afraid of *nothing*? It seemed she wasn't; the newspaper was tucked under Pamela's arm, hidden in plain view.

"I beg your pardon." The challenge also appeared to have surprised Dr Coates.

"You didn't mention swimming as an option. Unless perhaps I'd stepped outside at that point?"

Clearly ruffled, the doctor appealed to Father. "To be effective, the child would need to swim for an hour each day. And who has time to organise such treatment?"

"Hmm." Lucy's father, who spent half of every week in Birmingham, seemed inclined to agree. Daily commitment was beyond him. Even now, he kept glancing towards the landing, keen to be getting back to whatever it was he'd been dragged away from. And it was unlikely that Mother could be persuaded to take her to a public pool, even if a teacher could be found.

"I do," said Pamela. "It would do us both good to get out more often."

"You'd take on the responsibility?" Mr Forrester asked. "On top of your other duties."

"We'd go early in the morning. The pool will be less crowded and, that way, Lucille's other lessons needn't suffer."

The doctor cut in: "And how will you get there?"

Lucy looked to Pamela. *Yes, how?*

"We'll take the bus. It's only a short walk to the main road. Lucy needs to practise on the stairs, and to build on her distances. At the other end, the bus stops right outside the baths."

She supposed she could slide down the bannisters.

Her father's brow furrowed. He referred to the doctor. "Should we worry about the risk of using public baths? Especially at this time of year."

"I think we're a little beyond that."

Lucy felt her eyes widen. If he was saying that any damage was already done, then Dog could come home! She was about to suggest as much when Dr Coates turned to Pamela.

"The question I have for you, Miss, is –"

"Miss Finney." Pamela had *interrupted*.

The doctor's jaw dropped.

"Oh, I'm sorry, Dr Coates. I thought you'd forgotten my name. Do go on."

Frowning, the doctor complied. "The question I have for you," Pamela made the slightest of head movements as if she were prompting him, "Miss Finney," and here a demure smile, "is, are you *qualified?*" His tone suggested he thought he'd reclaimed the upper hand.

"I taught my younger brother to swim." Pamela sounded humble. "It was a great aid, both in terms of getting the strength back in his limbs and boosting his confidence."

The doctor frowned. "Your brother?"

Lucy's father turned to Dr Coates, lowering his voice. "Infant paralysis. It's the reason my wife thought Miss Finney would make Lucille such an ideal companion."

All thought of Dog suspended, Pamela came into focus for the first time. It should have been obvious when her governess had known the workings of wheelchairs…

"And did your brother make a full recovery?" The doctor's voice reined in Lucy's thoughts. She was eager to hear the answer.

"As you know, things are never quite that simple." Pamela lifted her chin. "His starting point was far worse than Lucille's. He has good days and bad, but he walked unaided within a year – and he's just made me an aunt."

Lucy had pictured Pamela visiting bookshops on her days off. Sitting alone in a café, walking in a park. But always alone. Never part of a *family*.

"And are you prepared to work hard at this, Lucille?"

Lucy was startled to find herself the centre of attention once again. What Pamela had proposed – daily visits to a public pool – filled her with horror. She felt herself plunging downwards once more, but kicked hard. She must do whatever it took to avoid becoming the girl in the square. "Yes, Father."

He glanced at his wristwatch, then covered its face with his opposite hand. "Miss Finney, we'll continue this discussion when I get back from Birmingham." He took the doctor by the elbow. "If you can bear with us until Thursday, Doctor."

"By all means. Four days is neither here nor there."

Not when so little is expected, thought Lucy.

"Then I'll show you out." Lucy's father reached for the door handle.

"With your permission." Pamela followed the men onto the landing. "If you don't advise against it, Dr Coates – and if you have no objections, Mr Forrester – I'd like to make a start tomorrow."

"Tomorrow?"

"That way, I'll be able to report back on how Lucy is in the water."

"You realise you may be building up the child's hopes?" The doctor had lowered his voice, but it wasn't so low that Lucy couldn't hear. An experienced eavesdropper, she knew how to still her breathing. "The girl you described. At least she's up and about. A leg brace may not be the *answer,* as you put it, but it *may* be the enabler."

Pamela maintained an even tone. There was no hint of emotion. "For Lucy, going out into the world to be pitied would be a compromise."

While the silence that followed breathed, Lucy wondered if Pamela hadn't gone too far. She imagined Father tight-mouthed, fretting over the meeting he had to chair or the speech he had to make or the factory he had to tour – or whatever blasted thing it was that took priority. Just as she'd known he would, he broke the stalemate, passing responsibility back to the physician: "Doctor?"

Lucy heard someone exhale loudly – Dr Coates, most likely. "We seem to be dealing with a very determined young lady. All I will say is there is no *harm* in it."

"Lucy's attitude is such a bonus." Pamela spoke as if the credit was Father's. "She's keen to push herself."

"You'll need money," Father said, herding them onwards. "You'd better come down to my study. *Lucille?*"

"Father?" She shot up straight, as if she'd been caught misbehaving.

"We'll talk again on Thursday evening."

"Yes, Father."

CHAPTER TEN

1949

Lucy looked at the expanse of cold yellow floor tiles between the changing room and the shallow end. Eyes were focused on her, hands cupped over mouths, judgement was being pronounced. Lucy stared at her left foot. Pamela had said that she mustn't drag it. She must make it *walk*. She raised her chin an inch or so. A woman on her back, arms like a paddle steamer; the lifeguard, whistle in mouth.

For the first two mornings, Pamela only had her hold the rail and kick. She was reminded how her limbs had once trusted the water; how she had trusted her legs. But commanded to swim, Lucy panicked, swallowing chlorinated water.

"Let's try it again." Pamela was standing in the shallow end.

Lucy held her breath until her hand grasped the rail and she could be sure she hadn't drowned.

Convinced she hated swimming, she failed to notice when she began to enjoy herself – when, eventually, to her delight, she managed a full width. A week later, she progressed from doggy paddle to something approaching breast stroke – half-circular movements ending with what could be described as a controlled kick. Widths became lengths.

Gradually, she added to her tally, no longer needing to stop and catch her breath at the deep end; touching and pushing off, as if playing tag.

Days assumed a new shape. Woken at five-thirty, Lucy stopped pulling a pillow over her head to block the harsh electric light. She cheated on the stairs, bumping her way down. Pamela wouldn't let her cheat on the walk and that hurt, but she timed herself and it didn't last long. The prospect of joining the jostle of commuters spurred her on. How appalled her mother would have been at the things she overheard on the bus! While Lucy delighted in the gossip and swearing and all kind of talk not fit for the dining room, Pamela seemed capable of focusing on her current book, unwavering. If there was no gossip, Lucy would study a face and the way a person dressed and sketch an entire life for them: name, date, occupation, pet hates, passions, the place they called home, the people they shared it with, the nightmares that dragged them violently from sleep.

The first time Pamela stood to get off several stops too early on the return journey, panic rose in Lucy's chest. "Where are we going?" she asked, clinging to a pole to haul herself up.

"You'll see."

An unknown. "Is it far?"

"We'll take it nice and slowly – but no dragging that left foot!"

They detoured down a narrow side street crammed tight with tall, dark buildings. Lucy's sense of the place was as immediate as her curiosity. A village within a city, was that it? Unscheduled, this diversion felt rebellious, disobedient – all those things a young girl denied spontaneity yearns for. She watched a man unloading what might have been a cream-coloured footrest from the back of a grocer's van.

Pamela hesitated at a corner, allowing Lucy time to catch up on her good right foot and her wayward left. "Cheese," she said, answering the question that hadn't yet been asked.

Cheese came in small squares or oblongs of pale yellow, in triangles with red rind, or the 'adults' cheese', putrid and blue veined. *Cheese,* Lucy repeated inside her head as if it were some wonderful new invention. The deliveryman carried it inside a narrow shop with an old-fashioned plate glass frontage.

Pamela pointed to hooks on the ceiling. "Do you see the hams?"

They looked nothing like the ham Cook prepared at Christmas, but Lucy nodded for fear of looking stupid.

A man in a white apron and with a strong accent said, "You come?"

She was abruptly shy. "I – I haven't got any money."

"You come!" He beckoned enthusiastically. "Looking costs nothing."

Lucy glanced back at Pamela, hoping to be handed an excuse to decline. But the governess didn't say, 'We really must be getting a move on'. Instead she nodded: "Go ahead."

Unfamiliar things were given familiar names. Jewel-like chains of dried chillies hung alongside strings of garlic tied together with blue twine. Behind a glass counter sat things Lucy had never heard of before: olives and anchovies. There were bags of something hard and shell-like called pasta, and tomato sauce that came in oversized jam jars.

"Is this what food looked like before the war?" she asked.

"No." The man threw back his head and laughed. "This is Italian food!"

"Food of the gods," the deliveryman agreed, kissing the tips of his fingers.

A few doors down, the mouth of an alley was blocked by a person smoking a cigarette. Though the person was dressed in a fur coat and wore towering heels, the face Lucy looked into briefly would have looked better on a man. Tripping over her own feet, she glanced back over her shoulder, questioning what her eyes had suggested. The person jutted his square jaw and blew a perfect smoke ring, followed by a smaller ring that floated through the first and dispersed. No one told her not to stare.

Pamela came to a halt outside a café with blue and white awnings. Maison Bertaux. "Here we are," she announced. "Your father suggested 'a little French conversation', so I've brought you to a place where you'll hear spoken French."

"Pam-e-la!" a waitress exclaimed (Lucy liked the name far better when its syllables were separated). "We wondered where you'd got to."

"Beatrice." Pamela turned, kissed the waitress warmly on both cheeks.

Lucy felt a stab of jealousy. To think, Pamela had this whole other life away from the square. Not only family, but friends too.

Meanwhile, a man in a chef's apron emerged from a side door. He strode over declaring, "Pam-e-la, *viens ici!*" and pulled her to his shoulder.

"Al-bear."

"And who is your young friend?"

She was to be included.

"This is Lucy. We're celebrating. She's just swum ten lengths." Was that *pride* in Pamela's voice?

The waitress called Beatrice used her round metal tray as a gong. "Bravo!"

"And she's also here to practise her French."

"Bonjour, Lu-cy! *Ça va?*"

She glowed at the sound of her own name, transformed. This was one question she knew the answer to. "*Ça va bien, merci,*" she replied.

"Oh," the waitress said, as if the voice she'd just heard was musical. "But you already speak excellent French."

Amid the exotic clamour, playing in the background was music: a woman singing very long, sad notes and who rolled her 'r's as if gargling with salted water. Lucy took her seat at a table by the window, but could wait no longer. Leaning towards Pamela, she said, "The lady? What's she singing about?"

"Love."

"Not just love." Beatrice went to hand Lucy a padded red menu. "The most marvellous love affair."

"Golly, I had no idea love was so awful." But that wasn't quite true. Kissing Barney had taught Lucy that love had consequences every bit as woeful as the song suggested. A boy who kissed you could suck the breath from your lungs.

Beatrice laughed. "At your age, I should hope not!"

"We don't need menus," Pamela said. "Lucy will have *chocolat chaud* and a croissant."

"Very good. And will you have your usual?"

"Please."

Lucy leaned across the table a second time. "What's a croissant?"

Beatrice cut in. "It's the second most important word in the French language. You'll see."

Though swimming left her ravenous, Lucy picked her warm pastry apart slowly, then licked a fingertip and rescued every last flake.

Within a couple of visits to the café, the girl was greeted like an old friend and shown to what was referred to as 'Lucy's table'. Her French, which had stopped at *'Hello, how are you?' 'My name is'* and *'What time is it?'* improved. She could now order her own breakfast.

September came and with it a complicated maths lesson. The government devalued the pound. What had been worth $4.03 was now worth only $2.80. Lucy looked up from the newspaper, frowning. "Does that mean we have less money than before?"

"No, a pound is still a pound. This will only affect your parents if they want to spend money *outside* Britain. The government wants to encourage British businesses to sell to British people. Of course, it will cost a lot more to pay back the money America lent us during the war."

That countries lent money to other countries was news to Lucy. "Why did we need to borrow money?"

"Bombs and guns are very expensive, I'm afraid."

Time passed slowly, but not as slowly as it had done. All these things and more were deliberated in the fourth-floor bedroom.

The People's Republic of China.

Riots at London's opening of *A Streetcar Named Desire,* "Is there no statesman in high places," asked Reverend Colin Cuttell of Southwark, "who will tell the United States to keep its sewage?" (Lucy rather admired his use of the word.)

Though larger boundaries were shifting, Lucy sensed movement that couldn't be charted on a map. There was a presence. A her beyond the self she knew. Something inside her that had been biding its time was awakening. It wasn't just that her hard work had been paying off. As well as her physical recovery, there was an impatience, a longing, a confusion of thoughts that needed to be set in order.

Sometimes she was aware of actively thinking the thoughts. Sometimes, it seemed they were inside her, waiting until she stumbled across them. Almost as if she was a bystander and they had thought of *her*.

"You're never without a pencil and paper these days." Cook shuffled through the door, out of puff after tackling the stairs. Laundry deliveries were becoming quite a chore.

Lucy begrudged this intrusion. Pamela's afternoon off

should be *her* time to do with as she wanted. But what Cook said was true; these days, she kept a notepad under her pillow with a pencil slotted into the spiral binding. At night Lucy was often wrenched from sleep, gasping for air or with a cold wind gusting through her soul. She might be buried alive, scratching at the lid of a coffin. Or a magician's assistant, sawn in half, blood dripping thickly on the sawdust. Entombed inside a submarine that was slowly filling with water, her knuckles rapping hollow on its metal shell. Trapping her terrors on the page made them shrink.

"Keeping a diary, are you?"

"No!" Lucy encircled what she'd been writing with her arms. Thoughts and dreams were private things.

"No need to hide what you're doing from me. I haven't got time to read it." And as if to prove the point, Cook walked unevenly from the room that was Lucy's in name, but never wholly hers.

She rested her forehead on the desk for a moment. That had been a lucky escape. Imagine if Freddie had walked in on her. She could almost see him standing on the landing, reading what she'd written at the top of his voice.

I was not always like this
Just a head in a box
I have an itch I cannot scratch
I have tears I cannot wipe away
Heaven help me if I catch a cold
You might say I'm up to my neck in it

Holding the papers high above her reach, he would let go of them one by one saying, "Oops, dropped it. Oops, there goes another. You might catch this one if you're quick off the mark. Oh, but I forgot…"

And then one evening Pamela didn't come home after her afternoon off. Seated at her desk, Lucy was chewing her pencil, wood and graphite – what she thought of as 'lead' – combining on her tongue. Her shoulders jerked as the telephone shrilled. Silly, really. Logic said that if a telephone never rang, it would be rather like a game of hide-and-seek when no one came to find you.

She heard the thud of Cook's footsteps on the lower staircase, then her mother's shout: "Let it ring!"

This latest development in Mother's behaviour infuriated Cook, especially since her knees weren't what they used to be: "I counted to forty! Nobody hangs on the line for forty rings unless it's an emergency. And do you know what the most annoying thing is?"

"No?" Lucy ventured. A short reply was best. Cook fired questions when she had plenty left to say.

"I hear the echo of the ringing long after it's stopped."

Keeping watch from her vantage point, Lucy saw that Cook wasn't the only one who counted. When the telephone began to shrill, Lucy's mother would stand in the doorway of the morning room. Often, the phone cut out at six rings, in which case she would emit a small *hmp,* as if satisfied, but more than six rings and Mrs Forrester would say, "It will only be Mr Forrester," dismissing him as she would an inconvenient relative. *What if it's an emergency?* Freddie's headmaster, perhaps. You'd have thought Mother might have woken up to the possibility since her illness.

Three, four, five, six. As she counted, Lucy realised that dusk had crept past unnoticed. In some absent-minded moment, she must have switched on the desk lamp and slid her notepad inside its halo, dragging out an illusion of afternoon. The quality of the darkness suggested that teatime had come and gone. Pamela was never late. So where was she? Was that her on the phone? But the ringing stopped, leaving a silence so loud it was overwhelming.

Lucy listened for evidence of activity in the house below. It was always possible that Mother had invited Pamela into the morning room for one of her 'quiet words' – a phrase that filled Lucy's heart with dread. It was almost preferable when her mother forgot the architect had given the house a top floor. But there was no muffled murmuring. Just the grandfather clock's steady tick.

Usually, when Pamela returned from her afternoon off, she would look in on Cook and collect their tea-tray from the kitchen. Depending on whether or not Lucy's parents were both at home, and whether or not they were eating in (rarely, unless they were entertaining), what was effectively a hand-over would be the housekeeper's final duty before she untied her apron strings. Perhaps Pamela had joined Cook for tea. Occasionally, they called a truce to mull over how Barney was getting on at school.

When Lucy's stomach began to grumble, her sense of abandonment intensified. Cook made no secret of the fact that she thought theirs a strange household to work in. The elderly housekeeper had put up with some fairly irregular arrangements over the past year, meals on trays and so forth, and not always uncomplainingly. Was it possible *Pamela* had decided not to put up with them?

Lucy swivelled round in her chair, bit her bottom lip and looked at the door to Pamela's room. Like the dining room door, this was a clear demarcation. But Lucy needed the truth, not a watered-down version.

She approached the room as if stalking a creature that might bolt. When she reached for the door handle, the ghost of her childhood sped past her. She and Freddie must have once had the run of the top floor, oblivious that their looker-afterers – all grown women – might have considered the room 'theirs'. She groped around for the light switch. Slope-ceilinged, shadow-dark, if she was the *out of sight, out of mind child,* this was the *out of sight, out of mind* room. Experiencing a kind of shame, Lucy remembered her father asking if the room was 'adequate'. Considerably smaller than her own, it had to be many things at the same time. Bedroom – her eyes fell on a ribbed hot water bottle – living space, office, and laundry. And gosh, it was freezing. The electric fire probably hadn't been on since yesterday. A short washing line strung high above it dangled nylons and knickers, things that made Lucy squirm. *But nobody packs wet clothes.*

As she turned towards the wardrobe, she distinctly remembered the feel of the carved rose under her fingertips. She must have been too young to be told, "Don't touch." She traced its smooth wooden contours, the tips of her fingers knowing precisely which direction they wanted to go. She hadn't thought herself old enough to have forgotten a thing that was so clearly part of who she was. As Lucy came to the next layer of petals, she withdrew her hand. *This isn't what you're here for.*

Inside the wardrobe were two day-dresses she recognised, a blouse and a skirt. Relieved, she clicked the door shut, but it struck Lucy: if Pamela had resigned, she might have made an arrangement to collect her clothes once she had a new address. Or, if dismissed (she did have a habit of answering Father back), she might have been asked to leave immediately.

Backing into something, Lucy twisted around. Only a chair but, hooked over one corner was – shockingly – a bra. Still in vests, Lucy was struck that the thing looked naked. She pulled away her hand, skirting the dressing table. No lipsticks, powder puff or perfume bottles here. Stacked on one corner were several dozen copies of a magazine – *Peace News* – a pile of envelopes and a large block of postage stamps. Cause for hope. Pamela would never abandon a task.

She picked up a magazine from the top of the pile and opened it to a page halfway through. *Ghost hands,* she read, thinking it was a story, but as her eyes drifted downward she saw the name 'Hiroshima' and knew. It was about the bomb that had wiped out eighty thousand people in an instant. When she'd asked Pamela to tell her about it, the governess had replied, "The only good thing you can say is that they wouldn't have known anything about it." But the people in the article hadn't died. They were children; children with skin peeling away from their arms and hanging loose. A strangled feeling filled Lucy's chest. Surely they couldn't have lived long? She wanted to look away, but couldn't, and she read about four more children, calling out for their parents as they cowered in the wreckage of their home. They saw a black four-legged thing approach. A stray dog, they assumed. It turned out to be their mother.

Lucy thought of her mother, upright, clipping across the hall. Lucy thought of Dog, paws down, tail wagging. *How could that be?* She turned the thought over. Was it possible Pamela had *lied?*

She shouldn't be in the room. It felt wrong. She put the magazine back on the top of the pile. Too neat. She nudged it so it was slightly off kilter and glared at it. Hateful, horrible thing.

Lucy made sure she closed the door behind her, walked out onto the landing and looked down over the bannisters, startled to find Cook, hands on hips and frowning upwards. Almost caught in the act, it took Lucy a moment to catch her breath. "Have you s–?"

"She's not with you?"

"No."

Cook's mouth fell open. It was comforting that she was expecting Pamela. Cook would be the first to know if she'd been sacked.

Cook glanced towards the closed door of the morning room. "I'd best come up."

"I'll come down," Lucy asserted, walking towards the top of the stairs. She wanted to put some distance between her and the magazine.

Cook sat Lucy down at the kitchen table and insisted she eat something, even if it was only bread with a scraping of raspberry jam. *Ghost hands.* Lucy stopped her. "No jam, thank you."

"Chances are, she'll have missed her bus, that's all."

"Yes," Lucy agreed, but Pamela could have missed several buses and not been this late.

Another half hour passed – another two missed buses. Lucy willed the phone to ring again but it didn't. She straightened up at the sound of voices in the hall above. "That's Mother and Father," she said, disappointed, but the look in Cook's eyes didn't escape her. "No, it's a Birmingham day," she corrected herself. Besides, the man's voice was softer and he was laughing.

"Your mother usually sticks her head around the door before she goes off to her committee meeting." Lucy wondered at Cook's disapproving tone. "You'd best let me do the talking."

"Cook, I'm just off ou–" The bread-and-butter coating of Lucy's mouth soured as Mrs Forrester swept a powerful drift of Chanel No 5 into the room. She was done up for the evening, lips red, skin powder-soft. A long sleek dress topped by a fur-trimmed cape and a large fur hat. Perhaps her thinking was that dressing the part was every woman's patriotic duty. *Now that the war is over we must Get Back to Normal.*

"Oh, Lucille!" Lucy might have just landed from another planet. This was the part where, unprepared, a mother crosses paths with her forgotten child. "I didn't realise you were downstairs, darling. Why didn't you come and say hello?"

"Lucy decided to have her tea with me this evening, didn't you?"

She sat very still. There was no law. No law that said you had to like your children.

"What?" Mrs Forrester acted surprised. "And Miss Finney wasn't invited to join in the fun?"

"She's worn herself out traipsing all over Hyde Park, so she's taken a tray up to her room."

To hear Cook deliver one lie after another turned Lucy's stomach to oil. It wasn't that Lucy didn't lie. How else could you stay out of trouble? But, then, *she* was in control.

"In fact we were just this minute saying it's been like the old days." Cook turned and smiled at Lucy in a way that demanded she smiled back.

"If only Freddie were here." *It's easy. You just open your mouth and the lies come tumbling out.* But she was newly aware of the exact width of her eyes, the precise curve of her smile.

"Well, it sounds as if you're having a lovely time." Lucy held her breath as her mother's heels clipped across the tiled floor. "I just came to say that I'm off to my meeting."

"And will it be the usual for your breakfast, Mrs Forrester?"

A bitter laugh died in Lucy's mother's throat. "Is there ever anything *but* the usual?"

"Probably not, now that you mention it. Just feels impolite not to ask." This, apparently, was something that could be confessed to.

"Lucille, just as soon as this rationing's over, you shall have a proper English breakfast." For one horrific moment, Mother looked as though she might sidle into an empty seat. "A sausage, a rasher of bacon, an egg, grilled tomatoes and mushrooms." It sounded like an entire month's worth of rations. Mother straightened up. "I'm missing something, aren't I, Cook?"

"A nice bit of black pudding. And my late husband was always partial to a fried slice."

"A fried slice." Her mother gripped the back of the kitchen chair and sighed her dinner-table sigh. "How heavenly."

"I might be able to manage a fried slice," Cook volunteered. "The rest will have to wait."

"I am *so* sick and tired of making do." Lucy's mother sounded as if she might stomp her high heels. "Aren't you?"

Lucy was surprised to find this question fired at her. Powdered everything was what she was used to – in fact, when Cook had fried her a fresh egg, supposedly a treat, the white was horrible and rubbery. She hummed what she hoped was an agreeable sound.

"Well, the car's waiting. I really should be off – although dinner's bound to be a bore and this has been rather fun."

Lucy noted her mother's slip. There had never been a committee meeting. She doubted there was even a committee.

"Always another time." Cook stacked Lucy's empty plate in the sink.

"Exactly! Not too late, now, sweetheart. I expect you'll be up with the larks."

If Pamela didn't come home, there would be no more swimming. In fact, there would be no more lots of things. What would a new governess have to say about newspapers and croissants?

"You *must* tell me how your swimming's going. Perhaps tomorrow?" Mother touched two fingers to her lips and fluttered them in Lucy's direction.

Everybody knew this was a lie.

Cook blew out her cheeks. "I thought she'd never leave." She hefted her apron over her head and hung it on its hook. "Right." She shrugged on her coat. "You stay here while I go and see what I can find out. If Miss Finney comes home, don't let her come looking for me. I'll try to be no longer than an hour."

It took a moment for Lucy to find her voice. "Why did you tell Mother that Pamela's upstairs?"

"Oh, it's 'Pamela' now, is it?" Cook fumbled with the clasp of her handbag, pulling out her headscarf and making a triangle. "There's no point bothering Mrs Forrester until we know what's what. All she'll do is fret. Most likely, it's nothing." The smile she gave Lucy as she knotted the scarf under her chin was too tight to be genuine.

"Where will you look?"

Cook rolled her eyes as if to say she'd never known a child who asked so many questions, but her voice was soft: "I don't want to worry you, love, but I'll start with the hospital and the police station. If anything *has* happened to Miss Finney, they'll be sure to know. Unless you can think of anywhere?"

There was only one place Lucy knew of where Pamela was known. "There's a café she goes to called Maison Bertaux. It's on a road called Greek Street."

"And where *is* this *Greek* Street?"

"In Soho."

"You'd have me traipse all over London." Cook seemed to think it through then nodded. "Alright. If I have no luck elsewhere." She stooped and kissed the top of Lucy's head, which added to the strangeness of the evening. "You'll be fine on your own. Just bolt the door behind me, there's a good girl."

The basement door led up an unlit staircase to street level. This was the door where masked burglars had broken in. The most exciting thing to have happened in an age and Lucy had slept through the whole thing.

She padded up the scullery stairs and across the empty hall. Often lonely, this was the first time she'd actually been alone in the house. She might have explored but, after the magazine, Lucy was no longer certain she wanted to look at things that were None of her Business. The windowsill in the drawing room gave the best view of the square. She perched sideways on.

It was a long two hours. Night pressed cold against the

pane. At each brisk footstep or slam of a car door, Lucy crushed her nose against the glass and squinted. Once, a dog cocked his leg against the railings. *I must get round to asking Father about Dog.* Eventually one of the noises turned out to be Cook, but no one was following behind. Lucy hopped down and hurried to open the front door. "No news?" she asked as Cook swept flinty night air inside the hall.

The housekeeper was flushed. She smoothed her headscarf as if it were hair. "No, no, there's news alright."

Lucy's heartbeat accelerated. "Miss Finney isn't hurt, is she?"

"She's fine. Fine." Cook walked to the side table and made fingerprints on the surface that only this afternoon she'd polished to a sheen.

Lucy didn't understand. If it was good news…?

Cook turned to face her, blinking rapidly. Lucy recognised the look of someone who was trying to compose herself. "I don't know why I'm trying to hide it. You'll know soon enough. All the same…"

As Cook pursed her lips and frowned, Lucy's heart was in her throat. "*What* will I know?"

"Miss Finney's been arrested."

"Arrested?" It seemed impossible. Pamela was a governess.

"Some protest or other. She – and a few others besides – chained themselves to railings outside the American Embassy."

Lucy thought for a moment. "Is that against the law?"

"It wasn't just that." Cook was shaking her head, the small movements of someone who can barely believe what they're about to say. "A scuffle broke out."

Lucy felt her brows pull together. "But if they were chained to railings, their arms would be –"

"Enough!" Cook raised both hands and splayed her fingers. Lucy must have flinched because she softened her voice.

"I'm only repeating what I was told. I said I'd track her down and I have."

Lucy felt guilty to have to ask another question. "What now?"

"All the sergeant would tell me is that he thought a night in the cells would quieten them down."

"Will Mother and Father have to know?"

"I won't be the one to tell them. I can't see what good could come of it."

Lucy was reassured. She was never quite sure if the two headstrong women liked each other.

"Besides, there's no point in all the upheaval of getting used to someone new. Not for such a short time."

A black shadow shot through Lucy's insides. "What do you mean?"

"Well, you don't want to be cooped up here longer than you need to be. You'll be going away to school soon, won't you?"

It was one thing to strip down to her swimming costume and parade in front of strangers. Once in the pool, even Lucy's good leg might look distorted or shrunken, depending how the lights reflected on the moving water. She pictured the things Freddie had described in his first few homesick letters. Sharing a dorm, communal showers. The taunts aimed at anyone who was different: the boy who was overweight; another with one ear that stuck out. *Slow-coach. Hop-a-long. Lop-sided loner. Surprised you don't swim in circles, peg leg.* Lucy knew beyond any shred of doubt that, for her, boarding school would be intolerable.

"Oh, come now. You must have realised…"

Lucy would refuse to believe it until she heard it from Pamela. "Of course I did," she said, lifting her chin. "Mother won't be expecting us home from swimming before half-past nine, so she won't think of coming upstairs before then."

"If I know your mother, she won't show her face until ten." Cook grabbed hold of Lucy's shoulders. "Right, this is the plan. If Miss Finney isn't back by the time I've made your mother's breakfast, I'll invent a little errand so that I can nip back to the police station and see what's what."

Lucy nodded as the housekeeper lifted her chin and tightened the knot of her headscarf.

"Take some bread and milk upstairs for your breakfast. And stay as quiet as you can until I come and find you."

CHAPTER ELEVEN

Interview for Granada Television,
1978, PART 1

As the applause died away, the chat show host indicated that Lucy should sit. Her first television appearance and it was on the Philip Harrington Show, where the guests were normally A-listers. She'd thought it odd when she received the invitation.

"I don't know," Dominic had said. "You were very good on *Opportunity Knocks.*"

"Ha, bloody, ha." Lucy was no Pam Ayres but it seemed she was about to become a household name.

She had obsessed over her choice of clothes, holding up outfit after outfit and liking nothing. Walking into the room, Ralph promptly removed the hanger from her hand, exchanging an utterly forgettable dress with a kaftan, an impulse buy she'd picked up from somewhere off Carnaby Street – a paisley affair in orange, white and black. Then came the accessories: a striped turban in two shades of orange separated by a thin line of turquoise, her white-framed oversized glasses, a chunky black and white necklace of interlocking squares. "More turquoise. You don't want to look too coordinated." But could clothes make the difference? Her concern had been whether the audience – and Lucy dared only consider the studio audience in their tiered rows – would think her poetry was 'relevant'? She hadn't expected an ethical issue to crop up so early in the show.

She nodded towards the white upholstery of the swivel armchair. "Is that leather?"

"No expense spared." This might not have been the BBC, but Philip's regional drawl still hinted at rebellion.

He must have *known* she was fronting the anti-fur campaign Ralph had just shot.

"A poster girl?" She'd laughed at her husband's suggestion. "I'll be the oldest model by twenty years."

"We need someone who adds kudos." He'd nudged her, coaxing, "You'll follow in Doris Day's footsteps."

Her mother's fox stole had come to mind – its full face and staring amber eyes, like marbles – and, though Lucy hesitated, there had never been any question that she wouldn't do it.

"Plus," Ralph pointed out, "your picture will be plastered on the sides of buses."

"Buses? Well, that sways it."

Lucy looked from the pristine leather upholstery to Philip's face. Of course he knew. He had an army of researchers. "No expense spared," she repeated. "Except perhaps to the animal." Rarely had Lucy been more aware of her clipped tone. "I hate to be a nuisance but do you have another I could use?"

Laughter rippled, the studio audience delighted that she was going to be as prickly as her reputation.

"Not at all. We like guests who keep us on our toes."

"Very efficient," Lucy remarked as two crew members, dressed head-to-toe in black, came running from the wings. One swiftly removed the leather armchair. The other simultaneously replaced it with a chair that looked far more in keeping with the set. "It's almost as if they were prepared," she observed.

He extended an arm. "Shall we?"

"Good of you to indulge me."

Once Lucy was seated, Philip made as if to sit, then straightened up. "You don't mind if I...?" He looked down at the white leather and gleaming chrome, then back at her.

Even this, Lucy saw, he had turned to his advantage. "It looks very comfortable," she said. "Just not my thing."

"So." Philip sat back in his armchair and swivelled the seat until he was facing her. "I wonder if I can start by asking you when your political awakening was?"

"Political." She chewed the word over, as if it was new to her.

While the camera was on her, Philip Harrington hefted the heel of one shoe onto the knee of his opposite leg. Finding herself staring straight at his crotch, Lucy quickly glanced up, registering amusement. He grabbed his notes from the table, propping them up on his raised thigh. "What I mean is, you seem to use your poetry as a vehicle for your political views."

"I think there's a responsibility to use whatever platform you find at your disposal, and poetry is mine." One of Philip's hands flickered – the prelude to another question. "Not so fast," Lucy cut in. Her skin was already suffocating under the layers of foundation and powder. "I know exactly what you're driving at. But I found myself dismissing the first answer I was tempted to give."

"Which was?" Known for flirting with his female guests, he flashed her his trademark smile and held his interwoven hands close to his chest.

"I was going to say that I was eleven years old, but at that age, would I *really* have considered what I was waking up to as *political?*" Lucy saw that the host was swivelling hypnotically. How could anyone be so at ease under the heat and glare of studio lights? "Some people believe that politics encompass everything, but I don't agree. There are causes I feel passionate about and I'd love to see a political party get to grips with them but, in the absence of that… it's more of a case of standing up for what one believes to be right, even if it means being thought of as an oddball."

From the back of the audience, beyond the glare of the lights, someone shouted, "No more seal-clubbing!"

Lucy grasped the opportunity and raised a fist in salute. As several people in the audience took up the cry, the nearest cameraman steered alarmingly away from her. "See how it works? I've rarely found myself standing alone for long." As she lowered her arm, one of Lucy's delicately flared sleeves caught on the arm of her chair. "In answer to your question…"

Philip raised his eyebrows.

"…it was my governess, Pamela, who opened my eyes to politics."

"Because, of course, you had quite a privileged upbringing, didn't you?"

She remembered his interview with Muhammad Ali, the boxer saying to him, "You're not as dumb as you look." *He's testing your pressure points.*

"I was never in danger of starving, I grant you," she fired back, trying and failing to free the sleeve of her dress. "And I was privileged to have an excellent governess, certainly. But I've met plenty of people who were penniless and had no complaints about their childhoods, while mine, well…" Dog chose that moment to slink through a doorway in Lucy's mind. There he was, settling by her feet, his tail sweeping semicircles on the studio floor. "Let's just say it was far from ideal." *Poor little rich girl.* If she wasn't careful, she would alienate the audience.

"If we could come back to your childhood in a moment, I'd like to hear more about this governess of yours. Who was she?" Out of camera-shot, the hand Philip extended brushed at the sleeve of Lucy's dress and subtly freed it.

"That's just the thing. I had no idea who she was or where she came from. For all I knew, she might have been blown by the east wind." Philip's face wasn't unpleasant, Lucy decided. The crows' feet at the corners of his eyes and those dark bags beneath them suggested that, for him, sleep wasn't a priority. "Everything she did went against the grain. She had no automatic respect for her elders, none for authority. In her view, the older generation had made a complete hash of the whole thing."

"She sounds rather like you, if you don't mind my saying so." He wasn't quite as attractive as he thought he was – or perhaps he understood that his attraction had little to do with appearance. It was his lack of apology, his 'take me as you find me' attitude.

"Not at all. I'm flattered by the comparison. She was my greatest influence."

"In what way?"

"At a time when nobody explained anything to children, she had me read newspapers. That was how I learned about the world."

"And when was this?"

"Straight after the Second World War. Great Britain was having to come to terms with the fact that it was no longer a world power. I had an inkling that my experience of home-schooling was quite… unusual. And then one day, after an afternoon off, Pamela didn't come home. I was afraid that, like Mary Poppins, she thought her work was done. But she hadn't moved on; she'd been arrested. Of course, if my parents had found out, they would have given Pamela her marching orders, and so we made sure they didn't."

Philip had been nodding attentively, waiting for the opportunity to pounce. "Who's this *we* you're talking about?"

"Cook and I." As Lucy saw her interviewer's eyes light up at yet more evidence of privilege, she did exactly as she'd been told not to do: Lucy looked directly into the nearest camera lens. "*She* was the one who made sure I didn't starve." Another ripple of laughter, this time louder.

"So why had your governess been arrested?"

"She and her friends chained themselves to railings outside the American Embassy. It was in protest against the US nuclear weapons development programme – although the reason for their arrest was that they refused to give the police their names and addresses."

His smile deepened. That disarming sparkle. "The old Mickey Mouse routine?"

"Not quite. Pamela gave her name as Manhattan Maid, New York."

Philip cut in. "*Manhattan Project* being the code name the Americans gave their nuclear development programme."

"Which caused something of an embarrassment. No one was supposed to know about it." Perhaps he wasn't the enemy. Just a man trying to create stimulating television to distract the work-weary. "Having seen the devastation these bombs could do, the idea of further testing was horrific. And it was *never* going to stop with one nation having the technology. One nation followed another." Lucy shook her head. "So, there we were," she played to the camera, "an eleven-year-old girl and an elderly cook. Trying to hush up this terrible scandal."

"You were quite heroic," Philip teased.

"Hardly – although I'll admit I thought we deserved more credit than we were given. It turned out that Pamela was quite unabashed about the whole affair. I remember her saying, 'What kind of an example would I be setting you if I didn't stand up for what I think is right?'"

"And your parents? Did they ever find out?"

"I honestly thought she might tell them about it herself. It was a real wake-up call – the idea that doing the right thing might mean breaking the law. But no, I don't think they ever found out – although the waiting and seeing was agony."

Philip turned his gaze to camera number one. "We're going to take a break right now, but I'll be back in a couple of minutes, talking poetry and politics with the woman who's often referred to as Britain's greatest living female poet." Lucy was uncomfortable at this accolade. It was an honour she couldn't accept. "Lucy Forrester, ladies and gentlemen!"

As the audience broke into applause, Lucy brought her palms together and bowed her head. She had just been getting into the flow of things. And from her experience of performance, Lucy knew that she would have to win their trust all over again.

"Don't go away," Philip said, and the band struck up the opening chords of the theme music.

CHAPTER TWELVE

1949

Why had they felt there was any need to lie? "Because you were arrested, of course," Lucy protested.

Though the governess needed a change of clothes, Pamela paused once she'd opened the door to her room. "I stood up to be counted, Lucy." She must have been exhausted but her eyes were bright. "Someone has to, however small a difference it makes."

Pamela had done something with the sole intention of being caught. Lucy was in such a habit of covering her tracks that this level of daring struck her as *extraordinary.*

"And it's not over yet." She hung her bag on the back of her chair. "There's every reason to hope we'll make the papers."

With everything else on her mind, Lucy failed to notice that she'd crossed the forbidden threshold. "So you *did* break the law?" She hesitated when she saw her breath fog the air of Pamela's room.

"Technically..." Pamela shrugged. "But we were prepared to. Not everything that falls within the law is *right.* Don't be trapped into thinking it is." She looked as if she was smoking a cigarette. *Ghost breath.*

"Then why will you be in the papers?"

"We had a happy accident." The governess beamed. "There was a security alert at the embassy, so the police were tailed by reporters. We were the first people they photographed."

Father always dished out two slaps. One for the crime itself, another for getting caught. He might not have objected to Pamela's protest, but he would most certainly object to a photograph of his daughter's governess being published in a newspaper. "But my father…" she began.

Pamela seemed unconcerned. "I'll explain myself. I've done nothing I'm ashamed of." She put her arm around Lucy's shoulder. The embrace was celebratory – as if she expected her to take up a battle cry. The pile of *Peace News* was there on the dressing table, a reminder to Lucy that Pamela had lied; for the eighty thousand, it had not been over in an instant. "What kind of an example would I be setting you if I didn't stand up for what I think is right? In fact, this may be the most important lesson I teach you."

The way Pamela spoke nudged Lucy's memory in a different direction. Her conversation with Cook came back to her. "Is it true that I'm to be sent away to school?"

"Ah," said Pamela, a slow, careful sound, and loosened her hold.

She had hoped for firm denial. "Is it?"

"Cook told me you were upset." Lucy's eyes prickled. She turned and walked back into her own room, resenting the fact that a private conversation had been repeated. She could hear Pamela's footfalls, following behind. "Lucy, I've loved being here with you, but I'm not a qualified teacher. You've pushed yourself so hard –"

Her world and everything in it was crumbling, and there didn't seem to be a single thing Lucy could do to stop it. "I wouldn't have done if I'd known this would happen."

"Don't ever say that!" Lucy's shoulders shrank inwards, but she turned to look at Pamela, who held her hands wide apart. "Where's the wheelchair now? Answer me that."

The worst thing? Freddie hadn't stood up for those boys who were being bullied at school. Instead, he'd joined in. *Darwin was right. It's about survival of the fittest,* he'd written. *Each man for himself.* The very opposite of standing up and being counted.

Pamela seemed to relent. "It won't be straight away. By the beginning of the next school year, even *you'll* agree that you've had enough of being cooped up here on your own. You won't be able to do everything the other girls can and I don't think you'll be quite ready for Wim–"

Blinded by tears, Lucy couldn't see what her governess held in her hands as she sank heavily onto the mattress of her bed, or the look of wonder on her face as she began to read, but she heard something unusual in Pamela's voice as she asked, "What's this?"

Lucy brushed her escaping tears away. The governess was holding the sheet of paper she'd been writing on before this whole business began. Lucy was horrified. She would never usually have left it lying about. It wasn't homework. It was… But there was no obvious way to describe it.

"You haven't copied it out from somewhere?"

"No –" The corners of her mouth quivered as half-remembered things came into focus. Searching for Dog, she could hear whimpering but couldn't find him. She was alone, crying for her mother who never came. *Rapunzel, Rapunzel, let down your hair.* Echoes of explosions she'd heard as a child; a fireball imprinted on her retinas. Things that terrified her.

"No, that was a silly question. I *know* this is you." Pamela gripped the corners of the page so tightly, Lucy feared it might rip. "What I don't know is –" the governess stalled for a second time, shaking her head.

"Sentences come to me. I write them down so I don't forget them, that's all." She'd written when she'd been angry too. Angry Freddie got the credit for saving the family. Angry his birth had been announced in *The Times* and hers hadn't. Angry that she was expected to behave a certain way; grow up to be a wife and mother. Angry that she'd got ill. Angry at the order of things and her lack of control.

"There are more like this?" Pamela shook her head, but it wasn't one of her usual controlled movements. "I've been blind. Blind to what's under my nose." Then she looked Lucy in the eye and spoke very slowly. "Please will you do me the honour of letting me read the rest?"

Lucy had never been treated as anyone's equal before. Freddie always dismissed her if there was anyone more interesting to play with – and these days he found most people more interesting than her. She threw her weight around with Barney, but only because she expected him to pull rank. Being a boy, he held the top trump, even if her mother's family did have its own coat of arms.

But being treated as the equal of someone who trumped her in terms of age was *unheard* of. It made her bold. "You said they died instantly," she accused.

"I beg your pardon?"

She gave a sharp little nod in the direction of the door to Pamela's room. Pamela walked to the doorway, then towards her dressing table and its pile of magazines. Lucy expected her to say that she'd had no right being in her room and reading what was none of her business. Instead, she squared the top copy of *Peace News*. "Many, many people died instantly." As if having second thoughts, Pamela picked up the top copy, and held it out at arm's length. Lucy felt as if she was being dared to take it, but she didn't know if she should, and still less if she wanted to. Pamela lowered her arm wearily. "These are the stories of the people who didn't die." Her voice brimmed with sadness. "The survivors."

Before this moment, Lucy had imagined that there were

people who'd died and people who'd survived, unharmed. She hadn't considered an in-between. *Could skin grow back?*

"And the bomb?" Pamela went on. "That's what I was protesting about last night; why I had to stand up to be counted, and why I'll do so again. Do you see?"

It hadn't crossed Lucy's mind to feel sorry for the survivors – they were supposed to be the lucky ones, after all – but she was a survivor and had some idea what that meant. "Some of the survivors must have died."

Pamela nodded. "It's estimated that the total number of deaths was more than double the original figure. And we don't know about the long-term damage that nuclear weapons do. Not yet."

This was too terrible a thing to be a lie. And if Lucy couldn't trust Pamela, then who could she trust?

Sliding open the top drawer of her desk, she bit her bottom lip at the sight of her own hurried handwriting. Lucy had thought that these pages would remain undisturbed, to be discovered after her death (when death still seemed likely). Perhaps stumbled upon by Cook, sent to clear out her room. Lucy would have resisted the idea that, far in the future, someone might be able to turn on a thing called a personal computer and search for her poems by title, first line or date. That her childish scrawl would be zoomed in on, the fibres of the paper and the ink bleeds scrutinised. That, at the press of a button, a transcript might appear in a neat little textbox to the right. That a digital lexicon of *Words used by Lucy Forrester in her Poetry* would exist. To the girl, clutching a pile of papers, these things would have sounded like science fiction.

As she looked at Lucy's offering, Pamela's expression was pure astonishment. "When did you find the time to write all this?"

"Your afternoons off. When I can't sleep. It's just words. The way they come out." It was nerve-wracking. For the first time, someone would glimpse inside the workings of her head, and they might like her less.

The governess held out her hand. "You capture your thoughts as they happen?"

"Yes." Lucy let go. She kept her eyes on the pages, but the deed was done.

"There's a phrase for that. It's called a 'stream of consciousness.'"

Was it true? Did other people do as she'd been doing – enough of them that someone had given it a name?

Pamela was nodding at her, smiling.

"Will you read them right now?"

"I'll make a start, but I've missed a night's sleep. I don't know how far I'll get."

Looking about her, Lucy couldn't see a single place where she would be comfortable sitting and waiting. "I'll be out on the top step."

She sat, elbows on her knees, chin cupped in her hands. This was what it was like when Cook caught her misbehaving and said, "I'm minded to tell Mrs Forrester," and she had to wait to hear whether Mother considered the matter serious enough for her father to be told. It might be four agonising days until he was due home. If only Cook or Mother could just give her wrist a good slap. Lucy wouldn't even mind the odd undeserved slap if it meant getting back to normal. But neither woman thought doling out punishments was their job, so that was that.

If only there wasn't going to be a photograph in the newspaper. And there would be another unbearable wait until she knew if Father had seen it.

She paused her thoughts to try and detect from the peculiar quality of the noiselessness how her words were making Pamela feel. The silence seemed overwhelming. It filled Lucy's senses in a way that made her long for distraction.

The picture of a floral arrangement on the wall to her left was horribly drab, she decided. As you worked your way upstairs, the pictures got duller and duller, the dullest of all reserved for the fourth-floor residents. This detail had been lost on Lucy in the days when she'd sprinted from the bottom of the house to the top – *You haven't got a train to catch!* – but, being slower, she now paid attention. At first, Lucy had only focused on one step at a time, the precise place where she wanted her foot to go, then she had counted the steps as she climbed, but later – as she dared to look up – she sought out markers. The picture of Mother as a young girl, a puppy sitting in her lap. The one with the three-masted sailing ship.

She would stop trying so hard with her exercises.

She would climb the stairs more slowly.

Then Pamela would be allowed to stay.

Which part was Pamela reading now? Lucy had never told Pamela about her submarine or the rear-view mirror or the boy who pitied her so much that he wanted her to have his glockenspiel. The waiting was intolerable. Probably what it's like waiting to hear if you're going to hang for murder.

"Lucy?"

Her pulse sped as it did every time the slam of the front door announced her father's return. *'And how have the children been?'* "Coming!" Lucy pushed herself to standing. She straightened her skirt.

'I will now pronounce my verdict.'

Seated on the end of Lucy's bed, Pamela had strewn the papers around her as if there was no order to them. "There you are, Machine Girl," she said. Lucy saw to her amazement that she'd been crying. "I wonder, do they have any idea?"

Lucy didn't know whether she was expected to ask who or what, so she waited to hear what had upset Pamela.

"Do you understand what these are?" She picked a sheet of paper at random; waved it like a flag of surrender.

Lucy shook her head.

"They're not just thoughts and sentences. They're poems." Pamela jumped to her feet and started pacing. "Well, we can stop going swimming, for starters. And you don't need to worry about being a tennis player."

Lucy struggled to see the connection. She looked forward to their outings. "But –"

"Alright, we carry on with your swimming." Her governess was shuffling thoughts as if they were playing cards. "But *then* we go to the library."

She was ready to agree, but Pamela went on: "Don't you see? All this time, we should have been concentrating on your English."

Skin pinched together in the centre of Lucy's forehead. "I know they're not very good."

"I didn't mean…" Pamela crouched down so that she had to look up into Lucy's face. "I'm not making myself clear. These are wonderful, Lucy. Wonderful. And I feel privileged to be among the first to read them."

"You *are* the first."

"So you haven't shown them to your mother?" Lucy barely had the chance to open her mouth. "No, I didn't think so. Do you think you could choose one – and by that I mean one that you wouldn't mind your parents reading?"

Lucy felt undiluted horror. "My *parents?*" She picked up a sheet of paper at random and sat beside Pamela, so that they could both read from it:

Dont you recognise me?
Look down
A little lower
Its me
Here

In the chair
But you look right through me
I am smaller than I ever thought possible
Are you afraid what people will think?
Will I reflect badly?
Now that I am imperfect
I see
I hate to break it to you
I was never going to be perfect
I am an inconvenience
Banish me to my attic purgatory
For all eternity
With only words for company
And a square of sky for comfort
Do not fear
I will not let down my hair
To the first prince who shouts Rapunzel
Write me off without a second thought
I will be your Out of Sight Out of Mind child

"Yes I take your point," Pamela said. "Perhaps you could write something new. Something less personal. We're going to need books, we're going to need to go out more."

"So you're not leaving?"

Pamela looked as if she was in two minds. "Not until I'm absolutely sure that your parents understand what you are."

It was a stay of grace. "And what's that?"

"A poet, Lucy. Don't you see? You're a poet."

CHAPTER THIRTEEN

1950

Pamela walked into the fourth-floor bedroom clutching a letter. "Oh, my goodness." She rocked herself back into the armchair. "If this is what I think it is."

Lucy bristled at the interruption. She'd been reading how the American President's advisors had urged him to threaten the North Koreans with the atom bomb unless they withdrew their troops, and how the suggestion had been met with cheers. As Pamela once said to her, "There's no one more dangerous than someone who believes they're doing God's work."

Dragging her attention from this horror back to the moment, she was aware that her voice sounded irritable: "What do you think it is?" But as she twisted in her seat, Lucy saw Pamela staring at the letter in her hands with a combination of nerves and awe. Her stomach tightened. "Aren't you going to read it?"

Woken from her trance, Pamela said, "Yes, I suppose I'd better." She balanced the envelope on one arm of the chair and glanced up briefly. "I hope you won't be too cross with me."

Lucy felt her eyebrows come together. What was this?

"I never imagined she'd actually reply – at least, not in

person..." Half an explanation – no – less than half. Pamela began to scan the page, her lips moving silently.

Was it about school? And if not that, was it something else that would have her creeping downstairs and removing her father's newspapers from the table in the hall? Pamela was taking forever. From time to time she made a throaty noise that sounded like agreement. Finally, Lucy could bear it no longer. "Pamela, just *tell* me!"

The governess lowered the letter to her lap and looked up, but her focus fell short of Lucy. "I sent one of your poems to Edith Sitwell."

The answer threw Lucy completely. "Who's Edith Sitwell?"

"Some people call her England's greatest living poet."

Lucy's insides went cold. After Father's reaction, she had sworn never to show her poems to anyone else. Pamela knew how she felt. *"Which* poem did you send?"

"Machine Girl. But it doesn't matter *which* poem. I wanted you to understand how good you are. And I wanted advice on how to go about teaching you."

Machine Girl. In the hands of England's greatest poet. Lucy trembled and for a moment she was back in her father's study.

"And you think it's *good,* do you?" he asked Pamela, implying that he didn't. He went to pass back Lucy's poem as if it was of no further interest.

"That's alright," Pamela said. "Lucille made a copy for you. And yes. I think her work is extraordinary."

"Well," he said, not knowing what to do with the thing in his hand. "If she's interested, if it keeps her occupied, I don't see what harm it can do. But not," he passed the poem to his wife, "to the exclusion of her other studies."

Though Pamela had respectfully herded Lucy out of the door, once they were back upstairs she had paced and fumed, "They're wrong, Lucy, wrong. You can't let these *people* put you off."

Those people were Lucy's parents. Other than the grumbles Cook let slip, she had never heard someone say that they were wrong before. Not in so many words. Now, Pamela seemed anxious about her reaction. Lucy's mouth was sandpaper dry. "Just tell me what she's written."

"Right." She took a deep breath. "She starts by apologising that it's taken so long to reply, but she's been quite ill." Pamela's knees were glued together and to one side. "Although it's given her the opportunity to catch up on her reading. Then she says – and I think I'll just read it: 'I must applaud you for recognising your pupil's potential.'"

A faint glow of importance kindled. *Father had been wrong!* Lucy sat up straight.

"'If I understand you correctly, Lucille's formal education has been interrupted by illness – a situation so similar to my own that it intrigues me. Lucille has come thus far on the merit of her own imagination, weighing one word over another and making the right choices. She hasn't been told that poetry is difficult or that there are rules (although I always say, write well enough and you may ignore any number of them). If you introduce a rigid lesson plan at this stage, I fear you risk sucking the joy out of it.'"

There were paragraphs that Pamela didn't read out, in which Miss Sitwell responded to doubts Pamela had expressed in her own ability. For example, she didn't tell Lucy that Miss Sitwell wrote, 'It matters not whether you can distinguish between the good and the not quite so good. Stop looking for technique if that isn't your forte. Instead, find the part that moves you, then say, *That's it. Keep doing that.*' When Lucy finally read the letter for herself, she heard those words spoken in Pamela's voice, because, over the next year and a half, the governess made frequent use of Miss Sitwell's words.

Pamela glanced over the top of the sheet and grimaced. "'I quite agree. Only one type of writing is to be found in newspapers. It is not the kind we wish to encourage'. You see, Lucy,

I had to admit that you've had a very limited range of reading material. She goes on: 'I suggest that Lucille is exposed to the greats. My early notebooks are filled with poetry that I transcribed: Sappho, Swinburne, Tennyson and Poe. You absorb so much in the process.'"

"Did she say anything else about my poem?"

"You don't think someone as important as Miss Sitwell would have troubled herself if she didn't like it, do you?" Pamela leafed through the fragile sheets of paper. "Here we are. She says that your sense of rhythm, feeling, and self is well beyond your years."

As Pamela went to put the letter back in the envelope, Lucy located a tiny core of confidence (rhythm, feeling, self), not something that could be mistaken for having a 'big head'.

"Oh, wait a minute," Pamela was saying. "There's something else." She pulled a single sheet of paper from the envelope and unfolded it. "Look. It's addressed to you."

Lucy swallowed and took the letter solemnly.

Dear Lucy,

You have already done one of the bravest things you will ever do, and that is to show your writing to another living person for the first time. It is an act of trust which says, 'Here. This is what I look like on the inside, I make a gift of my soul to you.' And while you fear rejection, you hope against hope that you won't be mocked or shunned.

The first person had been Pamela, and Pamela had wanted to know what she looked like on the inside. But when she'd made a gift of her soul to Father, he had gone to hand it back.

It was not your choice to share your work with me. I find myself imagining how I would feel in your shoes. Betrayed? (I hope not, because your governess seems to care very much for you.) Pleased that she thought she had recognised something rare and wanted another opinion? Nervous of the reaction of a stranger? That goes without saying. So let me put you out of your misery.

Your poem spoke to me – and by that I mean directly to me.

A small core glowed bright within Lucy. She had swallowed the moon. Father *had* been wrong.

It has that certain something I always look for but is so difficult to pinpoint; more of a feeling in my gut than recognition of technique. If you really do grab sentences from the air and manage to get them down on paper with such clarity, then you have something special, something that can't be taught.

Keep doing whatever it is that you are doing. Practise your craft every day.

The face Lucy conjured to go with the voice was solemn, with deep-set eyes. Very much like Virginia Woolf.

You may be tempted to censor your work, now you are aware it will be read by others, but don't hide whatever is strange and wonderful and unique about you. Never feel ashamed. Not everyone will love you, that's true, but the thing that sets you apart is the very thing that will touch every other person who is unable to voice what you have already grasped. When Emily Dickinson wrote, 'I'm Nobody. Who are you?' she invited all the misfits into her world. The misfits are your people too. Don't be put off by this word. Celebrate it. If all this advice feels overwhelming, imagine somebody exactly like you on a small island somewhere, and that you are writing for them and them alone. Find simple ways to say what you feel. Give your words room to breathe.

Perched on the very edge of her seat, more flustered than Lucy had ever seen her, Pamela asked urgently, "What does she say?"

But Lucy wasn't ready to share these promise-filled words. "She suggests I read Emily Dickinson."

"Good." Pamela nodded. Here was the instruction she had been waiting for. Something specific to work on.

One final piece of advice, Lucy, if I may. Less venom, more sorrow.

CHAPTER FOURTEEN

1950

The decision to have Dr Coates assess her while Pamela was at her mother's for Christmas seemed deliberate. Lucy had been ganged up on. The family gathered in the downstairs hall to watch her climb up and down the stairs. *Not too fast,* she reminded herself, bringing one foot down to meet the other, the way a much younger child would, and wincing occasionally. This fakery was a gamble, but what choice did she have? There had been talk of boarding schools. There were brochures.

Freddie, standing to the rear of the others, acted disinterested, throwing and catching a mottled red apple as if it were a cricket ball. She had re-read his first few letters as motivation and had no problem translating their content into insults that might be aimed at her: *Giraffe neck. Thinks she's a poet. Why don't your shoes match each other? What's that? A built-up heel?*

"Well, we knew it might happen," Dr Coates said as Lucy arrived at the first floor landing once more. "And I'm not suggesting it wouldn't have done if you'd agreed to wear leg braces," he continued. "I must say, I've been impressed with your efforts, young lady."

Gripping the apple, Freddie grinned unpleasantly. *You don't fool me.* Her brother had changed in the few short weeks since the October half-term holiday. It wasn't just the scattering of acne or his new deeper voice. Always a know-it-all, there was now something knowing about him. But although Freddie seemed to have crossed a line, she didn't think he would go as far as ratting on her.

Now level with Father, Lucy watched him draw a deep and disapproving breath. "So what *are* you saying, Doctor?"

"Well, the muscles in Lucille's left leg are still weak. If you look, you'll see that her left leg is noticeably thinner than her right."

She was to be talked about, as if she wasn't there.

"Don't slouch, Lucy," her father barked. "We need to take a good look at you." Lucy had got into the habit of standing with more weight on her left leg than on her right. While the machine part of her did as it was told, Lucy noticed how her mother angled her head, as if considering – and then rejecting – an item offered for purchase.

Girls, who'll have Lucy on their team? Anyone? Oh, that's very kind of you, Beth. Isn't that kind, Lucy?

"And though there's no discernible limp when she walks on the level, the stairs seem to cause her a good deal of discomfort."

"And?" her father prompted.

"I'm reluctant to admit it, but I think Lucille's recovery may have plateaued."

It didn't escape Lucy how Mother glanced nervously at Father, as if checking her own interpretation, or how he toyed with his moustache.

"Or…" Dr Coates shrugged his eyebrows. "It's possible she's suffering a relapse."

"A *relapse?*" Mother's voice emerged a shade higher than usual and her gaze shifted past the Christmas tree that had been delivered earlier that morning, its branches tied down with twine, and towards the nearest escape route.

Lucy was surprised her act had been quite so convincing.

"I don't mean to imply that she's infectious. But it's not uncommon for polio victims to experience recurrent symptoms. Pain." The doctor gave the impression of chewing over similar words and finding them equally distasteful. "Weakness."

Weakling. Cripple. Runt.

"How long can we expect this to go on for?" Lucy's father demanded.

"It's possible that it's a temporary setback but, equally, it may well be permanent."

Mr Forrester's clenched fist stopped halfway towards his mouth and he cleared his throat. "Shall we?" One extended arm herded the adults into the drawing room. The door closed behind them – a deliberate click – leaving the siblings alone in the hall.

She was to be discussed. Out of her hearing.

"You're laying it on a bit thick, old girl." Freddie's new way of talking was infuriating.

Lucy glared at her brother. He rubbed the Cox against his thigh as if preparing to bowl, then crunched into it loudly. The sharp tang of the fruit reached Lucy. "I don't know what you mean," she said.

"Oh, come on!" Juice dribbled down Freddie's chin, and he made a deliberate slurping noise that seemed designed to repulse. "You skip down the stairs the minute you don't think anyone's watching."

She shrugged, as if it didn't matter one way or the other. "It's like Dr Coates says I'm having a temporary relapse."

"You think they'll let your darling Pamela stay?" Freddie's sneer reinforced the gulf between them. "That's not how it works. Not in our family."

"Oh?" Lucy imagined the satisfaction she would get from kicking her brother on the shins. "Since you're the great expert on everything, tell me, how *does* it work?"

"There are boarding schools for cripples, you know. Only they don't bother with normal lessons."

Lucy knew exactly what her brother was up to. Freddie, who was learning to fence, was aiming straight for her weak spots. "I'm *not* a cripple," she fired back. Lucy's forehead pinched in a frown – she couldn't for the life of her remember the last time she'd seen the girl doing her brave and awkward circuits of the square.

Doubt, like the creep of evening shadows.

"Then stop acting like one. You're not doing yourself a fat lot of good." What Freddie really meant was *You're on your own.* He slapped one hand on the bannister, ready to stomp upstairs to his room – another door that would be slammed in Lucy's face.

A conversation came back to her. Down in the kitchen, she'd said to Cook, "I want another brother." What she really meant was that she wanted a *different* brother.

"I can't help feeling you're better off with Dog." Cook put pieces of the large marrow she'd been chopping in a basin, ready to be salted overnight.

"Father said he'd like more boys."

"Did he now?" The chopping resumed, more rigorously than before.

The memory jolted into position, Lucy had remembered those weren't his exact words. What he'd actually said was, "As far as children are concerned, you get what you're given." She'd repeated this for Cook. The same applied to brothers.

"You get what you *ask* for," Cook said.

Lucy looked at the closed drawing room door. Right this minute, the adults would be poring over school brochures. This one or... this – an extra brochure that Dr Coates provided: *"I hear it has a very good reputation. And I think we need to be… realistic."*

"If they don't teach regular lessons, what *do* they teach at these so-called schools for cripples?"

"Practical stuff. Trades. So you won't be a burden on your family."

"I'll go back to my day school. They'll take me." Lucy attempted to sound worldly.

He turned towards her, one knee bent. "Who do you think would look after you, stupid? Father's away half the week, Cook goes home in the evenings and Mother is… well, she's Mother, isn't she? And there's nothing we can do about it!"

Lucy's nostrils prickled. She'd made things ten times worse. Smells of cinnamon and ginger were beginning to waft up from the kitchen, but the girl stopped herself from running to Cook. The housekeeper hadn't warned her about schools for cripples. If lines were being drawn, people should be honest enough to declare their loyalties. It wasn't right to keep hopping across the divide. "So I'm in the way, that's what you're saying?"

He shook his head and looked as if he pitied her naivety. "You think you're special. Well, you're not. You'll be parcelled off, just like I was. The only say you might be allowed in the matter is *where*."

Lucy felt primed to run up the stairs after Freddie and pummel him with her fists, but the commotion would bring the adults to the door and she'd be exposed as a fraud. Freddie's message was crystal clear. *Toughen up. No one's going to stand up for you.*

All of a sudden Lucy couldn't bear to be in the hall. Her father's heavy winter coat hung in the closet, a solid dark presence infused with his favourite pipe tobacco. A careful thief, Lucy reached deep into one of the pockets. Empty. The other. Empty. She unbuttoned the coat and pulled at one lapel; felt the bulge in the smooth inside pocket. Just enough change for a bus fare, a *chocolat chaud* and one of Beatrice's delicious gingerbread men. She would go where she was always made welcome amid the cheerful clatter: Maison Bertaux. Beatrice would kiss her on each cheek and say, *"Regarde qui est ici."*

As she pulled the letterbox to, trying to make no more than a soft click, it struck Lucy: she was insignificant. Unlike Pamela, no one would miss her.

CHAPTER FIFTEEN

1953 – 1956

Lucy's feet came to a halt on the stone floor of the gallery as she passed in front of the photograph. Her neck twisted. Somehow she knew, even before she read the title – *The Poet as a Regal Corpse by Cecil Beaton.* Of course it was. Who else could it be?

One final word of advice, Lucy, if I may.

An extraordinary figure lying on a chequerboard floor, her head on a silk pillow, laid out under a spray of lilies. Flanked by two stone cherubs, the corpse spoke to Lucy, broadening her fourteen-year-old's definition of *misfits* to include the dead and the dispossessed – anyone who lacked a voice.

In the shop of the National Portrait Gallery she made a marvellous exchange: a coin in return for a picture-postcard. A single picture-postcard presented to her in a candy-striped paper bag. Lucy secreted it inside her coat so as not to bend it. She would add it to the trunk she was packing.

"Do you have everything you need, Lucy!" Mother was brisk, her hands clasped in front of her, turning about to check the hall for stray items. "The car's waiting out the front."

"Where's Father?" High in her chest, impatience

threatened to escalate to panic. She had already checked her watch a dozen times. She checked it again. "He promised he'd be here to take me."

"How should I know where your father is?" Now that she was going away to school, Mother would have the house to herself – while Father was hard at work. "Do you think he tells me everything?"

Father was a stickler for routine and couldn't tolerate lateness. If he said he'd do something he was known for doing it. "Hasn't he phoned?"

For some time now, Lucy had been asking herself questions and didn't like the answers she arrived at. She hadn't been looking forward to the conversation she'd planned to have in the car – in fact, even thinking about it made her queasy. But, on balance, Lucy had decided there was no option. She must risk maddening Father. If she described the committee meetings that required eveningwear, the phone that was allowed to ring and ring, the man's laughter in the hall, and he reacted by telling her she was being a baby, then at least... at least... The few sentences she'd rehearsed didn't seem to amount to very much, certainly not *evidence*. She turned to Cook hoping for assurance – what was it she'd said about theirs being a strange household to work in? But they had already said their goodbyes and Cook seemed unable to look her in the eye.

Mother softened her voice. "I imagine something's cropped up at short notice." She clipped over to Lucy, smiled an unnatural smile and cupped her face in her icy hands. "You know how it is in business."

She must have suspected something and told him not to bother.

"I'll come with you." She appeared delighted by the novelty of the idea that had just occurred to her; an offer a daughter should be grateful for. Mother turned to Cook as if expecting approval.

Two hellish years Lucy didn't care to reflect on. A prison sentence. A lesson in how not to learn. It wasn't just her classmates who thought her peculiar. Lucy quickly earned a reputation among the teaching staff for being impossible, questioning everything she was told, and yet strangely lacking in the basics. The picture-postcard was one of the few things that carried her through. When Matron opened Lucy's cupboard and found it pinned inside, she declared Beaton's image macabre.

"She's a poet," Lucy explained, amused that England's greatest living poet was playing dead.

According to the sturdy woman, poetry was an unhealthy occupation. "You might not be able to play hockey, but it would do you good to spend more time in the fresh air."

"What, that fresh air?" she asked as her classmates pushed back inside and clutched the silver-painted pipes, desperate to thaw out their hands. This was the same woman who had convinced the PE teacher to make a girl do gymnastics in her underwear rather than allow her to skip a lesson for lack of clean kit.

Sometimes Matron refused to take no for an answer. Ordered outside, rather than pace the perimeter of the sports field and watch the other girls play, Lucy concentrated on another unhealthy occupation: scavenging for fag-ends. With cigarettes being so hard to come by, there was quite a market for them. Polio had left her anxious about second-hand germs. Though Lucy couldn't bring herself to smoke second-hand cigarettes, she bartered with them to get herself out of sticky corners, and traded them for books and sweets. Occasionally, she sold them.

She refused to apologise. *Yes, I am a misfit.* If Lucy had her way, she would have sewn a banner in her needlework lessons, instead of this poxy cross-stitch flower arrangement they had her working on.

For a woman who claimed to want the best for every girl, it was interesting what Matron chose to ignore. Apparently she didn't see the girls who purposefully trod on the backs of Lucy's shoes because she couldn't walk fast enough for their liking. She was deaf to the frequency of the word 'left', and the emphasis placed on it by those around her. She didn't even see the harm when someone sewed up the end of Lucy's left trouser leg, so that she fell and struck her head against one corner of her bedside table, requiring stitches. It was just a prank.

"We don't need a witch-hunt. Whoever was responsible will be feeling ghastly enough."

Though Lucy had once complained of loneliness, she'd become used to it. Set apart, she *was* different. This wasn't a choice, but a fact. She had no small talk to share, no interest in gossip. The popular or athletic cliques would never accept her, and she didn't identify with the downtrodden and put-upon. They were all other people's people. Besides, she saw how fickle friendships were; how quickly girls changed allegiances.

"Lucy, where on earth is your left shoe?"

"I must have lost it, Miss."

"You *lost* it, you careless girl! What do you intend to do? You can't walk about with one shoe."

"No, I don't suppose I can."

Four days the shoe was missing, before it mysteriously reappeared, paired next to her right shoe after she returned from the showers one morning.

She said nothing. Just put it on. Laced it up.

That Miss Stillwell's letter was secreted away in the lining of her trunk was protection enough – her talisman.

All letters written by pupils were collected by a prefect to be read by a member of staff (and no doubt by the prefect). Any criticism of the school was censored with a black crossing out. Not that there would have been any point in complaining to her parents. Lucy knew exactly what her father thought of telltales. And, besides, any school would have its fair share of bullies; they were part of the public school system. Of the letters that arrived in return, Lucy looked forward to Pamela's the most.

I loved your latest poem. It felt almost cinematic. And now that's out of the way, I have an admission to make. I know very little about poetry, except that I know what moves me. I know even less about poets. The reason I chose Edith Sitwell was because, when asked why she wrote about Christ, she replied, 'Would you have me put my faith in the atomic bomb?'

It was odd to imagine Pamela living with another family, looking after another child. Her letters were a lifeline, Lucy's window to the outside world. She had asked Matron if it might be possible for her to have a newspaper only to be told, "Newspapers aren't for children. What I'd like to see is you making an effort with the other girls and spending less time on your own scribbling away in that notebook of yours." (This theme was echoed in her first school report: *We hope Lucille will take more interest in all sides of school life next term.*)

Strange, how a girl who chose to spend time alone was seen as a threat. If she *was* a threat, Lucy's thinking was that she couldn't be as powerless as she felt.

Lucy dared write to Pamela, *I'd like to read more about the bomb, if* Peace News *has any articles you might send me.* The teacher who vetted this letter must have been distracted because it was returned to Lucy with no crossings out. Within a week she had her reply. The closest thing she'd had to a newspaper article for some time.

Lucy read greedily of how the bomb's inventor, Leo Szilard, had bristled with fear the moment he'd grasped that his technology wasn't science fiction. But he reassured himself:

Nobody would risk using something this powerful, that was the whole point; possession alone would act as a deterrent. Then President Truman brought God into the frame, giving thanks that the atomic bomb had come into the hands of the United States not those of its enemies. Knowing what she already knew, Lucy felt sickened as she lay on her stomach and read his words. *We pray that He may guide us to use it in His ways and for His purposes.* Was it Truman Pamela had been thinking of when she'd said that no one was more dangerous than someone who thought they were doing God's work?

When Szilard learned what Truman planned, the scientist campaigned for a demonstration in front of the Japanese ambassador. But Szilard's arguments – that Japan *must* be given the opportunity to surrender – fell on deaf ears. *Possession alone* had gone out the window.

2.45 a.m. The crew of the Enola Gay took off, navigating the old-fashioned way – by the stars. For six months prior, holed up in Utah, they had trained for this. A top secret mission. Told that what they were about to do would end the war, the word 'atomic' hadn't been mentioned. But every one of them had an idea.

8.15 a.m. Morning rush hour. One thousand eight hundred miles and only fifteen seconds late. Navigator Van Kirk made a last entry in his log: *Bomb away.* Forty-three seconds later the plane was sent into a one hundred and fifty degree spin as the bomb exploded. The pilots of the three B-52 bombers filmed their God's-eye view as the shockwave travelled at over seven thousand miles an hour. It sounded as if the plane was being ripped apart. Minutes later they reported their mission a success; almost five square miles of city, obliterated. *Come on home, boys!* In a celebratory mood, they headed back towards Tinian, capable of ignoring the detail on the ground – eighty thousand men, women and children wiped out in an instant. Horrified by the news, a tormented Szilard covered his mouth with his hand. *My God. What have we done?*

From the moment of its invention, Pamela wrote in her covering letter, *the bomb was always going to be used.*

Tell me about the survivors, Lucy wrote back.

We don't have much information yet, and it's possible that we'll never know the full story, Pamela's next letter read. *Remember what I told you about newspaper articles and history books?*

But Lucy wouldn't be put off. *What* do *we have?* she wrote.

We have a man called Hershey who wrote a report for the New Yorker *in 1946. It tells what happened through the eyes of six survivors. Pick your moment carefully. This makes for difficult reading.*

Two years passed and, finally, Lucy's ordeal was over. She'd survived. As she drove away from the school, she didn't once look back. There was not one girl she wanted to stay in touch with.

Edith Sitwell's letter was back in its rightful place, in the drawer of her desk in her fourth-floor room. And the picture-postcard, with its telltale pin-marks in the white border, took pride of place above her desk. Lucy looked out over the square. She chewed the inside of her mouth; still no sign of the girl with the crutches. And she had never even asked her name.

CHAPTER SIXTEEN

1956

On the fourth-floor landing Lucy held her breath. She became just another balustrade. A conversation was taking place in the hall below. Something that wasn't intended for her ears.

"There's no point telling Lucille what you were doing when you were her age, Lionel."

"Why? How long do we have to make allowances?"

Lucy had a mind to march downstairs and protest, *What allowances?* Her hand had gripped the mahogany, ready to push off, but no. It would be more useful to hear what her parents said about her when they didn't know she was listening.

"Well?" Father demanded. "She can't spend all summer mooning about."

What about Freddie? He was abroad, 'broadening his horizons' and trying to work out how to claim an exemption from National Service, so he could start his BA in God-knows-what in the autumn. Surely taking a few weeks to find her bearings wasn't unreasonable?

"That's not it. It's because you're a man and because…" Lucy could almost hear her mother's reluctant shrug. "Well!"

"Why don't you say it? Because I'm *working class.*" With these words, Father slipped into an exaggerated version of his childhood accent.

Did it feel like putting on an old jumper? Did the wool make his skin crawl now he was used to cashmere?

"Oh, you were *never* working class." Her mother's icy protest betrayed the grate of his voice on her nerves.

Could you love a man if you cringed whenever he opened his mouth?

"I started out on the factory floor."

"Only so you could understand how the business worked!"

Her parents put on a united front, but to hear them; how had they ever thought they were suited?

"I'm not ashamed of my roots, even if you are. It's a pity we didn't instil a stronger work ethic in *our* children, instead of this sense of *entitlement* they both have."

The words stung like a slap around the face. Lucy's breath was the sound of an 'h'. *Sense of entitlement?* When so many things had been denied her, how could she have given that impression? She tried, and failed, to shake it off.

"We agreed they should both receive an education, Lionel."

"Freddie, by all means. But what good will it do Lucille? I mean, *poetry!*"

Disdain, all too clear, and not a word of support from her mother. Furious hot tears sprang to Lucy's eyes.

"I'll tell you what, if you don't deal with her, I will." The last word, punctuated by a shoulder-jerking slam.

Blinking, Lucy waited for her vision to clear then peered down. Directly below, Mother stood completely still; watching the closed door of her husband's study. Was she waiting to be dismissed? She must know better than to expect an apology.

"You think you're so clever," Lucy heard her say, her voice quite clear, quite calm. "It's my money. *My* money."

After a few moments Mother turned, walked smartly

towards the morning room and shut the door behind her. Two closed doors, divided by a hall.

Each time she found herself alone in a room with her mother, the questions began again. Would she follow her brother and go to university? Though she'd have to study something broader than poetry. *Chipping away, chipping away.* Her mother pointed with her cigarette holder. "I mean to say, we've been more than happy to encourage your writing, but being a poet is hardly a job, is it? So here's something to think about; would you like to be a deb?"

Lucy gave a sharp little laugh. She'd assumed that, because Mother married against her parents' wishes, she would want nothing so conventional for a daughter.

"It's not so extraordinary. Most women think about getting married at around the age of twenty." Mother narrowed her eyes as she drew on her Marlboro. My God, it was *marriage* they wanted to bully her into! "And you'll want plenty of time to get to know the young man in question."

Freddie's words about not being a burden sprang to mind. Too angered to wonder whether regret prompted her mother's words, Lucy retaliated: "So I'm a problem you want to pass on to someone else, is that what you're saying?"

"There's no need to take that tone, Lucy." Everything about her was so precise and deliberate: the way she removed the cigarette holder from her lips, the slight kick she gave as she uncrossed her legs. "What *I'd* suggest is that you consider *all* your options. If you'd prefer to find yourself a job, then by all means do so." This, coming from a woman who'd never done a day's work in her life! How would she feel, having to admit to her parents that she had a working daughter? "But make up your mind before your father makes it up for you." Lucy's mother had a knack of ending conversations in such a way that there was no need to slam doors.

A job would mean independence, but what was Lucy fit for? The idea that she was a poet had taken root so long ago, it was part of her psyche. She expected to have to work hard at it, but had assumed that, in time, she would find her way. Now, time was a luxury Lucy no longer had. She wrote with increasing ferocity, words crushed together as she reached the margins of her notebook.

When her mother next enquired about her plans she asked for a typewriter.

Mother performed a double-take. "A typewriter?"

"I've been thinking about what you said. I'd like to teach myself to type." She adopted her father's style, ending the conversation by leaving the room. It was gratifying to think of Mother staring at the space she'd vacated, waiting until she regained her poise.

"She wants to learn to type," she heard her mother report, as if this were the most extraordinary development. Lucy doubted Mother had the slightest idea about what went on in typing pools. Her father, on the other hand, did.

"Hallelujah. Something practical at last."

There it was, the extent of his ambition for her. *A little reading. A little French conversation. Nothing too taxing.* At the same time – she looked out through the rain-streaked window over London's blurred roofscape – they were happily bankrolling Freddie's European adventures. And when had Freddie shown the slightest interest in culture?

A typewriter was located. A portable Olympia. Pale blue, second-hand (in case this turned out to be some passing fad). While others practised with *the quick brown fox jumps over the lazy dog* Lucy bashed out her poems, line by excruciating line, the first time she'd seen them in anything other than her own messy longhand. Her lips moved, mouthing words she would one day recite. The Olympia's crisp unforgiving font made Lucy cringe at her juvenile self. *How could anyone have seen potential in this?* she demanded of Pamela's empty armchair. *Dylan Thomas is Dead.* Lucy shook her head at what had been her reaction to the news. *If I'm ever going to grow as a writer, I need to get out of this place!*

Lucy became her own editor. She chipped away at words, prodded at them, sulked over them. Her phrasing took on a new rhythm. She now knew where the punctuation, 'The nuts and bolts of the English language', as they'd been described to her, belonged. She had returned from school armed with terminology for the things she'd tripped over naturally: idiom, form, meter, pentameter, villanelles, sonnets, iamb, three-stress lines. It gave Lucy the confidence to dissect, dismantle and reassemble in a way that brought to mind what she imagined of her father's production lines. And yet she was careful not to over-engineer. Starkly tangible was the end result she aimed for. Her poems should have that dug-from-the-earth quality. When Lucy didn't like the polished effect a comma produced, she ripped the page from the pale blue Olympia and began anew. The growing pile of set-aside paper was as vital as the smaller perfectly squared pile of poems.

Rather than whisper words to the silent room, she dared stand and speak them to the far corner. She stood on her chair (why not?); pictured an audience. *Too earnest. It sounds as if you're trying too hard.* Then she climbed down from her chair, galloped it back under her desk.

To her father, the clatter of the keyboard was the sound of industry. He would stick his head around the door, demanding, "How many words a minute?"

A typo marring an otherwise perfect page, the urge to scream gripped tight. Lucy plucked a figure from the air. Anything to get rid of him. Then she slammed back the carriage. *I'll give you entitlement!* Once the desire to punch something subsided, Lucy would yank the paper out and replace it with a virgin sheet. *Less venom, more sorrow* was her motivation, the measure by which she judged her work.

Machine Girl. Lucy was astonished that she hadn't thought of the typewriter's potential before. She could type quickly, quicker than the words-per-minute-tally she fired at her father. But this was poetry. Every full-stop had to be scrutinised; every word needed to put forward a convincing argument. *The repetition at the end feels forced.* What Lucy ended up with was a refined set, together with a quiet exhilaration: *these crisp, clean words were hers.*

After the poems came the letters. Lucy submitted her freshly-typed sheets to *Poetry Review, Encounter, Nimbus, The London Magazine and Poetry (London), New Statesman, The Spectator, Scrutiny* and *The Critic.* The so-called 'little' magazines.

And back came the replies. Ignoring her muscles' burn, she raced up to the privacy of the fourth floor, wondering if anything she did – holding the envelope between her palms, sitting and staring at it, using her special letter opener – could change what was inside. The first few rejections stung. 'It's not one for us'. Lucy had thought her boarding school years had rewarded her with the skin of a rhino, but this type of rejection was new. She had invested such hope, training as hard as any athlete. *'Once published'*, Edith Sitwell had written. Publication was the thing that was supposed to get her out of here. Her exit strategy. 'You have an extraordinary lyric gift but have you tried…?' *So, it's not all bad news,* Lucy reminded herself. As always, the editor was sure her work would be snapped up by someone else.

"How's the typing coming?" her father asked over breakfast.

Lucy, whose dreams now filled with the image of her fingers moving feverishly over keys, took time over her mouthful of scrambled egg. "Improving," she said finally.

Her mother dabbed a linen napkin to one side of her mouth. "It would be nice to think we'll see some results in the near future, dear."

She advertised a typing service in a shop window and received several pieces of work. Enough to buy a little more time, but not nearly enough to pay her own way. Competent and thorough, if Lucy could be faulted it was that she couldn't resist making a few edits of her own.

And then one day – *Pinch yourself* – the postman delivered a Yes. Lucy laughed out loud. It was from John Lehmann, no less. The hand that had signed this letter had shaken the hand of Virginia Woolf! More important to Lucy was that Lehmann had been Edith Sitwell's biographer. Not just serendipity, this was validation. The promise of her name in print. *Her* name. *Actually* in print. She paced the fourth-floor room. She pressed the flats of her hands against the sides of her nose and wept, without trying to make sense of this rare cocktail of emotions. There was a cheque, something to present her parents with. But, no, they didn't deserve to share her news. This victory was hers.

"How's the typing coming?" her father asked as they crossed paths in the hall. "Much work?"

Lucy censored the part of her that still craved approval, if only to say, *See what I managed to do.* "Not too bad. I'm just off out to deliver the latest."

"Well, at least that typewriter wasn't a complete waste of money."

She would tell him about the next one. But then again… The second belonged to Pamela. Perhaps the one *afterwards*. There was never any doubt in Lucy's mind that she'd stumbled on a winning formula – Edith Sitwell + 1. This would be the first of many.

Meanwhile, the high that the sight of her name in print gave Lucy was matchless. She walked to the bank on air.

From the fourth-floor room to the post box, to the pages of magazines. But set in a different font by a stranger, Lucy seemed one-stage removed from the words. Sometimes she liked what she read and wondered how it had come into being, ignoring those hours of careful nurturing. Occasionally she didn't. Either way, Lucy was spurred on. She could improve.

Whenever she emerged from her fourth-floor domain, it was to clashes. At a time when every conversation had the potential to progress to an argument, television provided sweet relief. It was possible to sit in a room and not speak without accusations of moodiness being fired at her.

This particular evening, the planned viewing was *Sunday Night at the London Palladium.* Lucy and her mother were sitting side by side on the sofa. By now, Birmingham would normally have beckoned. Father liked to be installed before the start of the working week. But, there he was, sitting in his armchair, his ongoing presence unexplained. If she hadn't been so impatient for Tommy Steele's number, Lucy might have questioned it herself. She wasn't going to let anything spoil this for her, not even the constant crossing and uncrossing of her mother's legs (although she wondered that Father didn't say something). Then, all distractions forgotten, Lucy sat forward; Tommy Steele walked onto the stage, quiff bobbing.

Father hauled himself out of his chair saying, "We can do without this rubbish." Before Lucy had a chance to protest, he had switched off the television set.

"Quite right," her mother said, uncrossing her legs one final time and following him out of the room.

What a hypocrite! When Father was away, Mother tuned in to *Two-way Family Favourites.* Lucy, who'd grown up on a diet of Glenn Miller, often found herself singing along to Doris Day or one of the hits from *Oklahoma!* But mixed in with the more conservative numbers were records by Frankie Laine, Lonnie Donegan and Johnnie Ray. With no radio of her own, this was how she'd first heard Tommy Steele.

Lucy crossed the room and switched the set back on. If her parents didn't want to watch Tommy Steele, they didn't have to. Besides, they clearly had things to talk about. Now Lucy had to wait for the television to warm up all over again. She'd miss most of his performance!

"Lucy, I thought I made myself clear!"

Her father's return had been muffled by slippers and carpet. She refused to cower. Why should she put up with a tantrum, just because he hadn't got his own way? "It's just music," she said. "It's not as if he's pretending to be Mozart. I *can* tell the difference."

"There is a line, young lady. And you," her father stabbed the air that separated them with a pointed finger, "have just crossed it. Turn that thing off. Now!"

But if her parents managed to find fault with Tommy Steele, they were totally unprepared for *'the new American singing sensation'*. It would have been about the time of *Hound Dog*. Her father seemed paralysed by the sight of Elvis swaggering onto the stage. There was no music to offend his ears at first. Nothing other than the fact of him. Elvis stood behind the mic for a full five minutes, then he hit his guitar with a lick. A knowing sneer, two broken strings dangling, and, very slowly, he began to move his hips (the manoeuvre that had earned him the nickname, *the pelvis*). Lucy waited for her father to erupt. For now, he seemed incapable of anything other than blinking at the screen. Two girls in the front row keeled over, and men pressed through the crush to stretcher them away. Those further back clawed at their own faces, opened their mouths and screamed. It couldn't have been more shocking, unless Elvis had been naked and walked straight out of the television set.

As the camera zoomed in on the girls' wild eyes, Father reached one shaking hand towards the screen, a raised vein on his forehead pulsing. "Do you see?" Here was all the proof he needed to have Tommy Steele hauled into the streets and flogged.

Even while being accused of she didn't know what, every cell of Lucy's body was alert. When Presley faced the camera, his eyes stripped her.

Her mother's hand on Lucy's arm. "Do you see now why your father doesn't want rock and roll in this house?"

And Lucy did see. She saw her mother's dilated pupils, that hungry look she shared with the screaming teenagers. For the first time, something had arrived that had the potential to destroy her parents' peace of mind. It excited Lucy to know that Elvis might succeed where Hitler had failed. But, unlike her parents, she understood enough to appreciate the difference between Elvis and Tommy Steele. When he progressed from suits to leathers, Tommy Steele still looked like a toothpaste advert. It didn't surprise her when he became a matinée sweetheart. It surprised her when Elvis did.

Lucy decided not to share her news. She had received a letter from *Atlantic Monthly* – an American literary magazine she'd written to on a whim – to say that they'd just accepted Machine Girl and looked forward to reading more of her work. *I'm going to tunnel my way out of here,* she promised herself. *If it kills me.*

But rock 'n' roll wasn't what defined Lucy's year (though in late December she would see *Love Me Tender* and swoon). It wasn't even her growing awareness of that dark and dangerous thing called sex. (With little access to boys of her own age, the man she fashioned in her imagination was comprised of the more risqué elements of Tommy Steele and the less terrifying elements of Elvis.) 1956 wasn't even defined by the books and plays the critics wanted to ban. It was another awakening, a spark that Pamela had kindled. Lucy needed to claim a cause for her own. Proof that she had no *sense of entitlement*.

She found it in Suez, the vital waterway linking Europe, Africa and the Middle East. When the canal was nationalised, Anthony Eden declared an international asset at risk from an incompetent administration. Some nations needed saving from themselves. The Prime Minister broadcast his message on television. *'We all remember too well what the cost can be in giving in to fascism'.*

No longer could Lucy hide her frustration at her parents' unrelenting confidence in the 'establishment'. These people in power – the 'brilliant minds' they insisted were best equipped to run the country – clung to the idea that this small island of theirs deserved its jumped-up status. "You've both lived through two world wars. Can you stomach a third?" Lucy asked.

"What would you have him do?" her father demanded. "Let another Hitler take control?"

"Quite," Mother said.

Lucy was aghast. "You do understand the next war will be the war to end all wars? Einstein said it: General annihilation is a very real possibility."

"Scaremongering!"

"Yes, your doomsday predictions aren't helpful, dear," her mother echoed.

"The atom bomb wasn't used in Korea," Father contributed.

They really *didn't* see it. "America *planned* to use the bomb," she insisted. "Everything was in place, waiting for the word. It was dangerously close to becoming another Hiroshima."

As Lucy knew from the reports she'd read, in 1945, it had all came down to number-crunching. The Japanese had predicted that defending their country would cost up to twenty million lives. (Lucy disliked the vagary of 'up to'.) The Allied Joint War Plans Committee had given a range of figures, the upshot being that they calculated they would suffer 'up to' 220,000 casualties, forty-six thousand of whom would die. Sceptical, the US Secretary of War commissioned his own report. His intelligence put figures considerably higher: up to four million US casualties, 800,000 of whom would die.

Why did they differ so much? Lucy had written to Pamela from the homework room at school.

Because nobody knew the answer, she replied. *There had never been warfare like it.*

The ultimate chicken and egg scenario; already, an aerial bombing campaign had raged for six months. The question was, how many more lives needed to be wiped out before someone agreed that enough was enough? All along, the 509th Composite Group had been standing by. As Pamela had written, *From the moment of its creation, using the bomb was a very real possibility.*

But Father was adamant. "The Japanese did some fairly horrific things in the War, you know. They refused to sign the Geneva Convention."

"That doesn't make what happened *right.*"

"Well, if you hear of a way to fight a war without killing people, be sure to let me know."

"Do you have another topic of conversation, Lucy?" Mother said flatly. "One that's more appropriate for the dinner table."

Except when changing the subject, Lucy's parents were non-askers of questions. But even her father's beloved BBC was divided about Eden's decision to recapture the canal from Egypt. When schemes were proposed to discipline the corporation, he spoke as if the idea was his: "Perhaps the government *should* take over editorial control."

At the cinema, Lucy watched footage of parachutes floating like a shoal of jellyfish. She understood Pamela's dilemma. It was no longer possible to stand by and do nothing.

CHAPTER SEVENTEEN

1956

She picked an out of the way place, somewhere she wouldn't be recognised. The formidable-looking owner of the hardware shop was busy serving a customer. They seemed to be working down a lengthy list. Plenty of time to scan the ceiling-height shelves: kettles and slug-killer, picture hooks and sets of screwdrivers, but where were the locks and chains?

"Yes, love," an assistant said, coming through a door at the back of the shop. "What'll it be?"

Heat rose to Lucy's neck. "I can't quite see…" She looked around hoping for rescue.

"Start by describing it and we'll take it from there." His tone said, *Here we go, another time-waster.*

Oh, what the hell. "I'm looking for a length of chain. Something with a padlock on the end."

"For your pushbike, is it?" The man turned away from her and started rummaging in a wooden crate. What he slammed onto the counter was designed for a child's bicycle, but at least it offered a way forward.

"It's for a motorbike, actually."

Forget everything you know, Lucy told herself as she set her toothbrush back in its china beaker. She straightened up in front of the mirror in the bathroom, satisfying herself that the chain, wrapped around her waist and concealed under her baggy jumper, wasn't too obvious. *Forget logic. The whole point of the exercise is to get caught.*

At the sound of a sharp rap on the door, Lucy's hand flew to her chest.

"Are you finished in there, Lucy?"

"Almost!" Seeing a small trace of vomit in the sink, she twisted the hot tap as far as it would go. The point might be to get caught, but not *before* she was out of the front door. As the water gushed out, she used one hand to encourage it into the uppermost curves. Was that enough? Her mother had such a sensitive nose. She gave her neck a quick squirt of eau de cologne. A second, she aimed over the sink.

Another rap on the door. "Lucy!"

How did she look? A quick glance gave the answer: clammy and pale. *Imagine what Pamela would say!* If Pamela suffered from nerves, you'd never know it.

"I stood up to be counted, Lucy. Someone has to, however small a difference it makes."

"At last," her mother said as Lucy emerged, head down, so that her appearance couldn't be scrutinised.

"I'm off out in a minute," she said.

"About time your skin saw some daylight." Lucy had prepared herself to be evasive, but Mother slipped past and locked herself inside, either disinterested or in too much of a hurry to ask what her plans were.

Lucy fetched her coat from the closet in the downstairs hall. She got as far as the front door before another wave of nausea hit her. Perhaps she'd be better off with some fresh air. No, Lucy stayed her hand just shy of the door handle. With her mother in the second-floor bathroom, she would have to make it all the way up to the third floor. She took the stairs two at a time.

On her second descent, Lucy noticed the leather camera case on the table in the hall. Her father's Kodak Tourist. If she was going to pretend to be a tourist, she should look like one. The strap was so short, the case had to be hand-held, and Lucy needed both of hers to be free. She tipped the camera out (a better plan – no one would notice it was missing if the case was where they expected it to be) and hooked it around her neck, then pressed the mechanism to check that she still remembered how to release the lens, complete with its bellows, and how to press on the hinges to click it away inside the body of the camera. A neat design, rather like a jack-in-the-box.

Leaving the square behind, her feet fell into a regular rhythm. '*Imagine your fate's sealed, then there's nothing for you to worry about.*' 'Easy for you to say!' she answered back, but the camera had an unexpected power. Holding its strap gave Lucy a sense of security, as though she were inoculated against reality. Already, she had stepped outside herself. Now she must focus.

That arrogant bastard with his film star looks had dragged Britain into another war, less than ten years after the last one had finished. Did he care that Nasser had done nothing to deserve comparisons with Hitler? No! (She flagged down a bus that was heading in the right direction and found a seat on the lower deck.) The Suez Canal was on Egyptian terri-tory. All Nasser had done was lay claim to his country's most important asset. Compensation had been offered to the canal company's shareholders, and, with the exception of Israeli ships, international access had been guaranteed. Other canal users were satisfied, the UN was satisfied, but, oh no, not Eden! Even Eisenhower's public declaration that the US was firmly against military intervention hadn't deterred *him*.

"Where to, miss?" the conductor asked.

Temporarily herself again, Lucy's stomach grumbled, but there was no accompanying rush of heat, no fear that she might retch. "Westminster, please." She gave a strained smile, enough to be polite. Today she must channel anger.

Lucy had no doubt Eden had encouraged Israel to launch an attack, so that our great imperial nation could be seen coming the rescue of one of its 'little brothers', no matter that women and children were being killed in the process! Given her insight on how history was written, Lucy believed Eden capable of anything.

Wrapped up in her own thoughts (*I'm a tourist, I have every right to be here*), when Lucy stepped from bus to pavement, (*Who are these people, blocking the way?*) she failed to notice the man in the midst of the small crowd, standing on an orange box. Another individual who had been spurred into action. She would have been interested in the question he shouted: "I ask you, what steps are being taken to ensure that, if Nasser falls, the new Egyptian government will support British policy – and by that, of course, I mean the Tory government's? What about the Egyptian people? If you don't think they're behind Nasser, you've got another think coming!"

A pause at the junction of Whitehall and Downing Street; it wasn't Eden Lucy imagined stepping out of the black door of number 10, but Churchill: hunch-shouldered, homburg hat, large cigar, hand raised in a victory sign, but in a hurry; always in a hurry. Taking the opportunity to gather her wits, Lucy did as any tourist would do, raised the camera to her eye and trained the lens on her target. There he was; a figure of trust the world over. The British bobby, paid to guard the Prime Minister's residence. Helmet with its uncomfortable-looking 'chin strap' cutting into the skin just below his mouth, white shirt and black tie, silver rank insignia displayed on epaulettes, sliver buttons, chain for his whistle. Unseen were his truncheon and handcuffs. As she watched, he stepped aside to let a stout middle-aged tourist take his place, while her husband snapped away. So he *did* step away from the front door. And he was obviously a friendly sort.

Here goes nothing. She left the grind of Whitehall traffic behind.

"…combination of cheap construction and bomb damage." The policeman had missed his calling. He seemed happier in the roll of tour guide. "It all takes its toll."

"Took a hit, did it?" the man asked.

"Several near misses, actually. The biggest of the bombs fell over there," the bobby indicated with a nod, "on Treasury Green. Close enough to cause damage to the kitchen, the pantry and the offices to the Treasury."

Lucy came to a standstill and listened, her hands on the wrought-iron railings.

The woman's eyes were wide as she asked, "No one hurt, I hope?"

"'Fraid so. Three staff killed, but Mr Churchill got away with it. He was sitting down to dinner at the time."

"No!" the woman exclaimed as they swapped places, so that the bobby was back on the doorstep. "Just goes to show."

"Wrong place, wrong time," her husband agreed as she joined him, to Lucy's right.

She took a second, closer look at the street. Its shabbiness had passed her by. Vast swathes of London streets were subsiding. Sloping floors and warped doorframes were commonplace.

"There are only so many cracks you can plaster over." The policeman was playing to his small audience. "They say there's not a straight wall in number 10. They may have to knock it down and start again."

"They could do with something bigger," the woman remarked to her husband. "I mean, it is *terribly* small."

"No, no," he corrected her, as if embarrassed that she hadn't read the London guidebook he held in his hand. "It only looks that way. It's linked to the large house behind, the one we saw, overlooking Horse Guards."

Oh! she mouthed, as if such a thing was terribly clever, and looked to the policeman who nodded his affirmation.

"Mind if I –?" Lucy raised the camera halfway as if to finish her question, then aimed the lens at the policeman. The front wall of the house provided a sombre backdrop, as black as any factory, the accumulation of grime and soot, a toxic mix known as smog. Leaning against the railings, the cold coil of chain pressed hard against her hipbone and nipped the skin of her waist.

The policeman obliged by jutting out his jaw, but he saw that he was losing his audience. Something had captured their attention. "Oh, no! Not here, you don't!" He strode off the doorstep, towards a man dressed in black who was positioning an orange box. "Don't even think about it."

The man turned to face him. "I haven't said anything yet!"

"And you won't. I have the power to arrest you to *prevent* a breach of the peace."

This was it. Lucy wouldn't get a better chance.

Pricked into action, she fumbled in her pocket for the key, unlocked the padlock, and felt one coil of the chain begin to slip down around her hips. Her heart hammering, adrenaline pumping, she grabbed the ends and, tugging at the chain, managed to loop it around the place where an upright and a crosspiece met. She glanced up at the policeman's back, now yanking on the chain – *come on!* – when the street orator locked eyes with her. Her stomach lurched, but there was recognition: a kindred spirit. He raised his voice in protest. *"Law not war! Law not war!"* In a matter of days, the National Council of Labour would adopt the slogan as their own. Now, it bought her vital seconds.

The padlock hooked through the links, Lucy snapped it shut, checked that it was locked, then dropped the key behind her. Her eyes followed the slight glint that fell away to the level of the basement.

It was done.

"Law not war!" She punched the air, doing her best to suppress the tiny smile inside her before it grew into a victorious grin.

The policeman twisted his head sharply, opening his mouth as if about to say, *"You! And after I let you take my photograph."* Opportunity enough for the street orator to replant his orange box on the pavement and step onto it. Another look exchanged and they shared this triumph. A few paces towards her, the bobby became aware of the man's voice. *Law not war!* Marooned in the middle of Downing Street, his knees slightly bent, one hand reaching for Lucy and the other towards the street orator, he looked like a man who had been sleepwalking on a tightrope and suddenly found himself awake.

"I'm arresting you both for breach of the peace!" he shouted, in anger and panic.

"I'd like to see him try," a woman said to Lucy, and took up the chant. By now the bobby had his whistle between his lips. Its shrill sound cut repeatedly through the babble.

"I never imagined I'd be called out in the middle of the night to pick up my daughter from a police station!" Mother's grip on Lucy's upper arm was as tight as her voice. "Thank God your father's in Birmingham and we can cover this u–" Then she looked at Lucy anew. "Oh, I see." Open-mouthed, she gave a short bitter laugh. "Your timing was deliberate."

Lucy didn't deny it. Her feet slowed as she saw an unfamiliar profile in silhouette; an elbow resting on the open window of a saloon car, gleaming sleekly under the street lights.

"Mr Millard was good enough to drive me here," her mother said as the man let go of his cigarette, threw open the door and stepped out of the car. Lucy hadn't heard the name Millard before, and being on the back foot made it impossible to ask who he was. He moved quickly, grabbing the handle of the back door as if he preferred Lucy not to get grubby fingerprints all over his gleaming chrome-work.

How much of her mother's planned cover-up related to Mr Millard? From the back seat, Lucy looked in the rear-view mirror and saw that his eyes were steeled on her, judging in a way that a chauffeur would never presume to judge. They stared at each other for the best part of a minute.

Her mother broke the stalemate. "Let's get home, shall we?"

"I don't know what you hoped to gain." His tone was mocking as he pulled away from the kerb.

Lucy sat with her arms wrapped around her waist, looking out into the night. Why should she explain herself to a stranger?

Her mother turned in her seat, demanding, "Well?" as if she'd asked the question herself. "Have you nothing to say?"

It had only been a small stand. But she'd done as Pamela would have done; alerted the newspapers. There would be photographs. "I wasn't trying to *gain* anything. I stood against something I know to be wrong."

"Oh, good God!" Mother whipped her head away and turned to her companion. "Listen to her. My daughter's just been arrested and now she's the new authority on right and wrong!"

The next morning Mother sat opposite Lucy at the breakfast table, her silence at its most powerful. She snapped her newspaper (not her usual reading material of choice), making sure Lucy couldn't ignore the headline: *Let the Cry-babies Howl! It's GREAT Britain Again.* Lucy wondered whether to enquire after Mr Millard, but held her tongue. There would be a better time to use that information.

By the following week, the media's mood had changed.

This action has endangered the American Alliance, split the Commonwealth, flouted the United Nations, shocked the overwhelming majority of world opinion and dishonoured the name of Britain. Her father's flung copy of *The Observer* came to rest by Lucy's feet. "That's the last time I buy anything Astor's had a hand in!"

Mother did not echo. She looked pale and nervous, as if she had no way of predicting what her husband might do next.

Lucy bent to pick the paper up and read the words: *Sir Anthony Eden must go. His removal from the Premiership is scarcely less vital to the prospects of this country than was that of Mr Neville Chamberlain in May 1940.*

Her father's voice betrayed the fact that he was physically shaking. "Astor will be the one who's forced to resign, you'll see!"

She folded the broadsheet neatly and put it on her corner of the table, saying nothing.

There was no truce in the Forrester household. Her parents sat on one side of the table, she on the other. Even Cook remained frosty.

But Lucy wasn't alone when she demonstrated in Trafalgar Square. Thirty thousand people stood shoulder to shoulder as Nye Bevan spoke for each one of them.

"They have offended against every principle of decency. There is only one way in which they can begin to restore their tarnished reputation and that is to get out."

And she added her voice to the sound of dissent, raising a fist – "Get out! Get out! Get out!" – even as police arrived on horseback to disperse what the press would call a rabble.

CHAPTER EIGHTEEN

1957

Fresh from a matinée of *The Seven Year Itch*, Lucy was reporting back to Cook. As she helped herself to a glass of milk and a banana, Lucy mimicked the male lead: *"Because now I'm going to take you in my arms and kiss you. Very quickly and very hard."* As a rule, Lucy didn't approve of girly girls, but for Marilyn she made an exception. It was hard to get over how someone so sexy could also be goofy and vulnerable. "And her dresses! Especially the white one with the cross-over front."

"Don't you go getting any ideas." Cook's hands were stained red from the plums she was stoning. "No point lusting after fripperies."

"I don't know where I'd *find* a dress like that," Lucy said. "Let alone the nerve to wear it."

"Before you go upstairs, turn the radio on, will you?"

Lucy left Cook singing along to *The Nuns' Chorus*. Her head swam with images and sensations. The give of the plush red carpet underfoot. The tense hush as the lights began to fade. The thrill of sitting in the dark with unknown others, their laughter mingling with hers, watching the blue curls of cigarette smoke trapped in the bright beam on its way to the screen. On her way up to the ground floor, she imagined for herself a different body; experimented with swinging her hips in a kind of rolling action.

"Lucy, would you mind sparing me a few moments?"

Blood rushed to her face. Her father was standing sideways in the doorway of his study, his arm directing her inwards. Pleasure drained from the day, as final and fatal as those last few grains of sand in an egg timer. The room that had fascinated Lucy as a child no longer held any attraction. Dingy, airless and furnished with dark wood and leather chairs, she likened it to her headmistress's office. You were never invited inside for a good reason. Was it to be another discussion about 'the future' or had a photograph of her arrest made the papers?

"Sure," she shrugged, putting her glass of milk and the piece of fruit down on the table in the hall.

"An American film, was it?" His voice was sharp. "Well you can save the slang for when you're talking to your friends."

Bowing her head slightly, Lucy passed through the doorway. Newspaper columns had convinced Father that all American films were superficial, hedonistic and entirely to blame for the increase in juvenile delinquency. *At least they don't brush social concerns under the carpet.* He'd have her exist on a diet of Ealing Comedies.

Lucy arrived in front of her father's desk, hands behind her back, straightening up so that he couldn't find more fault with her.

He bypassed her, seating himself in his leather-upholstered chair. "Sit yourself down."

Lucy detected his usual impatient air. Their conversation might be unpleasant, but at least it wouldn't last long. She sat.

"How old are you now, Lucy?" He flicked open his tobacco tin and pinched a little loose-leaf between a finger and thumb. The earthy aromatic scent reached her. Lucy used to love watching him fill his pipe. The way he tamped down the loose-leaf with a thumb. "It still has to be springy, see?" he would explain in rare unhurried moments. Now, Lucy pondered how many other fathers needed to ask about their daughters' ages. "Seventeen," she said.

"Then we can have this conversation as adults. What I have to tell you, it's… well, my foremost concern is to protect you from the storm."

Pleasantly surprised, Lucy risked crossing her legs and let her arms overlap at the level of her waist.

"There is a situation –" the corners of his mouth twitched "– that it's best you distance yourself from."

Lucy frowned with what she hoped he would take to be concentration.

"For the past fifteen years or so, as you know, I've been living away from home for part of each week. And the thing is, I've been keeping two households."

"I imagined you had." Still so eager to please, she would later reflect, lifting the needle to replay this particular part of the conversation.

He glanced up from his pipe. "I must say, I've always thought you were more perceptive than your brother."

Masking huge surprise (although not altogether trusting what he said), Lucy volunteered, "Well, staying in hotels all that time would have been terribly expensive."

A sound in the back of her father's throat seemed to retract the compliment. "Perhaps I need to make myself clearer. When I say *households,* I'm not talking about properties or staff. Do you see? And the thing is, the press have got hold of it."

"The press?"

"The newspapers." His voice took on an angry tone, suggesting he'd been wronged. "I'm supposed to feel grateful they've given me notice. But there will be headlines and I'm afraid I don't know when or where this thing will end." He seemed disinclined to look at her. "So what I think the best thing would be – as far as you're concerned – is that we set you up in a little flat."

Lucy heard her own breath hitch.

He set his pipe aside for a moment. "Unless you were thinking of university like your brother? But I never had the impression that you particularly enjoyed school."

Struggling to follow her father's drift, she was a young girl once more, nursing a *chocolat chaud,* listening to someone speaking in a foreign language. "Not particularly, no –"

"That's settled, then. I'll make the arrangements." He opened the cheque book that lay on his desk.

On any other day, Lucy would have been happy to leave it at that, but a decision had been made about her future and she needed to understand why. "I–" she began.

He looked up, surprised to find she was still there.

"Perhaps you could explain. Why are the newspapers so interested in this second household of yours?"

"Your mother's been aware for some time, but now that other people know," he looked pained, "she's decided to divorce me."

Lucy blinked at the sound of the word. She didn't know anyone who was divorced, but had read enough newspaper articles to understand how it all worked. To avoid destroying his wife's reputation, the husband would feign adultery, making sure everyone saw him check into a less than reputable hotel with a less than reputable woman, to whom he'd paid good money to put on a convincing show. So that's what Father had done. And his next thought was to protect her.

"Your mother will stay here, in the house, and I'll make Birmingham my permanent home. With my lady friend."

Lucy's chin jerked upwards. "There's *actually* another woman?" This was her upright pillar-of-the-community father. The man who wore the serious black greatcoat, the person she'd felt she owed her loyalty to.

He pulled on the end of his nose, dragging one hand down over his moustache and chin, sniffing noisily. More information was communicated in the flare of his nostrils than in his tangled words. This wasn't simple shame. There was something else, but what? *Prominent Businessman Found to be Cheating on his Wife* would hardly be newsworthy but *Prominent Businessman is Discovered to be Bigamist…*

Lucy looked at her father, appalled. "Another *wife?*"

"No!" he said, his voice harsh.

Even as he objected, Lucy's blood was charging around her veins. Bigamy would be a crime. That wouldn't be her father's style.

"But…" he faltered. So rare was it for him to struggle for words, Lucy knew she wasn't far off the mark. Her father had a mistress. Right now, the idea seemed astonishing, but really, so what? Mr Millard hadn't been Mother's only unexplained visitor.

Part of her was curious. *What kind of a woman,* Lucy asked herself, *would* you *take for a lover?* She tried to picture her father with a Marilyn Monroe lookalike, but the only platinum blonde she could conjure was Ruth Ellis, whose brassy image had been splashed across the tabloids. That poor woman had killed the lover who'd driven her to distraction. When they hanged her, one thousand people stood outside Holloway, some like Pamela campaigning for abolition of the death penalty, others praying for her soul.

No, not Ruth Ellis. Mother was elegant, queenly. She had what used to be called breeding.

And then her father added, "Of course, there are the other children to think about."

It was as if Lucy was strapped into the fairground ride called 'The Cage'. Belted tightly in a standing position and being spun, while the axis was near vertical. "Childr–?" she heard herself echo stupidly, but the word stuck in her throat. The word 'household' meant *'family'*!

"Your three half-brothers."

One version of Lucy peeled away from her, pushed back the chair, letting it topple, and ran all of the way to the sanctuary of the fourth floor where she threw herself down on her bed. Another version ran to her mother's morning room, threw herself at her feet and clung to her skirt. A third version ran downstairs to the kitchen, where Cook would read her face and she wouldn't need to explain herself. Who could she trust?

Yourself. You must train your instincts.

You must ask questions.

Lucy forced herself to look down on the inner workings of the fairground machinery, then she was thrown onto her back, staring up at flashing lights and distorted faces. The other woman: brassy, blonde with pointed features. The three brothers: still in short trousers, clinging to the bars. *Count them: one, two, three.*

Not *mine*. No. *Yours.*

Head spinning, she looked at her father. This second household wasn't some casual or convenient arrangement. It was a *life*. He had more to keep him in Birmingham than he did in London. "Did you say," she began, her head pounding in a way that made her reach just above her ears with both hands. "Did you say that Mother's *aware?*" If that were true, then it was the most extraordinary thing of all.

"Not the detail, but yes."

Not the half-brothers, then. If Father was capable of concealing something this big, what other lies had he told? "There *were* businesses? There *were* investments, were there?"

"What do you take me for?" he growled, outraged that his own daughter should challenge him. "There *are* businesses. Very profitable, too."

There was no answer to that question. Every aspect of Lucy's childhood appeared altered. Even her father's insistence that the hospital should do something, find some medicine to *make* her better. She saw it now. An invalid child would have detained him in London.

Lucy gathered what ammunition she found lying about in the debris and hurled it, not worrying if some of it missed its target. "You *used* Mother's money to keep a second family."

"The profit from the businesses paid for the house. But we don't live like *this*." He looked with such distaste at all the things Lucy assumed he'd chosen for himself. For a moment, it seemed that he would sweep everything – the ebony-handled letter opener, his rosewood ashtray, the sheaves of paper – clean off his desk. "Your childhood has been extremely privileged compared with your half-brothers.'"

Here, at last, was the root of it. Lucy had spent the last year going out of her way to prove she wasn't a spoilt brat, when the reason for his cruel comment was that she and Freddie had more than his Birmingham family. She wanted to protest: *Privilege isn't all about money, you know.* Besides, there was no point trying to persuade her that he'd never felt comfortable with money when she'd seen him throw it around. Well, let him see what life was like without it! "They're *Mother's* businesses. She put up the capital."

"You needn't worry on your mother's account. She's had a good return on her investment."

Lucy resented the way Father distanced himself, referring to *her* mother. His marriage was a civil contract – a financial arrangement – while his second household was romantic, the relationship he'd taken risks for. While Lucy and her brother had legitimacy and so-called *privilege*, her father's other children had... was it possible that they'd had his time, his patience, his *love*? She tried picturing her father throwing a small child up in the air, but this was a step too far. "And how will you finance the businesses when Mother divorces you?"

His jaw dropped. She saw that her father expected things to remain civil, even after the last of the facts had leaked from the cracks. But what if the firm of solicitors Mother's family had used for the past seventy-five years advised her otherwise?

"These…" Lucy would never bring herself to refer to the boys as her 'half-brothers'. "These *sons* of yours? Do they have your name?" By which she meant did she and Freddie share more than a bloodline with them.

"They have their mother's name."

Her eyebrows leapt upwards. It was what she'd hoped he would say, yet this admission now seemed like a new slight. "And how are you known when you're at this second household of yours?"

"To the boys?"

"No, to the paperboy, the postman, your parish priest. I assume you don't go by the name, Mr Forrester?"

"Oh, I see. No." His expression suggested this would be quite improper; as if he was surprised she didn't know the proper etiquette for second households. "I use their surname."

When Mother had tried to insist that he took her ancient family name, he'd refused. And yet he'd done precisely that for this *other* woman. A name, presumably, with no history, no legacy. Jones, perhaps, or Thompson. Lucy's bloodstream formed a whirlpool. It was as if everything was being dragged down into the whole sorry mess. "And when you're the managing director of these businesses of yours? What do they call you there?"

"Look, Lucy, I daresay this has all come as a terrible shock. You're entitled to be angry, but it can't h–"

"I want to understand how you've managed to get away with it! For the *whole of my lifetime*." Never before had Lucy lost control in front of her father. All of those years of being *ladylike.* But something inside her wouldn't be denied. "Is this what you were thinking of every time you said to me, 'Don't get caught'? As if getting caught was as bad as whatever it was I'd done in the first place. Except *you* thought you'd got away with it? You thought you'd done such a thorough job of covering your tracks, going under a different name…" And then it occurred to Lucy. They might not be the only wronged parties in this horrible mess. "Your mistress? Does she know about *us?*"

"Of course she does. I made it quite clear that I would never leave your mother."

How thoroughly he'd convinced himself that he had followed some unholy protocol. "So honesty is owed to the other woman, but not to your own family?"

But the question was wrong. He had two families, staked apart as widely as he could manage. Lucy saw how he had begrudged the Christmases, the Easters, the summer holidays. All those occasions when he'd been here and yet absent. Behind the pages of a newspaper or a closed door. Obligation, not affection. Empty, like his greatcoat hanging in the closet in the hall. "Wouldn't *divorce* have been the honourable thing?"

His moustache twitched. *Ah! You don't like that word, do you?* Father had been vocal in his opinion that Princess Margaret should give up Group Captain Peter Townsend rather than marry a divorced man. Surely he must realise he should be rethinking his words? At no point had he suggested leading a double life as the civilised alternative.

"I was thinking about you."

"No." Lucy shook her head, no longer amazed by her own nerve. "You were wondering how to hang on to Mother's money."

Her father said nothing. Neither did he show the slightest remorse.

"What about these sons of yours? Have *they* known all along?"

"No. That's something we'll have to face up to."

We? A responsibility he wanted to dish up so that his portion of blame was halved. Lucy experimented with a sweet and wholly insincere smile. "Are you going to parcel us all off?" Then she relaxed the corners of her mouth. "Or am I the only one who's to have that privilege?"

"Things are rather more complicated at the business end." *That's right. Remove any hint of emotion.* "The youngest wouldn't be able to understand. And the twins both work for me."

All that time she'd been agonising over how she might earn her way, *he'd* been in a position to offer her a job.

"I imagine it will be rather worse for them than it is for you," he went on.

It was already abundantly clear that, geographically speaking, his emotions were in Birmingham. "Worse?" Lucy spat out the words. "Why would you possibly think that?"

"Why? Because they're illegitimate, of course." He stood and, resting his weight on his arms, leaned across the desk until he towered over her. "You might think things like that don't matter any more, but I can assure you, in the eyes of the majority, they most certainly do!"

"It's incredible. Even now, you're acting as though *I'm* at fault." Afterwards, she would remember how it was reported that Ruth Ellis said to a visiting bishop just before they hanged her, 'When I held the revolver, I was another person.' It was another person who spoke in Lucy's place, a future Lucy, and in the near future Lucy would look back on this conversation and think she was looking at someone else.

"Lucille!"

"I'd prefer to find out that my parents weren't married," she shot back, refusing to be intimidated, "than to find out their marriage was a sham."

"I'm sorry if that's how you see it, but I can't agr–"

You do not *get to hang on to the image of yourself as a respectable businessman.* "You've had plenty of time to think about the damage you were causing." *Years,* in fact. Questions swam lengths in Lucy's mind, kicking off from the cold tile, doubling back on themselves without waiting for an answer. Something was still amiss. A number… She grasped at it before it could slip away from her. "Fifteen years… 'For the last fifteen years', you said."

"Yes." Her father straightened up, one hand reaching for the comfort of his pipe.

"That would make the boys fourteen at the most. But if they work for you…" She left a gap for him to fill.

"I wasn't living with their mother at the time they were born. That came later. They're a little older than you, I suppose."

He supposed. Meaning that they were at least eighteen. In fact, it would make sense if they fell in the three-year gap between Freddie and herself.

Two things we share.

Blood, and shameful secrets.

Perverse though it was, it pleased Lucy to think that this was the second time her father had ploughed through this wretched conversation. "What did Freddie have to say about it all?"

"I've written to him."

"You've –?" She stalled, incensed on her brother's behalf. Freddie had crossed over to his parents' side, and now this was his reward. "You haven't had the *decency* to tell him to his face? Well, you can stop worrying that a little slang is going to influence *my* morals." Unable to tolerate being in the study a moment longer, Lucy shot up out of the chair and stormed towards the door.

"Lucille, I am still your father and I won't have you speaking to me like that!"

Stripped of power, his words bounced off her. *Sticks and stones,* as Freddie used to say. She turned. Red in the face, her father was bent over his desk. "The flat should be in Soho," she said. "And I'd like a spare bedroom so that guests can stay."

"Now, look here. I hardly think –"

"Let's get one thing straight." Every fibre of her being was shaking. "I no longer care what you think."

"I might have known! You *always* take your mother's side."

That's your parting shot? "You'll never know how wrong you are," she said. Lucy now thought she knew what had been more important than coming home to drive her to school: the appearance of a third half-brother. "But from now on, I take my own side. Soho. Two bedrooms. *And* a monthly allowance."

After slamming the door of her father's study, Lucy held one hand over her mouth, pressed it in place with the other, waiting to be sure she wasn't going to crumple. A moment passed and she appeared to be in one piece. This wasn't the bereavement she'd imagined five minutes ago. The hall was light and airy, and the front door led out onto the square, where late-afternoon life was taking place. Perhaps this was liberation. From now on, *Out of sight, out of mind* would apply to Father.

Since her return from school, Lucy had wanted to crop her hair. Only his disapproval had stopped her. A visit to the hairdressers was an appropriate way to start her new life. And where better than the place she'd chosen for herself? Soho, the only place she'd ever truly felt wanted.

CHAPTER NINETEEN

1957

Lucy took childish pleasure directing people to her new address: "It's the unmarked door to the left of the wet fish shop." Some years later it became a sex shop, but the smell of fish never quite washed off, and Lucy would say, "The door to the left of the wet sex shop." In her new life she felt undeniably free. There was nothing she missed from the house on the square. Except perhaps Cook.

Pamela and Lucy had met for one of their regular coffees in Maison Bertaux, which had become Lucy's local since her 'defection to Soho'. Pamela must have seen Lucy's expression fall. There, on the front page of a newspaper, held high by a faceless customer, was a Forrester family portrait. One taken the Christmas before her illness.

Her friend glanced over her shoulder and then back. When Lucy had told Pamela about her father's second household, she had only expressed concern.

"You're not shocked?" Lucy asked.

"On your behalf, of course I am. That's a terrible thing to find out. But as for your father? It explains quite a few things."

"But all those years..."

"If a relationship has to be kept secret, you know damned well you shouldn't be in it."

Now, Pamela's voice was low. "Don't worry, you're safe here." Lucy felt the squeeze of a hand on her knee under the table. Only the staff and a few loyal regulars at Maison Bertaux had known her as a shy ten-year-old, and they had already formed a protective circle.

But to have her past brought into this place of sanctuary when she was trying to put it behind her. "What if this is the first of many?" Her voice was a whisper. "There are far more recent photographs to choose from." Had her father imagined that Mother would prove such a worthy opponent? Relishing the role of martyr, she was thriving on media interest and the speculation of neighbours. There was no thought, no regard, for the impact on Freddie or herself. Not for the first time, Lucy wondered if she should change her surname, but she and it had been through so much together. It wasn't something that should be cast aside.

"No one here will recognise you," Pamela assured. "Not now you've had your hair cut."

It was true. The one spur-of-the-moment thing she'd done had worked to Lucy's advantage. Still, there was a rightness about her new life and she couldn't bear the thought that anything or anyone might threaten it.

Pamela started to talk about her new job at a friend's bookshop – Housmans. "I had to give notice to my last family because the child was so difficult."

"Difficult?" Lucy was grateful to be anchored to the here and now. "More difficult than me?"

"Ah, but with you I was needed. This one was plain spoilt – and the parents expected me to undo all the damage they'd caused."

"And I wasn't spoilt?"

"You were capable of being fixed."

Lucy smiled, reassured, although the word *entitlement* pricked at her once more, forcing her to accept an element of truth. London rent beyond her means, Lucy wouldn't be able to manage without financial help. And she'd had no qualms asking her parents for more than had originally been on offer.

Around their table was the clatter of voices and coffee cups, tables being cleared. With breakfast service coming to an end, there was a brief lull to look forward to before Al Bear (he would always be Al Bear to Lucy) needed to start preparing for lunch. All of the chopping involved in making onion soup, mixing the salad dressing, cracking eggs for the omelettes. Other customers were politely encouraged on their way so that staff could snatch a half-hour breather, but Al Bear topped up Pamela's coffee cup. "Not you two, you're family. But our Little Sparrow. She deserves to put her feet up, don't you think?" He put down the coffee pot and bent over the counter to re-tune the wireless. "*Voilà*. The news. Let us see what's happening in the world."

Now that the newspaper had been folded into a briefcase and its owner was leaving, Lucy felt able to relax. "Will you look for a position with another family?" she asked Pamela.

"Not just now. The bookshop suits me. But what about you? Have you had anything published recently?"

"Just last week." Lucy reached for her bag and pulled the magazine from it. That was the other thing about her name. In the smallest of circles, Lucy Forrester was beginning to mean something. With apprehension, she waited for Pamela's verdict. Hers was one of the few opinions she cared about.

Pride blazed in Pamela's eyes. "This is wonderful. You must come and give a reading at the shop."

"Excuse me for interrupting, ladies!" Al Bear called. He was hunched over the radio, turning the volume up. "This sounds like something you both need to hear."

They hauled themselves out of their seats, carrying their coffee cups with them.

"Something about a fire." Lucy and Pamela glanced

anxiously at each other. "I think he said *Windscale*. That's the nuclear power station, *n'est ce pas?*"

"My God." Pamela's words were a whisper. Her cup rattled in its saucer. "It's the reactor."

The chill that ran down Lucy's spine took her breath away. Windscale was where plutonium was made, using technology described as 'science fiction'. She listened intently. *Fire is raging at the Cumbrian plant. Staff are working around the clock to construct a firebreak.*

"How far away is this Cumbria?" Al Bear asked as the reporter turned to technical matters.

"I don't know." Pamela's voice was flat, almost neutral. "Three hundred miles or so, I'd imagine."

Lucy felt guilty relief. This disaster was taking place in some remote corner of Northern England. In between lay Oxford, Birmingham, Chester, Liverpool. Al Bear shook his head, then started to go about his business.

But Pamela made it their business. "That's no distance." Her hand was at her pale throat. "Even if they manage to get the fire under control – and that's a big if – toxic smoke will drift across the whole of Europe. London won't be immune."

Lucy barely dared ask. "And if they don't?"

"The reactor becomes a bomb. This is what happens when men play God." Pamela licked her lips nervously. "We won't get the facts from the radio. We'll have to insist on them." She snatched up her coat and bag. "Come on!"

Lucy grabbed a handful of loose change from her purse, gave it a quick glance to make sure it covered the coffees and threw the coins into a saucer on the counter. "Where are we going?" It was the first time Pamela had included Lucy in her plans.

"Downing Street. That's where everyone will be."

Familiar territory.

"Won't they expect you at work?"

"We'll go via the shop. I didn't mention, did I? It's very niche. We stock books on peace and pacifism. It's also where *Peace News* is produced."

So Pamela wasn't just selling books. Just as Pamela had said about her father's second household, *it made sense.*

"They have a banner or two that won't take much changing. And we'll need sandwiches in case we get arrested."

"Two minutes." Al Bear hurried towards the kitchen door, calling over his shoulder.

"But everyone's on their break."

"I will make them myself."

CHAPTER TWENTY

1958

"Are you sure you should go?" Slouched on the sofa, her flatmate Evelyn was wearing a gingham blouse Lucy recognised as her own. "The forecast's ghastly. Honestly, you'd think it was Christmas, not Easter."

Lucy could hardly believe it. Today, the people were going to take back control – the year's single most important event – and Evelyn was fretting over a little sleet. "Are you sure you can afford *not* to go?" she asked.

Raising her hand towards her mouth, Evelyn stifled a complacent yawn. "I'm only thinking of your poor leg. You know how it plays up in the cold."

"Sod the cold! I missed the CND's first meeting and I'm *not* missing this." While Lucy shrugged on her coat, another thing grabbed her. "Don't you want to hear Bertrand Russell?" she asked from the living room doorway.

"Not especially." Evelyn licked the tip of a finger and scooped up a page of *Vogue*. "I've heard him dozens of times."

"When?" Lucy couldn't keep the challenge from her tone.

"When I was younger." Her flatmate shrugged. "He used to come to our house for dinner *all* the time."

"You never said!"

"There was nothing *to* say." She turned another page, then looked up at Lucy who was staring, open-mouthed. "Alright. He looked like a cross between a vampire and a mad professor. Same inflections as Churchill, but less bullish. And *completely* out of touch with the real world. Will that keep you happy?"

Out of touch? Lucy's eyebrows jumped a good half inch. *You were only looking for someone to share the bills,* she reminded herself. *You weren't looking for a soulmate.* But still. Where did this apathy come from?

She'd be better off alone. Her stomach was a coil of nerves. Once Lucy announced her plans, there would be no backing down. Her audiences normally consisted of two dozen people. In cold church halls, audiences sat at a polite distance, stiff-backed, hands in laps. In bookshops, crammed into narrow aisles between the shelves, they'd perched on folding chairs. According to Pamela, somewhere between five hundred and five thousand people were going to show up. Lucy was one small person with such small things at her disposal to hold their attention. Allow herself to dwell on it and she really thought she might throw up.

"But you won't be on your own, will you?"

Lucy wasn't aware she'd spoken out loud.

"You'll find Pom-Pom." Pom-Pom was Evelyn's name for Pamela. In many ways, Evelyn never ventured far from the nursery.

Collar up, scarf looped, Lucy approached Trafalgar Square from the Strand. Already, her ears stung painfully. Clumsy in gloves she groped for the folded poem in her pocket, its inspiration Kenneth Tynan's protest in the *Tribune*. The government had volunteered for annihilation, but at least good old Blighty would be safe from invaders.

Lucy barely had her bearings when a young man in a Fair Isle jumper and a leather jacket thrust a sign towards her. "Like a lollipop?" Seeing her hesitate, he added, "Unless you've made your own banner."

Not only under-rehearsed, she was also ill-prepared. Lucy faltered, "I – I haven't." Her sick feeling had returned. She had no idea how far her voice would carry. Why on earth had she thought she was up to this?

"They're all the rage. I can offer you black and white or white and green."

"Black and white, thank you." She spun the sign around; the same design on both sides.

"What do you think? Gerald says it's a man holding out his hands in despair, but he can't do hands, so we've settled for a stick-man."

"It's not a stick-man. It's a *representation* of hands."

Lucy twisted her head. Another young man with his arms full of identical signs and plenty more stacked behind him, like the makings of a bonfire. "Halt!" He stamped one foot and lowered a sign, blocking someone else's path. "Who goes there?"

It was obvious that Pamela's directions would be impossible to follow. Lucy shouldered into the fray. Past a cluster of stern-looking nuns, women in raincoats and headscarves, men wearing Sunday best and carrying black umbrellas, students hunched in duffle coats, dangling French cigarettes from the corners of their mouths. *There's nothing to be afraid of,* Lucy repeated to herself as memories she hadn't intended to disturb surfaced. Shaken like a ragdoll in her father's arms. A fight to draw her next breath.

Perhaps it wasn't too late to turn back? A quick glance over her shoulder, breath snagged in Lucy's throat. An instrument of torture was attached by wires to a young man's mouth. Then he blew a note with an accidental quality about it and she laughed at her mistake; it was a *harmonica*. With a smile still ghosting her lips, she saw a father grip the ankles of a small child who sat astride his shoulders. Kicking his heels, the boy was unafraid. Impossible things came so easily to others that they didn't realise they'd been given gifts. *There's nothing to be afraid of.* Lucy needed a landmark. And there it was, the banner strung from Nelson's Column. *March from London to Aldermaston.*

While Lucy was looking up, a sheet of paper was crumpled into her free hand. She scanned the first line. *Ashes to ashes.* Another poet had got there first. She wouldn't have to go through with it after all. She could listen to the speeches, then go home and curl up for the rest of the bank holiday weekend.

"Song lyrics, so you can join in later," a young woman explained. "There'll be plenty of singing once the speeches are over."

She wasn't off the hook.

The crush tightened. People stepping on the backs of her shoes, her heel pulling painfully free, Lucy was back at boarding school. She stopped to stand on tiptoe, craned her neck. It would be impossible to pick Pamela out of the crowd. Besides, there was no way to battle her way through to the steps in front of the National Gallery. Laden with fish paste sandwiches and thermos flasks, people had arrived at the crack of dawn for front row positions. They weren't going to give them up without a fight. But look: two people were sitting astride a bronze lion. Like *The Chronicles of Narnia.* With a fresh wave of determination, Lucy began to carve her own path through the hullabaloo.

At close quarters, the lions' wet flanks looked hopelessly slick. Search as she might, there were no clues how the riders had got up there. Abandoning the lollipop sign by her feet, Lucy pocketed her gloves and tested the cold stone. Nothing to describe as a foothold. She explored higher, but all she could imagine was slipping, falling to the ground and being trampled underfoot.

From behind her came a tall young man who thrust his

knapsack and bedding roll onto the plinth, then launched himself upwards. There was a moment's stillness – a second or two – when he balanced like a gymnast. Lucy felt a sharp pull under her skin. There was only the way his hair was cropped close to the nape of his neck, the confidence and lightness with which he attacked the plinth, but Lucy was spellbound. It made no sense. She had yet to catch sight of his face. He might have been anyone.

Then he threw his legs to the side, and his trousers rode up to reveal sunflower yellow socks. Lucy had never seen anything so rebellious. Where would you get such things? Feet planted, the man brushed down his hands before turning and grinning. *"There are three good things in this world. One is to read poetry, another is to write poetry, and the best of all is to live poetry."* She was looking into the face of Rupert Brooke. Then, with a shout, he woke her from her trance. "What's keeping you, Ralph? Get your arse up here!"

A secret door closed as a second man elbowed past. *He wasn't looking at me.* Underneath his dog-tooth-check cap, this man – Ralph – was equally attractive, but there was no lurch in her stomach. As he moved the camera that hung round his neck aside, he must have caught her staring. "Hello, there."

She felt herself redden.

He looked again. "Don't I know you?"

"I don't think so."

"You see, that's typical." Ralph grinned. "I can't recognise people I do know, then think I know people I've never met before."

There was nothing threatening about him, and every chance this might be her one opportunity. "I – I don't suppose you could...?" Was boost the right word? Lucy gave what the feel of her face told her was an awkward smile.

He sized her up and loud-hailed up to his friend on the

plinth. "Dom, the Dairy Box Girl needs a hand."

She liked the sound of *the Dairy Box Girl* being applied to her – even if it *was* only because of her short hair. She was still smiling when Rupert Brooke locked eyes with her, rooting her to the spot.

"When you can spare me a minute," a voice said from close by.

It was a moment before Lucy could work out why there was a man kneeling at her feet. "Just a little wet down here," Ralph said, good humouredly. "Left foot on my knee." He clasped his hands together, locking his fingers. "Right foot in my hands and then…" He motioned upwards.

"Mind if I–?" She swallowed, gripping his shoulder for balance.

"Be my guest."

She tested his knee tentatively with her left foot. Perhaps he wouldn't notice her built-up heel.

"There are no prizes for elegance. When I hoist you up, grab whichever part of Dom comes to hand."

"It's Dominic." The man on the plinth cut in. The tails of his raincoat flared as he adopted the pose of someone preparing to field, but the name was enough to make Lucy's stomach constrict.

Ralph closed his eyes momentarily. "Can we do the introductions in a minute?"

"I'm just saying. You're the only person who calls me Dom."

Ralph turned to Lucy. "Ready?" he asked.

Don't think. Just do it. "Here goes. Oh Christ."

Lucy stood between the lion's paws, a dull ache circling her upper arm. She was terrified, but it was that particular brand of terror that knows it's part of a never-to-be-repeated moment. Never again would this particular crowd of people gather in one place. Never again would she feel part of *something*. She was here by chance. (Without Ralph she wouldn't be here at all.) But the sea of faces... *No,* she scolded herself. *Like J. Alfred Prufrock, you must dare, just this once, to disturb the order of the universe.*

"I might have known it." She felt a wingbeat in her chest. The speaker was Dominic, the Rupert Brooke double, who'd all but wrenched her arm from its socket as he hauled her onto the plinth. An Adonis, he was unattainable and therefore safe to admire. "The Dairy Box Girl's up to no good." He clearly meant her to hear him. "Who have you got us involved with, Ralph?"

Dominic had latched onto the name Ralph had called her. She imagined he often took credit for things Ralph said, just as Freddie used to with her.

"But you like troublemakers, Dom."

Don't let yourself be distracted. Holding her poem in both hands, Lucy looked out over the sea of faces, lollipop signs and homemade banners. Being published in magazines and having her work read by a few hundred people was one thing. Even getting a few favourable reviews. But to be heard... It was a pity Pamela wasn't here, but Pamela's voice rang clear inside her head: *"This might be your only chance. Grab it."*

"I do. I like troublemakers. I think she's ready. You'd better whip your lens cap off, Ralph."

"I know what I'm doing." The shutter clicked.

"There we are then. What are you going to sing for us, Dairy Box Girl?"

Lucy aimed her voice at the highest head she could see and spoke. "The City Dies Screaming."

The title was a springboard.

"You dangerous man,
You talk of your hands
As if they are righteous.
You talk of yourself
As if you are
God's right-hand,
And God
As if he's an American.

Look, just look, at the hellfire
Unleashed on Krakatoa.
An island created by a volcano
Ripped apart by another,
Tree stumps the only sign that life once thrived.
Divine Justice has its own
Perfect Symmetry, wouldn't you say?
An explosion so deafening, its barbaric roar
Circled the earth four times over,
Hauling deep-sleepers from pleasant dreams
To clutch their breasts and ask, 'Was that gunfire?'
Shhh, Go back to sleep.

At the helm of his sturdy ship
On hearing the unearthly roar, good Captain Jack
Convinced the Day of Judgement is here
Thinks last thoughts of his dear wife.
Was that the work of your American God
Without a thought for the lilies in the fields
Or the sparrows?
Or were those the lilies
That gave your enemies pleasure,
The sparrows that flew
In enemy skies?

Was it the wish of your God that
Winter would reign for five dark years?

'Send us, oh, most Powerful Lord,'
You fall to your knees
By the side of your king-size bed,
And voice your presidential plea,
'The means to destroy our enemies
So that we may protect what is ours
And flourish.'

You try your best to ignore
the whisper that says,
'Who are these enemies you speak of?
I created only neighbours.
And do not ask again,
Who is my neighbour?
I gave you my answer
In the parable of the Good Samaritan.'

This character
Tugs at your Sunday-school imagination
But not at your conscience.
'Then send me a Good Samaritan,' you say.
'Would you unleash a rain of hot ash?
Paint the sky with honest blood?'
And while God rues the day he gave man free will
You recall the letter
With Einstein's mark
And reply, 'No need.
You have already sent
the Hungarian.'

'Ah, the Hungarian,' sighs God.
'I liked his work on the
Intervention of Intelligent Beings.'"

Lucy paused here, took in her God's-eye view.

"The Hungarian is where
He is always found
At this ungodly hour;
Muttering in his laboratory.
If we have neutron-rich light atoms
Which produce secondary neutrons
There will be no stopping it.

And God looks down,
Shakes his weary head.
A chain reaction set in motion
So inevitable that
It may have begun with Adam and Eve.

Spared the trenches,
Szilard cannot look God in the eye.
He insists, 'This is a thing too terrible to be used.
The President gives his assurances.
(Pay attention now. It's you they are discussing.)
It's a deterrent,
Possession is the thing...'

'Oh, my son,' says God,
'You may be a scientist of the highest calibre
But you understand nothing

Of the nature of power.
After all,
You are no longer dealing with Roosevelt.'

'But I will draft a petition
"We, the undersigned"
I will stress the obligation of restraint.'
And in this moment
A new terrifying reality
Asserts itself.
Szilard is unmoored.
His stuttering heart knows
That the world is heading
For unimaginable grief.
The last earthly sound he will hear
Before his eardrums rupture,
Before his eyeballs melt,
Before he is thrown from his feet,
Is the city as it dies, screaming.

But you; you will say,
Good job, boys! Come on home."

Whistling came from behind her. She had done it. Whatever happened now – how she managed to make it back down to ground level – was immaterial.

"You're a poet!" Dominic said as he stepped over one of the great lion's paws to join her.

"I write poetry." Under his gaze, rain-slicked as she was, Lucy felt horribly self-conscious. "It's hardly the same thing."

He made a noise that suggested he'd known it all along. "*That's* what it was about your performance! I mean you definitely got away with it," – he said this in a way that suggested he'd thought it mediocre, which had Ralph arching his eyebrows – "but –"

"I was totally convinced." He tented his camera inside his duffle coat, trying to keep the drizzle off.

Contradicted, Dominic said, "Listen to the expert!"

The bronze had a wet sheen. Lucy found herself holding her breath as Ralph inched alongside the lion, by far the most likely of the three to fall. "*You* try shouting into the wind and rain."

"So, you're not published?" Dominic asked.

"In magazines, yes. I don't have my own collection. Not yet, at least."

"But there's more where that came from?"

Something of the arrogant schoolboy reminded Lucy of Freddie. "That's right," she retaliated. "I rattle poems off on the hour, every hour."

Arriving in the confined space, Ralph hooted. "That's the spirit, give as good as you get."

"No need to be so touchy. There was nothing amateurish about what I just heard."

"Nothing amateurish," Ralph cut in, "is Dom's idea of a compliment."

Something about Ralph made Lucy sense she'd known him her whole life, and hadn't he thought he recognised her? She'd developed a dread of coming face to face with her half-brothers. Bumping into them, accidentally. By her estimate, the boys were a couple of years older than she was. (Boys of her own age tended to be halfway through National Service.) Now that she thought about it, both had accents so slight, they were difficult to pinpoint. "Are the two of you brothers?" she asked.

"God, no." Ralph laughed. "What makes you say that?"

Relieved to have it confirmed, she said, "The way you argue."

"There's no point fluttering your eyelashes in Ralph's direction. He's a Wildeblood." Dominic, she saw clearly, demanded to be the centre of attention.

Lucy looked from one face to the other. "Am I supposed to know what that means?"

"Oh, come on, don't make me spell it out! A Wolfenden. An Oscar."

Ralph gave a tired sigh and lowered his voice. "Hello, I'm Ralph. I'm queer." He offered his hand.

A small thrill went through Lucy. "Pleasure to meet you, Ralph." She now knew what it was she'd recognised. He was a misfit, the somebody on a small island she'd been reaching out to.

"*I* see!" Dom was unrepentant. "It's fine when there's someone you're keen on, but when I'm trying to stake a claim…"

He was making fun of her, of course. She knew how she must look. Not a scrap of make-up, pixie-cut plastered to her face. Not to mention a good too many secrets concealed beneath inadequate layers of skin. "I should think about getting down from here before I fall." Lucy examined the view from the plinth; the tops of heads and umbrellas, the raised banners.

"Not so fast." Dominic's hand was there on her arm. "You haven't heard how I can help you yet."

She looked at the hand as if she couldn't understand how it had got there.

"I'm a critic, you see."

He laid words like tripwire, ready to jerk them upwards the moment she responded. "You mean that you criticise people?" Lucy's only weapon was sarcasm.

"I mean that I *critique*. The performance circuit mainly. I specialise in jazz and folk, but the clubs are perfect for poetry, and it's an area I'm keen to move into, so –"

Lucy found herself closing her eyes momentarily, in the

way that she'd seen Ralph do. "Let me get this straight, you review music?"

"That's right."

It wasn't just the way he looked, she decided. It was his energy. "And you know absolutely nothing about poetry."

"Not quite nothing. I was once locked in a broom cupboard and wasn't allowed out until I could recite *Ode to Autumn* by Keats."

She raised her eyebrows.

"It was a punishment," he continued undeterred. "I forget what for. But the point is I have contacts at the venues *and* the papers. Meanwhile," he nodded, "you obviously know what you're doing."

She stood up straight. "I should hope so."

"So?" He shrugged. "Teach me."

Lucy looked to Ralph, hoping for reason. *You can't teach poetry,* she wanted to insist. *You have to feel it.* But it was extraordinary. She had something Dominic wanted.

"Dom talks his way into most things." Related or not, Ralph's tone confirmed that playing second fiddle to Dominic was rather like being younger sister to Freddie.

"So resistance is futile. That's what you're saying?"

Ralph gave her one of those *What can you do?* smiles that would become so familiar, then added, "Also, he's quite brilliant." The crowd noise flattened suddenly, leaving Ralph speaking into the hush.

"Quiet please, ladies and gentlemen," Dominic said.

Ralph turned to the distant podium where men in dark suits were taking their places, and raised his camera. "Time for the speeches."

CHAPTER TWENTY-ONE

Interview for Granada Television,
1978, PART TWO

"And of course you're a huge supporter of CND. I see you're wearing a badge today."

"I've had this one for over twenty years." Lucy's fingers located the circumference of the button badge she'd had made into a pendant. She liked the way rust had bled onto the round emblem. "And this one," she pulled up her sleeve to reveal the small inked mark on her forearm, "just under that length of time."

"You have a tattoo?" Philip Harrington's eyes widened. He glanced at the camera in case the crew happened to miss it.

"When CND was founded, it was the only sane reaction, and this felt like a sane thing to do."

His hand a fist in front of his mouth, Philip feigned squeamishness. "Did it hurt?"

Lucy waited for the polite laughter to fade before replying. "Put it this way, I had two brandies for Dutch courage and still fainted clean on the couch."

"Are you pleased you had it done? Because you can't have them taken off, can you?"

"I wouldn't want to. CND is as relevant today as it was

in the fifties." This produced a scattering of applause, which Lucy acknowledged with a nod.

"When you say that CND was the only sane reaction, what exactly do you mean?"

Lucy had begun to wonder if Philip's constant swivelling was a by-product of nerves. "I grew up in wartime. My parents' generation lived through two world wars."

"Mine too."

"Then you'll remember how it was. People believed the Third World War was just around the corner and that it would mean the end of the world." Lucy shook her head. "Like most people, I was terrified of becoming another shadow on a wall."

"That's a reference to Hiroshima, isn't it?"

She paused out of respect. "Those poor people. And now, of course, data is proving how right we were about the nuclear threat. The high incidence of cancer among survivors and birth deformities in the next generation is already telling. And what *we* then did to the islands of the Pacific – not to mention our own servicemen. It was unforgivable. It's my belief that we'll see fallout for many generations." Lucy looked directly at the camera, pointing to one of her eyes and then at the lens. *We're watching you.*

Clearly uncomfortable, Philip glanced at his notes for a diversion. "There's always been a great tradition of war poetry, but you feature imaginary wars in several of your best-loved poems."

"I do, yes. Poetry takes time and, given that time might be short in a nuclear war, I thought I'd better make a head start."

"Do you still believe there will be a third world war?"

"Very much so."

"Within your lifetime?" he pressed.

Lucy felt the onset of a familiar ache, which spread rapidly. Access to intelligence came with responsibility. It wasn't public knowledge that the US was considering basing Cruise and Pershing missiles in Britain and elsewhere in Europe, while the Soviet Union was planning to base its new SS-20 missiles in Eastern Europe. Her throat felt dry. "I wouldn't like to speculate."

"I have to say, it wasn't your poems on the theme of war that I first discovered, but an earlier poem. The one about the machine girl."

"Oh, yes?" Though she'd received a personal invitation to appear on the Philip Harrington Show, Lucy hadn't taken her host for a fan.

"Who's the girl?"

"Can't you tell?" Lucy held out her hands and looked down at her lap.

"I wondered if you'd read it for us." And before she could object, he reached behind his chair. "I took the precaution of bringing my copy from home."

Lucy tried to look gracious as she accepted the slim volume from him and opened it. "Oh." She looked up, a little taken aback. "It's a first edition."

"I was hoping I might convince you to sign it for me later."

"Happily." Lucy could feel the beginnings of a blush. "Well, here goes." Lucy closed the book. She didn't glance at it. She cleared her throat, picked out the face of a woman in the back row; aimed her voice just above her head. "Machine Girl.

"Sugar and spice
And all things nice
Was what they wanted from ME
But I want does not get

A boy sucked the breath
From the bottom of my lungs
A machine gave me
The kiss of life

Underneath her layer of skin
This sitting down girl is made of
Pinking shears
A garden rake
Bicycle chains
Parts from under the bonnet of a car
Bits of stray shrapnel and shells
Dug up from the rubble
Fathers empty tobacco tins
Tin cans emptied of peaches and evaporated milk
Waste not want not

Stray Meccano pieces
Yards of twisted toy railway track
Parts from a broken cuckoo clock
Kept in a cardboard box
In a cupboard in the hall
For a time when they might come in useful
Waste not want not

I will be displayed at the next World Fair
Roll up, roll up and see
The miraculous Machine Girl!
You've heard of Pinocchio
A puppet brought to life
Now this is his opposite

And everyone will marvel
She has 700 words, you know
See how she holds a pencil and writes
All you have to do is put a shilling in this little slot
Behind her left ear

And she will pick up a hammer with her teeth
And play Three Blind Mice on the glockenspiel
All donations to the Red Cross

When she smokes a cigarette
It streams straight out of her ears
We call her Lucky Lucy
And keep her locked in a box"

"Wonderful!" Philip Harrington waited for the audience to settle, then resumed. "'I want does not get.'" He shook his head. "I can hear my mother using that phrase."

"I think it's one of those lines your parents say, and you swear to yourself you will never use it with your own children."

"And then you become a parent! And you wrote that when you were ten."

"I did, yes."

"They're very – how shall I put this? – *dark* words to have been written by a ten-year-old."

Despite Lucy's reworking, the darkness wasn't an addition. She had recited the original draft, written when her wounds were raw. "Do you think so?"

"Well frankly, yes!"

"I can't take *all* the credit. The words were in the dictionary. I only linked them together."

"You've mentioned that you had a governess, but you also described your education as 'unusual.'"

"My academic record is hardly glittering. I was the girl of the family, you see. Education was considered unimportant."

"Because you were going to marry and your husband would take care of you?"

"Of course." She indulged in a moment's playfulness before

becoming serious once more. "I wouldn't like you to think it was entirely my parents' fault. My schooling had barely got underway before it was interrupted by illness."

"Which is why you had a governess."

"Exactly. Until I was back in school – and by then I was in my teens – I wasn't aware how many basics I lacked. Punctuation, grammar, and so forth."

"And that bothered you?"

"How would you feel if you'd gone to school with an idea that poetry was the *one* thing you were good at, only to be told you didn't have the tools for the job? And so I suppose I rejected the idea of education. I have very few qualifications. People don't like that in a poet, especially those who feel they've been 'properly educated'."

"And your husband? *Has* he taken care of you?"

"Yes he has. Not just financially, but in every other way."

"So your parents were right?"

"Not at all. There was no guarantee someone would be willing to take me on. I can be quite a handful." *God, these studio lights!*

"I imagine you can." There were those crows' feet again. "Did you always know that you were going to be a poetess?" He began to toy with his signet ring.

"Plain poet's just fine. You know, T. S. Eliot said, 'I can understand you wanting to write poems, but I can't understand what you mean by *being a poet*'. It seems such a vain ambition." Lucy reached for a glass of water, but Philip got there before her. "Thank you." She accepted the tumbler he offered and sipped.

"So what changed? When did you realise this was what you were going to do with your life?"

"I suppose the moment everything fell into place was when I saw Dame Edith Sitwell on television. I thought, *Now there's a living, breathing poet* – in the flesh, as it were. She was extraordinary-looking, over six feet tall, quite elderly by then, nose like a beak. And when the interviewer said to her that people saw her as being eccentric, forbidding and dangerous, that was exactly how I thought a poet should *be*."

"But some people might say her poetry is inaccessible."

Determined to puncture anything that suggested poetry was elitist, Lucy cocked her head. "Do you think so?"

Crows' feet, undeterred. "What would you like to say to those people who feel poetry is difficult?"

"I'd agree. Poetry is all about ideas. It demands your full attention. Like music, you may not appreciate it fully to begin with. And, of course, some poetry *does* have a niche audience. Geoffrey Hill, for example. He has a reputation for being old-fashioned and obscure, but he's also lauded as our greatest post-war poet, which goes to show that what appeals to some, appals others."

"You're saying there's a poem for every palate?"

"Exactly. And if you like Pam Ayres or Edward Lear, then that's what you should be reading."

"Let's go back to your early work."

Lucy's fingers tensed. She was being steered in a direction she was less keen to explore.

"As I said, it really *is* quite dark. Most ten-year-olds wouldn't group those particular words together."

Lucy feared she might sound self-important if she said her subjects found her and not the other way around. She settled on, "I rather hope not. They'd put me out of a job."

"You seem to be rather good at deflecting questions. Do you always use humour as a defence mechanism?"

Lucy made sure the camera caught her smiling. "I thought everyone did. Seriously, though, it's a little late in the day for me to start being defensive. There isn't a single part of my life I haven't cannibalised in my poems, but if I were to explain to you what it means, I'd be defeating the object. People don't want the kitchen sink from poetry."

"What do *you* think people want from poetry?"

"You have to *feel* poetry. The good stuff makes your skin tingle."

"You're not someone who likes to explain herself, are you?" He smiled slyly.

"At one point in time, I used to carry a little rape alarm in my handbag." She sensed the impact of the word she'd used. The crackle of expectation it created. "Not because I was worried about being attacked, you understand, but I was given it by somebody. I forget who," she lied. Lucy remembered quite clearly. It had been her father. A prototype he'd got hold of. She was leaving home – her defection to Soho. He thought she should have it; a gift, from father to daughter. "Anyway, it made the most awful high-pitched shrieking. If anyone asked me about symbolism, I would set it off. You see, I can *try* to explain to you what I was attempting to get across when I arranged words in a particular order, but what would be the point?"

Philip widened the spread of his hands, like a benevolent priest. "There would be every point –"

"Why? They might mean something completely different to someone else." She paused to take another sip of water. *Damp down the irritation.* "Generally, what I do is wait until Dominic Marchmont has devoured my lines and spat them out, then I repeat what he says."

"Of course, for those viewers who don't know him, Dominic is your greatest critic."

"If by that you mean he criticises me more than anyone I've ever known, then yes. I always consult him when I want to know what I was thinking at the time I wrote something."

"But it's because of Dominic that you're so well known."

This angle – that she was Dominic's creation – grated. "Partly, yes," Lucy conceded, conscious of the camera, trying not to look begrudging.

"I only mean that you might not have come to the public's attention as early as you did unless he'd written about you so extensively."

"I'll let you into a secret." Lucy beckoned and leaned closer. She waited for Philip to mirror her. "He's obsessed by me. Always has been." She turned to the camera, then mouthed the words, 'Hello, Dominic'.

"So how does it feel when your greatest supporter tells you that he doesn't like your latest work? Because that's happened, hasn't it?"

"More times than I care to recall." They were back on track. "Firstly, let me say this: it's impossible for a writer to judge if what they've written is any good. What all artists need – whether they're painters or photographers or poets – is someone to hold a mirror up to their work. I was lucky. Dominic came along at exactly the right time."

"Which was when?"

"The late fifties. We met at a political protest."

Philip seemed intrigued. "So, he's also very political?"

Opportunist was the word Lucy would have chosen. "I don't think that's how he sees himself. You remember, Philip. It was very difficult to be pro-establishment when the government was making such an awful hash of things."

Philip nodded. "The decade of the angry young man."

"And a few angry young women to boot."

"But when the International Poetry Incarnation was held at the Royal Albert Hall, there were no women in the line-up."

As the cords in Lucy's throat tightened, one of her hands found its way to her pendant. She held it briefly, as if that had been her intention.

"It was billed as the first 'happening' in the UK," Philip continued. "There you were, a political poet, very much part of the scene. Did you feel excluded?"

"I wasn't excluded." She shook her head. "I was there, in

the front row. You can pick me out in Peter Whitehead's film."
An invitation *had* come about as a result of the event. Gregory
Corso told her he was compiling an anthology: Poets in the
Nude. Was she in? Apparently his naked reading in Paris had
gone down a storm.

When Dominic had enthused about Corso's proposal,
Lucy blinked at him. *Insect-life.*

"What have I done?"

"Corso had no idea what he was asking, but you…" Dominic sure as hell did.

"Oh, come on. Think of the publicity! And you'll be top of
their list the next time there's a big event."

I guess you Brits like to keep your clothes on, Corso replied
when Lucy declined by post. *You know, Edith Sitwell turned
me down too.* It was the closest she'd ever come to meeting
her idol.

"But not to be asked to perform," Philip persisted. "I
mean –"

"The whole thing was thrown together in ten days. Just
imagine the organisation. Ferlinghetti didn't have time to put
feelers out. He used the poets he published at City Lights."
Most of them thoroughly unreliable. "Ginsberg, Gregory
Corso. Then on the British side, Christopher Logue, Adrian
Mitchell, Tom McGrath…"

"*None* of whom happened to be women?"

"None of whom happened to be women," Lucy echoed as
if this had only just struck her.

Philip raised one eyebrow very deliberately.

"I get the feeling you'd like me to suggest there was another
agenda," Lucy goaded him. "Perhaps he didn't like my poems.
Have you thought of that?"

"Perhaps he didn't like *any* poetry written by female poets."
He was shaking his head and tutting lightly. "An international
event with no women."

He'd pushed the point beyond its limits. Lucy needed to move the discussion on. "An international event with very few nations represented."

"Well, now, there's another thing…"

"I sat next to the Russian poet, Andrei Voznesensky. He'd wanted to take part but the Soviet Embassy wouldn't allow it."

"Oh? Why not?"

"They worried that being on the same line-up as a bunch of beatniks would damage his reputation."

"In what way?"

Lucy responded to her host's blank look with an audible sigh. "Thank goodness this isn't the BBC! Let's just say that recreational drug-use was rather more acceptable then than it is now." Dangerous territory but, hell, they could cut whatever they didn't want to use. "It was seen as part of the creative process. In fact –"

"Can I just ask, were drugs part of *your* creative process?"

Lucy had intended to talk about *Howl*. Why the Russians hadn't wanted their rising star to align himself with Ginsberg and his free use of the C-word. "Let's talk about Dominic," she said playfully. "I like talking about Dominic. He was there too, by the way."

"What did he make of it all?"

"He found the contrast between the Yanks and the Brits highly amusing."

"In what way?"

"Well, they all looked like Beat poets. Long hair, beards, turtleneck jumpers, and all of them smoking pipes."

"You don't see many pipe-smokers these days."

"Not young men, at any rate. But although they *looked* the same, the Yanks were the bad boys, while the Brits sounded as if they'd been bussed in from an Oxford debate." Dominic had tried to cheer her up, of course. Tried to make her see that being excluded wasn't the insult she'd insisted it was.

Although, with her front row view, Lucy had plenty of time to contemplate how terrified she would have been in front of an audience of seven thousand. She imagined cowering like Harry Fainlight.

"Do you think Dominic's a particularly harsh critic?"

"They were lucky. He was having a night off."

"But in terms of your work?"

"Oh, I see. No. He's fair. What good would high praise mean if there were nothing to measure it against? Then, being totally defensive…"

"And you *have* been defensive."

"By which you mean that Dominic and I have had the odd public brawl." She smiled indulgently. "You have to understand that Dominic doesn't just pop round for coffee and say, 'Listen here, I didn't think so much of that last ditty you wrote.' I open up my copy of *The Observer* and read, 'The imagery is superficial' or 'Her unerring eye appears to have failed her'. And so, yes, I do get terribly upset, and out come the boxing gloves. Then at some point between rounds ten and fifteen, I begin to think, 'Damn you, Dominic, you may have had a point.'"

Philip raised one eyebrow. "The pair of you do seem to have maintained the most extraordinary love/hate relationship."

Lucy felt her upper lip twitch. "Yes, I suppose it would seem that way. Our relationship has been enormously productive. He's helped me become a better poet and he's made a very good living from writing about me." But Dominic's reviews would never have received the attention they did without the photographs that accompanied them. Ralph's wonderful intuition in terms of timing, not just capturing a facial expression, but the feel of that relatively short-lived era when poetry *was* rock 'n' roll.

The presenter had one hand on his hip, his elbow at a

ninety-degree angle. "And, a little bird tells me you're trusting Dominic to write your biography."

Lucy's childhood lunged, gripping her round the throat. Which little bird? And did Philip know that she'd refused? "Dominic hasn't managed to convince me that I'm interesting enough for people to want to read about." Her host was *enjoying* her discomfort!

"Oh, come now, you're far too modest. Isn't she, ladies and gentlemen?" Before he could swivel his chair to the audience, there was a sharp whoop from somewhere near the back.

Lucy shielded her eyes against the harsh studio lights. "My agent seems to be in the audience tonight."

"Here in my notes I have a quote. *I seem to keep getting myself into situations.* You said that, didn't you?"

She'd said it on the occasion of one of her arrests. "It was my I'm-not-very-bright-I-guess moment."

"So you were inspired by Marilyn Monroe?" His expression suggested how unlikely he thought this.

"I think there's something in all of us that wants to be Marilyn."

"Was she someone you particularly admired?"

"That would imply we had some kind of a relationship. I only knew the screen version, the one who looked as if she had it all. Let's just say that I enjoyed her films and leave it there."

"But as for your biography." Lucy tightened her mouth. She thought they'd moved past this. "You're part of this mysterious breed called poets and you're a person who's lived in the moment. So can we expect the whole truth, warts and all?"

The idea that one must unmask oneself, that one owes it to one's fans... Having crafted this persona – this counterfeit self – for the outside world, Lucy was hardly about to set the record straight. "I'm not sure I believe in a single truth, but

I do believe in the search for personal truth, whatever that might be. As for warts? I'm afraid they're a fact of life."

"Along with death and taxes."

"Exactly."

CHAPTER TWENTY-TWO

2014

After the initial relief came the guilt. What was there to do on a Wednesday that had been blanked out as a day of mourning for Dominic? It was hardly the time for household chores or catching up on emails. Even reading would have seemed inappropriate. In a sense, both cowardly and rebellious, Lucy felt as if she'd gone into hiding. While Ralph developed his photograph, she sat very still. If Lucy's office had changed over the past decade, so too had Ralph's. Rather than spending two hours under the glow of a red bulb, breathing a toxic brew of chemicals, 'developing' now meant retouching the shot using clever software.

Lucy's left hand rested lightly on the cushion where Dominic had so often sat. There was no indent, no lingering warmth to suggest he'd just got up to make a cup of tea. Not that Dominic had ever made his fair share. When he eventually caved, he made such a drama of forgetting who had what and how they liked it that he wasn't asked again in a hurry. Lucy looked about the living room and sighed; how like a museum it looked today. The artefacts of their combined histories. Well-considered, much loved furniture; pieces that were at home sitting alongside each other. Every item a reminder of where this happened, where that happened.

"What do you think?" Ralph's voice was there, in the room. She looked up, saw that he'd changed out of his suit. Soft grey was his preferred colour; a beret and a polo neck. "I think it's almost there." He handed her the print.

Something clenched inside her stomach. Down to the tiniest detail, the photograph spoke of a poet mourning her sparring partner. The man she'd loved to hate in public and had both loved and hated behind closed doors. She smiled inwardly, imagining her detractors saying, 'Whatever happened to growing old gracefully?' What no one would realise – the reason it appeared that everything in the photograph was in its perfect place – was that both emotion and destruction were absolutely authentic. This was Lucy, playing the part of herself. "Oh," she heard herself falter as he sat beside her. "It's –" But there were no adequate words. "Can I have this?" She looked at her husband with renewed wonder. "To hang in my study?"

"I'll make you a proper copy."

"No, this is the one. It's perfect." And then, continuing to look at it: "I've wrecked the garden."

"You *pruned* it," he said, patting the knee that was nearest to him.

"Pruned it," she repeated, stilling his hand by gripping it.

At a loss, husband and wife sat side by side on the sofa, eyes glazed, thinking their separate and coinciding thoughts. They sat uninterrupted, unspeaking, until mid-afternoon when the phone shrilled them out of self-imposed hibernation.

"We've been found out," Ralph said.

"I'll get it." Lucy put down what had for some time been an empty brandy glass.

"You don't have to."

"No, I do." Penance would be welcome. Lucy knew how badly she'd behaved.

Dominic's sister, Irene (or 'Reenie' as she preferred to be

called), bypassed any niceties. *"You didn't come. He loved you more than anyone else in the world and you didn't even make the effort to be there at his funeral."*

Lucy held the receiver away from her ear to take the edge off the shouting, but experimented with bringing it closer, closer still. Dominic's sister had never made any attempt to hide the fact that she barely tolerated Lucy.

"She hates me," Lucy had said, and Dominic made the distinction: "She doesn't *hate* you. She actively dislikes you." It seemed strange that, when Irene put so much energy into *actively disliking* Lucy, she should have wanted her at her brother's send-off. The silent truce they'd drawn on crossing paths in the hospice had clearly been rescinded.

A background uproar suggested the wake was in full swing. With an idea she'd be there for the long haul, Lucy sank into the Eames chair (another museum piece) by the telephone table. She buried her head in her spare hand wishing she'd had the presence of mind to top up her brandy glass and bring it with her. "Irene, I said more goodbyes than I care to remember. Nothing was left unsaid, certainly nothing I wanted to say in public."

"Now you decide you want to keep things private! For years I've only had to open a newspaper to see the two of you drinking champagne at some awards ceremony, or read about your public quarrels." Had a brother and sister ever been so different? Dominic with his polish and swagger. Irene with... well, with neither. "It wasn't about *you,* you self-centred bitch."

This venom stung. It sounded odd, coming from someone who comfortably discussed her faith with strangers. Lucy reminded herself, *She's just buried her only brother.* Except, of course, Dominic hadn't been buried. He'd been cremated.

Lucy drew a shaky breath. More than the sight of the coffin, she'd dreaded the moment when the curtain would be drawn, and she could see it no more. *The flames just soared, and the furnace roared – such a blaze you seldom see.* Even now, she knew that she wouldn't have been able to tamp down the urge to stride up the aisle and tear the curtain down. (In her mind's eye she saw burgundy velvet, though she doubted a municipal crem's funds would stretch to that sort of luxury.)

This morning, something of Dominic still had existed in the universe, something tangible, capable of being dressed in a suit. Now he was… *Ashes to ashes.* The average male weighs three-point-five kilograms after cremation, but Dominic had disappeared in stages, weighing well below average at the time of his death.

"It was about showing your respect, your support… for his family."

"I intended to come, Irene, honestly I did. I wrote something to say at the service." Lucy acknowledged a truth; she was jealous. In life Dominic had been theirs. (Never just hers. From the beginning, they had been a three.) But his ashes belonged to Irene. And what would she do with them? Decant them into an ugly vase? Scatter them in the town where they'd spent their childhood – the town that Dominic resented for its small-mindedness. Lucy knew that, even now, looking at the living room mantelpiece, surrounded by all of their trophies and souvenirs, Ralph would be thinking: *There, that's where he should be. Between the clock and the pewter candlesticks, where we can keep an eye on him.*

"Then what stopped you?" Irene spat out the words. "Dominic wanted you there and you… couldn't be bothered." Her voice dissolved into breathy sobs.

"Irene, that's just not true. When I got out of bed this morning I had every intention –" The truth wouldn't satisfy Irene. It barely made sense to Lucy now her surge of anger had passed. She hated to use her health as an excuse, but these were exceptional circumstances. "I had a collapse. Just a small one but my doctor thought it –"

"What sort of collapse?"

"The usual sort. Well, *my* usual sort."

"Stop speaking in riddles. I won't accept anything less than a stroke or a heart attack."

Lucy exhaled her shock. Was it possible to take exception to the reaction her lie had provoked? "I'm sorry I can't oblige you there, Irene." Yes, as it turned out, it was.

"What, then?"

"I had polio as a child. I suffer occasional episodes. Pain, temporary paralysis…"

"I didn't… I mean, Dominic never said…"

Irene had the grace to sound embarrassed, but there was no going back. "If you really didn't know, then you're in a small minority. The newspapers usually include this nugget of information, along with those pictures of us drinking champagne."

"They tell me that the moment you got home, you opened your address book and crossed out his name. Just struck it out."

A fresh angle of attack. The linen-covered book lay on the table in front of Lucy. She flattened her hand onto it, as if to absorb something through its cover. Described by someone else, their ritual sounded callous. Brutal, even. It was Ralph who'd started it, back in 1987. The first of his friends to go. The shock of it. He hadn't been able to say the words out loud. He'd simply left the address book open on the table, the name struck through with a thick black marker.

Lucy took a deep breath, as if she was about to dive underwater. "That's true," she said. All of those names. Quite a collection. And no way of telling which one was the *they* Irene had spoken of. "Did they also tell you it's what we've done ever since the first of our friends passed away? We strike through the name, then we draw a little cross and write the date. The time too, if we have it. I wish we hadn't started this bloody business because all it does is remind me how many... But I don't see how we can stop now. How would it look if I hadn't done the same for Dominic? Do you see?"

Now that Lucy had posed a question, Irene fell silent. Almost as if she didn't *want* to see anything from Lucy's point of view, because they were very different people. While she waited, Lucy saw movement from the corner of her eye. Ralph was disappearing into the kitchen.

"Just one moment, Irene. Here's Ralph. *Ralph!*" she called out, wondering how Dominic's oldest friend had escaped Irene's anger. "What are you drinking, Irene?"

"I honestly don't know. Somebody poured it for me. Why?"

"Ralph, be a dear and fetch me a brandy." She mimed their sign language for 'large'. "I'd like to toast Dominic with his sister. You don't mind do you?"

"No," they said in stereo.

"I'll join you," said Ralph, heading back towards the brandy bottle.

"How was the service, Irene? Was there a good turnout?" *Good God, I'm asking for details. What if the answer's 'no'?*

"People standing outside – people I've never met. A man thrust a microphone under my nose and said that Dominic had influenced a generation of critics. He wanted my take on it, but what would I know about that sort of thing?"

Lucy let her mind drift where it would. She recalled walking around Highgate cemetery with Dominic. It was the afternoon of the day the consultant had laid his glasses on his desk to confirm that the cancer was back. Most people wouldn't react to a terminal diagnosis by saying, "Come along. I want to go and check out the competition." But Dominic wasn't most people.

He hadn't wanted pity – according to Dominic, he'd had five bonus years, time he hadn't been entitled to. She'd wished that Ralph was there to say the sensible thing, but he was away on a shoot. Some unpronounceable place in Iceland. A band who'd wanted a set of photographs with a sixties vibe. And so it had just been the two of them. The day cold but bright and, underneath his favourite pink trilby and deep-blue mirrored sunglasses, Dominic had been muffled in a rainbow-coloured scarf.

"You bought me this, remember?" he asked.

How could she forget? A thing with an Indian look about it, a bright swathe tucked under his chin so that he could swig red wine from a bottle. She'd seen him undergo many transformations over the years. Even depleted, Dominic could still get away with wearing a woman's scarf. "I bought it for myself," she protested. "And anyway, how the hell can you take the news so calmly?"

"We're all going to die, Lucy." He put one cold hand to her cheek. "You know that better than any of us."

Her mouth had twitched. It didn't matter that she'd believed she wouldn't see her tenth birthday. This was different. Dominic was going to die at a definite point in the near future (his doctor had more or less earmarked a date) and Lucy was going to have to watch – for a second time, because the cruel first had turned out to be a false alarm. She'd pretended to concentrate on the leaf-fall and the worm-casts underfoot until she recovered her poise.

"Make sure they give me something large and showy. Weeping angels and a long inscription saying how lovely I was."

It had struck her how she'd been the one to insist he went to the doctors (so like a man not to have booked his own appointment). "How terribly you'll be missed," she quipped, though she didn't feel in the mood for joking.

"How I influenced a generation."

"*Lucy?*" Irene's bark was loud in her ear.

The address book was still under her hand. She found her voice, but didn't trust it. "Yes."

"I said, do you think it's true that he influenced a generation of critics?"

"Oh, almost certainly. Whenever I read one of his reviews,
it didn't matter if it was music or poetry, I felt as if I'd actually
been at the event. That was his skill. Creating false memories."
Getting away with it, that's what they'd always said to each
other. *We got away with it again.*

"Not bad for someone who made up the rules as he went
along."

Irene's words were underwater sentences. Lucy let them
float around her, like Pamela's encouragement as she powered
through the pool, length after length; like soft mermaid hair
in the bath as she rid herself of the clinical smell of chlorine.

*"'Fell asleep'! You will make sure I'm dead before my sister
buries me, won't you?"*

*But then she and Dominic had struck off down different
rows and Lucy stumbled upon a six-foot slab of black granite,
looking out of place among the ivy-choked Victorian cherubs.
What would have been its upper edge had been stepped, the
letters making up the word 'dead' cut away so that daylight
shone through. "I've found it, Dominic!" she shouted. "This is
the one for you!"*

*"Don't you think that's just a little tactless," Dominic had
said.*

Irene's words cut through, harsh once more. "I don't know,
I always thought he was an annoying bugger myself."

A laugh sliced Lucy's throat, surprising in its ferocity.
"It's the job of all older brothers to make their sisters' lives
a misery." And here was Ralph, offering her a glass. "Well,
I'll clink my glass with Ralph's and pretend it's yours, Irene."
As the edge of her glass met the rim of its pair, Lucy looked
her husband directly in the eye. Such tenderness there. Such
exhaustion. "To the most precocious, opinionated, infuriating, intolerant –"

"Outspoken, unpunctual…"

"Complete and utter arse," said Ralph, shoulders hunched, turning back towards the living room. It was a miserable day for him.

"What was that Ralph said?" Irene asked.

"That Dominic was probably the most brilliant man he'll ever have the pleasure of knowing." Or words to that effect. "Cheers." She lifted her eyes and her glass towards the ceiling, picturing Dominic as he was shortly after she'd met him. Bursting into a room with a champagne bottle in one hand, a pair of flutes clinking in the other, a Gauloises dangling from one corner of his mouth, eyes narrowed, coattails flying. Somehow, colour drained from the world once the possibility that Dominic might be up to no good was removed. "You didn't leave much of life unlived, Dominic."

Irene gave a bitter snort. "You two have the monopoly on *those* stories."

Yes. Lucy relished the small satisfaction of one-upmanship. *You'll get Dominic's ashes, but you never really knew him.* She could afford to be generous. "Perhaps you'd like to get together at some point. Mull over a few old memories."

"Perhaps." One short word, so much doubt. It had probably occurred to Irene that the main advantage of losing Dominic was never having to set eyes on his disreputable friends again.

Imagine Irene's face on hearing that she was to be honoured by the Queen! It would almost be worth it. "I should let you get back to your guests. It's usually about this time that strong coffee is needed."

"Huh. You know the Marchmonts."

Actually, Lucy didn't. Without going as far as cutting ties, Dominic had had as little to do with his family as possible. "I'm so grateful you called, Irene. I'll send my little piece to the newspaper, shall I?"

"They might find a use for it, I suppose."

Lucy leant heavily on the receiver after she had hung up. The conversation had taken it out of her.

"Did you salvage the situation?" Ralph twisted his neck as she entered the living room.

She sank into the cushions. "For now. But I lied and I feel bad about it and I feel…" She stalled. What did she feel?

"Worried you might have jinxed yourself?"

"No, not that. I suppose I just feel old."

"That can hardly come as a surprise. We *are* old."

Lucy let her head come to rest against his shoulder. "It's rather nice in a way. To have someone care about your soul."

"Irene once told me that the fact that Dominic Marchmont didn't believe in God didn't stop God believing in Dominic Marchmont."

Lucy sighed. "I imagine that arranging the funeral was the only time she got her own way as far as Dominic was concerned."

Ralph elbowed her. "Revenge! But a religious service. Dominic would have hated it."

"He'd have slipped out of a side entrance, flagged down a taxi and demanded to be driven to the nearest pub."

They were silent in the way that she and Ralph could be silent – companionably – and she and Dominic never could.

"Still angry with him?" Ralph asked at last.

"Yes. And no."

"*I* am. I'm bloody livid."

"You said it yourself. He stuck around as long as he could."

"I meant the honours thing."

"Oh, that."

"Yes, that!"

"Obviously, I'd like to give him a piece of my mind, but…"

"Just you and me now." He angled his head on top of hers, and when she didn't reply, added, "Not such a terrible thought, is it?"

Neither of them was alone, and yet without Dominic they were both depleted. "No," she said but, realising her tone was distant, decided she needed to commit. "You always were the better cook."

"Ah," he said, and she felt the pressure of his kiss on top of her head.

"And you do take the most beautiful photographs." She lifted her face and smiled, though it pained her eyes. "Will you go out tonight?"

"No, no. I'd be rotten company."

Overcome with tenderness, she looked at him, her most constant friend. He had loved her, not just in his own way, but in all the ways she'd needed him to love her. In all the ways Dominic couldn't. And he had loved Dominic long before she had. Lucy reached for Ralph's arm. "Then I'll be very grateful for your rotten company."

CHAPTER TWENTY-THREE

TRAFALGAR SQUARE, 1958

"*Scientific man cannot survive if he is going to make war. The worst possibility is that human life is extinguished and it is a very real possibility, very real. Assuming that doesn't happen, I can't bear the thought of many hundreds of millions of people dying in agony only because the rulers of the world are stupid and wicked.*"

Solemnity combined with an undeniable energy that pulsed from the crowd.

"*We will now hold a minute's silence for those who perished in Hiroshima and Nagasaki.*"

Stealing a sidelong glance, Lucy saw Ralph train his camera, a purposeful movement, smooth and stealth-like, but in no way disrespectful. She tracked the aim of his lens to others who stood tall, chins raised. Ex-servicemen, she presumed. It was only by remembering that they might stop this from ever happening again.

Five years old when the war ended, to Lucy, Hiroshima and Nagasaki had been half a world away, their people indistinct. The ghosts of the dead would outnumber the shoulder-to-shoulder people here today by... her mental arithmetic failed. Imagine if someone were to detonate a bomb, right at this moment.

Some instinct for premonition causes a flurry of pigeons.
Their wings' rapid tempo the only early warning.
In a moment they will be blind.
But what about me?
Will the last thing I see be the moment Nelson is felled from his high perch?
Or the bronze lions reduced to molten metal.
Or perhaps a jagged rift tearing through the paving slabs, exposing the lines of the Underground.
Will there be time to feel panic?
Before...Boom!

Lucy didn't fear death. She feared the alternative. Trapped in the wreckage of their homes, under wooden beams or tiled roofs; those who had survived the blast at Hiroshima cried out for help. Then fires broke out and gradually the cries died away only to be replaced by screams. For two days, fire raged four times hotter than the surface of the sun, until there was nothing left to burn. Silence fell over the rubble, deadly. The air glittered like a mirage.

There were many ways in which radiation could claim a life, some of them excruciatingly slow. There were no hospitals, no nurses. One lone doctor, battling on no sleep and what little medication he could lay his hands on, tackled injuries he'd never seen before, because there had been none like it. Victims vomited blood in makeshift facilities, waiting for help that didn't arrive. People were desperate for water. Food was easier to come by. Pumpkins and potatoes were dug up, ready-cooked from the blast. All of it, contaminated.

For nine long days the Japanese propaganda machine upheld a terrible pretence: *We are winning the war.* But even after surrender, the survivors were on their own. Lucy shuddered to think of what happened when the Japanese government failed to take control: the yakuza set to looting, removing gold teeth from the jaws of corpses, putting orphaned children to work in return for food – polishing shoes, prostitution. They wore face masks to help cope with the stench of tens of thousands of rotting corpses.

Two months later, many previously symptom-free survivors began to fall ill. They lost their appetites and ran high fevers. Their hair fell out in clumps. American scientists sat up and paid attention. They established the Atomic Bomb Casualty Commission, a name that seemed designed to confuse the islanders into believing it was a charity. Parents granted permission for children to take part, children who were made to stand on stage and remove their clothes. Nobody told the survivors that a decision had been made to study, not treat. By 1952, the scientists had gathered all the data they would ever need. Lucy couldn't believe the Americans didn't share it with their British allies. As far as she was concerned, everything that followed was a display of one-upmanship.

"This," roared Michael Foot, "can be the greatest march in English history!" A banner fluttered. *Walk with us.*

Never before had Lucy felt such a hunger to be part of something. Had it been only five miles to Aldermaston, she would have struggled. The fact that it was fifty made the decision easy. Her left leg wouldn't be up to it.

Then came the sound of a carnival, the kind of release that follows enforced silence. *We will not be ignored.* In the square below, people were jostling, moving.

"You heard the man!" Dominic said. Without hesitation, he sat on the edge of the plinth and launched himself off, then turned and held his arms towards her. "Your turn."

Daring herself to look over the sill, Lucy felt queasy. "Holy cow," she said, making light of frayed nerves as she bent her shaking knees to sit. Flattening her damp raincoat against her rump, she said, "What a time to find out you suffer from vertigo!"

"You're thinking too much," Dominic said laughingly. "Just jump."

"You're not helping, Dom," Ralph called down, then smiled at Lucy. "If I go next, there'll be two of us to catch you. Alright?"

"Yes," said Lucy, relieved that all she needed to do for the next few moments was sit, dangling her legs. Chill seeped through gabardine, and Lucy tried to imagine she was perched on the edge of a swimming pool, dipping her toes.

About to hitch his camera strap across his body, Ralph appeared to have second thoughts. "Do me a favour? Hold on to my camera, only for God's sake don't drop it. It cost an arm and a leg."

Lucy remembered gripping the rail at the side of the swimming pool, panicking about letting go. But she'd done it and hadn't drowned. Somehow she managed to take the camera and loop the strap around her wrist several times. Immediately, she felt less tense. "It's a good weight, isn't it?"

"Don't get too attached." Ralph grinned before he slid off the plinth, landing with bent knees. "I'd better have that back while you're still prepared to part with it. Now, what might work best is if you put one hand on each of our shoulders." He inched closer to the plinth and wedged himself into position, sideways on. "Dom?" He turned to his friend.

Dominic sighed and looked at Lucy, making something clench in her stomach. "Ralph *loves* to organise people. *Loves* planning."

Ralph, it seemed, was used to being spoken about rather than to. Lucy's feet were still some way above their heads. "OK, you're going to have to lean."

"I *am* leaning."

He closed his eyes and nodded. "Maybe a bit more. On my three."

Panic rose in Lucy's throat.

"One, two –"

"Oh, shit," she said, pushing off with her hands. Her descent wasn't at all like the clean-lined dive she'd visualised, but she was back on terra firma, apparently in one piece.

As she brushed herself down, Dominic said, "Ralph's very upset. You didn't wait until he said three."

"I'm sorry to have been so much trouble." She could barely look them in the eye for embarrassment. "I'll get out of your hair now."

"What's this?" Dominic frowned and it was damnably attractive. "If I'm not mistaken, that sounded like goodbye."

Lucy held out her hands and looked down the length of her body. "Oh, I was never going to walk."

"Why not?"

If you'd plucked up the nerve to jump when he said jump, the whole length of your body would have touched his. Was it possible that the thing she was so self-conscious about wasn't obvious? But she couldn't allow herself to be reeled in again. "Well, I'm not dressed for it, for starters."

"I'll lend you one of my jumpers."

"And I haven't got any money."

"Ralph will lend you money. Besides, you won't need much. We'll be camping in church halls and feasting on tinned spam."

Who were they, these people who took her as they found her? "Plus my flatmate's expecting me home."

"Your *flat*mate!" As Dominic dismissed Evelyn, Lucy thought that perhaps he had a point. "Look, you *have* to come. Your poem's rousing stuff. We need a performance in every town along the route. This march could be as much about you as it is about Ewan MacColl."

"And there was me thinking it was about peace!"

"Peace doesn't just happen. It takes artists, influencers." He leant towards her confidentially, then directed his gaze towards Ralph. "How many poets get to say they have their own personal photographer?"

Lucy felt giddy. She'd been waiting for something to happen. What if this was it?

In the background, a band struck up a marching tune, the drummer marking time as a chant was taken up: *'One, two, three-four-five. Keep the human race alive!'* People were snaking towards Pall Mall. The exodus had begun.

Ralph smiled. "We'd be very glad to have you along."

"Exactly," Dominic said as if that settled it. "One minute." He raised a hand in the air. "Someone I need to speak to. *Pat!*" And as he began to elbow his way through the crowd, he yelled over his shoulder, "Don't let her get away!"

Open-mouthed, Lucy looked to Ralph.

"Head on a permanent swivel. It actually rotates through three hundred and sixty degrees."

She laughed. "Is he always like this?"

"Pat's a folk singer. Dom's writing a piece about the British Protest Song, which is what he thinks today's legacy will be."

"So he doesn't believe in CND?"

"Does Dom believe in CND?" Ralph pretended to consider the question. "Insofar as it benefits him, yes. But Dominic's main cause has always been Dominic."

"And you?"

"I'm all for world peace. I'd be a fool not to be. But this is work. I'm here to take photographs in the hope that I'll sell a few." He widened his eyes. "I *have* to sell a few. We're two months behind on the rent."

Lucy felt a familiar twinge of guilt.

"Look," Ralph said, "it doesn't have to be all or nothing. The first overnighter's in Hounslow. If you've had enough by then, you can catch a train home."

A vague recollection. Once on a day trip to Syon House, she'd passed through the town centre. "How far's that?"

He shrugged. "Ten, fifteen miles."

It was hopeless. "It's not that I don't *want* to." She shook her head and bunched up her mouth. "But I've never walked anything *like* that distance. I'm not sure I can."

"Listen, don't let us bully you, but if that's too much, we'll stop in one of the parks for lunch."

Eyes sparkling, Dominic arrived back beside the plinth, untangling one of his arms from the crowd. "Canon Collins has asked for silence as we go through the centre of town, but once we're on our way... boom!"

Lucy shuddered. "How appropriate," she managed.

Ralph, opening the back of his camera, gave a snort of laughter.

"What?" Dominic turned to him. "I was just saying, a member of the clergy can hardly object to a few rounds of *When the Saints go Marching in.*"

Ralph pocketed the used film and reloaded. "That's not *exactly* what Pat has in mind."

"Every cause needs its song." Dominic swept his fringe out of his eyes. Here was someone who would have the power to make Lucy feel on the top of the world – and at her lowest ebb. She knew instinctively that she would get bruised. "So? Has Ralph convinced you?"

"I'll come as far as Hounslow," Lucy said with more confidence than she felt. He wouldn't miss her if she sloped off at Hyde Park.

"We'll see." Always, Dominic's grin would suggest he knew something she didn't. "I should have asked your name by now. You do have one, I take it?"

If she hadn't been so flustered, it might have crossed her mind to lie. "Lucy Forrester," she said.

"Why do I know that name?" Dominic snapped his fingers as if to encourage his thoughts. "Never mind, it'll come to me. Come along, troops! We must follow the Pied Piper."

For Lucy, Dominic *was* the Pied Piper.

"And he's off," Ralph said, as Dominic wove away from them.

"Who is it this time?" She'd lost all sense of how far they'd come. All the time they'd skirted Green Park and Hyde Park, she'd been on familiar terrain.

"This, you'll like. He thinks he's spotted Michael White. You know, the producer."

Lucy said she didn't.

"He's a man with a gift for spotting talent before anyone else recognises the slightest whiff of potential. But it won't *be* him."

"How do you know?" Four or five abreast, the marchers had kept to the road, while policemen held the traffic at bay. Occasionally, children darted between parked cars to rescue discarded coins before they teetered in the direction of drains.

"It never is. Dom makes most of his friends by chatting to people he thinks are Michael White." Ralph was keeping pace with her. She worried he was missing the good shots. "I'm not convinced he has any idea what he looks like. So, how are you doing?"

"Alright, I think." Her left side ached and her toes were numb. After breaking for lunch near the Albert Memorial – another opportunity to turn back missed – they'd continued past Kensington Gardens. All the while there had been people to wave at, Lucy felt that she was doing something vital. But the crowds had thinned and it was some time since she'd recognised a landmark.

"Don't worry." Ralph trudged beside her. "It's not a race."

Lucy tried to smile. At home there was an armchair, a hot drink, soup perhaps. And, since Evelyn would be visiting family for much of the Easter weekend, an uninterrupted wallow in a warm bath – oh, God, just the idea of it!

Slightly ahead, Dominic turned (another lurch in her stomach) and walked backwards, hands in pockets. "We need to worm our way forward. Karl's gone on ahead so that his band will be playing when the bulk of the walkers arrive at the next stop."

Lucy's mouth fell open. She was in danger of crying. "I'm going as fast as I can."

"That's *why*," Dominic exaggerated the word, "I was about to suggest we cheat." He nodded in the direction of a bus stop on the opposite pavement.

This must have been how Lawrence of Arabia felt on seeing a distant oasis in the desert. Lucy associated bus journeys with escape. The glorious anonymity of being wedged between strangers, listening to eye-watering scandal about people you'd never meet. Acting out a reason to look over her shoulder and see whether the speaker might be her Mrs Ogmore Pritchard, her Mog Edwards.

Aware of her arms being grabbed, Lucy was propelled across the road. Her earthbound soul soared. For a moment, she was at the centre of everything, and it was revolving around her. But as soon as they boarded, Ralph stood to one side. "You two go upstairs."

Lucy's sense of abandonment was acute. "Aren't you coming with us?"

"I'm going to stay here and take some shots out of the back."

As the bus lurched she clutched the handrail to steady her ascent. She had no idea how to behave with Dominic. Especially now, with winter clinging to her hair and clothes.

At the front of the top deck, Lucy filed to the right and cleared a porthole in the fogged window, pretending to be fascinated by the crocodile of walkers; the triumphant sea of banners; children carried high, like mascots; policemen's helmets and brass instruments spaced out at regular intervals. In later years when Lucy saw grainy black and white footage, she would think, *Yes, that was how it was.* The slick steel grey of wet tarmac, the muted grey of snow clouds.

"Shift over." Dominic nudged her sideways.

Hemmed in, Lucy was aware of every point where they

touched – her shoulders against his upper arms, her thighs against *his* thighs – and only a layer of cold damp fabric separating them. Her cheeks burned as they thawed. She must have been half-frozen. Without warning, Dominic leaned sharply over her lap. Paralysed by the thought of what came next, Lucy couldn't remember being more self-conscious. His scent was fresh cigarette smoke, a whiff of unfamiliar soap. It turned out that all he wanted was to retrieve a fold of paper from his back trouser pocket. "Today's running order," he said as he unfolded it.

Relieved and disappointed, Lucy was very aware of his fingers, tantalisingly close, his square nails, his pale wrists. She took the sheet, trying to appear businesslike. She wouldn't be the sort who swooned.

"See there?" He jabbed the page as she turned it over. "That's the list of officially approved songs. And there, those are the banned ones."

"I've always rather liked *Down by the Riverside*."

"Tough luck. The Communists have nabbed it." Dominic put out one hand and cupped her knee. Just cupped her knee. *Somebody breathe for me.* Elvis had been safe. He'd been trapped inside the goggle box. "It's all censorship," Dominic went on, oblivious. "Middle-aged, middle class men get to decide which books we read, which films we see, the music we listen to." No sideways sly manoeuvre, this wasn't the sort of thing she'd been warned to expect when a boy invited you to the cinema. Extraordinary, how the hand hadn't been there and now was. "I'm trying to do for music what Kenneth Tynan's done for theatre."

A small area of common ground. Lucy forced her gaze from Dominic's hand to his face.

"The thing is, record companies aren't sending their people to the clubs and the basements." Nothing in the way he spoke suggested that anything out of the ordinary was taking place.

She watched his mouth move, mesmerised. *"That's* where it's all happening. And that's where you come in."

It was as much as she could do to concentrate as he set out his vision.

They would be like a team.

Poetry didn't sell on its own. The thing was to create controversy.

She found herself repeating the tails of sentences. "Controversy?"

He would publish what were largely flattering reviews, but would always throw in one line which was open to interpretation. Her job was to pick up on that line and dissect it.

She swallowed the lump in her throat. "Dissect it?" *God, she was making a terrible fool of herself.*

"Go to town," he said. "Claws out, tear right into me." Each review would lead to exchanges between them. Even people who weren't normally interested in poetry would lap up their letters.

Lucy felt herself resisting. She'd had her fair share of reviews after her poems had been published in magazines. The advice was *not* to respond.

And then, turning serious, Dominic said he thought that a relationship should be hinted at.

"Between us?" she asked, stunned. Lucy was the girl with the orphan-boy looks, the giraffe neck, the wrong clothes and, when unrehearsed, the wrong damned words.

"There's no need to sound so horrified. Who else would I mean, you strange girl?" He said this so casually, his hand still a warm weight on her knee. "Our rows over the reviews will hint at lovers' tiffs. Not anything that can ever be confirmed."

"No!" Damn this shaking. She prayed Dominic would think it was because of the cold, or the shuddering of the bus in the stop-start traffic.

"On the other hand we should never do anything to deny it."

There was no mention of what would *actually* be going on. Was the part about lovers (a word that made her light-headed) supposed to be a fiction?

At the same time, Dominic continued, they would tease their growing audience with a little of what they wanted: a tour of the London club circuit. "And I'll be there in the front row, night after night and you'll address me. As if the rest of the audience is invisible."

Lucy swallowed. It would be a job to get her lines out, with him staring up at her. "Tell me." She felt the need to involve herself in the discussion about what was, after all, to be her future as well as his. "Do you have this kind of agreement with all of the acts you review?"

He laughed. "You'd have heard of me if I did."

"So you've never done anything like this before?"

"No!" He made the idea sound ridiculous, and Lucy's spirits sagged. "But I might have done. If someone like you had come along."

Lucy couldn't escape the feeling that he was toying with her. She didn't fear ridicule. That, she knew all about. But she feared he might think her gullible.

"Of course, we'll need to do something about the way you dress."

"I dressed for cold weather! This wasn't advertised as a fashion parade."

He glanced at her sideways. "From now on, you must look like a poet and act like a poet. You must be theatre personified."

Lucy chose clothes for their unremarkability. A tailored jacket, a turtleneck jumper, some cropped trousers or a skirt that fell below her knees. Nothing too tight on the legs. "You're very…"

"What?" he challenged, giving the impression he was digging for compliments.

She wasn't used to taking advice on what to wear from a man. "Direct."

"What's the point in being otherwise? And if we're going to be working together…"

It almost came as a relief when Ralph slumped bodily into the seat behind them.

"Nothing doing?" Dominic removed his hand from her knee in a way that had her questioning if she'd imagined it was ever there at all. He twisted towards his friend, casually resting his elbow on the back of the seat that separated them.

"Sit down or get off the bus, he told me." A cigarette between his lips, Ralph was shrouded in a halo of smoke. "Apparently I was about to fall out of the back and do myself an injury."

"Bad luck." The index finger of Dominic's hand shot up to indicate a lightbulb moment. "Bingo!" It was almost a shout and he followed it up with a drum roll performed with his feet. "Your name. Forrester." Something inside Lucy stuttered. "I've remembered where I heard it!"

A tiny part of the mechanism that held her past at bay sheared. Everything was about to come tumbling down about her ears. "Oh? And where's that?" she asked as casually as possible.

"There was a case that hit the headlines a few years back. A man who opened a cake factory to celebrate the end of sugar rationing."

We take our hats off to the housewives of Britain, for the fine job they have done in providing for their families throughout the years of ration-dictated dullness. But now we are heralding in a new age – and that, ladies, means not having to do everything yourself. Our ready-made cakes look homemade. We won't tell if you don't!

There it went: her imagined future. All of the poetry readings, the reviews, the affair, real or imaginary.

"*Having Your Cake and Eating It.*" Still sulking, Ralph spoke absent-mindedly, adjusting the controls of his camera.

The corners of Lucy's mouth trembled. In the end, the most extraordinary thing about her father's second household was that Mother had decided not to divorce him. Instead, each adult had carried on exactly as they'd always done – except that, in the eyes of the world, Father had his wife's blessing. He kept all the pies he had fingers in. Little wonder at the headline one of the tabloids had used.

Ralph's head jerked upwards, as if he had only just realised he'd spoken out loud.

"Yes!" Dominic punched the air, then turned to her. "That wasn't your *father?*"

Usually the eavesdropper, she'd never been party to a conversation that was worth eavesdropping *on.* Lucy said the first thing that sprang to mind. "My uncle, actually."

Dominic gave a triumphant *Hah!* "So he must have been your father's brother?"

There was no option but to take ownership of the lie. "Was. The family disowned him. Which was a shame because he was the only one from that side who was ever any fun."

"You never saw him again?" asked Ralph.

Mouth bunched, she shook her head. "They cut him dead. He was completely *persona non grata.*" This was what would have happened. Mother's family washed their hands of anyone they didn't approve of.

Dominic slapped his thigh, then threw back his head and hooted. The seat jolted hard against Lucy's back. "Now *that* I wasn't expecting," he said.

It struck Lucy: she hadn't simply denied her father. In that moment, she'd become a counterfeit self. Glancing over one shoulder at Ralph, she had the uncanny sense that he knew everything there was to know about her – but didn't give a damn about any of it.

CHAPTER TWENTY-FOUR

Granada Television Studio,
1978, PART THREE

Other objections aside, Lucy thought as she stormed down the corridor, a biography would imply that her best was behind her.

"I'm going to kill him," she said, closing the dressing room door. Something solid to lean against, something to put the flat of both hands on.

"Oh, I don't know." Ralph jumped up from the dressing table, where he'd been perching. "From what I saw, the audience seemed to enjoy it."

Blood was pounding through her veins. "Not Philip Harrington!"

He raised his camera to his eye. "Who, then?"

"Dominic, of course." Lucy let the back of her head come to rest against the door. Perhaps she *had* peaked. You were only as good as your last work. Yes, she would snatch the odd few lines from the air, but there was no guarantee that one or two lines would develop into a poem, "He's more or less told them the biography's in the bag."

"Hold it right there."

Obeying, chin tilted upwards, she felt less certain of her rage.

Ralph circled like an animal stalking its prey. She couldn't see his mouth as he spoke in a warning tone. "Now, you don't know it was him."

"Then who?" She pushed herself into the centre of the room and scowled at her reflection. She didn't like how they'd made her up. Too tasteful and absolutely no drama.

His knees a little bent, Ralph snapped away from behind her. "If I had to hazard a guess, I'd say it was Dom's agent."

"Ha!"

Ralph's reflection lowered its camera, pausing just long enough to make her pay attention to what was coming next. "He's under a certain amount of pressure." It sounded like an apology. Guilt was involved, that much was sure. Either for breaking his best friend's confidence or for keeping something from her.

"He's already accepted an advance?"

Ralph was hesitant. "Not that sort of pressure."

"What then?" She took off her glasses, set them aside, then reached for a pot of cold cream and a wad of cotton wool.

"Dom's broke."

She pulsed with resistance. "Broke?" *What were you thinking of, taking me to an expensive restaurant? And the champagne!* But Dominic had always lived beyond his means, certain his big break was weeks away. The first to reach for his wallet, money never remained in his bank account for long. Renting property rather than buying, adamant that flexibility was crucial. What if work came up in another city? Another country? Lucy's mouth was hanging open when there was a knock at the dressing room door. "Yes?" she barked. Talk about timing! Thank goodness she had yet to apply the cold cream.

The door nudged open and Philip Harrington's head appeared around it. "Lucy, I just wanted to say… oh, hello, I didn't realise you had company." He stepped into the room, giving Ralph a questioning glance. "I hope I'm not interrupting."

"Not at all," Lucy said, still fuming inwardly, *How could you be so bloody irresponsible?* "Have you met my husband, Ralph?"

"The photographer with the extraordinary eyes." Philip lit up and he lunged forward, extending a hand. "It's an absolute pleasure," the chat show host gushed, pumping his hand.

Lucy felt a swell of pride. To the world, her husband was only ever Ralph. As an adult, he'd dropped his family name. These days, people meeting Ralph for the first time regularly called him 'Mr Forrester'.

"Oh." Ralph dismissed the compliment with a shake of his head. "My wife's the one with the extraordinary eyes."

"I'm a huge fan of your work. Huge. I think your Robert Plant is my favourite."

"Well, thank you." Modesty wasn't something Ralph conjured up for effect. He still managed to be surprised that someone might have stumbled across a photograph of his while flicking through a copy of *Rolling Stone*.

"If I'd known you were here today... Lucy." Philip Harrington pressed one hand to his forehead and closed his eyes briefly, then deferred to her. "We didn't talk about Ralph's role in your career."

"Well, you can't cram everything into an hour slot." But he was already pointing towards Ralph.

"I don't suppose you could be persuaded...?"

Standing to attention, a fixed smile on her face, Lucy waited for an opportunity to say what she wanted to say.

Ralph looked at his feet. "Oh, I don't –"

"You've met all the greats. The stories you must have! We could call it *The Man Behind the Camera*."

"If it's all the same to you, the stories aren't mine to tell. *Behind* the camera's where I'm happiest."

"Fair enough." Something must have told Philip not to push his luck. He rocked back on his heels and reached into a trouser pocket. "But if you should change your mind."

Ralph never changed his mind. Not because he was stubborn, but because his instincts were fine-tuned. Philip waited for Ralph to take his card, then turned to Lucy. She tweaked her smile.

"So that was all. I just wanted to say thank you. You certainly kept me on my toes."

"Well, you asked some excellent questions." Lucy grabbed the opportunity. "Can I just ask?" She gave the impression of polite interest. "Who told you there was the possibility of a biography?"

"I think it must have been something a researcher picked up."

"Yes, but from where?"

"Guests' agents are the ones who usually volunteer anything newsworthy." He touched her forearm as if he was about to make a joke. "Not yours, I assume from your reaction."

"Have you ever heard of someone having a biography written about them while they're still in their forties?"

"But you've been giving us your poems for thirty years. It could be part one of two."

Emphasis on her early life was *exactly* what Lucy was afraid of.

Philip noticed that she didn't share his amusement. "Anyway." He rubbed the palms of his hands together. "A few minor edits and it will make great television."

"So, you'll cut the question about the biography?" She intended her question to be interpreted as an instruction.

"That's not up to me, I'm afraid. The final edit will be down to the production team."

Lucy made no attempt to suppress a noise in the back of her throat. There were those who thought that a damaged past was a valuable commodity. Given the facts, some might argue that Lucy had traded on the psychological fallout.

A quick glance at his watch. "Speaking of which, I'm due at the post-production dissection." Philip offered Ralph his hand a second time and Lucy his hand for the first, and was gone.

"Lu-cy." Ralph adopted the tone of an indulgent parent. "Publicity in return for controversy, that's how these things work."

Typical Ralph, not wanting to reflect on Philip's flattery. "Aren't you the least bit bothered?" she demanded, then softened her tone. "After all, certain parts of my story overlap with yours." Ralph and Lucy rarely talked about sex. Not the detail. They both respected the other's right to privacy.

"No one will be shocked to learn that I'm gay."

It was surprising he could sound so nonchalant. Married men didn't tend to 'come out'. Lucy and Ralph had been married for almost two years when 'homosexual acts' were decriminalised, but this didn't mean acceptance. Homo, fag and queer were still in use as derogatory terms. There was good reason to keep their private life private. Ralph's parents' minds had been put at rest and his career had taken off. "We've always kept our marriage out of the press. It's the one thing that's..." She bowed her head and shook it.

"Totally off-limits, I agree."

"I was going to say 'sacred'." She turned back to the mirror and began smearing her face with cold cream.

Ralph's voice was gentle. "You don't have to give them your soul."

"They've already had that," she said, closing one eye, dragging cotton wool across the lid. Part girl, part machine. The brother who changed allegiances. The ghostly half-brothers. They were all there in her poetry. But her fans had somehow formed the idea that these laid-bare things were red herrings and diversions, the real treasure buried elsewhere.

"What I mean is that *you're* in control of the material you give Dominic."

"You're forgetting about everything he *already* knows." As she wiped away the cold cream with fresh cotton wool, a more vulnerable version of herself emerged in the mirror's unforgiving light.

Thank God she *hadn't* confided in Dominic more often! There'd been many occasions when she'd been tempted; guard-lowered moments when she thought he'd glimpsed the truth. Lucy reached for her handbag where she'd stowed her own make-up, so that she could be her chosen version of herself.

Ralph's voice was muffled. "I meant the whatever-it-is you don't want Dom to know about."

Her hands shook. There were days when she felt as if she might open the clasp and something damaged would make an unexpected bid for freedom, rolling like a stray lipstick into the centre of the room, coming to rest between the feet of someone she barely knew. Thinking he was being kind, the stranger would pick it up and say, 'I think you dropped this,' and Lucy would look at the end of the tube, shake her head and say, 'No, that's not my colour.'

Odd that, after her father's confession, walking outside into the square had felt like the first step towards freedom. She had sat in a chair in a trendy hair salon, looking at her confident young reflection, and said, "I want you to crop my hair."

"How short would you like it?"

"As short as a boy's." She had thought all it would take was the snip of stainless steel. Her mane had fallen into her lap and to either side of the chair and she hadn't suffered a single second thought.

Slowly, she turned to her husband, resting one elbow on the back of the chair. "I've always felt as if you knew everything there is to know about me, without my having to say a word."

"I *never* felt it was my right to know everything about you. Whatever you're willing to share is enough."

She turned back to the mirror, pressed her lips together and blotted her lipstick, and her mother's waxy presence was there in the dressing room once more. The person Lucy had known was only ever an advertisement for the ideal family, the ideal home.

Darling, I had no idea about your father! It was as much as a shock to me as it was to you.

She thought, like Ralph, that she had fine-tuned instincts, but she never really knew whose affair came first. Lucy doubted her ability to recognise the truth when she heard it. In fact, she didn't want to know.

Unravel me to the first dropped stitch.

Knit me all over again.

A different-shaped garment.

Ralph was packing his camera away. "The fact that we've been married for over twelve years and I've never met a single member of your family tells me I shouldn't delve. And that's fine, by the way. All I know is that these things had to happen, otherwise you'd be a completely different person."

"You met Freddie," Lucy said, her throat raw.

"Did I?"

"You don't remember? Mind you, I'm not surprised. You were stoned at the time."

"I must have been. Did I *really?*"

"You were all over your latest. Emil, he was called. The one who made off with your wallet."

"My God, Emil. I remember him."

All the time she had accepted her parents' money, Lucy hadn't been free. She'd thought she could shake off the word *entitlement* by being generous with what she had. Letting the boys move into her spare room had put them on equal footing; three young people, none of them paying rent. An intensely creative and passionate time.

She sighed. "Dominic? Just how broke is he?"

Ralph hesitated before he replied, "On the verge of bankruptcy."

This alleviated Lucy's guilt. "Then a book isn't the answer. That would take too long. Isn't there anything you could put his way? Any contacts…?"

"Don't think it hasn't crossed my mind. The people I work with these days have their own PR."

Her mind strayed again to the Soho flat. "We could always ask him to move in with us." She gave a humourless laugh. "It would be like the old days." Bohemian, the three of them wearing each other's clothes, drinking cheap wine out of tumblers, cigarettes passing hand to hand, lips to lips. Moving closer and closer in each other's circles until, if someone invited one of them, they expected all three. The larger-than-life of it. Two double beds shared by three people, wherever there was space on any given night.

Her false smile slipped in stages.

It had stopped being fun. Coming home, tripping over sleeping bodies, finding that friends of friends had been invited to crash after a club closed; finding no room in either double bed and a couple sprawled on the sofa. *What's the problem? It's only for a night or two.* A slowly winding path from hedonism to resentment. Always, there was other people's noise. And, in the end, Lucy had longed for 'a room of her own'. Somewhere to write.

She saw Ralph's wince. "I've already suggested that, I'm afraid."

She tried not to react. "What did he say?"

"Oh, you know Dom. It wasn't as if I expected gratitude." And from this Lucy assumed that she could expect the imminent arrival of a house-guest. "But if you want my take on it – the book, I mean – I think Dom's convinced himself that you owe him this."

"*I owe* him!" Dominic's association with Lucy had propelled him from the underground music scene into literary circles. But Lucy knew herself to be capable of holding contradictory opinions. There was one sense in which Dominic *had* been instrumental in launching her career. He had seen something in her, a certain quality. He had been her Michael White.

"To be honest," Ralph addressed Lucy's reflection, "it's not just the money. He's been scratching around for a project for a long time. I don't think he imagined he'd still be writing about what *other* people were doing twenty years down the line."

"He thought other people would be writing about *him*." But Dominic's taste of failure had left him wary. Experimenting with something that came from himself was too great a risk. "You were supposed to be his sidekick. He's jealous."

"Perhaps. But not for the reason you're suggesting." He looked at her, making his meaning clear.

Applying the last touches of make-up, Lucy insisted, "Rubbish! He didn't want marriage."

"Not at the time, no. But he sees what we've got and…"

Lucy watched her husband shrug. She turned and put one hand on his arm. "This is going to sound odd coming from someone who's always said that whatever goes on in a marriage is no one else's business, but I would *never* have agreed to an open marriage with a straight man."

Ralph asked, "Would you have married him?"

It was a conversation that could only take place in a cramped dressing room. "I've never regretted marrying you. Not for one minute."

"That's not what I asked."

"Oh, I don't know. It's impossible to say." In her attempt to sound dismissive, she'd spoken sharply. "I've been very happy."

She squeezed Ralph's arm. "I *am* very happy." *And I would have been miserable with Dominic,* she thought, remembering that he was about to enter their lives again.

CHAPTER TWENTY-FIVE

1968

Dominic's wedding gift was a pair of battery operated walkie-talkies. They got a lot of use over the years.

"Base to darkroom, base to darkroom."

"Go ahead."

"This is your five-minute warning. Your parents have just pulled up on the drive."

"Bollocks, is that the time?"

"And your mother has one foot out of the car door."

"Fuck. I mean Roger."

"Shouldn't that be 'over'?"

From kitchen to sickbay:

"Do you read me, over?"

"Yes I read you, over."

"Time for your next dose in five minutes. Will you have soup? Over."

"I'm bored of soup. I never want to see another bowl of the stuff. Over. What kind of soup?"

"Celery. You're supposed to be keeping up your fluids. Over."

"Then I'll have wine. Over."

"That's not what the instructions mean when they say 'avoid alcohol'. Over."

From bathroom to Lucy's study:

"Emergency, emergency. Is there a wildlife conservationist in the house?"

"I was in the zone. This had better be good. Over."

"There is a spider in the bath, I repeat, a spider in the bath."

"I thought Will stayed over last night. Can't you put him to good use?"

"It's him who told me it's there. Please come. He thinks it might be a tarantula."

"Honestly! What's the point of having two men in the house?"

CHAPTER TWENTY-SIX

1958

"We need to celebrate," Dominic insisted as Lucy grabbed hold of his shoulder and clambered down awkwardly from the makeshift Hounslow stage – milk crates with planks laid on top. She laughed, exhilarated by the newness of it all. As she took the pint glass he offered, amber liquid slopped onto her coat. What difference did a little spillage make when it was already sopping? Tonight, nothing was going to dampen Lucy's mood. She swapped the glass over to her stronger hand, licking her fingers. "That's not beer," she said.

"Don't you like cider?"

"I do. It's just not what I was expecting." Tonight's stars were a promise. Beyond the strains of the band, the air echoed: *One, two, three-four-five. Keep the Human Race Alive!* It was a drumbeat, a heartbeat, and alive was how Lucy felt.

"Look at her." Dominic nudged Ralph, a knowing expression on his face. Every time she'd found Dominic looking up at her, Lucy felt as if he was the stage lighting that had been lacking. "She's hooked on adrenalin."

"You looked good up there." Ralph raised his glass in a toast. "You're a natural."

Even with her skin taut with cold, wearing the cold-weather clothes that Dominic had criticised, she felt uncaged and attractive. There was a whole world out there, and she wanted every last piece of it. A small island in the Pacific, shaped like a lobster claw, drifted further from her mind. To *Lady be Good* and *High Society*, Lucy allowed herself to be taken by the hand and looped under the arch of one or other of the boys' arms. Then, because she'd celebrated a little too much and the last train had left, she allowed herself to be talked into staying the night. It was the sensible thing to do. Far safer than a young woman alone on the night bus. But Lucy was still the sort of person who took up a black marker and drew boundaries. She drew hers at sharing Dominic's bedding roll.

"You know how to wound a person." Dominic staggered backwards, looking far from wounded.

"Share with me." Ralph looped one protective arm around her shoulder.

A little like a sleepover, a little like a dorm, the call of "Lights out!" did nothing to quieten the walkers. Floorboards, pressing hard against Lucy's hipbone, were infused with the sawdust smell she associated with sickness, tempered only with damp sock and unwashed bodies. In decades to come, she would scoff at talk of the number of pregnancies that started out in that very same church hall. True, several couples were entangled, giggling and whispering, but they were sandwiched between members of the clergy and nursing mothers. Hardly a recipe for romance!

Once Lucy had her shivering under control, there was something cosy about being cocooned in a grey woollen blanket, cider coursing through her veins, prayer-like hands contrasting cold under her warm cheek. There was comfort in the ticking and creaking and muffled private rustling. And this man who lay facing her. The word, "Well?" her cue, Lucy felt safe enough to recount roughly three-quarters of Dominic's vision. The smaller inexpressible portion she saved for her pen.

"Then you'll do it?"

"I'll *think* about it."

"Never worry about working with someone with a big ego."

"Big? It's huge."

"Keep it down over there!"

Ralph reduced his whisper to a hiss. "The thing about Dom is he always knows why he's in the room. He's interested in whatever's new. If there's an option of playing it safe or taking a risk, he takes the risk."

"Am *I* a risk?"

"No, we've already established that you're *good*. Tell me," Ralph propped himself up on one elbow. "Until today, what was your plan for world domination?"

Lucy's spirits dipped as she contemplated the less than glamorous truth. Twenty years old, living off an allowance, supplemented by renting out her spare room – and she wasn't sure how long she'd be able to stand having Evelyn for a flatmate. "Beyond getting up there and saying my piece, I didn't really have one."

"Then what have you got to lose?"

If Ralph was right, why was it impossible to silence one overwhelming question? "But what if I only have one shot?"

"What if this is the wrong choice? If Dominic blows it, no one will have heard of you and you'll get another chance."

"But Dominic's way…" Lucy was frustrated by her inability to nail down her concerns. Wasn't she supposed to be good with words? "It's not about the poetry. It's about the *event* and the *atmosphere* and what I *wear*. I don't know, it makes it less…"

"Serious?" Ralph suggested.

At last, Lucy felt understood. "He says I have to be *theatre personified*."

"Do you want to know what I think?" He rearranged the folded jumper that was to be his pillow for the night and lay down so that he was looking directly into her eyes. "You don't believe in luck. Because you couldn't predict you were going to meet us today, because it was pure chance –" *A miracle,* Lucy thought. "– you think you should ignore your instincts."

There was truth in that. Lucy didn't believe in *good* luck, not as far as she was concerned. "Go on," she said, her knees pressing uncomfortably into each other. "What *are* my instincts telling me?"

"They're saying, *Jump in with both feet.* And the fact that Dom mentioned the obvious. That you're clearly very striking –"

"Striking?" Lucy scoffed.

He made a triangle of his hands and held it up to his eyes, framing her. "Being different sets you apart, but it can also be glorious." He spoke confidently, leaving Lucy completely undefended. "And just to prove I'm totally objective, here's what you need to know. Dom believes he's irresistible to all women. If he hasn't tried it on with you yet, you won't have to wait very long." Transported back to the top deck of the bus, Lucy felt as if she'd been caught out. "I suggest you separate the two things, Dom and everything else he has to offer."

She made a joke of it: "He's not suitable boyfriend material, then?"

Ralph smiled, his lack of answer an answer. Lucy nudged aside a knot of disappointment. She thought of her last kiss with Barney, all those years ago. A different person before her illness, she'd had no qualms about taking what she wanted.

"You can want people to take your poetry seriously, but be less precious about how people see you as a person."

Lucy tried mulling this over, as if the idea were something

tangible. "So, you're saying I should separate Dom from what he has to offer *and* set myself apart from the poetry."

"Dom has his own agenda and it's Dom. If he pushes you in a direction you don't want to go in…"

"Push back." She wished she felt more conviction.

Still experimenting with ways of framing her, Ralph said, "And I'm not going to desert you. I'm the image part of the publicity machine."

The machine reference registered. Lucy angled her small chin. "Do you think you could make me look like a poet?"

"The most extraordinary poet."

As they left Slough behind, Lucy's eyes wrinkled against the onslaught of sleet. Cold crept into her marrow. Sleet turned to snow, snow to slush. Through her eyes, the column of walkers resembled the dispossessed, the exiled, those people of recent history Lucy had read about. The legacy of those moving boundaries she'd charted.

The three-week crusade from faraway Jarrow to accuse the government of the murder of their town. Cloth caps and makeshift capes, solemn and determined men trudging over slick cobbles through blinding rain, their banners limp. Deep-set eyes masked by fogged glasses, hollow cheeks. And then the Prime Minister, too busy to see them. All they could do was return home, wretched under the weight of their news. No one would be coming to the rescue.

She thought of the one and a half million wandering *Volksdeutsche.* Eastern European nationals forced from their homes. Expelled Jews, camp survivors, some only recently settled finding themselves unwanted once again. Moving, because there was nowhere they could stand still. A hand-cart laden with a suitcase, a desk lamp, a child's precious teddy bear; those few pathetic possessions.

Looking at Ralph's raised camera, Lucy imagined he was

capturing the things she sensed. She felt his commitment, his concentration, sure that he saw the world as she saw it. Fleeing Communist regimes, abandoning land farmed for generations, deserting towns when food supplies were exhausted; fear that cannibalism was considered an option. Scrambling to leave, queueing for visas, terror that borders would be closed. Unsure of a welcome, their journey's end a displaced persons' camp. In black and white and shades of grey, Ralph's photographs would tell the story not just of the Aldermaston march, but where it fitted in the context of others.

But the further she trudged, Lucy lost all sense that she was doing something noble. There was only the endless road. One foot in front of the other. With every step, a burning sensation through her too-thin soles. Inside a borrowed hat, her scalp itched; her left knee was a knot of pain, but still there was the need to keep up, to march in time. Ralph slightly ahead of her, she feared slipping further and further behind. And then there were the celebrities, people who were there to be seen, dropped off by black cabs. Their people touched up hair and make-up, unfurled professional-looking banners, glanced at watches as their charges set off – "Half a mile should do it" – in unsuitable footwear, men with expensive camera equipment in pursuit. There was little talk of banning bombs.

"Why talk about it?" Dominic, seemingly immune to the cold, shrugged. "Everyone's agreed on that." The point was to meet people and to hear songs. Skiffle bands, jazz bands, brass bands, every hundred yards a different strain so that, walking in between, folk anthems overlapped with hymns. Dominic's eyes sparkled. This brief moment in the history of music, this overspill of new into old, was what he would concrete in words. And then he was off, always someone he needed to speak to, someone to interview. The lure of the new. Dominic's agenda.

One thought kept Lucy going: Evelyn opening the front

door, the satisfaction of the look on her face and hearing her ask, "Where the hell have you been? I was beside myself with worry."

CHAPTER TWENTY-SEVEN

1958

After changing outfits a third time and still dissatisfied, Lucy violently pushed the hangers along the rail in the wardrobe. She unbunched her mouth to demand of her reflection, "I'll give you *theatre personified*. What the hell's a poet supposed to look like anyway?" On the march to Aldermaston, she'd performed in a gabardine raincoat, damp hair clinging to her face, a woollen scarf her only accessory. But the voice continued to nag. *More specifically, what does a poet wear to perform in a jazz club?*

She would have a better idea if she'd actually gone to a club, but the doctor had ordered bedrest. The triumphant return she'd imagined hadn't taken place. As Evelyn asked, "Where the hell have you been?", the walls loomed and Lucy collapsed in the hall. Exhaustion, the doctor had called it, demanding, "What made you do it? And in this weather! It was utterly irresponsible."

Evelyn had sided with him, in her jarring tone: "See? I *tried* telling you, but would you listen?"

It hadn't just been the physical effort, the lack of sleep or the cold. There had been terrifying nerves followed by spikes of adrenalin, and then the come-downs, all things Lucy needed to master. Pamela had been cross with her, but not for long. It had been too good an opportunity to pass up.

"Who are these boys you hooked up with?"

Lucy had shrugged. "A critic and a photographer."

"A photographer. He could be useful."

She was glad Pamela hadn't asked too many question about Dominic. She wouldn't have known how to answer.

Lucy held up another outfit in front of the mirror. How could she be so hung up on how she looked when she thought girls who obsessed over what to wear were shallow? A man wouldn't waste energy fretting about what to wear. And it was only because she was about to see Dominic that she cared.

"I can't afford a whole new wardrobe," she'd told him when he said she needed to make more of an effort to stand out. He was quite possibly *the* most infuriating man she'd ever met – and he had stiff competition from her family.

"You know, you could have been a debutante," she mocked her reflection, then laughed at the knowledge that she was free of every shabby ambition Mother had ever held for her.

Still laughing, she checked her watch – *shit, he'll be here any minute!* – and pulled a sweater over the top of her head, smoothing it down; zipped herself into a skirt. Even the thought of Dominic gave her the jitters. If he was to sit looking at her with that bemused expression of his, she would clam up completely, and tonight she needed to be good. Damn these nerves!

Dutch courage, that's what was required. She opened a kitchen cupboard and poured a large measure from a green-glass bottle. "And damn you, Dominic, for ever talking me into this." Tipping her head back, Lucy flooded her thorax with sweetness and warmth. Sherry reminded Lucy of soaking the sponge for the Christmas trifle, Cook allowing her a 'thimbleful', cautioning, "*Sip it slowly, now.*" She was poised to pour herself another when the doorbell jolted her stomach. Had he heard her?

Separate the sex from the other stuff, that's what Ralph had recommended. (He had actually recommended separating Dominic from the *other* stuff but sex was Lucy's translation.) She opened the door, every part the debutante. "Good evening, Mr Marchmont." She stood as she always stood, her weight a little more on one foot than on the other.

"I thought I'd better make sure you weren't having second thoughts." He walked past her into the hall, then looked her up and down. "Is that what you're wearing?"

"Don't you like it?" She crossed her arms in front of her, reached for the sweater's hem and pulled it upwards. "Is it just the jumper you object to?" Lucy cast it aside. Hell, she could do goofy as well as Marilyn. "Or should I change my skirt as well?"

"Now, hang on. I didn't *say* I didn't like it."

"Oh." She reached for the zip.

"I was checking to see if you'd already got changed." He seemed more amused than anything else. "Have you been drinking?"

Her skirt fell to the floor. "Just one very small sherry." She stepped out of the circle of fabric and moved closer, letting her hips sway.

"Look," he raised a hand to halt her and backed away, "I know you think I have a bit of a reputation, but I'm not going to take advantage the minute you've had a drink."

Lucy hadn't given Barney the opportunity to reject her. She was damned well determined that Dominic shouldn't. Yet inside was the child who feared being mocked and shunned. *Here. This is what I look like, I make a gift of it to you.* His pupils were already dilated. "You're not the one who's taking advantage," she said, giving him a push in the direction of the bedroom. "I am."

It was a dingy smoke-filled basement club, accessed via an unpromising spiral staircase. The ceiling was so low that

Dominic had to duck as they descended into excited chatter and cigarette smog. The walls were such a dark shade that if it wasn't black it might as well have been. Lucy thought this new underground world – London's hidden underbelly – marvellous precisely because it was the sort of place she could never imagine her parents. Dominic pulled her by the elbow, heading for the bar. Lucy wove reluctantly through students and arty types, wanting to take it all in. The room reverberated with sound. *This room is alive, and I'm alive within it.*

"What'll it be?" His breath was warm in her ear.

"Whisky mac," she shouted back, because it was something she'd never tried before and tonight everything should be new.

And then a man was shaking Dominic's hand, saying, "After the next song?"

"This is it," Dominic said. "Are you ready?"

Lucy knocked back her drink and handed him the empty glass.

"She's game!" she heard the man say as she walked away.

She was a poet.

She was a woman who had just had sex – with Dominic Marchmont, no less!

And now people were going to listen to her read.

Sticky with beer slops, the floor sucked at the soles of her pumps. Lucy excused herself and skirted the dance-floor to take to the 'stage', not a platform but a small cordoned-off space, quite a squeeze for the band. It was disconcerting to find herself looking directly in the eyes of the front row; to see fingers remove cigarettes from lips; the way those lips pursed as they released curls of blue smoke.

Lucy had only ever imagined that single misfit she wanted to reach out to. The sheaf of poems trembled in her hand as she realised she had only small things – her voice, her words – to stop the audience wandering off to the bar. She breathed in; she breathed out. Then she began.

"You dangerous man
You talk of your hands
As if they are righteous hands."

Earlier, helping her into her coat, Dominic had repeated, "Read as if I'm the only other person in the room." But, feeling her neck caressed by a plume of smoke, Lucy grasped that this intimacy was hers to take advantage of. She would grab each of them – this man here in the tortoiseshell glasses and the turtleneck sweater – with a glance.

"Divine Justice has its own
Perfect Symmetry, wouldn't you say?"

Lucy's height – or lack of – seemed to help. Necks craned to see where her voice – a big voice for a small girl – was coming from. Heads appeared in the gaps between shoulders. A tipsy girl who had pushed her way through to the front arrived stumbling, an inch from the microphone stand.

"Shhh, Go back to sleep."

Between verses, between poems, Lucy let her eyes stray to Dominic's table. He wore the excited look of someone who's realised he's backed a winning horse. She could almost hear his brain ticking, *Come on, come on, come on,* as he tapped an unlit cigarette on the table, letting it pass through his fingers and then turning it over again.

This evening had been on her terms. She had managed to unnerve Dominic. He had lost a little of his hold over her.

The next time she looked towards Dominic's table, the second seat was occupied. Beside him was the person who had brought her this far.

"And in this moment
A new terrifying reality
Begins to assert itself."

Distracted, Lucy almost lost her flow. She'd wanted to be in control of the introductions. But Pamela's expression said *Concentrate.*

As applause rang out, Lucy's mouth seemed intent on twitching into a broad grin. She looked to her exit where Ralph was making a circle of his index finger and thumb, focusing his lens on her. She walked towards him, head held high.

"Powerful stuff," he said, over the top of catcalls.

"I took your advice," she said, in a half-whisper.

"The cardigan. I noticed."

It was only after Lucy had emerged from the bedroom that she'd remembered Ralph giving her one of his confiding smiles. "If *theatrical* isn't you, it's important to make one small change when you step onto a stage. That way, you'll be a different version of yourself." With no time to dither, she'd settled on wearing a cardigan with the deep V and the buttons at the back.

Happy hormones with an adrenalin chaser were soon confirmed as Lucy's drugs of choice. Another evening, post-performance (and with Lucy wearing something she thought a little daring), Ralph arrived at the table, hands clutching pint glasses, a packet of crisps in the grip of his front teeth. Without a camera, his face looked strangely featureless. Rather like seeing a man immediately after he's shaved off his moustache. Lucy grabbed the crisps and ripped greedily into the packet. Eating had been overlooked in her early evening plans.

"Thirty-five minutes," Dominic had said after checking his watch, and Lucy had walked backwards, gently pulling on the collar of his shirt.

"So?" Ralph edged into his seat and nudged her, raising his voice above the trumpet's call. "What have you done to Dom?"

Lucy smiled down into her glass, secretly claiming the credit. She had done what a man would have done: seen something she wanted and taken it. "Done?" she asked.

"He's mooching about on his own." Ralph nodded in the direction of the bar.

"Ignoring each other in public's all part of his masterplan." Then, wrinkling her nose, she betrayed her perfectly convincing lie.

Ralph raised his eyebrows. "I thought as much."

"Did he tell you?" Her voice a whisper.

"Not a thing." He sounded offended.

The fact that Dominic had been discreet was good, wasn't it? And yet... Sex was something significant. Surely it – and, more specifically, *she* – should have been worthy of at least a mention?

"Are *you* going to tell me?"

The last thing Lucy wanted was for Ralph to think she'd 'given in', or whatever it was that girls who succumbed to Dominic's charms usually did. "It was up to me. I decided to get it out of the way."

"O-K." Ralph separated the syllables but his expression was unreadable. She worried that he was upset. What if it didn't work out with Dominic? If the tiffs were real, where would that leave them? Ralph was Dominic's friend, not hers.

"So is it?" he prompted.

"Is it what?"

"Was it a one-off never-to-be-repeated event?"

If the first time had been a practice run, the second had been a collision. Lucy found she could recall details simply by closing her eyes. Slowly, deliberately, she shrugged.

"You little minx! It's *already* more than once!"

"I need something to take my mind off the stage fright."

"There's no need to sound apologetic." Ralph slapped the table and hooted. "This is *great*. I mean the three of us, all being friends."

She felt as if she was breathing for the first time in a few minutes. "You don't mind?"

"You never know, you might be the girl to tame him."

Lucy glanced over her shoulder, confused to find Dominic looking straight at her, his smile almost shy. The idea of a tame Dominic Marchmont didn't appeal. Lucy liked him challenging, flirtatious. In fact, she wondered how sex worked without these things. How did ordinary people navigate their way into bedrooms? She couldn't imagine that her parents had ever left a trail of clothes, not even in the early days when her mother's ambitions had led her to a man with all the ideas. "Forget it." She turned back to Ralph. "We both know he's not boyfriend material." She shrugged. "*I'm* not even sure I want to go steady."

"Really?" Ralph said, a challenge accompanied by folded arms.

"Really," Lucy replied.

"Then it's just possible he's met his match."

CHAPTER TWENTY-EIGHT

2014

"Knock, knock."

Lucy looked up from her screen to see Ralph backing into her office, carrying a loaded tray. "It can't be lunchtime already," she said. Natural light had flooded the room, reflecting off its putty-coloured walls. She was struck anew, her study couldn't have been more different from her father's, with its wood-panelled walls and heavy mahogany desk. *I have lived the life I wanted.* The first truly positive thought to come to her for a while.

"Just coffee. I thought you might fancy a break."

It would be a good day for sitting on the patio. They could both do with the fresh air. Lucy sat back into her chair and placed her cool fingertips on the lids of her closed eyes, nudging her glasses onto the ridge her nose. The contrast of cold on warm skin was bliss. The heels of her hands moulded to the shape of her chin.

"Tired?"

"No, no." If Lucy ever felt tired, it was the possibility of discovering something spine-tinglingly wonderful that kept her going. "In fact, I've been reading the most extraordinary thing. A memoir in verse." Lucy had been exchanging emails with a young author, Colleen Mills, who was soon to publish. Today, Lucy had felt envy – Mills's writing was the real thing: raw, rare and precious. Lucy suspected it had been born out of a simple desire to write, that certain something that is lost once the hope of being published is planted. "I'm trying to think of a few words to do it justice. But it's as complete a work as I've read for a long time. What can *I* add?"

"You've just answered your own question." Ralph slid the tray onto one corner of her desk and unloaded it: a cafetière, an oversized bone china cup and saucer, a small jug of warm frothed milk. Then he produced a Manila file that had been tucked under his arm.

"What's that? A stowaway?"

"Ammunition." He flipped the folder open and pulled from it a thick wad of paper, then used the empty coffee tray as an old-fashioned in-tray.

Lucy raised her eyebrows. The absence of desktop clutter might create the impression that she was *less* busy than she used to be, but Ralph knew the reality. Her inbox was bombarded daily. Would she like to judge a competition? Contribute an introduction for a new anthology? Read at the Aldeburgh Festival? Attend a dinner at the Royal Society of Literature, at which she would be awarded a C. Lit.? Attack came from all angles, leaving little creative thinking-time. Only yesterday, having agreed to join a blockade at Faslane nuclear bomb base, Lucy had received the agenda for a compulsory training day. *Blockaders will be advised on safe use of 'lock-ons', climbing gear, superglue and paint to make it as difficult as possible for specialist police cutting-teams to free them.* How many other seventy-six-year-olds were forced to endure this sort of thing?

Until two months ago, Dominic's regime had dictated when work did and didn't happen. She'd had no option but to turn down the majority of requests. Ralph had urged her to carry on saying no, but word had leaked that she was available. Grateful, briefly, to have a focus, Lucy was now feeling the push and pull of being at everyone's beck and call. Ralph wouldn't add to her workload unless this were important.

She rotated the top few sheets so that they were facing her, pushed her spectacles down her nose. *Forgotten victims.* Damn it! Whichever part of her varifocals she looked through produced a blur.

"You need to get your eyes tested."

"I need to clean my glasses." She rubbed at the lenses with the cotton hem of her favourite old Breton top.

Her husband feigned impatience. "Give them here."

Lucy surrendered happily. It was his turn to take the role of parent and she, the disobedient child.

Ralph moved over to the French windows where he held her spectacles – thick white frames, retro styling – up to the light. "I'm surprised you can see through these at all." He fished in a pocket, hooked a black lens-cleaning cloth and a vial of something. A little burst on each lens, the smell of chemicals, fresh, not unpleasant. Then he massaged each lens in turn.

"It's this foundation," Lucy explained. "More of it ends up on my glasses than it does on my face."

After thirty seconds or so, Ralph inspected his progress and repeated the exercise. "That's why I keep giving you cloths." Lucy smiled inwardly at this small telling off.

Satisfied at last, Ralph returned the glasses to Lucy. She slotted them into place as if trying out a new pair. "Much better, thank you." She turned her attention to the paperwork: *Forgotten victims of Britain's Nuclear Tests.*

"As far as I can see," Ralph said, changing tack in his usual easy manner, "this hasn't had anywhere *near* the coverage it deserves recently."

"It's not *new* news," Lucy sighed. "Just old news that refuses to go away."

"No matter how much the Ministry of Defence would like it to!"

As he pressed down on the plunger of the cafetière, Lucy had the impression that Ralph was treading carefully. She studied his face as he studiously avoided hers, pouring the coffee.

At last he spoke. "It hasn't escaped my attention that you've been very down recently."

Little point in protesting. "I think it's fair to say we both have," she said gently. That very morning Lucy had woken with the terrible certainty that Dominic was in pain and missing them both desperately. It had never before occurred to her that the dead mourn the living as well as the other way round. Now, she felt Ralph's pain too.

"I'll mend." Ralph's attempt to smile made his sadness all the more transparent. He had looked ashen and bloodshot so regularly that it had stopped registering as unusual. "Don't you worry."

"But I *do* worry."

"You, on the other hand." Ralph handed Lucy her coffee, then forced a subject change with an accusing index finger. "You've always needed a good argument to pull you out of the doldrums."

She frowned. "It says here that the MoD are *still* blocking the veterans."

"As I said, a good argument."

Lucy sensed Ralph's restless energy, the way his eyes kept straying to the door. Now that she looked again, there was no second cup. "Aren't you stopping for coffee?"

"Actually, I thought I might go out."

'Going out' could mean any number of things. If Ralph thought it was Lucy's business he would say so. "Will I see you at lunchtime?"

"Dinner." He paused, one hand on the door handle. "You'll remember to eat, won't you?"

"Stop fussing. Go and do your thing."

"There's soup in the fridge. Don't forget."

She heard the metallic scrape of keys and the bump of something heavier, then turned to the stack of papers. "Right. Let's see what you've been up to."

While Dominic, Ralph and Lucy had marched to Aldermaston – fifty-six years earlier – *not* talking about atomic weapons, servicemen were being shipped to a remote island to take part in a special mission. Many were Second World War veterans, but the younger among them – only four or five years younger than Ralph and Dominic – were on National Service.

For one eighteen-year-old sapper in the Royal Engineers, it was the furthest he'd ever strayed from home. In truth, before joining up, he'd rarely ventured outside Devon. Perhaps into Cornwall, sometimes as far as the Dorset coastline. But the name 'Christmas Island' was reassuring. He imagined stockings hanging from the mantelpiece, chestnuts roasting. Except that this place turned out to be hotter than the hottest day at Whitsand Bay; a place of palm trees, lagoons and white sandy beaches. For Lucy, the word 'island' held a special meaning. She had spent years imagining somewhere like this. Now she took a yellow highlighter and marked these conflicting images. She sipped her soon-to-be-forgotten coffee and set the cup back in its saucer. The locals were fishermen; their nearest neighbours Californians, three thousand miles away.

For the first three months, the sapper helped with construction. The thousands engaged in Britain's thermonuclear test programme needed to be housed, fed, watered; twenty-two thousand in all, about ten thousand at any given time. Stripped to his waist in the midday sun, the sapper worked on a cookhouse and a refrigeration plant, mess facilities, shower blocks, latrines, a chapel and a beach cinema – rows of wooden planks and a projector screen. He joked that he was nut-brown with a skinny white arse. Since night-time temperatures rarely dropped below seventy-five degrees, there was no need for bunkhouses. Men slept in tents under mosquito nets.

Briefings were held in the run-down to the first test. Blackboards and pointers. By witnessing Britain's largest ever nuclear test, they would help keep their country safe. All they had to do was stand on the beach and observe. At the signal, they were to turn away and cover their eyes with their hands. (The pointer moved across a series of diagrams.) Any questions?

Eight years old when the war ended, the sapper had no comprehension of the scale of the devastation at Hiroshima and Nagasaki. But the older servicemen had been in the Philippines in 1955.

Whatever you do, don't look directly at the blast.

Like the instruction for a solar eclipse. Detonation was to take place twenty-five miles away – the distance between Okehampton and Plymouth. It didn't sound unreasonable. Not like being on the front line. The sapper only began to worry when he came across one man who was scribbling away.

Writing home? he asked.

I'm writing my will, came the reply. You might want to do the same, lad.

A little spooked, the sapper laughed, What, me? I've little to leave and no one to leave it to.

On the day of the first test, each man was issued with a pair of white cotton overalls; white, to deflect the light from the explosion.

Are you sure these aren't decorators' overalls? they joked as they zipped themselves into them.

Down on the beach, the sapper's main concern was the heat. Unbearable inside his overalls, he felt faint.

"This could be a live run. Cover your eyes."

All around him, men fell to their knees and began to pray. They seemed to know something he didn't. Now he felt both sick *and* faint. What's a mushroom cloud, anyway?

The bomb was dropped from a Valiant bomber (XD825) piloted by Squadron Leader Bob Bates, who would have seen the lobster claw shape of Christmas Island from his cockpit.

"The bomb has left the aircraft. Five, four, three, two, one."

It detonated fifty-three seconds after release, only 245 yards off target, a very acceptable margin. *Acceptable to whom*, Lucy thought.

"You may now turn round and face the burst."

Just looking at the photographs of the white flash, Lucy felt the strain on her eyes. What must it have been like to be there?

The sapper watched, and it was like nothing he'd ever seen before or hoped to see again. Awe-inspiring but, at the same time, hellish. There was a fireball at the base of the explosion, bright yellows, orange and red. Ripples emanated outwards, deadly. A gushing column of water sucked upwards from the sea. And the cloud – if it could be called that – was a volcano of ash and steam, miles high and so dense it appeared to be solid. Imagine the damage that thing could do on land!

Lucy didn't need to imagine. Over the years she'd picked through articles about Hiroshima, the facts didn't become any less shocking.

To the young sapper standing on the beach, twenty-five miles seemed like nothing. He'd once cycled from Okehampton to Plymouth to see the tall ships. Skirting the length of Dartmoor had taken just over an hour. As he sifted through fragments of memory – the hedgerows, a hawk hovering above, the mane of a pony – he became aware that something fierce and terrible was heading his way. With no instructions to move, he shifted his weight from foot to foot as if preparing to field a cricket ball. What felt like a gale slapped hard against him. He staggered and fell. Behind him, tents were torn apart. The cookhouse collapsed as if it were made of playing cards.

Christ, the things that man can do.

Strip off your overalls. That's right. Throw them on top of the pile.

The sapper was left in desert fatigues. Meanwhile, clouds fit for Judgement Day had gathered overhead. Thunder rumbled, then the rain began. Liquid hailstones, big as a shilling, dark as peat. Worse than Singapore during rainy season, his older colleagues quipped, their khakis mud-splattered. Out of the confusion, men wearing padded white suits came running. Hoods covered heads, large black industrial goggles covered faces. They were shouting, voices muffled through thick material.

What's that they're saying? The military men shrugged at one another.

I think they said we should get under cover.

Even inside the tents, the men in padded suits didn't take down their hoods. They remained zipped up.

Later: I've got a rather unpleasant job for you, I'm afraid, sapper. A bit of clearing up.

Right, sir?

The wildlife hasn't come out of it so well. The birds. Well, you'll see for yourself. They need putting out of their misery. A pickaxe handle should do the job. Good man.

He was propelled through the tent flaps by a double slap on the back.

A stench of scorched feathers hit him. What he saw was like some Old Testament plague. Still airborne, the birds were flying blind, eyes burnt out.

Lucy slid her cup away. Freshly ground coffee had always reminded her of the Soho years. Now the smell repulsed her. She'd read Hershey's account of how men's eyes had melted in the blast. Loath to admit it, she knew that the image of the cormorants would stay with her long after the image of the sapper had faded. She highlighted the entire paragraph.

There was a madness to the scene, men leaping and plucking cormorants from the sky. Aiming pickaxe handles at birds already strewn about in the mud. The sapper was a country boy. Of course he'd killed birds before, but not like this. A mess of feathers and gore.

Shovel them up, sapper. Put your back into it.

The things a man can do.

Still, it wasn't like being on the front line.

What about the fish, sir?

The fish?

Washed up on the beach, sir, hundreds of them. We can't leave them there to rot.

I don't see why the locals should get them all. Take some for yourselves. Make a change from the usual tinned rubbish.

Thank you, sir. Shame there's no chips.

Three days later, his face, neck, hands and chest were blistered, and his eyes wouldn't stop streaming. Queueing outside the medical officer's tent, men compared notes: stomach pains, headaches and vomiting. Mid-afternoon, the sapper went back to ask after a friend. His body was lying on a camp bed under a single white sheet. Dead.

Lucy knew it was all too easy to become desensitised. She paused, sat back in her seat. A moment to acknowledge a death.

Elsewhere, on another beach of white sand and palm trees, an RAF mechanic heard the words, "Right lads, this is it." He turned, crouched, covered his closed eyes with his hands. *Like playing hide-and-seek, but with none of the temptation to peek,* Lucy thought. When the flash went off, he could see his veins, his skin tissue, his bones, and through it all, diamond white, like a second sun. Searing heat built inside him, until he imagined it could only end when he burst into flames.

How could you prepare for the unimaginable? All that way from home, in a time of peace. Lucy found that *she* had covered her mouth.

Then, just as he could bear no more, the ferocity went out of the light and, with it, the heat and the terror. The mechanic stood on shaking legs to observe the mushroom cloud, but he could add nothing to the descriptions others gave. For the next day or so, every time he blinked, he could see an X-ray of his own hands.

Lucy remembered so clearly Dominic's skeletal hands. She turned another page.

Piloting the skies, a hand-picked crew had been tasked with gathering samples from the mushroom cloud. Christ, it was like going into the valley of death, but with zero visibility. All you could do was kiss your St Christopher and steer straight ahead, ignoring the needle on the radiation dose meter. *Think of your one-year-old daughter back at home.* But the pilots came out of the cloud changed. Men who suffered mood-swings and migraines; who would hold their heads in their hands and cry, "What's happening to my head?" and "I don't know if I can take this any more."

Some chose not to.

Placing the sheet of paper upside down on top of the second pile she'd created, Lucy rested her head in her hands, closed her eyes. The insides of her eyelids turned from ruby red to orange, but she couldn't help imagining they were white; couldn't help imagining the sight of her own bones.

She wasn't halfway through. Page after page, the accounts went on. Witness statements, letters of reassurance written to sweethearts and wives, later used by the MoD against their authors, letters written to MPs years after the event, medical reports, coroners' reports. How long had it taken Ralph to compile this stuff?

An idea was taking shape and form. An idea about what Dominic's legacy should be. She shook her head, trying to dislodge it.

After the first test, the servicemen were keen to leave the island, but most would witness four more tests. Driven to the beach, there was no longer any pretence. No more cotton overalls, they watched the explosions wearing shirts and shorts. And then it was back to Britain, to familiar green fields, the everyday, the beloveds. GPs were flummoxed by mystery spasms, fainting, infertility, unusual cancers. Lucy knew how men were when they went to the doctors. These men were proud and dignified. Determined to leave memories of Christmas Island behind, they didn't mention they were ever there. What would be the point?

Easier to gather data on those for whom leaving wasn't an option. For the islanders, the legacy of nuclear testing became apparent by the mid-sixties. At that time, Lucy reflected, Dominic Marchmont, *enfant terrible,* was a household name. He roused tempers, goaded, lacerated. But it was Ralph, whose surname was unknown even to those who admired his work (some of it hung here, on the reflective walls of Lucy's study), who was raking in the money. There was rather less money in writing reviews, even ones that raised whirlwinds.

It took time for the medics to join the dots, dots that made no discernible shape to begin with.

O'Neill: We now turn to the question of the height of the 28 April bomb. What height would you say the device was detonated at?

Stewart: It went off at eight hundred feet.

O'Neill: An official government report puts the height at eighty-nine thousand feet. What's your reaction to that?

Stewart: That's wrong. It was much, much lower. Definitely under one thousand feet.

While other countries compensated their servicemen,

the UK spent millions on defence lawyers. There was insufficient proof of causation. Then, when sufficient numbers of servicemen were rounded up, the MoD argued that legal action was time-barred. How, they asked, can a trial be fair when the majority of witnesses for the defence are dead? Mr Justice Foskett responded in no uncertain terms: "Given that the tests involved experimentation, they were likely to have been as well, if not better, documented than almost any other significant event in UK history."

But not accurately, Lucy reflected.

In January 2009, the veterans won their first victory. The Court of Appeal gave the go-ahead for their class action. Lucy toasted them with champagne. After that, the men who called themselves 'ghosts' had fallen off her radar. Time had been eaten up with Dominic's long drawn-out deterioration (there was nothing instant about his death). Now fewer in number, the ghosts had yet to have their day in court. Many wouldn't live to hear the outcome, and Lucy sensed this was exactly what the MoD wanted.

There was something she had never told anyone. Her best-loved atomic poem, Boom! People had thought how clever she was to break off mid-sentence. As if the world had come to an abrupt end. But that was the mirror other people held up. Lucy hadn't known how to finish what she'd assumed was the last verse. Now, fifty years later, she had a better idea how the story ended.

If estimates were correct, the legacy of Britain's nuclear tests would go on for twenty generations: leukaemia, cancer, premature deaths, fifty per cent more stillbirths and miscarriages than the norm, a new raft of hereditary diseases, congenital deformities, thirty-nine per cent of children born to servicemen and ex-servicemen with serious medical conditions compared with the national average of two point five per cent. Nuclear testing in the fifties was now proven to have made the most significant contribution to climate change. Fallout had been dug deep from the ice in Greenland. And, of course, the damage was irreversible.

Finish the poem, Lucy told herself. *Then present it in such a way that it's impossible to ignore.*

"Knock, knock," Ralph said, his hip bumping the door open. "I've brought you the soup you were supposed to have for lunch." He slid the tray onto the corner of the desk. There were two deep bowls, a good bottle of Gavi and two wine glasses.

"I lost track of time." Lucy widened her eyes, while he sidled the piles of paperwork together to make room.

"So I see." Ralph took a seat, and placed one bowl in front of her, a napkin at its side. There were traces of soil underneath her husband's neat fingernails.

"Been gardening?" she asked.

Ralph inspected his hands and laughed. "Rumbled again!" He sat down with a groan. "I went to see Dom. There were a few things I've been meaning to say to him. It would have been rude not to take flowers."

Lucy left a gap to see if more would be volunteered, but that seemed to be it. "Easier to get a word in edgeways these days," she said.

He made a throaty noise and poured the wine, leaving Lucy to ponder. The 'few things' might be unfinished business or the accumulation of everyday minutiae.

"I like to keep it looking cared for." There was a twitch at the corner of his mouth.

So this was a regular thing. She had put off visiting the memorial garden, dreading seeing the date of Dominic's death carved in granite. The finality of it. "I'm not brave enough to go on my own." She took up her glass and cradled its bowl. "Perhaps I could come with you next time."

Ralph responded with a crooked smile. He raised his glass halfway towards his lips, then remembered. "And what about you? How did you get on?"

No need to confess she'd found it heavy going. Ralph knew precisely what he'd given her. "I have a feeling I know what Dominic expects me to do about the honours thing."

"Which is what?"

"It's a platform, that's all. You didn't put this little lot together on your own, did you? He had a hand in it."

Ralph blinked at her, open-mouthed.

"It's alright. I know you had nothing to do with the nomination. I could see it came as a surprise to you."

"In that case, guilty as charged." Ralph bowed his head. "If we'd been born a couple of years earlier, we could have been there... We both dodged that bullet. As it was, I got to drive tanks across Salisbury Plain. No great shakes. Not like these men." He nodded at Lucy's notes. "I can see you've made a start."

"The makings of an open letter." Lucy's habit was to begin each sentence on a new line, a hangover from her pre-punctuation days. That's why Pamela had assumed she intended to write poetry. These days, people indulged her letter-writing style as an eccentricity.

Ralph's hand was gentle as he laid it on hers. "Eat first." Once satisfied that she was spooning soup into her mouth, he turned the letter around.

"At the moment it's really more of a thought process."

"Shhh. Let it speak for itself." He silently absorbed its content while spooning soup into his own mouth.

I will not debate what the greatest atrocity of the Second World War was.

Can we begin by agreeing to agree that targeting civilians is intrinsically wrong and constitutes a violation of human rights?

Then, can we agree that the indiscriminate murder of sixty thousand civilians at Hiroshima, with no proof that they were directly involved in the hostilities, was one of them?

He looked up. "Sixty thousand? I thought it was eighty."

"Twenty thousand of the dead were soldiers who were based in the city."

Can we agree that the decision of the Japanese to suppress news of the atrocity and to abandon the survivors to their fate was another?

Can we also agree that the decision of the American scientists to observe and not treat was another?

And if we can agree those things without too many arguments, save for those designed to justify atomic warfare, can we not agree that the continued testing of nuclear weapons is the greatest atrocity of peacetime?

And given that the results of radiation sickness were already known, can we not see that Britain's continued refusal to compensate its armed forces for injury, pain and suffering caused both as direct and indirect results of participation in those tests is equal to the actions and omissions of the Japanese and American governments?

"I wouldn't tweak it too much," he said. "What now?"

"One of the nationals. Then, I'll use whatever replies I get as material to add a final verse to Boom!"

"A collaboration?"

"Something like that."

"Social media. Send it to the right people and it will go viral."

CHAPTER TWENTY-NINE

1959

Lucy made an ill-advised dive onto the bed. A notepad lay open, turned to a crisp lined page. Raising herself up on her elbows, she mirrored Dominic's position. She wore the shirt he'd arrived home in an hour earlier. It was unbuttoned and she had nothing on underneath. "So tell me, Mr Marchmont." A post-coital smile curled her lips. "Exactly how does stage two of your masterplan work?"

Several of Dominic's more flattering write-ups of Lucy's performances had been published. Already, the manager at the club had noticed a change in the composition of his audiences. More and more people were coming to hear her read. The jazz was becoming secondary. "And since your fans also seem to enjoy a drink…" He was keen, he told her, to host a regular poetry evening. "If you know anyone else who might be interested."

Actually, Lucy could think of several possibilities. "I'll give it some thought," she said, not wanting to sound too keen. By now, she also had a weekly slot at The Macabre Coffee Bar. It had a different vibe: tables shaped like coffins, everything lit by candles and Bohemian Johnny looking like an extra from a Hammer Horror movie. She'd been inspired to experiment with make-up and 'theatricality'. Once, she'd pretended to be a statue, coming to life when it was her turn to take the floor.

Others, too, were sitting up and paying attention. Among those who introduced themselves at the bar was the editor of one of the 'little' magazines that had published several of her poems. Lucy accepted the offer of a drink and tried not to gush. Yes, of course she intended to submit more of her work.

Ralph's reaction had been that she should invite publishers to her readings. It was time she had her own collection. "They're probably drowning in paperwork, but if they see you have an audience..." He shrugged in his unassuming way.

"Come here," she'd said, planting a kiss on his cheek.

Groundwork was paying off. When the club's manager asked if she'd had any more thoughts about organising a poetry night (this time it was 'organising'), Lucy suggested he double her usual fee. She was gobsmacked when he said, "Done." After achieving so much in so short a space of time, Lucy was willing to go along with the next stage of Dominic's masterplan. "I suppose it's time for the first unflattering write-up," she said.

"Not unflattering, strange girl. 'Subject to interpretation' is what we're aiming for."

She rubbed one bare foot against the arch of its twin. Dominic's rules seemed to be subject to his whims. All the time they were at home in the Soho flat, it was fine for her to be known as his girl. Apparently, it was also fine for him to act as her agent at the coffee houses and clubs. Among their close circle or at private parties, Dominic happily draped an arm around her shoulder. But when they were out and about he might suddenly withdraw. "Trust me," he said, but it was unsettling to find she was alone when, a moment earlier, he'd been by her side.

"So I don't actually have to flunk a performance?"

"God, no. You just need to jump down my throat."

On the one hand, Lucy was relieved (she didn't want a reputation for being unreliable), but she couldn't help herself. "Isn't that a bit... I don't know... unprofessional?"

"You're a poet. You have sensitivities the general population can't even begin to imagine. They expect a little irrational behaviour." Dominic kissed her lips briefly. This small touch made her reach for him.

"Uh, uh, uh." He rolled away. "Playtime's over."

"Then perhaps," Lucy raised one hand slowly, taking the spare biro from behind his ear with a small flourish, "you should think about wearing a few more clothes."

"I would, but I seem to have mislaid my shirt."

"So?" She tapped her bottom teeth with the biro, resigned to being serious. "Have you decided on your line of attack?"

"I thought I'd lead with something strong, but later in the piece I'll slip in a sentence. Perhaps your preoccupation with metaphors."

Lucy was taken aback: "I don't have a preoccupation with metaphors."

"Hah!" He began to scribble furiously. "I've obviously struck a chord – which suggests you'll argue convincingly that I know nothing about poetry."

Though loath to admit it, after very little coaching, Dominic had succeeded in sounding as if he might just know what he was talking about. Of course, it had been impossible to get him to take poetry as seriously as she would have liked. "I can get away with murder – so long as it's entertaining." And he'd reeled off several quotes, memorised word for word. "'No poetry can be truly great unless it falls in the gap between subject and object, self and other'. 'Poetry is essentially a political act, like voting.'"

"Said in that tone of voice, of course they sound idiotic!" Dominic's arrogance infuriated Lucy in more ways than she could pin down, but when they sparked off each other her attraction to him grew. And as for his words, there was an authority about them.

His vision was as clear as it had been that day on the top deck of the bus. "Your fans will feel completely justified in jumping to your defence," he went on.

There was a danger. He was one of those clever journalists Pamela had warned her about. When Dominic expressed an opinion, readers translated it as fact. "You think they'll do that?"

"Act as if I've attacked you and they will. We want as many people to jump on board as possible."

"So it won't just be the two of us arguing with each other?"

"I never saw this as a two-way correspondence. The more the merrier."

"Won't that be awkward for you? With the newspaper, I mean." She traced the contour of his bicep, feeling the slight give of warm flesh as she followed the path of a vein. Dominic had surprisingly soft skin.

Freeze the frame right there.

Pause and take stock.

This was the moment Lucy would look back on as the divide.

Ralph would have captured it using his Rolleiflex, holding it at waist height and looking down at its mirror system. Dominic's fingers interwoven in the sweep of his fringe. His long, lean frame (some would say too thin). The bony ridge of his spine. The way his feet overhung the mattress. And, lying on her front beside him, Lucy, her boyish hair skew-whiff, looking less like a poet who insisted on being taken seriously. The hem of Dominic's white shirt skimmed the curve of her buttocks. Her legs were bent at the knees, feet raised in the air, ankles crossed. Everything up to this point had been dizziness, giddiness, liberation. When she lay next to Dominic at night she would find herself contemplating the back of his neck while he slept, obsessing about the very thing she insisted she didn't want. Not just a creative collaboration, but a partnership of another kind...

"No!" He brushed her concern aside. "All the newspapers care about is the number of readers, and if they see an increase..."

Surprised to hear him sounding so scathing, Lucy didn't see it coming. "Why did you choose journalism if you don't approve?"

"It wasn't my first choice, believe me."

"Really?" Lucy took a moment to consider this. "What was?"

"Art."

Strange. She'd been sharing her flat with an artist but had never seen any of his work. Ralph's photography was very much in evidence. Lucy had an arrangement to borrow a neighbour's bathroom because she'd lost count of the number of times that Ralph was using theirs as a darkroom when she needed it. Even when it was available, she might find herself brushing her teeth in a red glow, or else there would be prints pegged to the clothes line over the bath. "Art," she heard herself repeat stupidly. "I just assumed..."

"Fine art. Except that they didn't think mine was particularly fine."

Greedy to hear everything there was to know, Lucy missed the warning signs, the sharpening of the syllables. She turned her face towards him. "What happened?"

"If it's all the same to you, I don't want to talk about it."

Thinking Dominic could be persuaded, she rolled onto her back. "But –"

"We've had sex and you've made it quite clear that you're not in the mood for work, so..." The mattress bounced as he launched himself upwards, notebook in hand, pages hanging open.

Dazed where only moments earlier she'd been dazzled, Lucy laughed. "All I did was ask a question."

With a wide arc of his arm and without a backward glance, Dominic snatched a pair of discarded jeans. Empty denim legs trailed on the carpet on his way out of the door.

A second mirthless syllable caught in Lucy's throat. *Sex and work. Is that all you think we're about?* She stopped herself from shouting after him – Ralph might be in. Pulling the two halves of the shirt together, Lucy began buttoning furiously, but with a change of heart, tore the sleeves from her arms. Reducing everything to sex and work was cruel – and Dominic wasn't the sort to apologise. Lucy picked an abandoned biro from the folds of the sheet. "He doesn't want to talk about it." She rolled the pen hard between her fingers and thumb. The pain moved from side to side and felt good.

What Lucy needed was air. She dressed quickly. The living room was empty. Dominic must have shut himself in what was known as 'the boys' room'. Without making a conscious decision where she was heading, Lucy set out. She dismissed the idea of going to Maison Bertaux. If she ran into Pamela, her friend would extract the truth. Imagine the conversation, Pamela expressing sympathy but reminding, "If a relationship has to be a secret…"

"It's not as if either of us is married," Lucy would protest. "Anyway, it's temporary." But the more Lucy pleaded Dominic's case, the less confidence she felt. The novelty of lying and hiding had worn off. It no longer felt like the freedom of playing truant. And when she saw how Ralph had no choice but to lie about and hide his relationships, it didn't seem *right*.

She skirted the crowd outside the 2i's. Students, tapping their feet and jiving to the music that spilled through the open cellar doors, tucking into treats bought from Camisa's deli. Not in the mood for aimless wandering, the coffee bar seemed as good a destination as any. She was embarrassed to find Ralph leaning on the counter, smelling of freshly ground coffee and French cigarettes. "I hope we didn't drive you out of the flat."

"Bust up?"

Lucy shrugged. She had sworn to herself that she would not involve him.

"Well, don't worry on my account. I've been trying out a new camera lens. I was about to head for home, unless..."

"Actually, if you don't mind, a little company would be good."

They sat. Lucy placed a brown sugar lump in her inch of black coffee. She let it sit like a desert island until it looked soft enough to crush with her spoon. "What's all this about Dominic and art?"

Ralph's hand, holding a Pyrex espresso cup, froze.

It was unfair to hijack him, and Lucy knew it. She shook her head. "Don't answer if you don't want to."

"It's not that. I'm surprised he told you."

"The bare minimum." She took an extended drag of her cigarette, as if that could alter the facts. "Then he stormed out."

"It was oil painting." Ralph wet his lips, clearly still in two minds. "Look, if you're going to understand Dom at all, then you probably need to know this. And the fact that he's told you this much..." He placed his cup in its saucer, a careful movement.

Surprised by the suggestion that, rather than push her away, Dominic had taken her into his confidence, Lucy listened. Dominic's subject at college had been art, but art being subjective, the more experimental work he'd submitted wasn't appreciated. He'd never tasted failure before. The golden grammar school boy, he'd been academic, athletic *and* artistic. With all the options at his disposal, his father had railed, "Art's a hobby, not a job!"

"We've all been there."

"I haven't. Mind you, I was never academic."

"What made Mr Marchmont change his mind? Assuming he changed his mind."

"Our headmaster performed a small miracle. Said he'd rarely seen a student with so much promise. But once he was at college Dom stopped playing it safe and, well…" Ralph let a shrug speak for itself.

"Exactly how experimental was his work?"

"Pretty crazy. I remember him saying they were either going to love it or hate it."

"He set out to shock?"

"He honestly thought they'd be able to see the technique even if they hated the end result." Ralph's smile was a grimace. "The thing was, it was chronically bad timing. The examiners happened to be the most conservative bunch they'd had for years."

Lucy blew a steady stream of smoke. "They failed him?"

"Worse." Ralph ground his cigarette stub into the ashtray. He was still grinding as he said, "They thought his paintings were obscene. He was sent down."

"So he gave *up?*" Lucy shook her head in exasperation.

Another shrug. "He didn't want to risk baring his soul again. Not if it was going to be ripped out of him."

Lucy shot back: "What does he think you and I do every day?"

Ralph smiled sadly. "It wasn't only art he quit. It was his entire circle."

"Except you," Lucy pointed out.

"Ah, but I knew him long before art college. He couldn't get rid of me. Besides, I'm not a threat. Dominic doesn't put photography in the same category as art. And, I don't know… I suppose it's less personal."

"No, I won't have that." Lucy was surprised how much it

upset her to hear Ralph talk his talent down. "Speaking as one of your subjects, I know how exactly much work goes into what you do."

"Well, you're very kin–"

"You see, you say things like that and I want to grab hold of your shoulders and shake you!" Ralph looked startled. "I'm *not* being kind. You have a gift."

After a minute passed in silence he kicked her under the table. "Thank you. I like that you get cross on my behalf."

"You're very welcome." Somehow, this gave Lucy permission to go back to her original subject. "So, Dominic became a critic. What was that about? Revenge?"

"Maybe, if he reviewed art. I think *you're* probably safe."

"And he doesn't paint at all? Not even for pleasure?"

"All association with pleasure has gone."

She shook her head and spoke to the table top. "I can't imagine not writing. Even if I never get to publish my own collection."

"You will."

"Even if it receives the most damning reviews…"

Ralph's eyes were kind and concerned. *Imagine having had him as a big brother.* "Are you finding Dom hard work?"

"Do you have to ask?" Lucy laughed, even as the sex and work comment wormed its way back to the front of her mind. "I never know where I stand. When he's in a good mood, he is *the* most charming, but when he's in a bad mood, he's…" She clenched both hands and gritted her teeth. "You could never live with someone like that." Infuriatingly, hot angry tears sprang to her eyes.

Ralph's hand was there, on her forearm. Between two of his fingers was a tissue. "You're forgetting. We both do."

Not this temporary arrangement. Something… more. "You know what I mean." Lucy quickly dabbed at her eyes and blew her nose.

"I do. I know exactly what you mean."

Staring miserably into her empty espresso cup, Lucy wondered. If Ralph really knew, how could he bear living in such close quarters with Dominic? And with the two of them carrying on in the same flat! Was it always better to have something rather than nothing, when the something was so painful?

But that's exactly what you're doing, it occurred to her. And she knew she would go on doing it. They both would.

CHAPTER THIRTY

1961

The doorbell, ten fifteen. Late by some people's standards but, in the Soho flat, stragglers were welcomed long gone midnight, even on a Tuesday. None of its occupants had nine o'clock starts to get up for. The flat might be the last port of call on an evening that had already seen several changes of venue, or it might be the warm-up to a night of parties and excess. Sprawled on the floor next to Lucy, a couple were laughing to the point where they seemed incapable of moving.

"I'll get that." She hauled herself onto her knees and then up to her feet. "It will probably be for me. I'm a published poet, you know." Largely ignored, she made a deep bow.

"Soon to be," Dominic corrected her. "The ink on the contract's not dry yet."

"I'm a *soon to be* published poet." Her limbs were liquid. She upended a champagne bottle an inch above her mouth to check it was empty. "Let's hope whoever it is has brought more fizz." One hand trailing the wall, she floated away from the strains of *Only the Lonely*, humming as she navigated the dog-leg turn. It would be a friend or an acquaintance, or a friend or acquaintance of a friend or acquaintance. Dominic was incapable of passing anyone in the street if they looked remotely interesting (or if they bore a passing resemblance to Michael White). He would issue invitations to complete strangers.

Lucy grasped the door handle and swung backwards. "Freddie." Her smile became a gargoyle's grimace. The walls loomed. "What brings you to these parts?" Lines torn from an abandoned script.

Her brother had no place being in her new life. Lucy had left the house on the square while Freddie was away in Europe. Since their father's spectacular confession, no reason to write or phone had presented itself. Birthdays and Christmases passed by unacknowledged. She knew that, despite his efforts to dodge it, there had been National Service, and then university. Headlines aside, she had no idea what was going on in her brother's life.

Dressed in a suit, an overcoat and shiny brogues, he radiated tension. "The downstairs door was unlocked," he said in a way that implied she'd been careless.

"It saves running up and down the stairs."

"That music's a bit loud, isn't it?" Freddie pushed past into the hall, head low. Lucy had no need to see his expression to know there would be no pretence at pleasantries. He must have been sent to check up on her; to make sure she wasn't *wasting her time*. Well, she wasn't. The publishing contract would prove it.

"Come in!" she said, closing the door. *Christ!* Lucy sprang forward. *What would Freddie make of the scene in the living room?* From the way he came to a sharp halt, Lucy understood that her brother had expected a single female flatmate, reading a paperback, drinking camomile tea. She craned over his shoulder and, for an instant, thought how ridiculous it was for a man to wear a beret indoors.

This sense was only fleeting. Ramshackle it might have

been but, to Lucy, the scene spoke of domesticity. People doing whatever it was they did (reading, drumming, giving head massages, the laughing couple inhaling from the drawtube of a bong). In years to come, Lucy would be surprised how many of Dominic's 'discoveries' cropped up in newspaper columns, accompanied by Ralph's photographs of the Soho scene. Some of them found the levels of fame Dominic had imagined for himself.

Dominic, who had no trouble working in chaos, lay on the floor scribbling away, a spare pen behind his ear. Next to him an ashtray was sitting on top of a rush mat, an attempt to protect the carpet from burns. If Freddie looked closely enough, a second abandoned cigarette would provide a clue of where Lucy had been positioned. Only a minute ago, they had been doing their usual two-man show. Dominic, writing something provocative about her soon-to-be-published collection. Lucy, letting a swift retort fly. An image of Freddie's hand felling her house of cards came to Lucy. He could expose them. *Not only do they know each other, but they're flatmates. In fact, if I read the situation correctly...* Freddie was more than capable of reducing her long-awaited success to something sordid and tatty. *Calm down. Freddie won't have a clue who Dominic is.* There was a more immediate concern, which had nothing to do with poetry.

She prayed that Freddie hadn't already singled out Ralph from among the half dozen stragglers. He was lying on the sofa, his head resting in the lap of his latest boyfriend – 'the one', he had confided to Lucy.

A jobbing actor, Emil was an exquisite blend of Thai and French parentage. In fact, the boyfriend would disappear before the week was out, neither he nor Ralph's wallet ever to be seen again. The pair were passing what was quite obviously a spliff between them, fingertips to fingertips. Ralph's chin was tipped upwards. Perhaps he was imagining how he would photograph Emil's perfect jawline. Visualising the end result was part of Ralph's creative process. If he could see it, he could capture it. This was Dominic's one complaint about his friend. "He never looks at a person without working out how he's going to light them."

Astonished how blind Dominic could be, Lucy had said, "It's not as if you ever look at someone without wondering how to describe them."

"None of us is ever really off duty, not even you, strange girl."

She strode across to the record player, intending to silence Roy Orbison, but the arm slipped through her hand. A startling scratching noise jerked heads towards her. "Sorry," Lucy winced. "Everybody, this is my brother."

Everybody murmured a greeting. The intellectual drifters and artistic misfits, drawn together by ideas or opportunity. Freddie wouldn't attempt to understand that this life was the antidote to Lucy's childhood. She imagined defending her choices but, glancing around the room, something troubled her – and not for the first time. Fed up with being told they'd never had it so good, the stragglers tended to know what they were *against*, but not what they were *for*.

"Freddie, this is my flatmate, Dominic." Lucy indicated his patch of the floor, where there was at least a suggestion of enterprise.

Already on hands and knees, Dominic stretched out a steady hand. "Pleasure," he said, his fringe falling into his eyes. "About time we met one of Lucy's family."

She felt relieved at how reluctant Freddie's shake was; how keen he was to pull his hand away.

She glanced back to the sofa. Ralph was finally reacting. Having swivelled round, he allowed momentum to carry him to sitting.

"And over there is my other flatmate, Ralph." Ralph was

dressed in three-quarter length trousers. Lucy had an idea what Freddie would think about the three inches of pale leg above his brown suede desert boots. She'd heard his views on 'pansies'.

"What happened to Evelyn?" Freddie asked, softly enough so that the others might not hear.

"She found herself a husband." Close up, her brother's face had a grotesque quality.

"Something you might want to think about."

You sanctimonious shit. Why had she ever looked up to her brother? Probably because, to a begrudged child, his destructive streak was attention of sorts. But Dominic had said he couldn't marry her. His timing had been remarkable. He'd said it immediately after he told her he loved her. Giving with one hand, taking away with the other. Lucy aimed a saccharine smile at her brother. "Perhaps you'll pick one out for me."

Lucy saw Ralph from the corner of her eye. Having pushed himself to his feet, he looked in danger of toppling. His voice was drowsy and slow as he asked, "Can I get you a drink of anything, Freddie?" but he thought better of it and rocked back down.

"Actually, what I need is a quiet word with my sister. Is there somewhere…?" Freddie looked about.

Freddie would like nothing better than to get as far as the bedrooms so that he could report back on who shared with whom. Lucy relied on her allowance. In fact, though they didn't know it, all three flatmates did. The boys were under the impression that their pooled earnings covered the rent and bills. "I'll grab my coat." She wanted him out of the flat. "We'll catch last orders at the pub on the corner if we're quick."

"Look, you don't need to do that," Dominic volunteered. "We'll make ourselves scarce. Time, please, ladies and gentlemen. You too." He began to make sweeping motions in the direction of the door. Bare feet stepped reluctantly into sandals. Then he said pointedly, "Oh, for God's sake, Ralph, you're such a lightweight. Grab his other arm, Emil."

Between them, the two men hustled Ralph into the hall, bouncing off walls as they navigated the turn. The sound of laughter welcoming them out onto the landing was cut off by the slam of the door.

Her brother looked uncomfortably stiff. "You'd better sit down," he said.

Perching on the edge of the sofa, Lucy braced herself for a lecture.

Freddie clapped one hand over his mouth. She was about to comment on his wedding ring when he dragged the hand downwards. "He's dead. Massive heart attack." Freddie remoulded the shape of his chin.

There was no need to ask who. Waiting for the news to permeate, Lucy pinpointed all the ways in which Freddie resembled her father: his height, his mannerisms, his superiority. It was curious that no particular emotion followed. *I need facts,* she thought to herself. "When was this?"

"Last night."

Monday, then. "So he was in Birmingham." Part girl, part machine, her beating heart seemed to have calcified. *If I can't feel,* Lucy asked herself, *how will I be able to write?*

"That's right. *She* called me."

Lucy didn't want to know what the 'other woman' had been doing with Freddie's telephone number. "And Mother? Did she call her?"

"No. She asked if I wouldn't mind telling her. She didn't think Mother should be alone when she heard the news."

"How did she react?" Lucy asked her brother.

"Five minutes of hysterics. I suspect the tears were over the question of what's to be done, rather than grief."

"And what *is* to be done?" she asked.

"Mother wants him back. Birmingham say they're going to put up a fight, so she's set her solicitor on them."

Lucy's theory was that Mother's motivation for refusing a divorce was spite. She hadn't wanted Moira Lee to achieve the degree of respectability marriage would have enabled. Instead, she'd been outed as a home-breaker, her sons bastards. And, of course, Mother had dangled the threat of withdrawing her capital, ensuring Father's Birmingham family hadn't enjoyed any sense of security. While Mother… well, she'd had the sympathy, the legitimate children and her old family connections to fall back on. And now, a solicitor would decide where to bury a man and under what name. "Only in our family!" Lucy sighed.

"So it seems."

Curious to hear how her brother was faring, Lucy asked, "What about you?"

He had buried his hands in his pockets as soon as he started talking and had yet to remove them. "Everything will be dredged up again – just as people were beginning to forget. Except last time I was still at university. Now I have a reputation to worry about."

No hint of sorrow, just an instinct for self-preservation. And still no mention of a wife. "Can't you just deny everything?" It was a tactic Lucy had employed with some success.

"What, with Mother intent on telling her story?" He cast a bitter nod in Lucy's direction. "You're lucky. You escaped all the attention by cutting your hair."

"You'll have to grow yours," she said, though it was laughable to imagine Freddie with anything other than a short back and sides.

"Anyway, there was a message. Mother wants to know if we'll stand together on this."

At last, a small shudder. "She's asking if I'll attend the funeral?"

"That's the gist, yes."

"The media will be out in force."

A mirthless laugh. "I imagine they will!"

"Then, no. I don't think so."

"To be honest, that's exactly what I thought you'd say."

A flurry of second thoughts; if Lucy didn't consider herself to be part of the family, Mother might withdraw her allowance. "What was your answer?"

"As I see it, we're damned if we do and damned if we don't." He headed out into the hall.

"You're going?" As she pushed herself out of her seat, Lucy's feet seemed determined to trip each other up. "The first time I've seen you in over two years and that's it?"

He stopped in front of the door, lowered his head and turned. "He's dead. What else is there to say?"

A pinch and a punch for the first of the month and no returns forever.

"I thought you might at least share your news."

He looked at her blankly; shook his head. "That was the news."

She nodded towards his ring finger. A congratulatory smile. "I see you're married."

He toyed briefly with the gold band. "Some of us still go in for conventional morality," he said as he worked the door handle.

Slam!

Stunned, Lucy leaned back against the wall. She bent her knees, slid downwards. "Morality?" she said to the empty hall, incensed that Freddie had claimed the moral high ground even as he walked away. "Don't make the mistake of confusing convention with morality."

Lucy retrieved phrases from their conversation, examining each in turn. "Who's this 'us' you mention?" Freddie had remained on their parents' side of the divide. What example of marriage did he think they'd offered?

She pictured a sister-in-law. Not *her* sister-in-law. She had as little to do with this woman as she did her half-brothers. Sweet, submissive, and in a year's time, cheated on. Imagine bumping into Barney on a street corner, in a basement club, in the post office queue. Lucy's nostrils flared. He would never look her in the eye and ask, "What else is there to say?" He would have shared his news and then he would have asked for hers and she would have told him, *My collection's going to be published.* And he would have said, *My mother would have been proud of you.*

Enough time passed for Lucy to wonder if she'd dreamt the visitation, but why then would she be crumpled in a corner in the hall of an empty flat? She shivered, hugged herself. The boys must have negotiated a lock-in with the local's landlord, or perhaps they'd been invited to a party. Brandy, that was the thing. Brandy and then bed. She pushed herself to her feet.

Much later, Dominic clambered in behind her. Chilled feet, the smell of toothpaste and a waft of stale smoke. "What time is it?"

"Late." He wrapped himself around her. "I didn't mean to wake you. How was your brother?"

"Unchanged, unfortunately."

"I'm glad you said that. I wasn't convinced the two of you are related."

"Sadly, it's true."

"What did he have to say that was so urgent?"

It was time for the truth. "Remember the uncle I told you about?" She turned, slotted herself under the warm niche of his arm.

"Having his Cake and Eating it?"

She winced, remembering how she'd caught Dominic trading on the headline to secure a booking for her at the 2i's coffee bar.

"Is there nothing you wouldn't use?" she'd demanded.

With this memory replaying itself, Lucy found that she couldn't come clean. Far easier – safer – to maintain a pretence. Besides, what had been a pretence was now her truth. "He's dead. Massive heart attack."

She felt Dominic's torso stiffen. "Shit! Just like that?"

"Just like that. Boom." Her voice was flat, but in her mind there was a great explosion.

"How old was he?"

"He would have just turned fifty, I suppose." She was ten years old, standing outside Father's study, wanting beyond anything else to be invited in to sit quietly in the leather armchair and watch him fill his pipe. She was seventeen years old, storming out of the door.

"I'm sorry." Dominic pulled her closer still. "You were fond of him weren't you?"

Why didn't he love me? Why weren't we enough for him? "I was, yes."

Two days later, late evening, the doorbell rang again.

"I'll get it." Ralph, who had been staring intently at his feet, hoisted himself off the sofa. "I expect it's Emil."

Dominic and Lucy looked at each other. All three had been to the Odeon in Leicester Square to see *Victim*, the first film that dared use the word 'homosexual'. Ralph, whose choice it had been, had been subdued on the walk home. For him, fear of blackmail was a constant. He might return home to find 'Ralph is queer' painted on the front door. An incriminating photograph might easily find its way to an employer.

"Bad choice," Lucy said, her voice low.

"But it's good that it's being written about," Dominic said, his voice low. "People will start to see that it's–"

Lucy's diaphragm tightened. Ralph was standing in the living room doorway, with two uniformed policemen behind him. Something else her father had done must have been unearthed.

As Ralph stood aside to let them pass, one of the policemen nodded at Lucy. "Miss Forrester." His tone was dry. She was about to be outed as a liar.

Dominic ground his cigarette into the ashtray and pushed himself to his feet. "You're a fan?" He smiled as if addressing an autograph hunter.

"Let's just say we've had the pleasure of Miss Forrester's company at the station before."

Heat rose to Lucy's neck.

Ralph cut in. "Now, hang on –"

But the officer was undeterred. "What was it you said to me outside the American Embassy? 'I have a habit of getting myself into situations'. Let's hope this doesn't turn out to be one of those occasions."

Relieved, still she met his gaze with effort. So far, she'd succeeded in keeping the various parts of her life entirely separate. Just as Dominic had with his art.

"So who lives here?" he asked.

Crossing his arms over his chest, Ralph stepped in. "The three of us."

It was almost a relief when one of the officers said, "You don't mind if we take a look around, do you?"

"Not at all," said Dominic. "If you don't mind me asking what you're looking for."

"Drugs."

It was a drugs raid! The three exchanged glances. A new report by Sir Russell Brain had concluded that drug-use in the UK was low. Out to prove him wrong, the drugs squad raided the homes of members of famous bands. They must have been judged 'bohemian' enough to receive an unannounced visit.

Small quantities of cannabis and LSD were found in a wooden chest with a gemstone inlay, supposedly Indian. It wasn't hidden away, but sat squarely on a side table. Buoyed on by their success, and despite Dominic's assurance that it was all there, the three stood by and watched as various packets of rice and lentils were split open in the kitchen (Lucy would use this in her poem, Arrest), and Ralph's darkroom was taken apart.

"Nothing else, gov."

Ralph's fists were clenched by his sides.

"As I told you." Dominic stepped in, for once fine-tuned to his friend's feelings.

Though LSD was legal, the cannabis was reason enough to haul them off to the local station.

The policeman who recognised Lucy angled his head to ask, "Will you be bringing your own handcuffs?"

Lucy's fingerprints and photographs were already on file. Processed more quickly than the others, she used her phone call to contact the only solicitor she knew – her mother's. Some hours later, he arrived with news that they were all free to go but that, since Lucy obviously had enough money for what he called non-essentials, her allowance would be halved.

"She's taken the fact that you're grieving into account."

Lucy's head jerked up. *Was that blackmail?* But he made no demands and so she humbled herself. "That's more generous than I expected."

Back at home, reluctant to end the celebratory mood, Lucy knew there was no way around it. "We need to talk," she said, speaking to the carpet.

"This sounds ominous," Dominic said, bounding onto the sofa.

"The thing is, I haven't been completely honest with you."

"I had no idea we'd been living with a criminal, for starters."

She closed her eyes briefly and shook her head. "I've been arrested at a few protests, that's all."

"But that's priceless! It will make brilliant publicity."

Ralph, seeing Lucy's obvious fluster, said, "Just shut up, Dom, and let her speak."

Gratitude didn't make what Lucy had to say any easier. "It's about the rent for this place. What we earn between us doesn't cover half of it."

There was a moment's respite while the news sunk in.

"Then how have you managed it all this time?" asked Ralph.

"My allowance." Lucy shrugged, embarrassed and guilty to admit that her family had money.

Dominic blinked, astonished. "You've been funding us?"

"My mother has. After tonight, she won't be nearly so generous."

Ralph seemed unsurprised. "I thought we'd been lucky to stumble across the only London landlord who fancies himself a patron of the arts. How far short will we be?"

The figure Lucy mentioned produced whistles.

"So it's bar work and busking for all of us." The way Dominic rubbed his hands together irritated Lucy. Now that their ordeal was over, he seemed flattered that they'd been targeted by the drugs squad. It meant he'd arrived.

Lucy had her own theory: either Emil or Freddie had tipped them off.

"And Ralph, you'll be back to lurking outside stage doors, waiting to pounce on unfortunate luvvies."

"Actually, there's another option." Ralph rolled back the sleeve of his jumper to reveal a telephone number inked on the inside of his wrist. "Remember those guys in the cells?" And to Lucy, who had been separated in the women's quarters, he explained, "Ours wasn't the only flat to be raided tonight."

While Lucy had the women's cell to herself, Ralph and Dominic had found themselves with company.

"Well, this is cosy, isn't it?" Dominic had said as the door clanged shut behind them.

"Like the changing rooms at the municipal baths," one of the men said. "Shove up, boys."

Dominic kept the pair he sat next to entertained with tall tales but, on hearing that their cellmates were band members who'd just signed their first major deal, Ralph paid close attention. Told by the lead singer that their publicity photographs looked staged, he'd sympathised: "You need someone who'll come along for the ride." And Ralph knew exactly how to blend in. Observing others gave him an acute sense of occasion. He always dressed the part. "They almost need to be part of the band."

"Right. You've hit the nail on the head."

"That's the kind of work I do. I'm a freelance photographer."

"You should give me a call. Here, I'd better give you my number."

"No pen."

"Don't let me leave without writing it down."

Dominic made a shrugging movement with his mouth. "Potential?"

Typically reserved, Ralph said, "Could be interesting. It would mean having to skip a few of your readings, Lucy."

Later, with Dominic gone to bed, sitting next to Ralph on the sofa, Lucy noticed that he was holding his wrist, just above the place where the number was written. "So?" she asked and raised her eyebrows.

He shook his head, smiled sadly. "Straight as they come."

"What, then?"

"It's just that he was so casual, the way he went about it. We were at the front desk – I was leaning on it – and he asked the officer if he could borrow a pen. He had the lid end between his front teeth, grabbed hold of my arm, pulled back the sleeve and wrote. Just wrote his telephone number on the inside of my wrist. I could never have done that. I'll never be able to do that. Not openly."

Lucy put her hand on top of his.

She heard the air leave his nostrils. "And the thing is, he wouldn't have done it if he'd known I'm gay. He'd have kept his distance."

Lucy knew better than to say anything. This was Ralph's life.

"All the time, the lid was still in his mouth."

She remembered what Dominic had said. It *was* good that film scripts were being written. "Things will change."

"Not in my lifetime, they won't."

Ten days afterwards, Freddie phoned, explaining in his economical manner that Mother's solicitor had sorted out the whole thing. Birmingham weren't going to get a look-in. Struck by a pang of compassion, Lucy tracked down a Birmingham church that was hosting a memorial service for a Mr Lionel Lee. It wasn't difficult.

She slipped into the back pew. There they were: an unexceptional-looking woman and three very ordinary boys. Moira wasn't a brassy blonde. The boys weren't younger versions of Freddie. There was no coffin to fix their grief on – Mother had seen to that – just a floral tribute. It sat astride a box so that anyone present might imagine an empty coffin. The vicar spoke movingly about a stranger who was warm, caring and community-minded; whose life had touched the lives of many. Here was a family united by loss; black attire for her, grey suits and black ties for them, the mother's arm draped around the youngest boy's shoulders, bowed heads and, when they turned to leave, ashen faces. Afterwards, the unveiling of a brass plaque in the memorial garden. More than they could afford, Lucy suspected. Beloved husband – so she did call him 'husband' – and father of Mark, Matthew and Luke. (Had they been building up to a John?) The family was claiming a stake, stating publicly, *To hell with whatever you've read in the papers, this was real and it was ours.*

Lucy was the imposter; the intruder. Whatever they had, it had never been hers.

CHAPTER THIRTY-ONE

1962

"*It was illegal!*"

Lucy woke, disorientated. It was Pamela's voice that had dragged her from sleep. For a moment, she was back at the house on the square.

"*Where is she?*"

"Nice of you to pay us a visit so early in the day," came Dominic's reply.

Lucy pushed herself to sitting. She was in her own bedroom. Dominic's half of the bed was empty, the cover thrown back. His underwear was on the floor; his dressing gown was hanging on the back of the door. "In here!" she shouted. "Won't be a minute."

The door opened and in walked Pamela. She perched on the end of the bed and twisted around. "It was illegal," she repeated, her eyes shining.

There was no need to ask what. The question they had demanded an answer to was this: was the US's deployment of atomic bombs in Japan legal? "I'm just letting it sink in," Lucy said, swinging her legs onto the floor.

Pamela threw herself backward and lay staring at the ceiling. "Eight and a half years." She sighed loudly.

"Let's celebrate. We'll go out to breakfast." Lucy pulled a jumper over the top of her head. "By the way, did Dominic answer the door?"

"I think so." Pamela lay there, basking.

"You *think so?*"

"Yes, it was Dominic."

"Was he... wearing anything?"

"Can't remember."

"It won't be recognised under international law," Dominic said. He had joined them at Maison Bertaux, reasoning that he might as well have breakfast now that he was awake.

"It's not just the finding." Pamela pointed with her tea-spoon. "Several crucial issues have been examined in detail –"

"*Great* detail," Lucy cut in.

"– in a court of law. Was it military necessity?"

"Was the harm to civilians and civilian property proportionate?"

"Exactly. And was the environmental damage excessive in relation to the military advantage anticipated?" Pamela and Lucy clinked their espresso cups together.

In 1953 – the same year Lucy started at boarding school – five private individuals had brought an action against the Japanese government on the grounds that it had waived their rights for compensation. Initially, the Japanese Prime Minister had called on the Red Cross to denounce the US for committing a crime under international law. But then he'd sniffed a possibility. Might it be possible to get the US to drop its demands to try Japanese war criminals if he offered not to make any complaints about the use of the nuclear weapons? Yes, it might.

An agonising eight and a half years later, it had finally been ruled that the use of the atomic bomb *was* illegal – but the five were told that they had no claim for compensation under international law.

Dominic tore a strip off his second croissant. "So it was a complete waste of time."

Pamela was taken aback. "Of course it wasn't! Not everything's about personal gain." Her expression as she looked across the table at Lucy was accusatory. How could Lucy want to be with someone who thought this way?

"Stop trying to be provocative, Dominic," she said quietly.

"I'm asking questions, that's all."

"That wasn't a question."

"Alright." He slapped his hands on the table. "Then tell me how it *changes* anything."

"It gives us *hope*," Pamela said, infusing the word with magical qualities. "The first real hope we've had. *Finally*, people are starting to see sense."

CHAPTER THIRTY-TWO

1963 – 65

Fearful that whatever she said would reek of jealousy, Lucy had bitten her tongue. Even now, what remained of the sugar-and-spice child thought she might be accused of sulking, and so her manner was jokey. "Were you out with one of your leggy blondes last night?" she asked.

"If you don't trust me, strange girl, the whole plan falls apart."

Trust. So there it was.

At the beginning, Lucy had convinced herself that, because the decision to move the relationship from one thing to another had been hers, she was in control. She hadn't realised that the rules of Dominic's masterplan would take a sideways shift. Apparently, not being seen together in public wasn't enough. They now had to be seen with *other* people. 'To throw people off the scent'. In practice, *they* meant Dominic. Lately, Lucy had taken to leaving the club immediately after her reading. Why put herself through the agony of witnessing him leaning in close, while she imagined him deploying the line, *Wait! You haven't heard what I can do for you yet.*

"I can't possibly be carrying on with *all* of them." Dominic reached for her, but she pulled up the sheets and covered her shoulders.

"And that's supposed to be reassuring?"

"Besides," he insisted, combing his fingers through his hair. "I've gone out of my way to flirt with women who aren't my type."

"Oh?" she managed to say. The women he picked were all of a certain type; painful reminders of Lucy's boarding school years. "And what is your type?"

He rolled onto his side. "Five foot two, pixie haircut, extraordinary brown eyes, lips made to be kissed."

She was in no mood to be teased; certainly not to be kissed. "Slight limp?" She twisted her face away.

"How else can I convince you?" He sank back on his pillow.

"Choose the ugly ones." She stared at the ceiling, angry with herself as well as him. Her gaze was drawn to a cobweb which spanned the coving. She had only small things – her voice, her words, her intrigue – to hold Dominic's attention. Lucy was losing him. She could feel it.

"What? And fool no one?"

Ralph nodded in Dominic's direction. "Here comes tonight's cover story."

"Don't tell me," she said. "A glamorous blonde." On an ordinary weekday, without theatrical make-up and clever lighting, the person who stared back at Lucy from her mirror looked nothing like Ralph's magnificent poet activist who was splashed across the pages of newspapers and magazines. When they met her in the flesh, people were often underwhelmed. But not tonight. Tonight, in the grand dining hall of the University of London, she intended to parade herself. "Where are they sitting?"

"Three o'clock."

"Two can play at that game." Lucy made as if to stand. She wore as sleek a dress as she had ever worn (sleek being a word that attached itself more naturally to her queenly mother). It was all spaghetti straps, backless, floor-sweeping. Her large eyes were heavily kohled. It was her first award nomination. She was adamant that no one would look her up and down, search for something to say and finally settle on, 'I thought you'd be taller'.

"Be careful." Two words, a hand on her arm, but Ralph's eyes said more. Things Lucy didn't want to acknowledge.

"I'm always careful." She didn't feel careful. A glass and a half of champagne and already she felt reckless.

Ralph made a second, softer appeal. "Don't mistake the kind of person you'd like to be for the kind of person you are."

Colour rose to Lucy's cheeks and neck. Strange, how gentle words had the power to sting. Confused, she settled back into her seat. "Dominic's my critic. You're my photographer. How come my critic and I can't be seen together, but you and I can?"

A waiter had arrived, starched white linen draped over his forearm. "More champagne, madam?"

Lucy shoved her glass towards him. As he topped it up, foam rushed to the rim of the glass, wave-like, and then receded. She wondered if the waiter thought they were married; that he'd interrupted an argument. "Thank you," she said, hoping he could detect her unspoken apology.

"And for you, sir?" There was something military in the way the waiter's heels came together, his curt bow.

While the waiter poured Ralph's drink, Lucy recognised a famous poet (old guard, condescending) as he entered the room, people nodding enthusiastically, hanging on his every word. One fawning waiter – a student, she suspected – showed him to his seat, two tables away. The poet eyed the place cards to either side of him with disgust, prompting the waiter to swap them with others.

Ralph sipped from his full glass and turned to Lucy. "I know the official answer." He had a knack of picking up conversations exactly where they left off, no matter how long the interruption.

"Which is what?"

"No one knows what I look like, but even if they did, who worries about a photographer being biased?"

Dolled up as she was tonight, Lucy was recognisable; impeccable save for the CND badge drawn on one side of her face. The thing that would ensure people put two and two together. *Yes, I am she.* Few poets ever got to be household names.

"Unless they stick their heads in gas ovens," as Dominic had pointed out.

"Is that part of your masterplan?" she'd replied.

Now she turned to Ralph. "Once, just once, it would be nice to have him sitting by my side." Lucy realised her lack of tact. "I didn't mean –"

"I know you didn't."

Ralph wore a tuxedo well. In fact, he wore everything well, but he wore a tux particularly well. "I'm so glad you're here." She blinked back tears. "I hate this type of evening."

His gaze had strayed back to three o'clock. She always detected a sadness in the way he gazed at Dom, and so Lucy knew from his neutral expression that he was studying the blonde.

"Well?" Her fingers were cold against her warm throat. "What's your verdict?"

He cocked his head. "She thinks she knows what men want, but there's nothing to choose between her and a dozen other women. She's made sure she's interchangeable."

He made it impossible not to smile. They were allies. Both wanting the unattainable, settling for scraps from the table.

She leaned towards him. "Have you ever been attracted to women?" It was the first time Lucy had asked the question. She couldn't have raised the subject a year ago. She might not be able to raise it tomorrow.

"Not Dom's clones, no. But I'm often drawn to the aesthetics of a face or a figure. I *appreciate* beauty, but take the camera away and…" He shrugged.

"No chemistry," Lucy said. It wasn't a question because there was no need to ask. Ralph had just described the essence of how she felt about *him*.

"None."

The dinner fell short of mediocre, as dinners at mass-catered events often do. It was necessary to refer to the menu cards to see what they'd been served, and still they were surprised. The red wine was undrinkable.

"I hired a tux for this."

"I bought a dress."

"Ah, but you'll get plenty of use out of that."

"What?" The champagne was taking hold. "At all the other award ceremonies?"

The woman to Ralph's left turned out to be a food critic with not inconsiderable clout. As she sketched out a review, everyone pitched in with contributions. One brave soul asserted that the red wine was drinkable once you got the hang of it. Since no one else was prepared to take the risk, he took on the challenge. Lucy began to enjoy herself. It was only when the speeches began that she remembered why she was there.

Amazed when her name was called out from the podium, Lucy froze. She had practised her gracious loser's expression in front of the mirror. She was not prepared for this.

Ralph was transformed by a look of pure joy. "Holy crap, Lucy!" He gripped the tops of her arms.

She twisted her head; there must have been a mistake.

Cheers from the table. Hands drumming on white linen. These people whose names she'd let wash over her. She steadied herself, holding Ralph's forearm. "What do I do?"

"Up you get." They both stood, clinging to each other.

Tears glistened in Ralph's eyes. "Sod Dominic. I'm glad it was me sitting next to you." He hugged her and she was shaking and couldn't work out how to let go of his arms.

"I'm going to throw up."

"No you're not," he said, his eyes holding her in a steady gaze. "Notes."

"Handbag." She opened it and retrieved them.

"Smile?" he said.

She tried to move her mouth but her face muscles refused to cooperate.

"That will have to do. Your audience awaits." He turned her towards the stage and she felt as giddy as a child playing blind man's bluff.

Tentative steps.

A pat expertly placed on one of the cheeks of her arse as she passed by the Famous Poet.

She grazed her hipbone on the back of an unoccupied chair, grabbed to steady it as it rocked.

Stepped on the hem of her dress as she made her way up the stairs to the stage.

The scratch of bristle on her cheek; a trophy placed in her hands.

Eyes narrowed against the glare of flashbulbs.

A sea of faces.

Her scribbled notes a hopeless blur, she made a ball of them and threw it backwards over her shoulder.

Laughter.

And as she spoke, Dominic there in the periphery of her vision. His knowing look. His claim on her. His precious bloody secret intact.

Ralph's head was thrown back. He whooped as if howling at the moon and turned to clink glasses with anyone who was prepared to clink a glass.

It was an ugly little trophy but Lucy couldn't help stealing glances at it, even as she referenced Dominic's review in her acceptance speech. (Was that someone collecting money? Had people placed bets on her?)

Later, walking up a narrow flock-wallpapered corridor, returning from the ladies, the Famous Poet cornered her.

"Very well deserved, young lady."

The ghost of the slap on her arse cheek made Lucy wary, but he would make light of it if she challenged him. *'What that? Bit of harmless fun'*. Too useful to alienate, he sat on the board of a firm of publishers ('a sleeping partner' it was rumoured he liked to whisper to young women). "Thank you," she said, regretting the dress.

He moved his arm to block her escape and Lucy's nostrils protested at the combination of stale sweat and mothballs. "You were impressive up there." Behind the compliment was an unspoken 'for a girl'. She looked for a way to slip past, or at least to move the conversation somewhere more public. "But it must help that we know your face. You'll have to let me into your secret."

"What secret's that?" She disliked the proximity of his face.

"How you grab so many inches of newspaper column, of course!" He extended one fat finger, and pulled lightly at the silver chain around her too-long neck.

As she held very still, it was an effort not to say, 'Getting arrested helps'. *Tread the path of least precariousness. Remember how the head of champagne raced to the rim of your glass and then receded.*

He dropped the chain casually, his smile thoroughly unpleasant. "I suppose it's being so photogenic," he said.

She thought he would stroke her skin as he withdrew his hand, and knew she would flinch, but he did not and she flinched anyway. She hated the Famous Poet. In particular, Lucy hated the fact that he might be right. She was good, but it couldn't be said that she was more talented than any number of undiscovered poets who lived and breathed words. The difference was that Lucy had that certain unconventional something that made people look twice. Only now was she learning not to shy away, understanding that it might be an advantage.

"That's your photographer friend I saw you with this evening, isn't it?"

A safe question. One she could respond to. "It is, yes. Ralph."

"Ralph. That's right." The Famous Poet knew exactly who she was talking about. Though embarrassed, Ralph would secretly be chuffed when she reported back. "Boyfriend?"

This was where it should be possible to point out that she wasn't up for grabs. *No but you've probably heard of my boyfriend. Dominic Marchmont, the critic?* "I'll tell Ralph that you like his photos. Now if you'll –"

The arm was a gate. "Were you at Oxford?" The Famous Poet had been professor of poetry some twenty years ago. "I knew Ursula from Oxford."

She knew how this conversation went. Not only had Lucy stolen the small ugly trophy from someone more deserving, she had jumped some imaginary queue. "No, I wasn't."

"Ah, so you're a Cambridge girl?"

Normally Lucy would offer reassurance that the natural order of things was still intact. Not tonight. "Soho, actually," she said, looking at him on the level.

His indignation, then uncertain laughter. She was joking, of course. "Just remember. It doesn't matter how clever you are, you'll never be accepted. Not while you persist with this silliness." He indicated to the CND logo, his hand hovering as if he might reach out and smudge it.

At that moment, a waitress excused herself and the Famous Poet removed his arm.

"It's been an honour meeting you," Lucy said, intending to

be overheard. "But I'm neglecting my guest."

Lucy had never expected to be accepted, but a pattern was forming. Fate would allow her to reach the finish line so long as she understood that, even as she danced sideways, with people she didn't know grabbing her hands, a commentator in his high box would make the announcement. Someone else had taken gold.

Ralph smiled up at her. "There you are."

"Take me home," she said.

Unwanted advances were only half the story. The next evening, at her regular Wednesday evening slot, dressing down in a sweater and cropped jeans, Lucy found herself an object of curiosity.

"Of course, she's not married," one gossip mused.

Back at boarding school, Lucy had imagined that her trials were tests. Here, on her own turf, she expected to be safe.

"How old did you say she was?"

A figure was mentioned. Younger than Lucy's years.

Women really were the worst, she thought. Of course, women were not *actually* worse than men. It only seemed that way because of the deliberately trodden-on heels, the left shoe that had mysteriously gone missing – and because this particular pair of gossips were the type of women she hated seeing on Dominic's arm. Predatory, leggy blondes, dressed in elegant black, prizing their own company so highly they expected drinks to be bought for them. Girls who were used to getting what they wanted, in other words. Didn't they realise she was standing right behind them?

"You'd have thought she'd want to be getting on with it."

Heads cocked for a mental assessment. It was agreed that Lucy looked impressive on stage but, actually, once she was part of a crowd…

Lucy shouted her order for a post-performance drink at

Cockney Gerald: "Whisky mac, when you've got a minute."

"Right you are, Lucy."

As she found a dry patch at the bar to lean on, the women's elbows tightened. She turned to them with a venomous smile. "Keep your pity for someone else. I've been shagging Dominic Marchmont for years."

The women went from astonished laughter – embarrassment at being found out, shock at Lucy's crude choice of words – from a poet! – to relief. Obviously, Lucy was making a joke at her own expense. The second woman wiped the corners of her eyes and said, "Oh, you're hilarious." The reaction seemed genuine, which made Lucy, conscious of her sloppy sweater, feel dowdy and straight-laced. A violent urge to slap someone rose up through her gut. Only the thought of having to own up to Dominic made Lucy go along with the laughter, earning herself the reputation of being a little unbalanced – something expected of a poet – but a good sport.

They had just made love. Lucy lay in Dominic's arms, her focus soft, not thinking of anything except the general impression of whiteness: the tented sheets, the four walls of the square room and its ceiling, the connectivity she felt with everything. She was lazy and perfect-limbed when Pamela's words came to her: *If a relationship has to be a secret, you shouldn't be in it.* For once, she felt relaxed enough to ask, "How long do we have to keep this up for?"

He pulled her closer and, burying his face in her hair, groaned. "Do you have somewhere you need to be? I was just thinking how nice it would be to lie here all afternoon."

Lucy had assumed that, because their bodies had been so perfectly tuned, Dominic would understand what she meant. "Not *this*," she said.

"Then what?"

"The creeping around. The aliases."

"I don't know, I thought it added a certain frisson. It

doesn't bother you, does it?"

Lucy stuck out a stubborn elbow, craned herself up. "Yes, since you ask, it bloody well does." Not prone to histrionics, it occurred to her, *I'm going to make a scene.*

He seemed put out. "If people see us together then our cover's blown. You know that."

"We got away with living under the same roof for *three* whole years."

"Soho's always been a good place for secrets, but people know who we are now. That's why we agreed I should move out."

Lucy closed her eyes so the sight of him wouldn't be a distraction. "Let me put it like this. At what point will we be able to walk down the street hand in hand like an ordinary couple?"

She felt him take her hand and trace a figure-of-eight on its palm, overlaying the original pattern again and again. "But we're *not* an ordinary couple." Lucy opened her eyes to his, which insisted with an irritatingly earnest quality, *And we don't want to be.*

"Why do you have to make this so difficult?"

"Difficult?"

At other times Dominic was keen to stress the differences between them. How for him the light dies, but for a poet it's always 'dies the light'. "All I want to know is when I can look forward to sitting at a table for two in a restaurant, for fuck's sake. It's not as if I'm hankering after a proposal."

"Good."

Lucy snatched her hand away. The voice inside her that objected *"Good?"* was extremely high-pitched. She thought she'd conditioned herself to absorb shocks, but somehow Dominic always managed to catch her out.

"I have to admit that, when I first met you, I didn't think this through," he said. It was only as he started unfolding her fingers one by one that Lucy realised she'd made a fist. "At that point, I would have suggested we carry on as we are until I got a regular column with one of the nationals and you'd had your first collection published."

The air left her nostrils. Was he saying that if she'd asked the same question at her publication party, or as they cracked open a celebratory bottle of champagne on the evening of Dominic's appointment, he'd have taken her hand in front of everyone and said, 'Quiet, please, I have an announcement to make'? But she'd been patient, well-behaved – what Cook used to call 'ladylike'.

"Now there's more to lose," he continued. "Our great advantage is that we don't want the same things as everybody else. There isn't this urgent rush to pin everything down and stick a label on it."

Lucy's body, so light and fluid only a quarter of an hour earlier, was now leaden. It was true, she had no desire for a white wedding. Certainly none for children. But playing the penniless bohemian and settling for stolen moments wasn't enough. Lucy had worked through her rebellious refusal to live as her parents wanted her to live. This extended dress rehearsal – what Lucy would always think of as 'treading water' – had become a bore. She had begun to feel the tug of some ancient longing, and she could only think of it as wanting her own ground beneath her feet. "It's been four years, Dominic." She did not say, 'And I'm *twenty-five*'. "Are you suggesting we carry on as we are indefinitely?" she asked.

"Not *indefinitely*, no."

Pleased that this possibility seemed equally unpalatable to Dominic, Lucy decided to experiment. She tried something she thought a woman who was good at getting what she wanted might say. "It would be quite a coup if we announced that the critic and the poet were a couple."

"The buzz would only last a week, then nothing else I write about your work will be taken seriously!"

In that moment, when his expression was almost pitying, the intensity with which Lucy disliked Dominic shocked her. "Perhaps it's time you stopped writing about me," she told him. "There are other poets, other musicians. And there *are* other reviewers who write about *my* work." Some of them far more complimentary than Dominic was.

He seemed capable of ignoring her point. "It's not that your publicity angle isn't a good one. I just think it needs to be managed carefully."

Lucy resented having their relationship described in clinical terms. She threw back the covers and swung her legs over the side of the bed. "You be sure to let me know when you've figured it out. Because I'm not planning on living this way forever."

"Is that an ultimatum?"

His voice, drowsy and amused, made Lucy fear that she might appear ridiculous if she demanded on being taken seriously. Easier to be coy. "Ultimatums usually come with dates attached." Standing there naked, Lucy thought, *Perhaps I should give you an ultimatum.* But the truth was, she would be afraid the date would pass. Better to end this thing herself than to become Plath's Mad Girl. She could not stand by and watch – no, *participate in* – the slow decay of something that had been as close to perfection as she'd dared imagine. It would have helped if, at this moment, Dominic didn't look quite so beautiful. "But if I get a better offer, I may have to consider it." She didn't care that her voice was bitter.

Whatever those women thought, Lucy wasn't short of offers, and not all of them from lecherous old poets. Only one interested her.

"If he doesn't marry you by the time I turn thirty, I will!"

He'd even said it in front of Dominic, who warned, "Watch out, she'll hold you to that!" as if she was one of those women who was out to ensnare.

She decided to hand him one final opportunity. "Do you still love me, Dominic?" It was what she always wanted to know. Was this thing real? Would the end be worth holding out for?

"What's brought this on?"

"It's a simple question." Her voice emerged, flinty. Rather that than sound needy. "Yes or no."

He sprawled across the bed like a starfish, his face upside down, hair hanging down. "You must know that my interest in you has never been purely proprietorial."

"Even now..." Best to walk away. She had her answer.

"Lucy! Lucy, come back!" But he was laughing.

It's the worst feeling, she thought as she tried to stop her lips from trembling, *when your heart belongs to someone who doesn't want it.* Because, loath to admit it, she'd been aware of the truth for some time. If her heart sang for Dominic, it was Ralph she was in tune with.

CHAPTER THIRTY-THREE

1965

It had been said jokingly at first, but then one evening Ralph came home wanting to develop the day's photographs. He found Lucy hiding in the bathroom in tears.

"What's he done now?"

She'd been telling herself that enough was enough. Jealousy was tearing her apart. Sooner or later, despite Dominic's insistence that she was paranoid, it was inevitable that one of his flirtations would escalate. The one blonde with something slightly different about her. And yet Lucy was afraid to end it. She shook her head.

Instead of interpreting this as *leave me alone*, Ralph perched on the side of the bath. "He's a fucking idiot, he really is!" He wrapped an arm around her shoulder and she could feel him shaking. She rather liked knowing he had taken her side. "I can see that I really *will* have to marry you."

She laughed and wiped her eyes. Here was a man she'd shared a bed with on any number of occasions, putting the world to rights in the early hours. They'd often joked that they were like an old married couple.

"Seriously, I mean it. You could do a lot worse."

She rolled her eyes. "Oh, I know I could."

"So it's settled. If the two of you haven't sorted this out by the time I'm thirty, then you marry me."

Lucy's smile slipped. By his own admission, Ralph wasn't brave enough to stick his head above the parapet. His parents had no idea. Unwittingly, they dropped reminders of their expectations. After all, an unmarried man over the age of thirty attracted rumours. Ralph had never cared what people thought of him, but his mother and father were small-town folk. Although he'd left their world behind, Ralph cared very much what people thought about them. And as for those rumours, Ralph had every reason to fear they would stick. Dominic, on the other hand, did not. Seen about town with his interchangeable blondes, he was very much the playboy. No one had ever spat in his face and called him a pansy. He'd never known the fear of blackmail. And this contrast – the fact that, to Ralph, thirty was a great looming deadline and, to Dominic, it meant nothing – was something Lucy resented. Dominic seemed so determined to sidestep commitment that the *Having Your Cake and Eating It* headline might easily have been written for him.

Ralph's solution – it could hardly be called a proposal – was a security blanket, a delicious betrayal. It said: *You deserve better.* At first Lucy only wanted the words. A way of claiming something back, they made her feel extravagantly guilty. It was impossible, of course it was. But it was precisely that impossibility that appealed to Lucy. She remembered Dominic saying, *'But we're not an ordinary couple. And we don't want to be.'* She hadn't liked his use of those words but, applied to her relationship with Ralph, they were a far better fit.

Neither Ralph nor Lucy was single, not in the sense that other people would understand. Ralph displayed surprisingly poor judgement when it came to men, refusing to see their flaws. Lucy kept her theory about his choices to herself. And

Lucy, well, for Lucy there had only ever been Dominic.

Sex was sex; glorious, messy but most probably a temporary state of affairs. What if it was the hiding and lying that kept them both keen? Lucy had a clear idea of what Ralph meant when he said marriage. To him it was sacred. And there was no fear of taking a risk on an unknown. Since Dominic had moved to his rented room, it had been just the two of them and, with the exception of moments like these, there had been calm. Lucy also knew what marriage to Ralph would *not* mean. She wouldn't be made to feel as if she was difficult and demanding. She would never be censored or hemmed in.

Lately, their late-night conversations had turned to specifics. There was an urgency, and it was on Lucy's part. She couldn't look at Ralph without being reminded this newfound calm was temporary. He had just signed the contract for a new house. Although Lucy had often bemoaned her lack of privacy, now that living alone was to be her reality, it had lost its appeal.

"No children," she said when the question came up. They were sitting at either end of the sofa, toes touching, drinking red wine, but by no means drunk. The first time she'd ever said 'no' to anything Ralph suggested, she pulled herself up sharply; this was a life they were discussing.

"You might change your mind. The clock starts ticking later for some women than for others."

"I don't have a clock and I'm not a huge fan of families – at least, not in the conventional sense."

"But if there was an accident?"

She wondered at him in every sense of the word. Few men would be so willing to take on another man's child. "That would be different," she said. "But the other man might not be happy to give up his child."

"He wouldn't be much of a man if he was."

It didn't need to be said. The other man would be Dominic. Although if Lucy were married, all that would have to stop.

She nursed a darker fear. Already, Lucy sensed ageing in her bones. It wasn't difficult to imagine a time when she would be in need of a carer, someone nurturing. Even if he changed his mind, Dominic wasn't right for the job. Needing to be sure they were talking about something real, Lucy added, "You know, there's a possibility that I might not always be as well as I am now. I could have a relapse."

Ralph took one of her hands in both of his. "That's the deal. In sickness and in health."

All the time she was with Ralph, Lucy felt that it was right, but when Lucy woke alone, or by Dominic's side, she felt sick to her stomach. This was mutiny they were plotting. And yet she seemed to have unwittingly set a course towards it.

"Something else is bothering you, isn't it?" Ralph asked.

"Yes," she admitted. *I'm terrified.*

"How to break it to Dominic?"

She nodded.

"We'll do it together." Then he said, "I think it needs to be said. Dom loves you, Lucy." Anticipating her protest, he put one finger on her lips. "Hear me out. If, when we tell him, he says that he wants to marry you… If you think that marrying Dom will make you happy… I don't want you to hesitate. Understand?"

Lucy nodded and the finger on her lips moved with her.

"Promise?"

Lucy nodded again.

"Don't say anything." He removed the finger slowly, as if he was worried that she might startle and bolt.

In the days leading up to Ralph's thirtieth birthday, Lucy was plagued by nerves. She couldn't write, couldn't relax. *No one's forcing you into a decision,* she reminded her pale reflection.

Whatever you do will be of your own making. But wasn't that worse somehow?

Dominic caught her at her dressing table agonising over what to write in Ralph's birthday card and said, "It's just a bloody card. Look, it already says 'happy birthday' on the front." He took a pen from behind his ear and slid the card to one corner of her desk so that he could sign his name.

Lucy bristled. "Now it looks as if it's from you."

He gave a look of complete incomprehension. "You want top billing, is that it?" He took back the card and added an ampersand above his name.

With her fountain pen, she wrote 'Lucy', and blew on the ink. The card now read *Lucy & D Marchmont*. Ironic that Dominic was quite happy for her name to appear with his. *Above* his.

"What have you bought him as a present?" Lucy asked, distracted.

"The fattest cigar I could find."

"Does Ralph like cigars?"

"It's a gesture, that's all. Listen, I've got to rush. I need to hand in my copy."

"Haven't you already done that?" she asked. Dominic crammed the day before a deadline, subsisting on coffee and cigarettes. That should have been yesterday. And this morning, while Lucy visited l'Escargot to add personal touches to the table decorations – balloons, streamers and packets of sparklers – Dominic was supposed to have been handing in the results.

He checked his watch, then slapped one hand over its face. "Shit! If I don't get over there now, they'll be hammering down my front door." He stooped to brush his lips against hers. "I'll see you at the restaurant."

She was left staring at the door, wondering *What the hell did you do from yesterday afternoon until now?* Something told her she might not like the answer.

Instead, she knelt by the side of her bed to retrieve the extravagant book she had bought Ralph from its hiding place. She removed the tissue packaging to reveal the title: *The Decisive Moment*. Shipped all the way from New York. Though photography wasn't her area, Pamela knew someone in the trade who'd been able to source a first edition, and it was pristine. Lucy opened it to the page where the photographer's signature appeared. *Henri Cartier-Bresson*. She smiled at the thought of the thrill Ralph would feel when he saw it. Then she took the old map of Soho she'd stumbled upon in Stanfords, and set about wrapping the book, carefully positioning it so that all of the familiar street names would be uppermost. She spent a good half-hour cutting little arrows out of red paper (from a picture of a dress in a magazine) and taping them in place, so that they pointed to the flat, the pub that they'd called their local, the club where she'd first read. A record of their joint history.

"I'm getting married." The words spilled out of her. They were lying together in bed, a moment when it felt wrong to withhold this kind of information.

Dominic rolled onto his back. One hand was on his forehead. "Who's the lucky man?"

"How many do you think I had to choose from?"

"Ralph?"

"I would have thought that was obvious."

"But you're... I mean, he's –" Dominic fell silent. Lucy had an idea that adding to what she'd said would only make matters worse. "Probably a good idea," he said finally and did not sound disapproving.

"Really?" Lucy had expected sarcasm or anger. She had *wanted* those things.

"Well, you can't seem to get the idea out of your head and he's a steady kind of chap. Especially now he's minted."

Dominic *knew* that money wasn't a consideration. It was putting down roots that appealed. She approached her next question tentatively. "I was wondering if you might give me away?"

"What about your brother?"

Lucy recoiled: "What *about* my brother?" She had hoped Dominic would have interpreted her request as an indication that he was still going to be an important fixture in her life.

"Well, I imagine Ralph will want me to be his best man. I can't be in two places at once."

"I don't see why not. You'll be like Danny Kaye in *Wonder Man*." Nerves were making her spout nonsense. "I'm sorry. That wasn't funny." Lucy offered him another opportunity to object. "So you don't feel weird about it?"

"It depends how far you go with the vows." Lucy opened her mouth, but before she could pick up on this, Dominic reached for his packet of cigarettes. "I mean, if neither of you has the slightest intention of keeping them, doesn't that make a sham of the whole thing?"

"That's nobody's business but ours."

"So nothing changes between us?"

Lucy had assumed everything would change. Now she rested her chin on his chest, afraid to look him in the eye. Was it hypocritical of her to want everything? "It doesn't have to. Unless the thought of sleeping with your best friend's wife bothers you."

"It would if my best friend wasn't Ralph."

Later, on arriving home, Lucy sheepishly admitted to Ralph that she'd told Dominic.

"I know," he said, carrying on with dinner preparations. "He telephoned."

"The two of you are alright, are you?"

"You haven't driven a wedge between us, if that's what you're afraid of. Are *you* alright?"

Her smile was fake. Didn't men challenge each other to duels for less? "I have to say, he took it better than I expected."

"But he didn't ask…? I mean, he didn't say…?"

It was Lucy's turn to put her finger on Ralph's lips. "He said he thought I was doing the right thing. But he *did* ask if we could carry on as we were." She took her finger away slowly.

"I'd always imagined you would."

Lucy found that it was possible to feel both comforted and confused. "Did you?"

"Of course." He cupped her cheeks with both hands and kissed her forehead, "We both know who and what we are. We'll make it work."

Dominic gave her away, whispering a litany of complaints. "This has to be the most bizarre scenario ever. The man sleeping with the bride gives her away. To his gay best friend!"

"You can always object," she said, smiling the fixed smile of brides, at the same time feeling numb. "They give you the opportunity."

He straightened his tie, cleared his throat. "Do I just interrupt the registrar?"

"I think it's polite to wait for the *If any person here present* bit."

Part of her dreaded he might do it. The other part longed for it. But Dominic didn't create a scene. He didn't say that it wasn't too late for her. They didn't sit on the back seat of an ordinary bus crammed with ordinary people, contemplating what had just happened. The fear, the occasional grin, the hopeful gaze. Instead, Dominic placed her hand in Ralph's.

The moment she looked at Ralph, Lucy felt absolute clarity. He wasn't the route to happiness. He was happiness itself. And, as Lucy looked at him, she wished there was some way of communicating this to him.

Afterwards, they decamped to Dean Street where they

drank champagne and ate a fish supper in the Yorkminster, agreeing they'd never tasted finer chips. Ralph, who disliked being in front of the camera, remembered that he should probably send his parents evidence that he'd 'done the deed', as Dominic put it.

No one thumbing through the wedding album would say that Dominic looked upset. In fact, a casual observer might be forgiven for thinking he was the groom. The only person to appear mildly put out was Pamela, by then in her early forties. Sixties Britain was still backward enough to write off an intelligent independently-minded woman who led a full and active life as an 'old maid'. (Double standards meant that no one suspected *her* of being gay. She had simply been passed over.) Pamela enjoyed playing up to the 'old maid' image by looking disapproving. This was not one of those occasions. The photographer, a passing barman Ralph persuaded to set down his tower of empties, captured the moment Dominic lay across their laps, planting an elbow in Pamela's to raise himself up. He didn't give a thought about *where* he planted his elbow. It was a shame, really, that the tower of pint glasses featured so prominently in every shot. Like the Leaning Tower of Pisa.

But it didn't matter how enthusiastically Dominic threw confetti. Even while Lucy was thinking, *Finally, finally I can be myself*, things between the three began to change.

CHAPTER THIRTY-FOUR

1965

Slumped back on the sofa, Dominic perched his feet on the coffee table, pulled off his woollen hat and ruffled his hair. It was the lull between Christmas and New Year. He'd insisted Lucy stood on her own doorstep while he sang *God Rest Ye Merry Gentlemen*. The full rendition. As usual he showed no sign of feeling the cold, while Lucy clasped her hands together and shivered. Now inside, she poured two glasses of forty-year-old port. It had been her Christmas present to Ralph, but this was an emergency.

"Only two glasses?" Dominic said and sipped, humming his approval.

Lucy's back stiffened. She'd reminded Ralph to call Dominic, but he'd been preoccupied. Now she came to think about it, she couldn't remember how he *had* replied. "Didn't you know?" She planted the bottle on the sideboard and hesitated before turning. "Ralph's away at the moment."

"Honestly, he is the worst kind of host. When he invited me to stay for New Year, I assumed he'd at least be here!"

"I've been abandoned." Lucy concentrated on keeping her tone light. "For a rock and roll tour, no less."

"What is it this time?" Dominic patted the empty cushion beside him. "Out of season seaside towns?"

In fact, it was Ralph's first international booking. Afraid of not doing himself justice, he'd been doubly nervous at the thought of having to use borrowed equipment. Kneeling amid organised chaos, he ticked item after item off on a list: two camera bodies, two flashes, four lenses, numerous filters, spare lens caps, spare straps, a folding reflector, a cable bag. Lucy had only just managed to convince him that he wouldn't get darkroom chemicals through customs. No surprise that cancelling Dominic hadn't been a priority. But it wasn't in Ralph's nature to forget. And if Ralph hadn't told Dominic, that signalled a change in the balance of their relationship.

Lucy sat stiffly, her knees locked tight and angled towards him. "It was all very last minute… A photographer went down with food poisoning, Ralph agreed to fill the gap, and the next thing he knew…" she stalled.

"Don't tell me that rabble of a band *finally* have a hit single."

"No, Dominic. Ralph's in Australia. He's on tour with the Stones."

Dominic's laughter was confidently scathing. This was Ralph who never did anything without running it by him. She sat uncomfortably, waiting for reality to dawn. When it did, the laughter stopped abruptly.

Lucy gripped the stem of her glass in agony. Should she dive in with an apology or words of comfort? Neither seemed appropriate. Dominic might assume she was gloating. Better to be practical. "It's a few months' solid work." She watched helplessly as Dominic stood and moved in the direction of the sideboard. "He could hardly turn it down."

"Because you look as if you're a little short at the moment." Dominic reached for the port bottle and turned it until the vintage label was in Lucy's eyeline.

That was unnecessary. There were times when Lucy filled with self-loathing at the thought that she hadn't worked for every penny. Well, sod Dominic, because Ralph had! It was a while since he had witnessed the exhaustion on Ralph's face as he emerged from the darkroom. But Dominic always thought his own craft far harder, though his deadlines came only once a week.

As he topped up his glass, Lucy opened her mouth. Before she could protest, the ruby liquid was within half an inch of the rim. Drunk on port, Dominic could be downright unpleasant. "You've said it yourself." She felt ruffled. "You have to take the work when it's available."

After planting the bottle within easy reach, Dominic took his seat again, feigning cheer. "In that case, I shall enjoy having you all to myself."

Lucy decided to wait a moment before telling Dominic. They weren't alone. She sat facing the photograph of Jane Birkin that Ralph had hung to the left of the fireplace. It was his Christmas present to himself. He had declared that, now he had the money, he would buy the best to remind himself of 'the gold standard'.

He followed her gaze. "Is she new?"

Lucy hummed her affirmation, waiting for Dominic to comment that this was yet more evidence of their increasing fortunes.

All he said was, "She's stunning."

Doe eyes kohled, lips parted, Jane was sitting in front of the blurred arches of one of London's bridges, leaning forward on her hands. "Talk about looking the part." It was such a direct look she gave the camera, self-aware, some might say resentful. Lucy's chest rose and fell. "I asked Ralph if he thought she practises that expression in front of the mirror. He told me that Eric couldn't get her to smile."

"Oh? Why's that?"

"Apparently she thinks she looks goofy."

"Did I hear voices?" Pamela was framed in the doorway, her hair flattened on one side, suggesting she'd just woken from a nap. Jolted out of her melancholy, Lucy realised she'd lost the opportunity to warn Dominic. "How are you, Dominic? Happy Christmas. Oh, is that port and lemon you're having? What a good idea."

By now, there was no point trying to salvage the bottle. Lucy pushed herself upwards and forced a smile. "I'll find you a glass."

"Stay where you are. I can help myself."

"It's alright. Dominic's just used the last of the lemonade."

"Stop treating me like a guest. I should know my way around the kitchen by now."

Lucy gave in, tucking her legs up beside her. "Alright, then. There's another bottle in the larder."

Dominic turned round in his seat. "Why have you got to stop treating Pamela like a guest?"

Lucy lowered her voice. "Her landlord's selling up. Gave her virtually no notice. And we're not short of space, so…"

"He was a crook." Pamela strode across the room to claim the port. Lucy reminded herself that it was the season of goodwill as Pamela topped up her glass with lemonade. "I won't be taking advantage. It's just until I'm back on my feet."

"We'll see. We won't be turfing you out in a hurry."

And while Pamela and Dominic exchanged tales of dodgy London landlords, something within Lucy reached out, scanning the horizon, looking for a man with a camera. God, how she missed Ralph, her voice of reason, her sanity. He'd barely been gone a day.

She zoned back into the conversation at the point when Dominic said, "I'm trying to remember what I'm *for*."

Her hand clasped for the glass she'd been holding. Someone had removed it. She must have drifted off. A game of Scrabble had been set up on the coffee table. A cheese board, a spoon standing upright in a jar of chutney, the tattered skeleton of a bunch of grapes, a few walnut shells.

"What you stand for?" Pamela asked, quite reasonably.

"No, what I'm *for*. What my purpose is. What *function* I perform."

Warning bells sounded in Lucy's ears. She might have been able to prevent Dominic from launching into a downward spiral if she'd had the courage to stop him topping his glass up to the rim.

"Must you have a purpose?" Pamela said, exchanging a cream cracker for a Scrabble tile.

Lucy pulled her cardigan about herself. God, her limbs felt as if they were weighted. Was she coming down with something?

"Says she, patron saint of hopeless causes." There was an unpleasant slur in Dominic's voice. This was dangerous territory, but Pamela might prove herself a match for Dominic at his worst, and so Lucy pretended to go back to sleep.

"Haven't you heard? They're the only ones worth fighting for." Pamela, Lucy noted, had the ability to sound wounded while holding her own.

"What exactly have you managed to change, you and Lucy and your small disturbances?" Dominic said flatly.

Lucy felt something physical – a tug – at being brought back into the conversation. As if she was being hoisted upwards. She opened her eyes.

"We stood up to be counted," Pamela said. "We've reminded parliament that they're not representing the views of the majority. And we've let governments on the other side of the world know that we know exactly what they're doing and that we won't stand for it." She paused and gave a frustrated shake of her head. "And now you've got me on my high horse, you're going to repeat your question: What are *you* for?" Groggy as she was, Lucy was taken aback to see Pamela lean over the Scrabble board and place one of her hands on Dominic's. "We're your friends, Dominic. The people who love you. We're not making demands. We're not judging. Infuriating as you are, the truth is we wouldn't have you any other way. All we ask for is your company."

Dominic shrank backwards, apparently surprised that Pamela considered herself a friend. Not nearly as surprised as Lucy, who'd always thought Pamela disapproved of Dominic – but perhaps it was only their ongoing relationship she disapproved of.

"It's your turn." Pamela was busy shuffling her Scrabble tiles sideways. "A word would be nice."

"If what you say is true, why couldn't he face telling me?" Dominic said quietly.

There could be no doubt that he was referring to Ralph. Lucy was gripped by irrational jealousy. Something subtle had changed in the dynamic of the household. A new understanding had been forged.

When Pamela excused herself at the end of the evening, Dominic turned to Lucy and, without a prelude, asked, "Why are you so angry with *me?*"

"I'm not." Her voice betrayed the lie.

"I can *feel* it coming off you in waves. *I'm* the one who's entitled to be angry."

"Oh, I'm glad." Arms folded. "I'm glad you're so clear about that."

"There, I knew it!"

"Alright. I've never had your trust. That particular door has always been slammed in my face. I always thought you found it difficult to confide in anyone but Ralph. Until this evening, I never knew how easily you could give it away."

"You're asking *me* that?" He shook his head, apparently dumbfounded, but then shrugged whatever he was feeling aside. "I suppose I like Pamela."

"You *like* her?"

"Yes. She's direct. Anyway, is the fact that we get on such a bad thing? I thought you might be pleased."

Pleased, thought Lucy as Dominic pushed himself up and left the room, saying, "I'll sleep in Ralph's room." *Pleased*, she thought, appealing to doe-eyed Jane Birkin for sympathy.

CHAPTER THIRTY-FIVE

1973

Another evening, another black tie event, Ralph away on a two-day shoot. Lucy felt up to the job of fending for herself, the only woman among a group of the 'old guard' (white, male, late middle-age). Holding her wine glass at chest level, she made sure she was displaying the symbol of her married status. With two collections to her name, both of them award-winning, Lucy had earned the right to be here. Not that it felt like a prize. Being seen, offering support, doing the rounds was part of the literary scene, she accepted that, but Lucy could never relax in a room of writers. Their acceptance felt begrudging, as if an allowance had been made. She wondered if she *should* be there. A token female paraded as a shiny example of their 'open-door policy'.

Quizzed endlessly on various topical issues by a man who clung to her elbow, Lucy felt as if her soul was slowly suffocating. Oh, to sit and be silent for five short minutes. The ladies room developed a magnetic pull. "Would you excuse me one moment?" she said.

"Oh, of course, of course. Shall I?" The limpet nodded in the direction of her wine glass and held out his hand.

"Thank you," she said, unable to think of an excuse to

decline, though it would mean returning to the conversation she was so desperate to escape.

As she left the room, Lucy overheard one of the older poets say, "What do you think?"

"Yes. Very interesting."

"Of course, what she needs is a thoroughly good seeing to."

Breath caught in Lucy's throat. Beyond the plush velvet curtain divide, she pressed herself against the wall to hear who would stand up for her. Later, when the moment presented itself, she would discreetly thank them. To her consternation, she heard laughter and general consensus, with several volunteers.

Darkness pressed up inside her. It was always Lucy who had married the gay man. Never Ralph who had married the straight woman. She would have loved to see their faces had she marched back in and thanked them for their concern, but actually they needn't trouble themselves because she was shagging Dominic Marchmont. In all but their closest circle, their affair remained secret. Lucy was actually far less bohemian than friends assumed. Amused, she did little to correct the rumours. So long as nothing got back to Ralph's parents. Now she wished some of the more salacious whispers *had* leaked and spread among the older poets.

"All of them self-congratulatory, as if they were planning on performing a public service," she complained to Ralph on his arrival home.

"I know the type. They're the same bastards who assume I'm a danger to them." He poured her a large whisky. "So what did you do?"

Lucy's expression was one of disbelief as she said, "I marched back in and asked if whoever it was who had pulled the short straw could please get a bloody move on, because I had a cab waiting, and the meter was running."

Ralph laughed and clinked his glass against hers. "Oh, how I've missed you."

To Lucy, the moment was bittersweet. Her on/off relationship with Dominic was currently fraught after his admission that one of his flirtations had gone beyond drinks at the bar. It was only one night, and what right did Lucy have to complain? After all, she was married. It was in her power to put an end to the affair, but she'd let it drag.

"I'm sorry I wasn't there," Ralph said. "I would have beaten them up for you."

"I shouldn't need protection while I'm at work." She appreciated Ralph's sentiment, but this hadn't been an isolated incident. Just last week she had heard it said that she'd married Ralph in the hope of turning him, but that she'd failed. The response had been that he was the prettier of the pair. That, at least, was true.

Marrying Ralph had been a choice; the decision to champion marriage as they believed it should be, but it didn't feel particularly easy. Nothing she did was ever good enough. The trouble was that, despite everything, Lucy cared what people thought of her, and that extended to people whose opinions she happily admitted she had no respect for.

Calmed, she asked, "So what should I do? Withdraw from the many-faced poetry community, or carry on using it for the connections?"

"Start your own literary salon."

"I'm not having those people in our home."

"There must be others. Women, for a start."

"I don't like other women."

"That's taking it a bit far."

"True. I like Pamela."

"Does it have to be either/or? It's not as if you have an ogre of a boss and wake up every Monday morning dreading the thought of going to work."

"You think I should stand their contempt and pity as long as I can?"

"I'm saying you have *options* that people bound to a regular job don't have. Seal yourself into your study when the muse grabs you, come with me to the shoot in Copenhagen next week, hang out with your 'Greenham cronies', help Pamela at the bookshop."

"Doesn't it always rain in Copenhagen?"

He cocked his head on one side and shrugged. "You might even consider going to pick up an award if they're nice enough to offer it to you. Provided it's not too ugly."

"They're all ugly."

"Then no more awards."

"You're right. And I'm being ridiculous."

"No, you're not. This shouldn't happen."

But it did. And over the next decade, even after many of their circle had separated and divorced, it continued to do so.

CHAPTER THIRTY-SIX

1987

D ominic burst through the door of Lucy's office and threw a copy of *The Observer* onto her desk. "What's this?" he demanded as it skittered to a halt.

Bracing herself, she took off her reading glasses and sat back in her chair. So this was it. The showdown she'd been anticipating.

I risk all in the hope it will resonate with the few. What does Mr Marchmont risk?

At least the waiting was over. Now it would begin. "It looks very much like a newspaper to me."

When was the last time he created art? When do I get the opportunity to critique something that Mr Marchmont has created?

She turned it the right way up and was momentarily distracted by a headline. The front page was loaded with details of the coroner's report following Liberace's death. For pneumonia, read AIDS. She'd been right to think that love and death were close relations.

But there were Dominic's hands, trembling with rage, his feet shuffling with pent-up energy. "Page forty-three." He jabbed at the paper. "Your response was totally –" Dominic cut himself short, as if there were no words to express the magnitude of the injustice he felt.

"Totally what?" Though shaking inside, Lucy was sure of her ground. After all, she was in her own home. Dominic was a guest. "Were you going to say 'uncalled for'? Because I'd say it was long overdue."

"We had an *understanding*." He crammed so much anguish into a single word.

And I don't mean the reviews, in which he dumbs down whatever his subject is, assuming his readers are incapable of understanding it in its original form.

"No," she corrected him. "Understandings are implied. We had an *agreement*."

"That I would attack and you would defend. But this... this is a counter-attack."

"Counter-attack being a recognised defence strategy."

"Call it whatever you like, you've crossed a line."

"Pots and kettles, Dominic. We agreed never to go to press without letting the other know what they were in for. You rescinded on that years ago!"

He loomed in the way that her father used to loom when riled. "So, this was deliberate."

She gave an astonished laugh. "You're making me sound like a sulky teenager." But she'd known precisely what she was doing, precisely where to aim. "When *you* knew something would upset *me*, you thought that was justification to use it because my reaction would be genuine. Besides, art's a generic term. Who but the two of us know I was referring to something specific?"

He pointed. "And I know *exactly where you got your information from*."

Did he really imagine that she and Ralph didn't discuss him, the third person in their marriage? "Oh, come on!" Lucy's weapon was outrage. "I've had to open the newspaper and read what even *you* must accept have been increasingly cheap jibes. *We rather fear that marital bliss has led to over-sentimentality and only hope that the honeymoon period will soon be over.*"

"Twenty sodding years ago, I wrote that!"

"There you are. Let's pin a date on when it all began."

"So, instead of *saying* something, you've brooded over this. Then what?" The question contorted his face. "You woke up one morning and thought, *Today's the day I throw it all back in his face?*"

"I'm sick of it. I'm sick of you deciding when things are on and off between us, and I'm sick of you thinking you can call the shots." Although this moment had been building for a long time, Lucy was suddenly afraid of where momentum might carry her. "And do you know what? I'm *glad* I've made you angry because now you know how it feels to be on the receiving end."

"You think *I* call the shots? Jesus!" Dominic's hand flew to his head and grabbed at a fistful of hair. "You married my best friend and you both expected me to be alright with that? We were sleeping together, for God's sake!"

"Work and sex, you said. That's all I was to you."

He startled. "I never said that."

She raised her eyebrows, astonished that his memory could be so selective.

"Once! Once I said that."

"You said you could never give me what I wanted."

"They were *words*. I was twenty-four years old and I didn't think I deserved you."

"You were nearly thirty when I married Ralph. You had every opportunity to object –"

"So it was, what…? Blackmail? If you don't think you're ready, I'll marry the next guy?"

Lucy wondered if this was the moment when she should

interrupt and say, *It was more complicated than that, and you know it.*

"But it's OK, we can continue to fuck. How do you think that made *me* feel? If I was a woman you'd agree that I was entitled to feel used, but no!" Dominic paused, his lips pressed together in a way that suggested he was censoring himself.

Now Lucy had heard Dominic's take on it, what she'd done seemed appalling. She'd thought herself modern. Refusing to live as her parents lived, Lucy had found her own definition of family, but seemed doomed to repeat their mistakes.

"How do you think it made me feel that my best friend felt he had to make up for my shortcomings?" Dominic went on. "That he had to *protect* you from me?"

You have no idea. No idea that Ralph adores you. She must steer away from this fact, lest it show on her face. "I shouldn't have had to find out you were upset by reading about it in one of your reviews."

"You ungrateful bitch. My reviews *made* you."

"You might have helped me find an audience, but it was Ralph who kept me in the public eye."

"Ralph?" His voice was incredulous.

"You've *always* underestimated him. He's the greatest talent of the three of us. Certainly the most successful. And another thing." Though she was in full flood, Lucy's heart wasn't in the argument any more. "You've made far more money from my poetry than I ever have, and you lived rent-free while your career took off, so don't pretend there was nothing in it for you." Lucy felt herself colour. She had only meant to refer to the Soho flat, but Dominic was currently living rent-free under their roof. He might think she begrudged this, which wasn't the case at all.

Each stood their ground. Lucy determined not to speak first – though part of her wished she could take it all back, or at least make subtle corrections.

Dominic broke the stalemate, sounding exhausted. "How long have we been doing this to each other?"

There seemed to be a finality about the question. Something inevitable, something unstoppable. When Lucy gave her answer, it would mark the end. She took a moment, turned and looked out of the French windows at her rose garden. "Thirty years." It sounded like a gulf. Like reading the dates engraved on a tombstone. She forced a safe tone, "But the first three were pretty amazing." Her nostrils flared and prickled at this admission.

"Then it's time something gave."

"Are you resigning as my critic?" Even as she was speaking, Lucy regretted joking. It was far too late to right things.

"You once asked me how I could confide in Pamela so easily. Do you remember?"

It had been the first Christmas after she and Ralph were married, and they had spent most of it apart. "Yes," she said, without understanding the relevance.

"I asked how you could ask me that. But I had the emphasis wrong. What I should have said was 'How can you – Lucy Forrester, *Having your cake and eating it*. How can you possibly ask me that?'"

Wham! – chin grazed by floorboards, tongue bitten. There had been no seeing it coming. She remembered distinctly how, at nine years old, she had opened her mouth to holler and no sound came. "How long have you known?" she gasped.

"The week after we met. I was working at *The Observer* and asked if I could look through their archives. Then I visited the library, to double-check."

Lucy had written what she couldn't say. It was there, in her poetry, the truth hidden in full view. She had waited for him to react, to say as Pamela had said: *I know this is you.*

Dominic lifted her chin, forcing her to look him in the eye. "And so, you see, I've always known that I only ever had your counterfeit self."

A line from her own poetry used as tripwire. Lucy flinched from the truth; the thing that had stopped them being a couple had nothing to do with Dominic's masterplan. He'd been waiting for her to tell him. Lucy said it as simply as she could, in words her ten-year-old self might have chosen, "I had to leave the real me behind. I wasn't that person when you met me."

"I understand that. If you'd told me, I would have said that I thought you'd done the right thing. But you can't give ten per cent of yourself and expect one hundred per cent in return."

It didn't matter that her sins were of omission rather than commission. She'd insulated herself in layers of lies. Her breath constricted. Everything from her neck downwards ached. Once, pre-polio, after accidentally knocking a vase over, Lucy swept up the pieces and hid them. She remembered the agony of having to lie every time she was asked if she knew where the vase was. Once was easy. You just crossed your fingers behind your back. By the tenth time it had begun to wear her down but there was no choice but to run with it. For Lucy, lying had become a childhood survival technique. Unwittingly, she'd carried it into adulthood.

Dominic must have known it was her father and not her uncle who'd died, and had been denied the opportunity to comfort her as one comforts a lover. "Why didn't you tell me…?"

"Ah, the million-dollar question." He turned to the French windows, hands clasped behind his back. "I could give you the long answer, but what it boils down to is simple. I wanted to know that you trusted me."

"Does Ralph know?" she asked, and when she heard Dominic's slight snort, she pressed, "Did you tell Ralph?"

"Of course I told Ralph!" The words exploded from him, then he relented. "What shocks me is that you didn't. All these years. I didn't think there were any secrets between you."

315

It was Lucy's turn to remain silent. She'd been as open with Ralph as she was capable of. She trusted him more than she trusted any living soul. And yet he too had only had her counterfeit self.

"I'm leaving," Dominic delivered his decision with calmness. Possibly even with kindness. But, God, the wrench of those words. He turned to face her. "Living under the same roof… It would have been better if I'd made the break when you moved here." Dominic laughed painfully, then shook his head. "It seems odd saying this now, but I was afraid I'd cause offence." He turned back to the French windows and Lucy's rose garden one final time, and she stole a look at the nape of his neck. *That neck!* "It's funny. Even now, I find myself wanting to ask you to come with me," and Lucy couldn't help the lurch in her stomach at this small rekindling of hope. "But…"

She was surprised to find that the fight hadn't yet left her. "There you go again. Skirting around the thing that needs to be said."

"Oh, for Christ's sake!" He turned, and his eyes were everything in that moment. "Get down from that high horse of yours. Can you see? I'm saving you from having to make a decision that will either hurt me or the last person in the world I want to hurt."

Usurped by her husband, Lucy felt paralysed. *I don't want you to go.* All she could cope with were practicalities. She asked the questions Ralph would want answers to: "Where will you stay?"

"Tonight, a hotel. Then, who knows? Perhaps one of the papers will have an assignment for me. Perhaps I'll take a holiday." He smiled the way that you can only smile at someone you have known for an awfully long time. The thought that this might be the last of these unspoken intimacies filled Lucy with pain. "I shall avoid going to my sister's for as long as possible, but it may come to that."

Lucy gripped the underside of the desk so that she wouldn't claw at him. The word *Stay* screamed inside her head. "Do you have money?" was the question that left her mouth.

"Lucy, I'm a fifty-two-year-old man."

"Of course. I didn't mean to sound so bloody patronising."

His hand hesitated over her right shoulder, before touching it uncertainly. Lucy couldn't help but compare it with the confident way he'd once cupped her knee on the top floor of a double decker while she sat in a stupor, listening as he painted visions of a future she wanted to be part of.

"You'll say goodbye to Ralph for me?"

Then the pressure was gone. The touch of Tennyson's vanish'd hand. Without waiting for a reply, he began to move towards the door. Lucy's lips peeled apart but she could think of nothing that hadn't already been said. There was just the sound of her breath.

Left alone, Dominic's absence felt so vast that Lucy wondered if she'd conjured him up to fill the loneliness. Memories jostled to bookmark themselves. Odd that most of the good ones featured all three of them; that relatively short period before marriage, before money, before any hint of fame. Sitting on the sofa in the Soho flat, between Ralph and Dominic, *Revolver* playing on the turntable, three heads lolling back against the curve of the sofa. None of them particularly liked to dance. None of them could sing, but given a few drinks they would happily raise their voices to *Got to Get You into My Life*. And Lucy would cheat, looking from one chin uplifted, eyes-scrunched-closed face to the other. *How beautiful, how incredibly beautiful men can be.* Thinking she had it all.

The launch party her publishers had thrown, not her own, the memory of which was clouded by her father's death. This was for some other poet. Hangover champagne and grim canapés combining lethally. All terribly polite, everyone in evening dress, outwardly – at least – on best behaviour. In fact, everyone but the few friends Lucy recognised looked like bankers. The more she felt there was an expectation that she would play the role of 'supporting poet', the more Lucy felt that she would succumb to an attack of giggles, and so, in her attempts not to smile, despite the champagne's hold, the more serious she appeared. This continued until she could stand it no longer. Leaning her head onto Ralph's shoulder. Lucy bit down hard on a shoulder pad.

"I think it's time to throw the cloth over the canary cage." Ralph reached out and tugged the hem of Dominic's dinner jacket.

Dominic was better at this sort of occasion than either of them. He was playing his role – 'literary critic' – rather more convincingly than Lucy was hers. "Excuse me one moment," he said to the person he was speaking to – Lucy saw that with his round glasses and brown curls, the man bore a slight resemblance to a recent photograph she'd seen of Michael White.

Ralph leant towards him. "We're leaving."

I'm leaving, Dominic had said.

Turning back to his abandoned conversation, Dominic indicated to the table where champagne bottles were laid out. "Mind if I…?"

"Go right ahead." The man stepped aside. "That's what it's there for."

But instead of topping up his glass, Dominic grabbed the neck of a full bottle and said, "Well, it's been good to finally meet you."

She remembered running from the function room like someone possessed. She hadn't attempted to run since those circuits of the garden at the house on the square, when she'd pretending to be a fighter plane. She would answer for it in the morning but, for now, it felt like freedom. Lucy had no real idea where she was heading. When a narrow side alley yawned, suitably seedy, she pulled them into its mouth, panting, speechless with laughter.

"Was that really *the* Michael White?"

"The one time you drag me away!" Dominic gripped the bottle between his knees and ripped the foil from the cork.

"It didn't look anything like him," Ralph said.

"In my breast pocket," Dominic nodded, his face red with effort. "Look at it."

Lucy drew out a business card. "Michael White!" She jumped up and down.

Even the moment when the cork gave seemed something new to laugh about. The champagne foamed out and Dominic stopped it with his mouth. When it was Lucy's turn with the bottle, more spilled down her chin than went in, and so Ralph threw her over his shoulder and carried her home, but it was Dominic who put her to bed.

And now Ralph was standing in front of her desk. Proof that Dominic wasn't someone she'd dreamt up, because how could one of them exist without the other? He wore a soft grey polo-neck jumper, not so different from one he might have chosen at twenty-two, twenty-three, but this was fifty-two-year-old Ralph. Ralph with his camera bag slung over a shoulder, back from a shoot. It was dark outside, a measure of how long Lucy had been sitting there.

"He's gone, I see," he said. It wasn't a question.

My God, what have I done? She felt herself crumble, the beginnings of accepting what had happened even as she fought the facts.

"I knew as soon as I walked through the front door."

She reached for Ralph's hand and his fingers closed around hers. Something real. *How will this change things?* she thought. *Not just for me, but for us.* "I did this," she said.

"No, no." Ralph's arms circled Lucy's shoulders and she clung greedily to his waist, the side of her face against the warmth of his stomach. "We all did. It was such a long time coming that we managed to fool ourselves that we got away with it."

The newspaper was still on her desk. One line stood out: *Carrillo responded: "I firmly believe that somebody wanted to pull a fast one on us. They probably pulled something they thought they could get away with."* Had Ralph seen it? Everybody, it seemed, relied on 'getting away with it'. But there was a fear – all too real – that Ralph might be taken from her too. He'd said it before: he was only here because of 'the sheer randomness of AIDS'. *Please, God, no,* she thought. *Not Ralph.*

CHAPTER THIRTY-SEVEN

1988

To fill the void Dominic left, Lucy joined forces with Pamela and threw herself into the fight more vigorously. Theirs became such a well-rehearsed routine, planning was almost redundant. After an exchange of times and dates, the clincher was whether Ralph was available. In the past, small disparate groups of accomplices had tipped off newspapers in the hope that at least one would send a photographer. Lucy and Pamela both had their little black books filled with contact details for freelance photojournalists and staff photographers. Relationships were reciprocal. They both had something the other wanted.

Little more needed to be said than, "John, it's Pamela," or, "Andy, it's Lucy Forrester," and they would say, "What time and where?"

But Ralph, Ralph had access his competitors envied. He took the shots and actively submitted them to newspapers. And the name 'Ralph' carried weight. More and more often the front page was theirs.

Up until now, Lucy's arrest sheet had been modest.

In 1961, shortly after the release of her first collection, Ralph had suggested they combine a holiday in the States with a few readings. It made sense. No publisher was going to fund a poetry tour for a virtual unknown. In those days, travelling to America meant a sea voyage. It was like travelling to another planet. Dolphins acting as markers, flying fish, a succession of astonishing sunsets as they crossed the mid-Atlantic, temperatures far beyond anything she'd imagined, the night skies as she and Ralph lay side by side on deck, the oil fields, with hundreds and thousands of pumps lining the shore nodding in welcome, almost majestic. Once there, it 'made sense' for Lucy to join a women's peace march. She wasn't charged but she was arrested and quizzed for five exhausting hours about her reasons for being in the country.

"We're combining a holiday with official business," she protested.

"Uh-huh. Well, ma'am, we'd strongly encourage you to leave the minute this 'official business' of yours is over."

Back at home, with a look that suggested he could barely contain himself, Ralph passed her a contact sheet. "Look what I've got."

She saw the demonstrators at the foot of the Washington Monument, but that clearly wasn't what had him fit to burst. "You'll have to give me a clue. What am I looking for?"

He pointed to a picture of a window. "If I tell you that's the White House."

"My God!" She laughed disbelievingly. "You struck gold."

He had caught John F. Kennedy. A thoughtful pose from a man who had no idea he was on view. Lucy hoped to God that he *was* a thoughtful man. In June that same year, when he and Khrushchev reached an informal understanding against nuclear testing, she was reassured that he wasn't another Truman.

"I don't know about gold," Ralph said, kissing the contact sheet, "but it will pay for the trip."

Two years later, when the world held its breath in disbelief,

Ralph's photograph was reproduced extensively in the British press and it paid for more besides.

It was about this time when Pamela made a connection with another photographer, not that she knew he was a photographer at first. He was simply a large ungainly Scotsman who wandered into Housmans from the Caledonian Road and asked for directions. They bumped into each other a second time when he was commissioned by *The Times* to cover a CND march. Pamela and Lucy, naturally, were marching.

"It's you!" he called. It was his voice rather than his face that she recognised.

"Left at the lights and keep going," she said. Was she *blushing?*

"I'm Angus. Angus Boon."

"Boom?" Pamela asked. (To Lucy, this lovely man would always be Angus Boom.)

Over the next mile, they established that he was ten years Pamela's senior. He had served the Army Film and Photographic Unit during the Second World War. Later postings had taken him to Korea and Vietnam. From miles one to two, Pamela put forward a spirited argument. Apart from a wink in Lucy's direction Angus gave no obvious reaction. When she finally came to a stop, he handed her his hip flask. "That was quite some speech. You'll be in need of a wee dram." And while she was busy, he said, "Although I'm not the one you need to persuade. I've always been on your side."

After almost choking on what turned out to be a very good classic malt, Pamela wiped her mouth with the back of her hand. "Why the hell didn't you say so?"

"I didn't like to interrupt. I suppose you could say I liked the sound of your voice."

Lucy had the impression that no one had ever told Pamela they liked the sound of her voice, and sensed this was something she'd been waiting to hear for a very long time. It was

Lucy who handed Angus her little black book and asked him to write down his telephone number.

"Quite a collection," he said. "Got a pen?"

Lucy dug deep in her handbag. "Useful contacts."

"Think I can be of use to you and your friend, do you?"

She made sure that she could read his handwriting. "Oh, I hope so. In fact, would you like to come to dinner?"

"You're a good cook, are you?"

"Absolutely hopeless. My husband's the cook."

For the first half of the seventies, Pamela and her placards found a home in Kilburn with Angus and his camera equipment. They were an unlikely couple, but in Lucy's experience, it was the unlikely couples who made it work in the long term.

There was vague talk of marriage when they 'got round to it' but a middle-aged unmarried couple weren't frowned on in the same way that youngsters might have been. "Besides," Pamela insisted, "at my age, I'd look ridiculous in a white frock."

Experience of exposure to real danger meant that Angus thought nothing of being called out to a police station in the middle of the night. And, though by no means immune to fear, Pamela tried to rationalise the risks that Angus's job ("You can't call it a job. It's more than that") entailed. She feared for him most when he was away from home, and sometimes the fact that he was away from home was all she knew.

"Don't ask me where I'm going. I can barely pronounce it."

"Will you please write it down?"

"What makes you think I can spell it?"

Angus was killed by an IRA bomb in 1976. Not on the other side of the world, but a visitor at the Daily Mail Ideal Home Exhibition in the Olympia Exhibition Centre. His was probably the first death that Lucy allowed herself to mourn and she grieved long and hard with her friend.

1979. Two days after the Three Mile Island accident – the

worst meltdown in US nuclear power plant history – she and Pamela (who had taken to wearing black) handcuffed themselves to railings outside the American Embassy. Various failures, both mechanical and human, had resulted in the escape of an 'unknown quantity' of radioactive coolant. When the statement that there was 'no cause for alarm' changed to 'it's complex', there was no real need for Pamela to say, "I think we all knew *this* was coming."

Schools closed, people were ordered to stay indoors, farmers were warned to keep livestock and feed under cover and 140,000 women and children were evacuated. Like many of the protesters, both Pamela and Lucy were arrested. Lucy had to be stitched by a police medic after a bolt cutter overshot its target and clipped the skin of her wrist. There was more blood than there was pain, and she was rather proud of her war wound.

By 1980, with a very real possibility of US nuclear weapons arriving on British soil and being carted along country lanes for regular testing, CND membership saw astonishing growth. Forty per cent of participants in a BBC poll believed nuclear war possible within the next ten years. In a Gallup poll fifty-seven per cent thought a world war imminent. Little wonder that three hundred firms began marketing nuclear fallout shelters and radiation suits.

Then came Bruce Kent's 'call to arms'. "It will cost time, energy, money, friends, ambition and career prospects, but these are not important compared with what we're saying … We must curb the arms race or face annihilation." The women had a simpler call to arms. "Pankhurst calling, Pankhurst calling," they whispered into transistor radios, and, "Bring your black cardigan" (the code name for bolt cutters).

The arms race was firmly back on the agenda in October 1981 (only two months before the first reported case of AIDS in the UK, and still nine months before the death of Terry

Higgins). Lucy and Pamela were among a quarter of a million people who took to London's streets in what would become an annual march. By October 1983, Pamela was no longer by Lucy's side, but her old governess would have been proud to see how 400,000 people stood up to be counted. More than twenty hours of footage of Hiroshima had been made public. Taken in March 1946, considered too shocking, it had been marked 'secret' and locked away in a vault in the Pentagon.

A regular at Greenham Common over the years, Pamela was still well enough to attend Embrace the Base. Lucy thought Ralph's photograph – this linking of hands around the nine-mile periphery fence – one of his most striking. Taken from ground level at a corner, the view of the women's jawlines and the hard right angle. Lucy, who blamed the IRA for Pamela's death as much as she did Angus's, often looked at this shot, the last Ralph took of Pamela. When he found her with it in her hands, he would sit with her in silence until she spoke. Both thought the photo a good summing up of the person Pamela was and the life she'd led.

"You made her look determined."

"Unapologetic," Ralph said.

Lucy wondered if Cook was still alive and, if so, how she was.

Ralph captured Lucy chained to the base fence. Pressed up against the wire, standing beneath a banner. 'We Say No to Cruise Missiles'. As part of the 70,000 strong human chain that stretched from Greenham to Aldermaston to the factory at Burghfield. Sitting among a tight knot of women whilst her neighbour was dragged away by a policewoman. Her mouth open in song as a slow-moving lorry pressed into the crowd. Suspended Christ-like between two policemen, the badges huge on their uniform helmets, expressions suggesting that they didn't know quite what to do with her. Drinking a steaming mug of tea with Sarah Hipperson. Part of the Greenham camp for over nineteen years, Sarah would never replace Pamela in Lucy's affections, but she was someone with whom Lucy could be herself. In most of the photographs, Lucy stood out. Dressed in wellingtons, her trademark CND symbol drawn on her cheek in black eyeliner. There was only one photograph in which she didn't recognise herself. She was among two hundred women who entered the camp dressed as teddy bears.

"I'd know you anywhere," Ralph said. "Even in a bear costume."

"Bloody Heseltine!" Lucy shook her head. "Saying he couldn't tell the difference between a peace protestor and a terrorist. We showed him."

"I must admit, I worried when Heseltine said he'd have you all shot."

And then of course there was Chernobyl, the worst nuclear power plant accident until Fukushima. The immediate death toll was thirty-one, but 200,000 emergency workers were sent in, 116,000 people evacuated from the exclusion zone, leaving 270,000 in the worst contaminated area – and that was before anyone considered the numbers affected by the radioactive fallout, which drifted over Western USSR and Europe. Even taking the most conservative projection, it was said that there would be fifty thousand 'excess cancer cases', resulting in twenty-five thousand 'excess cancer deaths'. Lucy's placard simply read, 'Nuclear: This is the price'.

As the growth of Lucy's arrest sheet accelerated, so too did her scrapbooks of clippings. Ralph shared the understanding that Lucy needed to use her public profile, and so she was always among those who refused to disperse, labelled a 'troublemaker'. Always a misfit, she didn't fit the typical profile of her kind of troublemaker: a mother in her mid-thirties, whose children had been born during the Cuban Missile crisis, consumed by fear that they too might become shadows on pavements.

Yeats said, it takes fifty years for a poet to influence an issue. Lucy still had a good eighteen to go. But Dominic, who continued to 'critique' her work, seemed to have lost all enthusiasm for the publicity angle. *We had hoped that the name Lucy Forrester would be associated with poetry rather than political stunts, but it seems we are to be proven wrong,* he wrote in March 1988. Lucy tensed as she read the word 'stunts'. "Bastard!" she said out loud as the newspaper rattled in her hands, an involuntary outburst. "He's done it again."

Ralph folded his own Sunday paper, put it on the arm of his chair and asked, "Who's done what again?"

"Why me? Why can't he find someone else to write about?"

"Ah. Dominic."

Even now, the name made Lucy's stomach constrict. "He's implied that I only take part in protests to get publicity for my writing." Her eyes were wide with indignation. "He's more or less suggested that I don't have any genuine belief in the cause."

Ralph sighed loudly. Still friends with Dominic, he was piggy in the middle. It was unfair and Lucy knew it, but her husband was more than capable of objectivity. "That deserves a reply."

"That's not how this works. We *always* agree a strategy in advance."

"Well, on this occasion, it sounds as if Dom forgot to run it by you."

"Forgot," she scoffed. "A photo of me being dragged off down the street by two policemen will *always* get more coverage than one of me collecting the Somerset Maugham. It's as simple as that."

"Then that's exactly what needs to be said."

"Did you say he's away until Thursday week?"

"I thought he said Tuesday. Either way, it can't wait. Your response needs to be in next Sunday's *Observer*."

"Damn him! He *knows* that people repeat what he's written as fact. Now I have to waste my time on damage limitation."

Ralph rubbed his chin. "Rather than a letter, I wonder if you should contact the editor. There might be scope for an article about how limited the media's coverage of poetry is."

"Won't that suggest Dominic's right?"

Ralph frowned and beckoned. "Read me what he's written."

Reluctantly, Lucy opened the paper. "'*We had hoped that the name Lucy Forrester would be associated with poetry rather than political stunts*'," she exaggerated the word, "'*but it seems we are to be proven wrong*'."

"He doesn't say the fault's *yours*. He could just as easily be criticising the media."

"He *is* the media."

"Much as he'd like to think so, he's just one very small cog. And it doesn't matter what Dom intended. It's how you respond that counts."

As Ralph spoke, Lucy felt a surge of energy, the kind that says, *Get to it.*

"You supported CND before I met you," he continued as if reeling off a list. "Your two careers have run in parallel, you've been successful in both, and it's a crime that only one has had the recognition it deserves. Something along those lines."

She was on her feet. "I'll make a start on some notes. I'll need facts if I'm going to make that call tomorrow."

"It's just as well you've kept all your clippings. You'll be able to offer a comparison: protest versus poetry. And I can take a few shots of your scrapbooks, just to drive the point home."

Lucy had reached the door when the impulse hit her. She turned, marched smartly towards the armchair Ralph was sitting in, held both sides of his face and said, "I married a genius." Then she kissed him fiercely on the lips.

CHAPTER THIRTY-EIGHT

2014

Lucy and Ralph were reading in bed, propped up on pillows as was their habit. Not *like* an old married couple, but a proper old married couple. Distracted by images of blind cormorants and ghost hands, Lucy had read the same paragraph several times.

"What's up?" she heard him ask.

"This?" She used one finger as a bookmark and examined the cover. A woman dressed in a red raincoat posing on rocks in a way that would have health and safety executives breaking out in a sweat. "*Olive Kitteridge.* It says it's as perfect a novel as I will ever read. That's a challenge if ever I saw one."

"I didn't ask what you're reading, I asked what's up?" Ralph made a point of taking off his glasses. "Why all the deep sighs?"

"Sorry, I didn't realise." She found her place easily. The shape of that now-familiar paragraph. "I'll try and keep the noise down."

He looked at her, waiting.

"My poem." She shook her head. How to explain? It wasn't for lack of material but the damned thing was resisting revision. "It's as if it doesn't want to be finished."

"Good. I liked it the way it was. The drama of the ending." He mimed an explosion.

"But it won't suit the occasion."

"Then perhaps it's time to separate the poetry from the politics."

"And do what?"

He was silent for a few moments. "Are you busy tomorrow?"

"Other than the usual, there's nothing in my diary."

"Good." Ralph reached for his bedside light and settled back on his pillows. "We're going on a little outing."

The last of 888,246 poppies, planted by a small solemn boy, adrift in the vast red moat. It surrounded this stone fortress, the building that housed England's memories, from William the Conqueror to Reggie and Ronnie Kray. But today – this bright and beautiful day with its cloudless sky – the Tower of London was transformed. The sheer scale! Lucy reached for Ralph's hand. It wrapped itself securely around hers. Blood Swept Lands. Seas of Red. One flower for each soldier who lost his life in the First World War. Thought of this terrible quota altered Lucy's breathing, but the moment coincided with an elderly straight-backed Beefeater beginning to read from a list. A clear, true voice.

It could only be a gesture, a tiny fraction of the whole, but the quiet dignity of names, ranks, and regiment transformed the moat into a living breathing thing. Great-grandfathers, grandfathers, fathers, colleagues, brothers, sweethearts, childhood friends, best friends. Unintentional rhythms revealed themselves in the syllables of the names. Lucy's chest rose and fell, keeping time. *We will remember them.* The crowd repeating, "We will remember them," each person's startling certainty reminding Lucy of something from the depths of her memory. An old man whose name she never knew, someone seen on Sunday mornings at church. He responded loudly to whatever the vicar said – *Lord graciously hear us* – while everyone else mumbled. Prompted to join with the other voices, Lucy silently added Dominic's name to the litany. *We will remember.*

And then, a lone bugler standing on top of a small mound, a green break in the red poppy field. The mournful strains of the *Last Post*. As the Beefeater stiffened his hand in salute, a lump lodged in Lucy's throat. The toll of the bell. Its solemn echo, and in the background, the call of gulls mourning the tidal loss of the Thames mudbanks, muffled traffic from The Minories, the clank and clang of building work as the city forced itself skywards from new foundations. There was a way of doing honour. She tightened her grip on Ralph's constant hand and looked away momentarily, towards the two towers of the Bridge and beyond to the glass peak of the Shard.

CHAPTER THIRTY-NINE

1998

Ralph glanced up from the onion he was quartering. "Who was that on the phone?"

Lucy leant against the kitchen worktop to steady her thoughts as much as her legs. "A journalist with a tip-off." She blinked in protest against the onslaught of sulfenic acid.

"Sounds intriguing."

"Apparently I'm being considered for Poet Laureate." Said out loud, the words sounded extraordinary.

"Good God." The knife stilled in his hand. "They've only just buried poor Ted."

"Is *that* how we refer to him now?"

"Never speak ill of the dead."

"No, you're right. And I should put it out of my mind." She opened a low drawer, where saucepans were arranged like Russian dolls. The smaller ones scraped against each other as Lucy set them aside to get at the two larger ones.

"Sorry," Ralph said. "What I meant to say was congratulations. It's about time."

She shook the praise away. "Don't plan on drinking all that sherry just yet. And, for God's sake, don't mention it tonight."

"Am I not allowed to express a little pride?"

"Blair compiles the shortlist. As you know, I've not made myself too popular."

"There is that. Did they let slip who else is being considered?"

"They *tell* me," she couldn't help a little cynicism, "that the appetite is there to appoint a woman." Lucy turned on the tap, filled one of the pans and salted the water.

He laughed, a single syllable. "They said that last time."

Lucy smiled as she lit the gas. "Apparently the bookies are taking bets."

"Oh? And who are the favourites?" Ralph was ready with a thick slice of butter for the onions.

"Me and Carol."

"She doesn't come without controversy – assuming she and Jackie are still an item."

"As far as I know. We haven't spoken for a while. You know how it is."

"I do. It happens all too easily and, before you know it, it's too late. Do something about it."

"I will."

"Good. Who else?"

"Ursula Fanthorpe. I don't think you know her. Another lesbian. Slightly older. A latecomer to poetry, but prolific. Carol's bet one hundred pounds on her." Repeating this snippet, Lucy knew she shouldn't feel slighted. Carol and Ursula were old friends. "And apparently *The Guardian* are going to champion her."

"So, unless I'm wrong, you're the only non-lesbian female option."

"The non-lesbian, married to a homosexual, habit of chaining herself to railings option. What do you think of my chances?"

"There's always a safe option. Who is he?"

"Andrew Motion."

"*Whitsun Weddings?*" Ralph slid the sliced onion into the sizzling butter.

"Close. That was Larkin." Lucy's thoughts were racing. "The post comes with a heap of publicity. The phone wouldn't stop ringing, for starters."

"You'd think about accepting, then?"

"It would give me another platform to push from." She was restless. "I've never been any good at writing to order, but I don't know… The idea of being the first woman."

"That would certainly be something."

"*If* it's offered to me. And that's a very big *if*." But even as she protested, there was a small place in Lucy's mind where the job was hers. "Besides, they've changed the rules. It would only mean having no private life for ten years." She picked up the stray end of a carrot, crunched into it; remembered something. "Anyway, you were about to say something before the phone rang."

"Yes, I was." Ralph spoke carefully, as if in two minds.

She waited, chewing the vegetable into pulp.

"I bumped into Dom today."

Lucy felt a small but perceptible change in her blood-stream. She swallowed. "Oh?"

"I had a feeling." Ralph grimaced. "He tried to make it look as if he just happened to be passing, but, I don't know…"

Lucy pictured it. A busy London pavement. A pause of recognition. A greeting between two friends who hadn't seen each other for some years. The slap on the back.

"There was something not quite right."

"In what way?"

"I had the feeling he'd been waiting for me, if that doesn't sound too strange. To be honest, he looked bloody awful."

She laughed fondly. "He'd put on a lot of weight the last time I saw him." It had been some official function. And it wasn't only the weight-gain Lucy recalled. He'd grown his hair long enough to tie back in a bunch.

"You haven't changed a bit," he'd said.

"You have," Lucy replied, relieved that for the first time in memory the lurch in her stomach was absent. Finally, she was over him.

"If he had, he's lost it again. He looked ill." Ralph looked at Lucy in the way he did when checking she'd got his drift.

Ralph had had his own health scare in the early nineties. When the doctor used the word 'pneumonia' Lucy had felt sick to her stomach. But although he'd needed a drip, Ralph assured her it was common or garden pneumonia.

"Common or garden," she'd heard herself repeating, and putting one hand to her chest.

As she'd raised her eyes and laughed, the nurse had looked disapproving. "Your husband's very ill. This is what happens when you don't rest up after the flu."

"Yes, yes, I'm sorry." But not *that* kind of ill. This was the kind penicillin could cure.

After that, they'd both made an effort to look after themselves. Lucy had resumed her swimming. Slow, steady, length after therapeutic length. The smell of chlorine and the rubber of the cap she used to protect her dyed hair. The pull of the goggles. "Drinking too much?" she enquired, hoping for a relatively simple answer.

"No," Ralph said softly, and she understood that he'd been underplaying his concern. "He looked like death itself."

Lucy, who, a moment earlier, had thought she'd known both the cause and the remedy, found she was unable to move.

"You'll be able to judge for yourself. I've invited him to dinner." Ralph continued, finding his place in the recipe and moving onto the next small task, measuring out the blend of herbs.

She'd been looking forward to the evening all week. The guest list was made up of her small, close-knit community; her hand-picked tribe. Old wisdom, new talent, probable mentors, possible patrons. Harry Chalmers had sent his apologies, but had suggested a sharp-eyed youngster from a fledgling Bristol press, one half of a husband and wife team…

Now she ran the sharp edge of a thumbnail her over her lips. Her mother had been incapable of being around illness. People had thought her highly strung. Lucy was suddenly afraid. Not only of what she would see, but that she wouldn't be able to disguise how it made her feel.

"One more won't make any difference," Ralph went on. "And I suggested he stays the night. I hope that's OK."

Understanding from this that Dominic wasn't working and had nowhere else to go, Lucy began rooting about in a drawer for cutlery. She needed activity, something to occupy her restless hands. "I'd better lay another place at the table."

"I've done it."

Dominic hadn't set foot in their home since he said the words, 'How long have we been doing this to each other?'. "Then I'll check the bed in the green room," Lucy said.

"Also done."

She picked up a tea towel, wiped her hands and flung it back down. "Then I'll go and get changed."

Lucy moved between the twos and the threes, topping up prosecco glasses. The task lent her the appearance of being sociable without the need to engage with anyone for more than a few moments. Anticipating Dominic's arrival these last few hours, she'd been listening out for him. Guests reduced to props, Lucy would rather they left, or perhaps *she* could leave. One or the other.

When she finally heard Ralph say, "Dominic," in his hail-fellow-well-met voice, Lucy felt unprepared. Bottle in hand, she smiled and said, "I won't be one moment," as if she was putting a caller on hold.

In the doorway she paused, steeling herself. The opposite

wall was taken up with the one photograph Ralph always wished he'd taken. One of Michael Joseph's photographs for *The Beggar's Banquet*; the setting, the wreckage of a medieval feast. "Dear God," she said as she looked at Keith Richards sprawled on his back, eyes closed, holding an apple skewered on a knife to his mouth. That was the extent of her cry for help. At the very front of the shot, Richards's tankard angled towards the camera, empty. In contrast to his horizontal position, a French pug sat bolt upright in Richards's lap. The dog's expression was one Lucy recognised: singularly unimpressed. She saw it so many times on her father's face. On her brother's too. The detail was magnificent, everything from the stained trousers, the texture of Richards's crocodile-skin belt, the knit of his cardigan so clear that it could be chain mail. "It's the contrasts," Ralph would say, over and over, something that Lucy with her love of textures and layers appreciated. It was the contrast Lucy now feared. The before and after.

There was no one to hear her prayer. There would be no help. A stretch of hall lay between her and Dominic. She must walk down it, not knowing what awaited.

"Lucy!" Ralph called out, his voice sing-song.

"Coming." She stepped into view, turned.

She'd hoped that Ralph had got it wrong; that it would be appropriate to compliment Dominic on his weight loss. Before her stood a man, not the ghost of Christmas Yet to Come as she'd feared, but nothing left of the boy she'd glimpsed when he was relaxed or sleeping. Realising that she was gripping the neck of the bottle too tightly, Lucy set it down on the telephone table and forced her feet to move. *Look him in the eyes*, she told herself sternly. They were newly deep-set.

"Here she is," Dominic said, though his jaunty voice didn't mirror the level way he returned her gaze.

This man was undeniably Dominic. And yet part of what had made him Dominic had gone. A spark. Ralph hadn't been mistaken.

"The celebrated poetess," he said, which enabled Lucy to respond: "Oh, God, not you as well!" and to lean in, put one hand on a wrist – so heartbreakingly thin it felt as if there was only bone – and kiss Dominic's cold cheek. But, the last time she'd seen him aside, he'd always been thin. Too thin, many people said.

"Poet, poet, poet," he said, closing his eyes so that, for a moment, she could drop the mask and take in the face as a whole. "Poet Laureate," Dominic said as if tasting the words, then he smiled and that, at least, was genuine.

She glared accusingly at Ralph, then returned Dominic's smile as he opened his eyes, acutely aware of the corners of her mouth.

"Stop that nonsense," Dominic said. "You can't blame a husband for being proud of his wife."

"If they decide on a woman, it will be Carol."

"Christ, I'd better check I'm not burning something." Ralph strode off up the hall. He collided with the corner of the telephone table, swore loudly and, as he paused to rub the spot, said, "Show Dom upstairs, will you?"

She'd been abandoned with a man who was, and yet was not, her critic and lover of forty years. And because she didn't move, or comment on the size of his suitcase, Dominic said, "Shall we?"

It felt odd to have Dominic lead the way. At the top of the stairs, he turned left towards what had been his room. Sometimes *their* room.

"Actually, we've changed things around. That room's ours."

He pretended to be shocked. "You sleep in the same room these days?"

She scratched behind one ear. "Awkward, all this talk of domestic arrangements." Lucy led the way to the opposite end of the landing. Her back was turned on Dominic as she said, "We've discovered we rather like it. Of course, we often used to back in the Soho days." Lucy had only meant to draw on nostalgia but, every word seemed infused with unintended meaning. She opened the door, cursing herself. "We've put you in here."

It was a large bright room. Dominic parked his suitcase in an upright position, sat on the mattress and bounced a couple of times, as if trying it out for comfort. "What if I get lonely?"

She thought of suggesting they use the walkie-talkies, but abandoned that idea. Too personal. "Leave the door open." She folded her arms under her breasts. "You can shout."

"So strict. You sound just like Pamela."

"Do you know? I was thinking about her earlier. I'm the same age as she was when she died." The word hung in the air. Determined not to cave, Lucy gave a nod, indicating to the hall. "I should –"

"Have we forgiven each other yet, Lucy?" And as she felt a sharp tug at the corners of her mouth, Dominic added, "I only ask because the last time I saw you, I felt that we hadn't."

"Not yet, no," she replied, because stubbornness was a convenient mask for the raw ache in her throat, the pressure pushing down on her lungs.

"Good." Dominic nodded. "It's good to get that out of the way, I think. Clears the air. Now we can go downstairs and enjoy the company of the glittering literati."

Lucy laughed, surprised anew that she was capable of making such a clear bright sound, and still more when Dominic tapped the mattress beside him. Instead of sitting, Lucy flung herself backwards, folding one arm over her face so that the ridge of her nose fitted in the crook of her arm and her eyes were covered.

"You look tired, strange girl." She moved the arm away to find his hollowed-out eyes looking down at her, concerned. "Are you sure you're quite well?"

And again she was laughing; staring at the ceiling,

uncontrollable belly aching, and she thought once again how human beings laugh when what they really want to do is weep.

"And Ralph. He's keeping well? I mean he looks fit as a butcher's dog, but you know... I worry."

"He's well," she assured him, and although she couldn't quite bring herself to ask how he was – not yet, at least – she knew that the three of them would manage to find a way to live together. And it would not be the way of old. There would be no need to tread water this time. "Welcome home, Dominic," she said.

Andrew Motion was appointed Poet Laureate on 1 May 1999. Lucy was unsurprised.

CHAPTER FORTY

ITV STUDIOS, 2013

Lucy waited behind the studio set, gripping the back of the moulded plastic chair she'd brought from home.

"And now I'd like to welcome back one of the nation's best-loved poets and best-known activists. Ladies and gentlemen, Lucy Forrester!"

"You're on." A hand alighted on her shoulder. "Remember: wait at the top of the stairs for the audience to react."

Hearing the studio band strike up, she centred herself, then stepped into the glare of the spotlights and the applause, carrying the chair with her. Lucy had brought the legendary chat show host no other retirement gift. Just this single memory. What did it matter that, to anyone other than their generation, the joke would be lost? Although a veteran of television appearances, Lucy had been moved that she was one of five guests – the others all A-listers – Philip Harrington had requested for his final show. "Why me?" she'd asked when she got the call. "He's a great admirer of your work," came the reply.

On his feet to greet her, Philip brought his outstretched hand to his forehead. He was laughing. Lucy gave a quick glance to the nearest camera, nodding to its faceless driver.

A hand was raised in response. Someone who knew Ralph, perhaps. About to begin her final descent, she was overcome by a sudden rush of vertigo, and with it, an inexplicable fear.

Glad to reach the studio floor, Lucy spoke with a confidence she didn't feel, "I took the precaution of bringing my own chair this time."

"Didn't anyone tell you?" Philip's face was a map of laughter lines. His shock of white hair was testament to the passage of time. "We ditched the leather years ago."

"Well, in that case." Lucy set aside her own chair and they both sat. He no longer rested his heel on the opposite knee, exposing his crotch. Apparently, he needed no notes. There was a tiny table between them, an impractical thing, just large enough for two glasses of water. They were seated so closely that he had to lean back on one elbow to get a better view of her.

"How long has it been, Lucy?" This was a man whose successful television career would have been unimaginable to his father, a publican from a small mining community in the north-west.

"It has to be at least thirty years," she replied.

"It can't be!"

"I was on with Douglas Adams and, yes, I think it was The Human League."

"I have to say, you're looking marvellous."

"*When I am an old woman,*" she quoted, patting down layers of fabric.

"Of course, these days you're almost as well known for how you dress as you are for your poetry and political activism."

Lucy described her style as cultivated eccentricity. She'd earned the right to wear whatever she liked, and she wore it with confidence. *Yes, this is exactly how I wanted it to turn out.* The retro glasses, the turbans, contrasting (clashing) textures and fabrics, oversized plastic accessories. "I've been less afraid to experiment as I've grown older."

"So what brought about the change?" Philip still liked to use his hands while he talked, she saw. He could go from wringing them out to holding them apart within the space of a few simple words.

"Well, there's my husband's influence. As you know, Ralph's used to photographing world-class models. If he doesn't like what the dresser's done, he won't hesitate to make a few changes. He gives the impression he's throwing a few things together, but that's him. He has a feel for how things should look and when they're right." Age made Philip look hunched rather than relaxed as he leaned towards her. Lucy reminded herself to sit up straight. "It's also a case of being comfortable in my own skin. I had childhood polio – a disease that's been all but eradicated."

"Thankfully."

"Absolutely. It left me with one leg slightly shorter than the other. I was terribly self-conscious. You never would have caught me wearing a miniskirt or a bikini. But so many friends are no longer with us, it seems like such a silly thing to be vain about."

"I promise not to keep harping back to the question of age, but you've reached the stage when many people would be thinking of retiring. *I'm* retiring." He basked in the inevitable applause and whistles.

"So I hear." Lucy felt safe enough to flirt. "I rather hope your hellraising days aren't behind you."

He feigned embarrassment: "Don't let the suit fool you." He lifted the lapels of his exquisitely tailored charcoal grey jacket. "What I was *going* to say, Lucy, is that you show no signs of slowing down. So what keeps you going?"

"I've never had what you'd call a proper job. What would I retire from?"

"Your writing, your causes..." he suggested, circling one hand in the air as if there were more examples he might choose from.

Lucy had learned when to pause for effect. She paused now.

"It's your turn to say something." He leaned towards her. "That's how interviews work."

"I'm sorry, I thought you were just getting warmed up."

"I was giving you a cue!"

"Well, in that case… Writing's how I express myself. I wouldn't give that up even if I didn't have an audience. And while things are still unresolved, I can't give up my causes. It's like Martin Sheen said, 'Acting's my living, but activism keeps me alive.'"

"I'd heard that you two were pen pals. How did you meet?"

"We were arrested at the same demonstration. I found myself sitting in the back of a police van with him."

"A police van? I imagined celebrities like you got special treatment."

"I rather suspect we did. We had a bench each."

Something about Philip's laughter made her think it was for the camera. "So what happened?"

"Well, I was there, in the back of the van, when the doors were opened and in climbed Martin Sheen. I probably stared a little too much, because you don't expect to find yourself with a Hollywood film star sitting opposite you. At least *I* don't."

"Oh, to have been a fly on the wall. How did the conversation go?"

"To break the ice, I offered him a sandwich." She held out an imaginary Tupperware box. "'Would you like a sandwich, Mr Sheen?' – because I always take plenty of sandwiches and he had none."

"What kind of sandwiches were they?"

She raised both hands at the absurdity of the question. "I can't remember what type of sandwiches they were!"

Philip lowered his voice. "For the sake of the story."

This was going to be a fun interview. Not like last time. "Alright." She played along. "Let's say they were tuna and mayonnaise."

"Did he like them?"

She rolled her eyes as if to say, *Now what!* But Philip nodded encouragement, and so she said, "Yes, Mr Sheen said they were the finest tuna mayonnaise sandwiches he'd ever eaten, and I assured him that I'd pass the compliment on to my husband, because he'd made them."

"You called him Mr Sheen?"

"I'm of that generation who wait to be invited to use some-one's first name. I wanted him to know that I *recognised* him but that, just because he'd been beamed into my sitting room, I wasn't going to presume I *knew* him."

"And yet your husband's only known by his first name."

"That's *his* choice. He hated having his surname barked at him."

"Barked?"

"You know. The way men do." She raised a hand to her mouth and used it as a loudhailer. *"You there! Harrington!"*

Philip scratched the side of his noise. Lucy marvelled how anyone could be so unself-conscious in front of a camera. "I take his point. Did 'Mr Sheen' know who you were?"

"He said he did, but I had a feeling... You know when these famous actors get that glazed expression?"

"Oh, I do." Applause broke out as Philip did a very poor impression of someone glazing over. It was his night and the audience intended to indulge him.

"Anyway, he was terribly nice. We compared histories. He'd been arrested sixty-three times and I was only ten behind so I think I made a good impression."

"Is there a record for who's been arrested the most times for political activism, do you know?"

"I don't – but Martin Sheen must be fairly near the top."

Philip smiled. "You've mentioned being arrested. What about actually being charged?"

"You'd have to ask him."

"I'm asking *you*."

"Have *I* been charged?" Lucy laughed. "Oh!" She made no attempt to dodge the question. "The law's a funny thing. I've been charged with resisting arrest when I wasn't guilty of the thing I was arrested for in the first place. It's rather like being at school and getting the blame for something someone else has done, then not being allowed to stand up for yourself. The whole idea is to resist arrest without resorting to violence."

"Because you believe in peaceful protest."

"That's right."

"Explain how that works."

"Often it's as simple as what we used to call a sit-down. Quite literally, a large number of people sitting down. On one occasion at Trafalgar Square, there were twelve thousand of us and one thousand three hundred arrests."

"Talk me through what you do when you're arrested."

"I go limp in the police officers' arms." She demonstrated, allowing her shoulders to sag. "Often, you'll find yourself being scooped up by two officers, your heels dragging along the pavement. I've ruined several pairs of perfectly good shoes that way."

Philip waited for the laughter to die away. "You've mentioned occasions when you were arrested for things that weren't criminal, but were there other occasions, perhaps…?" His question ended on an upward lilt.

"We always look for alternatives. At Torness, for example, rather than scale the fence, we climbed on top of hay bales donated by local farmers."

"So there was trespass?"

"We call it 'polite direct action'. There was no destruction, no violence. You'd be surprised how many present-day politicians were involved in the Torness protest."

To Lucy's disappointment, Philip didn't take the bait. "I hear that on one occasion you hijacked a crane. Tell us what you remember about that."

"It was bloody freezing." Lucy hugged herself at the memory, and earned her biggest laugh so far. "The crane was supposed to be unloading a fuel carrier at Sellafield. I joined members of CORE –"

"Core?"

"Cumbrians Opposed to a Radioactive Environment. Trips nicely off the tongue, doesn't it?"

"Very nicely." He nodded playfully.

"Well, we had to swim across Barrow dock."

"You swam across the dock?"

"Yes, to get to the crane, and up we climbed. It took eight and a half hours before the policeman on the ground noticed us, and by that time we were thoroughly miserable. And *he* couldn't come after us because he was afraid of heights." Lucy shook her head. "I wonder how we had the nerve. But I'm glad we did. Back then we thought of environmental damage as being local. Now we have evidence of irreversible damage that's been done to the planet."

"So, for the record, Lucy, can I ask if you have a criminal record?"

"I do – although my intention is to *prevent* nuclear crime."

"By protesting?"

"No, protesting only raises awareness but if one of us gets as far as the courtroom, then there's the opportunity to call experts in international law and help prove the illegality of nuclear weapons."

Philip was now serious. "Do you think that will happen?"

"I certainly hope so."

There was a trickle of applause. Only a trickle.

"You must know that you and Martin Sheen have more in common than activism? He also suffered from childhood polio."

"I did know that, yes." Lucy would never have introduced the subject of someone else's medical history, but Philip clearly didn't own such scruples. "We're of a similar age and were both caught out just before the vaccine was introduced."

"But you made good recoveries."

"We were lucky. At a time when the practice was to immobilise limbs, we both exercised. Later, it was proven that physical therapy substantially reduces the after-effects of polio."

"Many famous people I meet seem to have suffered a serious childhood illness of one type or another. Do you think it creates ambition, perhaps?"

Lucy considered the question. "Indirectly, perhaps. Knowing you've dodged death is a defining moment, but it also sets you apart. I coped by putting my thoughts down on paper. It was different for Martin. He was one of ten children, at the hub of a busy family."

"We've given Martin quite enough publicity, and it's not as if he needs it. Let's get back to you. I want to pick up on those unresolved issues you alluded to. What are they?"

Lucy found herself nodding as she gathered her thoughts. "I'd like to see the British government compensate the ex-servicemen who witnessed the atomic tests during the fifties. We're way out of step with how other countries have treated their veterans, and that seems very unjust."

There was a smattering of applause from the audience, rather less than Lucy might have hoped for. Perhaps the leap from Hollywood to nuclear veterans was too much. She acknowledged the reaction with a nod.

"We can't *all* and chain ourselves to railings –"

"Then you'll probably never meet Martin Sheen."

"But, seriously, how can people get involved?"

"By supporting the work of the British Nuclear Test Veterans' Association. It represents people who've worked with radioactive material for the nation's benefit. And, of course, we now know that the consequences are genetic. They'll carry through twenty generations."

"Twenty generations, that's…"

"Five hundred years. If you're looking for a measure, five hundred years ago, Henry the seventh was king. The thing is to educate yourself about the work of the BNTVA. Perhaps to read about the veterans' experiences, then find opportunities to talk about it. Social media can be an incredible power for good."

"You said earlier that you've never had a proper job. Many poets work as professors. Didn't teaching appeal?"

"With my arrest record, do you really think I'd have been offered a teaching post?"

"So you sacrificed your career?"

"When I started standing up for the things I believe in, I had no career *to* sacrifice." Lucy reached out a hand and placed it on Philip's arm. "I seem to remember being very defensive the last time I was on your show."

"Don't tell me you've mellowed?"

"Not mellowed exactly, but I'm getting more direct as I grow older, so let me say this: I've been extremely lucky. What with the money I inherited from my parents and the fact that my husband does very nicely, I've never been under pressure to earn a great deal. That's not to say I don't work. In fact, I work damned hard. It's just that the things I do don't pay."

"But you've been instrumental in launching the careers of young poets."

"I do what I can, but I support young writers by mentoring rather than standing at the front of a lecture theatre. You can't underestimate the value of a few words of encouragement given at the right time."

"Do you think it was your arrest record that caused you to be passed over for Poet Laureate?"

Lucy had been prepared for this. Half a dozen interviewers had asked similar questions over the past fortnight, each armed with a few 'fun' facts. How Wordsworth only agreed to accept the post after the prime minister assured him it came with no obligations, and so he didn't write a single word for the court. How Ted Hughes offered to share his 720 bottles of sherry with the Queen Mum. The role would soon be vacant again. "I wasn't surprised when Andrew Motion was appointed. He was the least controversial candidate."

"But you were considered, I believe?"

Lucy regretted her reflex to scratch an itch under her eye. It might make her appear defensive. "Along with several others. There was never an official offer."

"Andrew Motion's residency comes to an end next year. Would you *like* to be offered the job?"

"At my age, I'm not sure I have any business signing up to anything for ten years. Ralph and I recently debated whether or not to risk taking on another cat. But I'd like to see a woman in the role."

"And who, in your opinion, would be deserving?"

"Carol Ann Duffy." This time the studio responded with an echo of applause.

"Why does she top your list?"

"She's honest, she's authentic and she has great integrity. She'd take the role on her terms." Like Wordsworth.

"What do *you* think about gay marriage?"

The question took Lucy by surprise. "You shoehorned that one in, Philip." *And given that you're considered to have the most natural interview style in the business, it was quite unprofessional.*

"I suppose it is quite a leap. Fear of running out of time, perhaps. But Carol Ann Duffy was in a relationship with a woman when she turned down the role in 1999."

"That's not something I'd want to comment on." Although

perhaps she should? "Except to say that I believe everyone should be allowed to enjoy an open relationship with the person he or she loves, whichever sex that person may be."

"You're very happily married."

"I am." Lucy felt herself tense. She now knew why she'd been invited back on the show. Philip didn't *admire her,* as his assistant had said. There had, after all, been a reason for the vertigo.

"And you married Ralph knowing he was gay."

Confirmation was the line they took if asked directly. On the occasion of Ralph's one arrest (post 1967, thankfully), he'd grabbed a microphone from a waiting television crew and said, "Love takes many forms and I love my wife." Lucy had been immensely proud of him for those few simple words. She was proud as she replied: "I did, yes."

"If gay marriage were to be legalised, would you divorce?"

She felt entitled to snap. "Absolutely not."

"But you've *both* been in love with other people?"

We have both been in love with the same *person.* Her mind strayed. Had Dominic taken his medication? "Let me get this straight. I married my soulmate. I married for love. I did *not* marry for sex."

"But you see your marriage as being successful? You see it as being a *marriage?*"

Lucy felt her chest rise. The cameraman had zoomed in. She breathed out, very deliberately. "That's harsh, Philip, even by your standards."

"It's a simple question. I meant no offence."

"I know plenty of straight married couples who choose to be celibate, or whose relationships have changed or adapted over time. No one suggests they should divorce. Actually," she corrected herself, "that's not true. The media suggests that couples who aren't at it like rabbits the entire time should consult divorce lawyers immediately." Philip had sat back in his chair and now steepled his hands. He clearly had no intention of intervening while she was working herself up. "I would go as far as to say that when people married the first person they wanted to have sex with, it was a terribly bad system. Marry for sex and you'll be disappointed."

"What did you learn from your parents about marriage?"

"My parents' marriage was an act of rebellion. They were so wrapped up in that idea, it was only later that they discovered they didn't love each other. Once they produced an heir and a spare – I was the spare," she deferred to the audience, an attempt at humour, "they had as little to do with each other as possible. So that was what I imagined marriage would mean for me. Wearing a mask. In fact, until Ralph came along and changed my mind, I swore I'd never marry. In many ways, we have a very old-fashioned relationship based on the value of respect." Lucy had calmed herself. "It's very open. Very honest. I feel cherished, I feel supported and I feel cared for. What more could anyone ask?"

"Lucy Forrester?" Philip Harrington's eyes were sparkling. He thought he'd just made great television.

Having finished what she wanted to say, Lucy was breathless. "What?"

"I do believe you've mellowed." He pushed back his chair, making it clear that he expected her to follow his lead. His expression was almost paternal, as if she'd passed some kind of test. Applause erupted, but as he stepped towards her and reached out his arms, Lucy felt the blood pulse behind her eyes: *You don't get to ask those questions and then hug me like an old friend.* A wave of anger took control of her arm and, before she knew what was going to happen, Lucy heard the palm of her hand make contact with Philip Harrington's cheek. He didn't even have time to step out of the way – or perhaps he saw the slap coming and thought it would crown his final show. Perhaps it was what he'd wanted all along.

He covered the place she had struck then looked at his hand, as if he expected a trace of blood.

"What did I tell you?" she said pleasantly and picked up her chair. "Non-violent protest, ladies and gentlemen. *Unless* there's no alternative." Then she walked smartly off the set, leaving her host gawping at the camera.

"Well, no, of course I had no idea she was going to do it. It's not as if she's Grace Jones or Emu. This is Lucy Forrester we're talking about. Queen of peaceful protest."

All three were seated on the sofa, Lucy sandwiched between the two men with dinners on trays, watching an early evening magazine-style show. The chat show host had turned guest. So much for retirement!

The interviewer was a young comedian. *"You were quite hard on her. Did you feel you'd pushed her over the edge?"*

For the seventh time, Lucy watched the clip of the moment she slapped Philip Harrington. Already a YouTube hit, it was shown in slow-motion, giving her the opportunity to study the shock on her own face. She remained curious as the hand that was undeniably hers did something she couldn't recall asking of it.

Dominic removed his oxygen mask briefly. "You should have broken his nose."

Lucy still found it difficult to adapt to the fact that he needed help to breathe. They were children now, Lucy and Ralph taking turns to be the adult. Today it was Ralph's turn.

"Finding my guests' pressure points is my job. Anyway, you heard her. She said she'd mellowed. I took her at her word."

"I believe what Lucy said was that she was more direct."

"She's certainly that. She has a good right hook." And again Philip Harrington put his hand up to touch his face.

Lucy was open-mouthed. "That's the wrong side, you fool! Honestly, anyone would think I *had* broken his nose."

"Are you sure it wasn't staged? I mean, you've been dining out on the story all week."

"No, I can assure you. You can see the look on my face – and I'm no actor."

"You deserved an Oscar for that performance," she scoffed.

"But you went to drama school."

"See!"

"Where I failed quite spectacularly."

Lucy nursed the knuckles of the hand that had struck Philip. Despite her protest, she'd had time to reflect on the question about the success of her marriage. The truth, like most truths, was complicated. Without Dominic, marriage to Ralph might have felt lacking in something. Having discovered that she was considered attractive, she had wanted – no, *needed* – to feel desired, although that feeling was now so dim, it might have belonged to another person. The third person had been an essential component in her marriage, but her instinct to protect that sacred thing was as strong as ever. She would happily strike out at anyone who threatened it.

Ralph patted Lucy's thigh. "Are you sure you don't want to tell your side of the story? I wrote down that journalist's number."

"This hand," she held it up, "acted alone. How can I take credit for what it did? And how could I defend it? Besides," she deferred to Dominic. "This is the best PR I've had for ages. Right?" Lucy no longer narrowed her view to avoid the sight of his jutting cheekbones. She had trained herself not to recoil.

Part-man part-machine, he moved his mask aside. "Finally, you're learning. My work here is done."

She refused to acknowledge that she must prepare to live without him. "I've made it onto a list of Top Ten Assaults on Chat Show Hosts. How many poets get to say that?" This brave, deceitful face of hers. This calcified heart, crumbling.

This counterfeit self. Dominic had been told not to hope for too much. It was unacceptable. It occurred to Lucy that she'd been brought up to believe in miracles. He had beaten the odds once before. All a believer need do was touch the hem of Jesus's cloak. She took the woollen cuff of Dominic's jumper between two fingers.

CHAPTER FORTY-ONE

2015

Lucy walked from the en suite into the bedroom, head covered as she towel-dried her cropped white hair. After draping the damp towel around her shoulders, she felt a rush of tenderness. There, on the bed, were her clothes. Each item exactly where it should go. Imagine how carefully Ralph would have laid out a child's school clothes. The pinafore dress, the shirt and tie, the cardigan, the ankle socks. If there was one thing Lucy regretted, it was that he hadn't experienced fatherhood. Perhaps he would have shown her how to be a mother. Her eyes pooled. She was prone to tears these days. *Stupid old woman.* She brushed them away. *There's work to be done.*

Lucy had settled on a silk-lined indigo blue suit tailored in a modern interpretation of forties styling. The nipped-in waist. The flared skirt of the jacket. Ralph had draped the short cape – her superhero cape, inspired by a Fathers4Justice campaigner around its shoulders. A pencil skirt Lucy would never have had the confidence to wear in her teens. The indigo pill-box hat with its bright pink yin and yang logo and fishnet veil was set on her pillow. Just below it, the new thick-framed raspberry-coloured spectacles, delivered by courier at the eleventh hour. The string of pearls was at the neckline of the jacket, to avoid an overly coordinated look – something both she and Ralph detested. The raspberry gloves lay at the end of the jacket sleeves. On one side was the pair of handcuffs Lucy would use, together with her handbag. She picked the bag up and checked its contents. There was the key, the formal invitation to her investiture at the Palace (she'd confirmed she was happy for the ceremony to be filmed for broadcast on the BBC, ITV and Sky), a packet of energy sweets and two cereal bars. On the other side was a bluff: heavy silver bangles, designed to look like handcuffs. Lucy pulled aside the cape, exposing the lining with its repeat pattern of the CND logo, interspersed with names belonging to the victims of atomic testing. This had been an extravagance, but Lucy understood only too well the power of the names of the dead. Underneath was a plain pink camisole. Matching indigo tights extended from the skirt. High-heeled lace-ups, also in raspberry, were paired on the floor at the foot of the bed. Typical Ralph. He'd thought of everything.

"Ah!" he said as she walked carefully down the stairs. There was a sideways turn to her step, forced by the combination of heels and fitted skirt. Ralph was dressed impeccably. Seeing him standing there brought a lump to Lucy's throat. The purity in her admiration remained untainted. It wasn't that Lucy hadn't seen Ralph at his worst. Over the years, even before their marriage, she'd ministered to his various illnesses, but she couldn't say that she'd seen every crease of him.

"Turn round for me," he instructed, and she obeyed, play-acting to cover her shyness, extending her arms so that the lining of the cape was on display. "Exquisite. Miriam's done a wonderful job."

She toyed with the silver bangles. "Do you think so?"

"The jeweller too."

"Not too obvious?"

"No!" he insisted, and she felt calmed. If Ralph didn't make an adjustment, then it must be right. "You've got your scroll?"

Lucy opened her handbag, allowing Ralph to inspect inside. She saw that he'd packed a tote bag. There was bottled water in it.

"You're all sorted. The taxi will be here in five minutes. Feeling nervous?"

"Very." With the admission came a fresh release of butterflies.

"We should drink a toast." He turned toward the living room. "Brandy?"

"Please," she said, though doubted she would taste it. She looked herself up and down in the full-length mirror, and thought, *Finally, you look the part.* Then Ralph was there, smiling, holding a glass toward her.

"To success." He clinked her glass.

"To us," she said, meaning all five: the two of them, Dominic, Pamela and Angus. Then she tipped back her head and let the amber liquid burn a trail down her throat.

Attendees had been asked to leave their cameras at home, but not Ralph. He looped his around his neck. Ralph wasn't Ralph without a camera.

They approached via The Mall, one of a steady procession of black cabs. It was impossible to sit back and relax, so Lucy pretended to pick out the various landmarks they passed – to their left was St James's Park.

Ralph spoke to the driver through the dividing window, "As close to the memorial as you can manage, if you don't mind."

Lucy stepped out, straightened her skirt and found herself looking up into the roar of a bronze lion. This beast was flanked by a woman carrying a sheaf of wheat and a scythe – a good woman of Britain. She smiled as Ralph paid the driver.

"Ready?" he asked and noticed the lion. "I'd say that's a good omen, wouldn't you?"

"An unexpected symmetry."

This was unlike any other protest Lucy had ever taken part in. Security at the Palace had toughened up since the Fathers-4Justice campaigner had scaled its façade. There was the narrow ledge next to the balcony, where, dressed as Batman, he had unfurled a banner proclaiming himself a Super Dad. Lucy wondered at his nerve. But nerve was all it took. *Besides, you have every right to be here.* "Ready," she replied, striding forward.

Beyond the wrought iron railings was one of four stiff-backed Queen's Guards, his rifle topped with a bayonet. Lucy's hand strayed to her pearls as she recalled footage of a guard jabbing its point at the throat of a would-be trespasser. She forced herself to think of Freddie's tin soldiers as the guard stamped and hefted his rifle onto his shoulder. But she had no intention of scaling the railings. If she wanted to enter the Palace grounds (which wasn't part of her plan), Lucy wouldn't be trespassing on a designated site. All she need do was to show her invitation. And outside the gates, she had every right to peaceful protest.

Recipients and their plus ones were arriving on foot at the central north gate, where they queued, ready to be herded through rope cordons by police officers wearing high-vis jackets. Inside the gates, several press photographers were clustered together. She thought Paul Stoddard from the *Evening Standard* had recognised her (although it was just as likely that he'd spotted Ralph) and hoped to God he wouldn't draw attention to them before she was ready.

Once their photos were taken, those about to be honoured glanced about nervously, hopefully. Inside, they would be separated from their guests and would walk stiffly up the grand staircase, plush red carpet giving beneath the soles of their gleaming shoes, marvelling at the ornate gilt balustrades (far too much gilt, in Lucy's opinion). Shoulder to shoulder, they would gather to be briefed by a representative from the Lord Chamberlain's Office. Plenty of opportunities to practise laughing politely as he described the ballroom as being situated 'somewhere between here and Victoria Station'. Then they would be called in groups of twelve and led in strict single file.

"It's not too late to join them," Ralph said, only a half joke.

"This isn't a look of longing." But knowing there was a medal with her name on it renewed Lucy's sense of purpose. "People are relying on us." Taking Ralph by the elbow, she threaded through tourists who milled around.

"Jeff's here," Ralph said. "John too."

Surprised he was able to pick out members of BNTVA so readily, she said, "You've been doing your homework."

"Good on you for thumping that bastard, Harrington," one of the pair said. "He had it coming."

In front of the railings, Lucy reminded herself of their construction. A stone plinth just over her knee-height. In between each twelve-foot rail, an ornate quarter-height rail, topped with the shape of a spear. Behind the lower section, a short run of wire. There was nothing unusual about the sight of a tourist gripping the railings, but none of them were dressed as Lucy was. Cadences of half a dozen languages reached her. Several tourists had balanced on the concrete plinth, cameras held high for a view of the Horse Guards. Lucy looked about, trying not to make her interest in the crowd too apparent. But there was Jeremy with his camera raised. She nodded and tried to suppress a smile. Ian and Mikaela too.

Ralph crouched low, indicating directions with one hand, crab-like in his movements. Then he strode towards Lucy, repositioned her hat, adjusted her veil and her cape, retreated and shook his head. As she posed for him, she saw Eddie raise a hand as he arrived, taking up a front row position.

From beside her, a couple of tourists jumped down and pointed to her and then to their cameras. She smiled and nodded, just a patriotic British eccentric, the backdrop to a selfie. "I've spotted four photographers," she told Ralph the next time he approached.

"Four who prefer what you have to offer to the official function. Not bad."

A policeman laughed as he recognised her. "I dare say I should be keeping an eye on you."

"Don't you know?" she said, as Ralph made some minor adjustment to her shoulder pads. "I'm on the guest list."

"You?" He laughed and shook his head. "Now I really have heard everything!"

"Would you like to see my jewellery?" She flashed her silver bangles at him. "I had them made specially." He dismissed her with a limp wave and turned back towards the tourists. Lowering her voice, Lucy spoke in Ralph's ear. "Alright, he's moved on."

Ralph fished in his jacket pocket for the key and unlocked the real handcuffs. Lucy's left wrist pinched as he snapped them around both rail and wire. It had to be her left hand that was out of action. Few people were as right-handed as Lucy.

"Not too tight?" he asked.

"No." Lucy smiled, though, with her hand twisted behind her, standing was uncomfortable. Discomfort was part of the job. She wondered if her hand could be considered to be trespassing, and gripped the rail.

Ralph had stepped away and was crouching once more. He moved back towards her and handed over the scroll. As he positioned the bag of provisions near her feet, Lucy was surprised to see a flash of silver around his wrist.

"Matching bangles?" she asked.

"Actually, I thought you might like some company."

"Ah, that's sweet." Lucy was genuinely overcome as Ralph locked his own cuff into place.

"The invitation said plus one."

She recognised Ralph's new assistant – the good-looking Asian – as he threaded his way through a group of onlookers. Ralph slipped the two keys into his hand. "Quick as you like, down the nearest drain. And take my camera. You know what to do with the shots."

"Yes, boss. Highest bidder."

"Everything's set to stream the live footage?"

"Sorted. But I wouldn't worry. Every single tourist has a camera phone. Even if there's a blip, you'll be all over Facebook within the hour."

"I'd better get started," Lucy said and steeled herself. Would this raggle-taggle of celebrity-spotters and mainly Japanese tourists care about her message? Would they even understand it? – or would they be happy provided that something – anything – happened?

"Ladies and gentlemen," she projected her voice, aiming high above the tops of heads, somewhere beyond. "My name is Lucy Forrester, and for the past fifty years I have campaigned against nuclear weapons. The Palace has invited me here today to honour that work, and so I think it only fitting that I carry on just as I've always done." She nodded to her wrist in such a way that it was impossible to ignore the fact that she was cuffed to the railings, then dropped a slight curtsey. Camera phones obscuring their faces, two tourists collided. "Unfortunately the Ministry of Defence has continually failed to recognise the sacrifice made by twenty-two thousand servicemen and women whose job it was to take part in, or to witness, nuclear tests in the fifties." Out of the corner of one eye, Lucy saw movement as the first of the police officers began to stride towards her. She also saw Ralph's head turn.

"Keep going," he said.

The policeman stopped a short distance away, took a wide stance and, with a knowing nod, folded his arms. At some point he would decide it was time to silence her. For now, Lucy knew to reel him in. "Other countries have compensated their veterans. Roy Prescott of Burton upon Trent was the first British soldier to be awarded compensation by the US government. He received forty thousand pounds under the US Radiation Exposure Compensation Act. While on National Service on Christmas Island, Roy witnessed thirty-six tests – thirty-six! – over an eleven-week period. His lung cancer is a rare type caused by exposure to radiation, but the Ministry of Defence insist that there isn't sufficient evidence of causation. They want more.

"The US government have also paid Pat Spackman forty-seven thousand pounds after her husband, Derek, a former RAF navigator, died from throat cancer. Stationed in Darwin, it was his job to test levels of radioactivity after nuclear tests around the Marshall Islands. The MoD, however, have refused Mrs Spackman a war widow's pension.

"And if that isn't shameful enough, in January this year, the Prime Minister of Fiji awarded each of the twenty-four surviving veterans three thousand pounds, saying, 'Fiji is not prepared to wait for Britain to do the right thing.' Let me repeat that: *Britain is not prepared to do the right thing.*" Lucy looked directly at the policeman, who appeared to arrive at a decision and turned back towards the central north gate. He was moving fast. Lucy pressed on. "Originally, I intended to read one of my atomic poems but, recently, I heard the names of First World War casualties being read out at the Tower of London." A small reaction. "Did anyone go to see the poppies?" A few nods. "Wonderful, weren't they? I feel the atomic casualties deserve a similar honour."

Lucy's research hadn't resulted in a complete list. The majority of British servicemen had returned to England and scattered. Lucy had collected nothing like the full twenty-two thousand names – but she didn't expect to be allowed to speak for long. With only one hand free, she cursed under her breath. All of that research, a full walk-through, and she hadn't thought how she would hold the blasted scroll! What would Pamela have said? But Ralph was there, ready to step in.

"Teamwork." He smiled at her, and there was a trickle of laughter from the crowd.

Even shoulder to shoulder, it was going to require considerable teamwork to hold the scroll between them and keep it moving. "We should have rehearsed with the cuffs," she said.

"Don't worry. I'll follow your lead."

She cleared her throat and began. "Gerald Adshead." Each name had to be enunciated carefully – as carefully as Matron had spoken to her father. "Alexander Richard Barton. Don Battersby. George Baulch. Andy Leonard Beaumont. Eric Blackhurst. Norman Blackburn." Every name had its own story. She remembered Norman's; he had died of stomach cancer. "John Butler. Derek Chappell." But the concourse in front of the Palace didn't have the solemnity or the atmosphere of the Tower. These people were on holiday. They had dressed their children in fake fur bearskins. Nerves made Lucy add to what she'd planned to say. "Now, Derek's still alive, but I decided not to discriminate between the living and the dead.

"Brian Coates. Brian," she told them, "was an RAF engineer. His job was to strip down and clean the engines of planes which had flown through mushroom clouds.

"Anthony Brian Cox. He was only forty when he died.

"Eric Denison. Poor Eric. He received the equivalent of twelve thousand X-rays to his brain while flying through mushroom clouds on sampling missions. After suffering years of headaches with no relief, he took his own life." She paused and noticed that there was very little noise from the crowd.

They didn't understand every word, but they had sensed that something was happening and were listening, some of them with heads cocked on one side.

"Colin Duncan. Colin was given kitchen tissues to clean down radioactive aircraft. *Kitchen tissues!*

"Ken Earl. Edward Egan. Dennis William Farrant." Lucy felt bad that no details sprang to mind for those few men, but she paused when she came to the next name on her list. She had been unable to find a connection, and yet she couldn't help wondering.

"Frank Forrester." The name caught in her throat. "Died on 13 October 1952 at Monte Bello. He was exhumed and reinterred at Onslow Cemetery a year later." All of that time she had nursed a nagging resentment that she'd been born a girl, *this* was what being born a boy might have meant.

Marching feet. Lucy saw Ralph's assistant turn his video camera in the direction of the sound. Glad to have got as far as Frank, she felt her heartbeat accelerate, but whoever was heading their way moved towards the north central gate, taking the long way around. There might be time for the names of five more wronged men, perhaps ten, but still Lucy didn't rush.

"John Marr Garside. Robert Joseph Geddes. John Henry Gellender. John Hall. Robert H. Halley. Able Seaman 'Bobby' Halley died on Christmas Island in 1962 and was buried at sea. His family never had the opportunity of attending his funeral or having him buried at his home cemetery."

A flash of red and gold livery, she saw a man raise his gloved hand to his mouth and bend his head towards her.

"Miss Forrester." Polite and low.

"One moment," she addressed the crowd and saw that the press photographers had followed him from the north gate. Paul Stoddard was among them. Good. To the man from the Queen's Household, she said, "It's Lucy Forrester. And I'm married." The police officers were standing a short distance behind. They would be less polite, she imagined. "This is my husband, Ralph."

She felt a tug on the scroll as Ralph acknowledged the member of the Royal Household, who said, "Mr Forrester."

"Just Ralph," he replied.

"Yes, of course." To Lucy he said, "His Royal Highness would like to invite you inside, if you're ready."

Lucy's heart was pounding. "Please convey my gratitude to His Royal Highness. I just have a few more names to read out."

"I'm sure Prince Charles would like to hear those names."

"And I'd be happy to read them to him." She was firm. "Just as soon as I've finished." Lucy returned her attention to the scroll. "A little higher," she said to Ralph, making as if she was about to go on.

"What I'm trying to say, without making too much of a fuss, is that I think you've finished out here."

"Oh, but we were invited," she insisted, bringing Ralph back into the conversation, as if checking the detail with him. "I have the invitation here." Without a free hand, she nodded to the handbag that hung in the crook of her elbow.

The press photographers were jostling. "I believe you were invited *inside*."

"'To the Palace', the invitation says, and here we are."

The member of the Queen's Household turned his back on the crowd. She realised he was wary. No longer the queen of peaceful protest, she was a woman who had hit a chat show host in full view of a camera. "Let's stop pretending there's been some awkward mix-up. We're doing our very best to avoid a scene."

She matched his tone. "And you'll understand that I never go out of my way to avoid a scene." Then she raised her voice. "I'm afraid I don't have my bolt cutters with me. I don't suppose you…"

The man turned and looked at the police officers, who, in turn, looked at each other blankly.

"Perhaps your friends have some kind of multi-purpose key that fits handcuffs?" Lucy suggested. "They're usually very obliging."

The man made a throaty noise and marched off swiftly, her cue to continue. Lucy's bravado was waning. "Michael William Harris. George Albert Harrison. Arthur Hart. Arthur, bless him, developed two hundred tumours after witnessing explosions during his National Service in the Royal Navy. He stood on the top deck as HMS *Diana* sailed through the aftermath of the tests. But, again: no proof.

"Derek Hatton. Now Derek's was the clearest verdict. Ruling on his death, the Derby and South Derbyshire coroner established that his underlying fatal conditions were a type caused by exposure to high levels of ionising radiation.

"Douglas Hern. Wing Commander Thomas Hine." Hine, she knew, was one of many who suffered ulcerated legs, a condition his family believed was brought about by walking through radioactive water, but now it seemed more important to get through more names than tell the stories. "John Hindmarsh."

The sound of feet walking briskly over the compacted salmon-pink gravel. *This is it,* Lucy braced herself. "Wally Holdsworth," she said as if unfazed, but gripped her scroll to stop it passing through her fingers.

"Roy Howard. Alan Ilett. Brian Jagger." Bolt cutters. Here they were. "John Ian Jen–"

"Hold still, please."

Freed, she held her left arm across her body as if it were in a sling, flexing her fingers repeatedly, stretching them and then making a fist.

Maximum publicity, that's was they were there for. It would be a shame to have access to so many photographers – not to mention the live streaming – and *not* be arrested. As the policeman moved to cut through Ralph's handcuff, she rolled her shoulders to relieve the aching in her shoulder. Peaceful protest. *Unless there's no alternative.* She looked at the member of the Queen's Household. There was little chance she would inflict any serious damage. *But would I be capable of intentionally hitting someone?* Lucy Forrester, seventy-six years old, poet activist, survivor and misfit asked herself.

Yes, as it turned out, she would.

ATOMIC VETERANS

Around 22,000 men, many of whom were on National Service, were ordered to stand and watch as scientists detonated nuclear bombs in the Central Pacific during the 1950s and 1960s. Little or no protective equipment was provided. They were simply instructed to turn their backs and cover their faces with their hands.

While some servicemen suffered symptoms immediately or soon afterwards, for others it was a different story. They appeared to be fine for decades before developing cancers and other rare diseases. Over time, as dots were joined, many veterans became convinced these illnesses and disabilities were related to their exposure to nuclear radiation, but questions and concerns were met with silence and denial.

The British Nuclear Tests Veterans' Association (BNTVA) is the premier UK charity representing people who have worked with or alongside radioactive material for the benefit of this nation, campaigning for recognition and restitution, as well as sharing its knowledge and heritage.

The veterans' bid to be recognised by the European Court of Human Rights was denied in 1998, which said it had no jurisdiction in the case.

Then in 1999, researcher Sue Rabbitt Roff at the University of Dundee surveyed 2,500 veterans and their children, reporting unusually high rates of infertility and birth defects.

Britain's *Sunday Mirror* newspaper took on the veterans' case in their Justice for Nuke Vets campaign led by columnist Richard Stott (1943–2007). The government continued to deny any links between the veterans' health and radiation exposure.

In 2007 two scientific studies demonstrated links between the veterans' exposure to nuclear radiation and health problems:

- A Massey University study of New Zealand nuclear test veterans found genetic damage at three times the normal rate – comparable to victims of the Chernobyl nuclear accident.

- An independent study by Green Audit looked at long-term effects of radiation exposure in British veterans and their families, finding significantly higher rates of miscarriages and stillbirths, infant deaths, childhood cancers, and inherited genetic deformities.

As a result of the studies, 700 New Zealand and UK veterans launched a class action lawsuit against the British government claiming NZ $36 million in damages. The Ministry of Defence countered with a statute of limitations defence.

Following a parliamentary inquiry in early 2008, the government agreed to fund new studies into veterans' health and agreed to pay interim compensation of £4,000 each.

At the time I completed research for this novel, the government had announced that they would set aside £25million (£5million per year over a five-year period) for an Aged Veterans' Fund. There are approximately two million qualifying veterans, including a reducing number of Atomic Veterans.

In addition to applications from individuals, the BNTVA can apply for funding for projects such as respite care or counselling, and make those services available to its members. Whilst any such services may indirectly benefit the families of the Atomic Veterans, once the remaining veterans die, all funding will cease.

Without an admission of negligence from the MoD, there will be no help for their families who have suffered a genetic curse of birth defects, which scientists estimate will last for twenty generations.

You can find out more or make a donation at
https://bntva.com

ACKNOWLEDGMENTS

To the many Atomic Veterans I was unable to name in this book, including George Edward Kinnersley, Roger Kingston, Ronald 'Shady' Lane, Frank Leeming, Gordon Allen Lowe, Alexander Mackinnon, Ken McGinley, Bede McGurk, Britford Victor Merrit, John Morris, John Neal, Christopher Edward Noone, David Hugh Owen, Malcolm Pike, Eric James Pownall, Dawn Pritchard, Bob Redman, Archie Ross, Bert Sinfield, Anna Smith, Brian Taylor, John Taylor, Ray Whitehead, John Allan Willard. We will remember.

I drew inspiration from a number of sources, including *The Life of Kenneth Tynan,* by Kathleen Tynan; *Edith Sitwell: Avant Garde Poet, English Genius,* by Richard Greene; *Mad Girl's Love Song: Sylvia Plath and Life Before Ted,* by Andrew Wilson, *Love from Nancy: The Letters of Nancy Mitford,* edited by Charlotte Mosley and *Vivienne Westwood* by Vivienne Westwood and Ian Kelly. I used various newspaper articles, personal accounts and websites in my research about the experiences of veterans, including:

https://bntva.com/

https://pacificnukes.wordpress.com

http://www.janeresture.com/christmas_bombs

As I so often do, I must admit to taking liberties by putting words into the mouths of real characters, but I hope I have done so respectfully and in historical context.

A mounting debt of thanks is due to my team of beta readers, especially Beth Allen, Karen Begg, Sheila de Borde, Anne Clinton, Kath Crowley, Sheila Christie, Kevin Cowdall, Sue Darnell, Sarah Diss Evans, Mary Fuller, Sarah Hurley, Magda Knight, Jo Lambert, Liz Lewis, Deb McEwan, Lauren McQueen, Sarah Marshall, Matthew Martin, 'Happy' Harry Matthews, Jenn Moore, Les Moriarty, Amanda Osborne,

Lynn Pearce, Will Poole, Sally Salmon, Julie Spearritt, Eleanor Steele, Adi Teodoru, Joe Thorpe-Legg and Clare Weiner.

Extra special thanks to my copy editor John Hudspith, and to Dan Holloway, Carol Cooper (http://pillsandpillowtalk.com) and Liz Carr for editorial advice. And not forgetting my cover designer Andrew Candy, proofreader Helen Baggott, JD Design for interior formatting, Jill Marsh for her fabulous book description and Rebecca Souster and all the team at Clays.

The Cremation of Sam McGee is a poem by Robert W. Service, published 1907 in *Songs of a Sourdough*.

'Tennyson's vanish'd hand' is a reference to Alfred Tennyson's poem, *Break, Break, Break*.

The Lovesong of J Alfred Prufrock is a poem by T. S. Eliot.

When I am an Old Woman I Shall Wear Purple is a poem by Jenny Joseph.

Finally, thanks to the ever wonderful Colleen Mills, whose memoir in verse *Solace* moved me to tears, and who allowed me to reference it.

ABOUT THE AUTHOR

Jane Davis is the author of seven novels. Her debut, Half-truths & White Lies, won the Daily Mail First Novel Award and was described by Joanne Harris as 'A story of secrets, lies, grief and, ultimately, redemption, charmingly handled by this very promising new writer'. She was hailed by The Bookseller as 'One to Watch'. Of the following three novels she published, Compulsion Reads wrote, 'Davis is a phenomenal writer, whose ability to create well rounded characters that are easy to relate to feels effortless'. Her 2015 novel, An Unknown Woman, was overall winner of The Writing Magazine/David St John Charitable Trust Self-published Book of the Year Award. Jane's favourite description of fiction is that it is 'made-up truth'.

Jane lives in Carshalton, Surrey with her Formula 1 obsessed, star-gazing, beer-brewing partner, surrounded by growing piles of paperbacks, CDs and general chaos.

For further information, or to sign up for pre-launch specials and notifications about future projects, visit the author's website at www.jane-davis.co.uk.

A personal request from Jane: "Your opinion really matters to authors and to readers who are wondering which book to pick next. If you love a book, please tell your friends and post a review. Facebook, Amazon, Smashwords and Goodreads are all great places to start."

OTHER TITLES
BY THE AUTHOR

Half-truths & White Lies

I Stopped Time

These Fragile Things

A Funeral for an Owl

An Unchoreographed Life

An Unknown Woman

Sign up to my newsletter at www.jane-davis.co.uk/newsletter
and receive a free eBook of I Stopped Time.